GODS

OF THE

SEA

By

DEIDREA DEWITT

ISBN 978-1-7342866-6-3 (Print)
ISBN 978-1-7342866-7-0 (ebook)

www.deidreadewitt.com

The sense of the world is short,—
Long and various the report,—
        To love and be beloved;
Men and gods have not outlearned it;
And, how oft soe'er they've turned it,
        'Tis not to be improved.

— "Eros" by Ralph Waldo Emerson

To the father I never knew

and the Father who took care of me in his place

EIGHT DAYS

CHAPTER 1

INTRODUCTIONS

"The red one," I said. "After all, there's no better color for a lady to wear when seducing a husband."

My handmaid, Lina, raised an eyebrow and pursed her lips in an agitated frown that always amused me.

"Listen to you," she said, clicking her tongue, her gray curls bouncing around her face disapprovingly. "Sounding like a lass of thirty when you're barely brushing twenty and one."

She pulled the crimson dress from my piled choice of clothes, the silk glistening like pieces of eight. My lovely seamstress, Caroline, had been more than generous with the detailing on the gold embroidered flowers, matching them perfectly with the golden lace bodice sash and stomacher. She had even shown me a way to drape the train so I could dance with my choice of gentlemen tonight. If it were anything like my previous birthdays, I would certainly wear out my leather boots by the end of the night from the line of suitors waiting to impress Father.

Unfortunately, he was never impressed. This would be my last night to change his mind on it too.

"And don't be gettin' no ideas about seducing a

husband," Lina continued. "Your father has already made your arrangements."

It was my turn to frown. "Yes, I know. Hence, the reason I should attempt to seduce another and get his approval before the night is over. Father might have mistakenly picked a brainless, dull businessman."

"A brainless, dull businessman will keep you from starving to death when your father passes. Ever think of that?"

I sighed. I knew Father had been struggling with finances since Mother passed away a little over five years ago. Mother had been the glue that held Father's business together, and when she passed, our worlds fell apart both emotionally and financially, resulting in Father's expedition to find me a well-off husband.

"I know why Father wants me to marry," I said, "but I don't think money is any reason for it."

"Aye, you ain't wrong. But is love a better reason? Feelings are fleeting, dear one. Better a boring man with wisdom and a heavy pocket than a gorgeous wild card with no common sense."

Lina helped me into my petticoat and began to drape my dress.

"Are those the only two choices?" I asked. "Surely the world is not so black and white."

"Of course it is. What else do you think all those grays are made of?"

"Do you really think Father has chosen a suitor already?"

She sucked on her cheek as she finished fastening the stomacher, not saying anything.

"Oh, you're truly awful sometimes, Lina," I scolded.

"Keeping secrets on my birthday."

"Then don't think of it as a secret, dearest. Think of it as a surprise."

"Can't you give me a small hint?" I pleaded.

She looked up into my eyes, thinking about it for a long moment.

"Please?" I nudged with a smile.

She rolled her eyes, straightening my sash. "A man of fortune and character. I believe your father has made a good decision."

I clapped with a smile. "Then he must be responsible and dependable. Yes, I can see Father choosing someone fashioned much like himself in that way. But is my suitor handsome, do you suppose?"

"Be glad to marry a man of character and fortune even if he looks like a goat, dearest."

I was suddenly overwhelmed by the thought of a wealthy goat-faced husband, my stomach souring.

"What if he's terrible, Lina?"

"Then pray he's a workaholic and you never see him."

"Or, on the other hand, perhaps I meet an amazing stranger tonight who is absolutely crazy about me, and asks me to run away with him?"

"Then pray he's a workaholic too. You'll need a man with a solid salary. But enough what-ifs. Time to step down the stairs into reality."

She spun me around and grasped my shoulders. She then smiled, warmth pouring from her eyes for the first time that evening.

"Oy, you look so much like your mother, Esmeralda," she said. "Let's pray you marry a man as decent as your father."

It was the finest compliment I could think of. Mother had always been a lady of elegance, fashion, and beauty. Eyes sparkling with laughter. A smile made of the finest pearls. A rich imagination and an adventurous spirit that craved the unknown. I admired Mother more than anyone.

I looked down at my mother's emerald necklace, the one that Father bought her the day he proposed. The necklace that had inspired my name.

"Did you hear that, Mother?" I whispered into the jewel. "I've been given the greatest of all compliments."

Light reflected from the jewel as if Mother had heard me. I hoped she had.

I held back my aching smile, turning back to Lina.

"You know," I said, suddenly feeling like a good tease was in order. "When I marry, Father will be quite lonely. Why don't you two—"

"Ayyy, enough o' your babble." Lina waved her hand at me. "Get down the stairs. The guest of honor should be at her own birthday celebration."

I smiled and nodded, giving her a single wink before heading toward the stairs.

Father may had been struggling recently, but it didn't show in the party downstairs. There was live music and dancing, the guests taking part in fine wine and cheeses. Half the aristocrats in the city were there, their clothes finer than the wine Father specially ordered; each *monsieur* and *mademoiselle* wore gold, silver, and jewels. For a moment, I considered throwing an auction just to see who would donate their highest treasures to win me. I knew a few gentlemen in the crowd who would cut off their own pinky fingers for the chance to marry the daughter of the great Simon and Charlotte Dupont, who both came from long lines of aristocrats, wealthy business owners, and personal officers of the kings themselves. Our family was legendary in every way, and the world knew it.

I leaned over the second-floor stair rail like a child at Christmas.

"Which one is my future husband, do you think?" I asked Lina.

I searched the room, looking for a gentleman who might pique my interest. Thankfully, the most unattractive men had women on their arms, meaning I was safe from their claws.

My eyes wandered around the room, stopping at a man on the side of the room standing near the balcony. His broad shoulders stood stronger than anyone else's in the room, his eyes and short hair darker than the night settled behind him, his skin as pale and delicate as moonlight. He raised wine to his lips, and something in my chest fluttered as he swallowed. He was certainly a sight to look at, and I didn't mind it.

His head raised. His deep black gaze met mine and he looked at me in a way that stole my breath.

But not from romantic notions.

It was more like looking into the eyes of the devil.

"Stop gawking," Lina said. "Your father is waiting."

"Of course," I replied. I swallowed as I tore my eyes away from the stranger. "But what's a party without a proper entrance?"

She rolled her eyes. I giggled at her lack of appreciation for dramatics.

I stood at the top of the staircase, placing my hand delicately on the banister. Pulling back my shoulders, I straightened and cleared my throat ever so gently. Even though the sound was no louder than a breeze, it stopped everyone in the room. They turned to look up the staircase at me.

The room was quiet until I nodded and gave my best smile, then a wave of coos and applause trickled over the room. Except, of course, from the broad-shouldered, dark-eyed stranger. He only sipped his drink.

"Thank you all for coming so far to see us on this day," I said to everyone. "I'm grateful that our family has so many good people to call friends. Please stay as long as you like. My handmaid will take your thoughtful and expensive birthday gifts on the way out."

The crowd chuckled as Lina shot me a warning look. I shrugged with a single shoulder and scrunched my nose at her in jest. The joke was charming. Everyone thought so.

The only person who didn't crack a smile was my dark-eyed stranger. My wit always pleased the crowd. Was he made of stone? Perhaps he was going through a tough time with his family? I made a mental note to introduce myself to him later to determine if I could assist somehow. To not laugh was simply too terrible a life to live.

I came down the stairs, greeted by men and women of the highest class. There were so many familiar faces: my father's coworkers, naval comrades, and fellow community volunteers. Father was generous to the community, and his friends were generous to us, especially after my mother passed. I was grateful to every one of them for it.

It was impossible to avoid a small line of small talk

as I made it to the center of the room where my father stood rightly proud as he always was. He wore his naval uniform—saved for only his best occasions—with his hair pulled back in a formal ponytail as if he was still working for the king himself.

But my father was better than any king.

"You look absolutely dashing, Father!" I said, flinging my arms around him as soon as the trail of guests stepped aside.

"Always the flatterer!" He chuckled, tapping my shoulders warmly then looked me over. "But what's all this? This dress is most becoming, but I can't remember giving you my permission to grow up."

I leaned in to kiss his cheek. "I only grew because you gave me so much sun, Father."

He gave a hearty laugh at my teasing, and I took his arm and drank in the sound. There was nothing better than the sound of my father's happiness after so many years of heartache. Seeing him weep at Mother's funeral still haunted me. I'd do anything to never see tears in my father's eyes like that ever again.

"Come let me introduce you to someone," he said, taking my arm.

We walked to the side of the room, and my heart pounded harder every time we took a step forward. I didn't want to jump ahead of myself, but we were walking closer to the dark-eyed stranger I had seen from the balcony. Everything in me wanted to know more about him, even if his bottomless black eyes warned me to keep my distance.

Could he be the one Father chose? I would not be upset at all, if that were the case.

My heart was frazzled with excitement when we fully crossed the room, stopping in front of him. He was even more beautiful up close. His skin was delicate like silk, but his jaw and eyes were strong as iron. He was taller than I anticipated, with a firm posture that emitted great power. And now even closer, I could see that there was definitely something haunted behind those rich, chocolate eyes. I couldn't help myself from wondering about his ghosts.

"I'd like you to meet my former naval captain, Theodore de Villiers, and his son, Jacques."

I had been so enthralled by the dark stranger that I didn't even see the older gentleman standing next to him. I sheepishly curtsied and held my hand out for them to kiss. The older man gave a polite peck. Jacques, however, only raised it next to his lips. He didn't kiss it.

"Your father has praised you a considerable amount, Mademoiselle Esmeralda," the older man said. "I was afraid he was exaggerating, but I'm pleased to find that he's quite accurate in his praises."

I smiled, tickled by the compliment. "My father should save some of those praises for himself. All of my accomplishments are from his spoils."

The older gentlemen nodded in amusement, while Jacques only narrowed his eyes.

"Yes, your father was the best of us at sea," Monsieur de Villiers replied. "Saved quite a few of us—"

"And was rescued plenty of times in return," my father finished. "We're even in terms of life-saving, I assure you."

"You're a hero among us, anyway."

"Stop your flattery, will you? You've already earned

my respect and friendship, no need to keep earning it."

"Then I might earn your agitation just for sport."

The men laughed together, while I caught Jacques's eyes. He had his head cocked to the side, sipping his wine and watching me like an owl about to capture a mouse. His gaze was becoming less exciting and more unnerving. There was something in his eyes…bitterness, perhaps? Anger? But whatever for? I had never met the man.

"Have you danced, my dear?" Father asked me.

I turned back to him and shook my head with a smile. "Looking for a suitable partner, Father. All in good time."

"Perhaps someone nearby would be suitable?"

By the glimmer in his eye, I knew he was teasing to something, but I decided to tease back.

"Are you volunteering, Father?"

"Me? Heavens no. You know I haven't the slightest ounce of rhythm."

Monsieur de Villiers cleared his throat. "As much as I would enjoy the honor of the first dance, I'm afraid I've forgotten all the steps after this blasted knee injury. Jacques, my boy, would you do the honor?"

Jacques—looking bored at the thought—nodded and left his drink on the table. He held out a hand as if he was asking me to pay him a debt instead of for a dance. I took it with a smile, regardless.

He walked us to the middle of the dance floor, his steps long and somehow disinterested.

"I warn you," Jacques said in a dark, gravelly voice that unironically suited him as we came to the middle of the dance floor. "Once we dance, you'll lose interest in taking my hand again."

I giggled behind an open hand, assuming he had a

dry sense of humor. "Is your dancing so bad?"

He turned to me slowly, his eyes changing from amused to something like the winter sea—chilled and unforgiving.

"No," he whispered. "But once you find out who I am, you'll make your distance. Same as everyone else."

I swallowed, catching the seriousness in his tone. "Oh? And just who might you be?"

He gave a proud smile. A real grin. "Someone who holds your fate in the palm of my hand."

CHAPTER 2

ARRANGEMENTS

Jacques was a solemn dancer, hitting each step with perfect precision but without any flare in his step. Was he truly the man Father had picked for me? I didn't mind his face, but the lack of warmth or—well, quite honestly, the lack of any emotion at all—behind his eyes was quite uncomfortable.

"Thank you for the dance," I said with a curtsey and a smile when the music ended. "I'm honored for your time."

He gave a hollow smile in return, and with a quick bow, he left me for the bar once more.

My fate was in his hands, was it? There was only one reason he would say such a thing.

As the night trickled on with suitors and other gentlemen fighting for my attention, I couldn't help my eyes drifting to wherever Jacques was, wondering what kind of future I could possibly have with a man so dark and serious. He didn't seem like the affectionate type. Would he enjoy spring walks to see the blossoms? Winter fires and long stories? No, probably not. He was just...a gargoyle. Father wouldn't pick such a man for me, would he?

After an hour or so of dancing and drinking, I couldn't handle the curiosity burning every corner of my mind. I tracked down Father, linking my arm through his.

"Father, can we speak?"

He nodded with a rosy complexion, leaving his current company but bringing along his drink. We went to the first-floor parlor room, shutting the doors behind us.

"Is the party to your liking, my love?" he asked.

I swung my arms in contentment. "It's the best party you've ever thrown, I'll say. I've never felt more like royalty."

He glowed. "In my eyes, you're better than any royalty."

"I know it," I said proudly. "Which is why I trust your judgment on the man you've arranged for me."

He shifted, swallowing uncomfortably. I paused, allowing him a moment to prepare for my question.

"He's here tonight, isn't he?" I asked.

Father nodded slowly. "He is."

"And he agreed to the wedding after meeting me?"

"He agreed before meeting you."

"He must be an incredible good man for you to allow such an arrangement."

Father nodded. "He will bring you security and stability in every sense. I have no doubt you'll be well taken care of."

I swallowed, playing with my gloves. I then let out a sigh.

"Oh, no need to be coy about it, Father. I know who it is."

Father raised an eyebrow. "You do? And you're not angry?"

"Angry?" I giggled. "Oh, angry, no. He's quite handsome. You certainly know my tastes. But his personality is so dry. And there's a bit of darkness in him I can't put my finger on. You know I've always been good at reading people, Father, but I can't get a sense of anything from him. Why, when we were dancing, he said the strangest thing—"

"Dance?" Father chimed in. "My dear, you never danced with him."

I cocked my head to the side. "No? Whatever do you mean? You weren't setting me up with Jacques?"

Father rubbed his face, the years appearing suddenly in his frown. "Oh, my dear...no. You wouldn't be the wife of Jacques de Villiers, but instead, the wife of *Theodore* de Villiers."

The words struck me, making my mouth nearly too dry to speak.

"Wait," I croaked out. "You want me..."

I lost my voice.

"Theodore is a man of great wealth and power," Father returned. "He also has strong character and is quite popular with women in his city."

"Women his own age, I'm sure! Father, you can't set me up with a man twice my age!"

"A man your age has no assets."

"Jacques as well? Surely his father will pass down his assets..."

Father sipped his wine, swishing it to the side of his cheek. "He has no inheritance."

"No inheritance? Even the youngest have an inheritance. Not unless he's—"

Father's eyes flashed. All my words dried up in my throat.

Jacques was a bastard son. That would be the only reason he wouldn't get an inheritance.

Father's eyes softened alongside his shoulders.

"It's not often that Monsieur De Villiers has the opportunity to spend time with Jacques without gossip and slander," Father continued. "I had hoped that this family would be a safe place for them both."

I folded my arms as I thought about it. It was quite a social rebellion to take in a bastard son. Lina was a bastard child herself, and I remembered the gossip and cruelty she faced from other staff members in our home when our mother decided to hire her. Thinking of her suffering—her lack of prospects and options—I couldn't speak ill of such a family.

If Monsieur De Villiers was acknowledging Jacques in public, then he indeed a generous man. But marriage?

Father's hands on my shoulders brought me out of my thoughts.

"If I had another option, my love, I'd give you an inheritance so large that you never had to set foot at the altar. But I'm afraid…"

He sighed in defeat. Recently he had held back his despair behind a wide, forced smile, but now he couldn't seem to hold back his true feelings. It was clear there were no other options for us.

"We're broke, aren't we?" I asked.

He chewed his lip, his eyes glossing over. "This might be the last birthday you see in this house, my love."

I clenched my teeth, nodding. Even without him saying the words, I could guess it: Father had spent the last of his money to celebrate my birthday.

How could I defy a man who loved me so? How could I take what was his for twenty-one years and then give him nothing in return?

At that moment, I had a vision of him as an old man with no home, healthcare, or food. It crushed my spirit. I could never allow him to reach that point.

"All right, Father," I whispered brokenly. "I'll do as you wish."

***

It was hard to celebrate after that.

I wanted to forget the course of the future and spend my last moments as a single woman in reckless abandon, but the weight of the future was too heavy.

I instead removed myself from the party and walked out onto the ballroom balcony to look out onto the glorious ocean on the horizon in all its wonder, eventually turning my eyes up to the stars and getting lost in my own thoughts.

Marriage was the right thing to do. Father had given everything he had for our family, and I knew if there had been another way he would have ripped the sky apart to give it to me.

But losing all his money to save Mother's health, and his business taking a turn for the worst...

"What are you wishing for?" a velvety voice behind me asked.

I turned to face a man I had never seen before. His almond eyes and lips were dark and sharp, like he could cut me with both a look and a kiss. His clothes were a grade lower than those of the other guests, a rough leather coat in place of the usual crisp silk. He had earrings in both his ears that were lightly brushed by wild chestnut hair, and a scar running up the skin of his neck that had been darkened by the sun.

"At least, that's what I assume you're doing," he continued as I assessed him. "That's the only reason a woman would stare at the stars so intensely."

He came and stood next to me on the balcony, the strong scent of the sea drifting in with him. At this proximity, I realized that he was only a smidge taller than I, and that his blatantly low-quality coat was hiding a slim physique. His features were strong but quite boyish in the corners of his eyes and lips.

No, he was not a man that my father would approve of at all, let alone invite into our home. So why was he here?

"Have we met?" I asked.

He gave a heart-melting grin, sure to charm any barmaid. "Not yet, milady. But I know all about you."

"Oh?" I raised an eyebrow, encouraging him to continue.

"You're a descendant of Neva, aren't you?"

I frowned. I had expected him to say something about Father's fame or fortune, or perhaps our family's business. I hadn't expected him to bring up my great-great-grandmother's name. A name I barely remembered, quite honestly.

"How do you know that name?" I asked.

"She's quite famous where I'm from. She was one of the Guardians of the Eros, wasn't she?"

I burst into laughter. He turned to me with surprise.

"The Eros?" I asked, hiding my amusement behind my hand. "You mean that silly fairy tale about a mythical

16

stone that controls the creatures of the ocean? The old sailor's fable? However did you hear about that?"

He stared at me, not amused. "Where I'm from, the waters talk."

"Maybe you should stop drinking it then."

"And every legend has a bit of truth to it," he said matter-of-factly. "Didn't your family ever talk about the Eros?"

I dabbed the tears from my eyes as I laughed. "Oh, of course they talked about it. It was an amusing story for family gatherings and such. Even I myself believed the fairy tales when I was a child; however, I'm too grown up for that sort of thing now. If that tale were true, my family's reputation would be higher than the king's."

"You give the king too much credit," the stranger returned. "The Eros is more important than anything he's ever done."

I rolled my eyes. "If you came to irritate me about an old silly legend, it's not appreciated."

"Then you're going to hate the duration of our relationship."

"Relationship?" I teased. "Have you decided that there will be such a thing?"

"Aye," he said with another careless smile.

A charmer. How ridiculous.

"Do you use this line with most girls," I asked, "or am I just lucky this evening?"

"You seem rather lucky to me." He turned to face the party inside, leaning against the balcony rail. "Seems like you live fat and pretty in this castle in the sky, yes?"

I glanced over my shoulder. "Yes, well…luck changes."

He pursed his lips and nodded. "Aye. It does."

The edge on his voice made the hair on my arms freeze. I tried not to show my sudden suspicions.

"*Monsieur*, forgive me, but I believe you haven't given me your name."

"How rude of me. Let me introduce myself." He straightened, giving a formal bow. "My name is Captain Adrian Moreau. I'm here to kidnap you."

CHAPTER 3

KIDNAPPED

"What a terrible joke," I said, straightening my headpiece and dress.

"Who's joking?" the self-proclaimed captain replied, his eyes clear and curious.

I scoffed at his foolishness. "I suppose you always announce your crimes before doing them?"

"No, but I thought I'd make an exception. It's your birthday after all."

He gave a fearless smile, leaning in closer. I pulled back.

"What a terrible way to flirt," I reprimanded. "You could have just asked me to dance like a regular gentleman."

He sighed, sighing with exhaustion as he slouched against the balcony rail.

"I'm not interested in your affections," he said. "I'm afraid you've mistaken me. Here. Perhaps this will help?"

He straightened and opened one side of his jacket, revealing a hidden dagger at his waist. My stomach sank when my eyes met back with his. Darkness clouded his face, the playfulness on the edge of his lips turning as sharp as his knife.

He wasn't joking. It was written all over his face.

I held my jaw tight, heart pounding. "If it's money you want —"

"I'm interested in far bigger things than that."

His arrogant smile curled at the ends of his lips, making my palms sweat.

I laughed ironically, trying to break my nerves. "So you expect to walk out of this place with me as your captive and not raise any suspicions? I assure you, there are at least a dozen naval gentlemen inside who would rush to my aid."

He leaned back against the balcony rail again, looking back into the ballroom full of people.

"Yes, I've thought about that," he said. "That's why I think we should make our exit here."

He looked over the side of the railing and then back at me. I looked down at the drop below.

"You're out of your mind!" I yelled. "You can stab me for all I care, I'm not going anywhere with you!"

I turned to scream for my father, only to have my mouth covered and an arm constrict around my waist.

"Easy, darling," the captain whispered in my ear. "Let's not wake the sharks."

He pulled me back toward the edge of the balcony. I clawed and cried out in muffled screams, but he was relentless and much stronger than I cared to admit.

He pulled us up on the ledge of the balcony. The world spun when I glanced below.

Praying for any last hope, I looked back toward the entrance just in time to see Jacques walk out onto the balcony. His eyes met mine, a wave of confusion disrupting his apathetic expression.

I bit the captain's hand. He snarled, pulling his hand back.

"Help me!" I yelled desperately to Jacques. "Get my fath—"

My captor covered my mouth once more, his soft laugh flooding my ears.

"Is she yours, mate?" the captain yelled to Jacques, who was now halfway to us. "I'm going to borrow her for a bit. Hope you don't mind."

And with that, the captain jumped from the ledge, taking me with him.

*****

SEVEN DAYS

I woke up to the smell of cinnamon and cheap alcohol.

My eyes fluttered open, my heartbeat pounding in my head as I looked up to a wooden ceiling. With a stiff neck, I turned to look around the room, which was not lavish or expensive by any means. There was a desk covered in maps and navigation equipment, a few large chairs, and a couple barrels of what I assumed to be liquor based on the smell of the room. The only elegance in the room was the thick red tapestries hanging from the ceiling like upside-down rainbows, and the wild fruits in wicker baskets.

As my eyes followed around the room, they came back to the bed, where a man was sitting and watching me sleep.

Captain Adrian.

I screamed and shoved a foot out, kicking him clear off the bed.

He hit the floor with a grunt and a few swear words, coming back to his feet and towering over me.

"Is this how you greet a man in the morning?" he asked, wincing. "You kick like one of the horses of the apocalypse."

"Where am I?" I commanded. "Why did you bring me here? How long were you watching me with that disturbing look on your face?"

He chuckled, coming forward and leaning over the bed, straightening the stray curls of my hair with a long finger.

"Is it the first time a man has watched you sleep?" he asked. "You must be thrilled at the good fortune of never being approached by a pirate before."

I slapped his hand away. "No! Yes. Wait—"

He chuckled and licked his bottom lip, stepping away from the bed. I sat up and turned to jump off the bed and run, but my head spun with so much vertigo that I could only return back to the bed, palms in the bedsheets to hold myself steady.

"It seems you can't take heights well," Adrian said, pouring an odd light-brown drink into a glass. "You passed out the moment we jumped from your balcony."

He came back over to the bed, sitting down next to me. His thigh grazed against mine. I pulled back, sitting further down the bed.

"Don't worry, darling," he said, taking a sip of the drink. "I want something from you, but it ain't your body. I don't find you that attractive, to be honest."

"You're no morning sunrise either," I snapped back. "If you're wanting ransom—"

"Money would be preferable, but your father has none. Isn't that right?"

I didn't answer. How did he know that?

He took another gulp from the glass, then offered it to me. I looked at it in disgust. First he says I'm unattractive—even with how obviously well-dressed I was—and then he wants to hand me his dirty glass?

"Drink," he said, nudging the glass at me. "It ain't poisoned, and you're probably dehydrated."

I caught the smell of it and nearly gagged. "What is that?"

"Water."

"The hell it is."

He chuckled. "It's water with rum and lime. The rum purifies the water, and the lime wards off disease.

Unless you want to drink sea water and give yourself scurvy, I suggest you drink it."

My tongue suddenly felt like sandpaper, and I hesitated before taking the glass. Under his eyes, I eventually took a sip, the flavor overwhelmingly bitter, sour, and unpleasant.

"Drink faster than that, darling," he said. "I'm not your handmaid."

I downed the glass, hoping the alcohol would settle my nerves. When I finished, he took the glass and leaned forward to get my attention. I stared back into his sharp, deep eyes, the brown in them swirling in mischief.

"Now," he said. "About what I really want."

I waited.

"Take us to the Eros," he said.

I broke out in a laugh, spitting the remnants of the alcohol-water in his face. He pulled back with a grunt.

"The Eros?" I echoed, still laughing. "Are you dense? You truly believe in that old fairy tale?"

He used his sleeve to clean his face. "It's not a fairy tale. It's a real stone. One worth a lot of money when I get my hands on it."

"And what does that have to do with me?"

"Neva," he said, repeating my great-great-grandmother's name. "She was one of the Guardians, was she not? That means you can take us to it."

"You'll have a hard time finding something that doesn't exist," I replied flatly. "My great-great-grandmother died at sea and never told our family of a location. Even if I believed in the Eros, which I must tell you, Captain, I do not, I couldn't tell you where it is."

Contrary to the clear message in my words, he smiled.

"I don't need you to *tell* me the location, darling. I can get it from you in other ways."

He grabbed my wrist, twisting it so that my palm faced up, and extending my arm until it was flat. With his other hand he traced a line from my elbow to my wrist, sending shivers down my spine. His eyes dragged down my arm like he was going to eat it, his gaze meeting my eyes once more.

"Your blood will tell me where to go," he said. "The blood of a descendant of a Guardian will be enough to find what I'm looking for."

I struck his cheek. "Don't touch me like that, you pervert."

"Gah! Such a violent woman," he hissed, rubbing his face. "Usually I'm into that sort of thing, but you have no charm to go with it."

"No charm!" I returned, insulted. "I assure you, dear captain, I am one of the most charming and attractive women on this side of the Atlantic. If you had half a brain, you could see it."

"Maybe that's the problem. All the men you know only have half a brain."

He grabbed me by the wrist again, this time bringing me to my feet. The world spun a second time, and I stumbled, crashing into his chest.

"Such an attitude, yet you're falling for me already," he teased.

I struck his chest to create distance between us.

"Don't flatter yourself," I replied, stumbling once

more.

He reached out and tugged on my hand again, chuckling. "Let's go."

"Go where?"

"To get directions," he said, a deadly smirk engulfing his entire face. "Your blood will tell me all I need to know. It's time to make it talk."

CHAPTER 4

OLDER BROTHER

The salty air hit my face as soon as we stepped out of the room.

How did I not realize we were on a ship?

The ocean stretched out for miles into the horizon, the sun glistening on the water. In front of us were at least a dozen men shuffling back and forth around the deck, yelling at each other in playful banter. They laughed and burst into random songs as Adrian brought me down to the deck.

"Welcome aboard the *Quetzalcoatl*," the captain said with a wave of his hand and an overly exaggerated smile. "If there's anything you need, please don't hesitate to keep your pretty mouth shut about it."

He yanked on my hand, pulling me further along. The singing and banter stopped as we walked past, everyone looking over their shoulders to look at us. I straightened my dress as much as possible. If I was going to be gawked at, it might as well have been for looking good.

"At long last our queen arises!" a cheerful voice sang beside us.

The owner of the voice was a man dressed in wildly colored robes, an apron across his waist, and long fiery hair pulled back in a reckless ponytail. He smirked with a sparkle in his bright green eyes as he saluted me, followed by a bow at the waist.

"Luc," the captain said to the man, nodding. "Have you seen my brother?"

The man wiped his hands on his apron and nodded firmly. "He's in his room, preparing for the end of the world."

"As always," Adrian said, rolling his eyes.

The man named Luc waved a finger at the captain. "You should acknowledge his efforts. You wouldn't be captain if it weren't for him."

"Are you my cook or my mother?"

"What's the difference? I feed you either way."

Luc then turned to me, biting his lip and giving a playful wink.

"And who might the ocean goddess be?" Luc asked. "Will you properly introduce us?"

"No flirting with the hostages," Adrian ordered, snapping his fingers in front of Luc's face.

Luc shrugged. "You can't blame me for having sight, Captain."

Adrian tugged on my arm, leading us away. Luc waved us away with a warm smile and another bow. I found myself smiling despite the circumstances.

"Where are you taking me?" I asked after Adrian brought me down the stairs.

"I don't appreciate you asking it like you're in charge," Adrian replied. "Just follow my orders, *hostage*."

"And if I don't?"

He turned back to me, gripping both my wrists in his hands. It wasn't painful, but it was certainly possessive in a childish sort of way. A hollow deadly smile played across his lips. An ineffective scare tactic.

"Such sass…" he hissed. "Remember that you'll be staying in my quarters, princess. So don't give me any ideas on how to punish you."

He chuckled to himself while I sneered at him.

"Or," he added with a thoughtful nod, "I could leave you with my brother. That would punish you both."

He leaned over and opened the door, throwing me in first. The moment I stumbled through the door, a blade struck next to my ear. I jumped, the point of it only inches from my face.

Following the blade to its owner, I was met with a man with bold eyes, darker than the ocean at midnight.

He pulled his sword out of the wall and stood back to his full height. He was slightly taller than Adrian, his body was stronger and more defined. He was also a bit more elegant, wearing a silk button-up shirt, the sleeves rolled up past his firm biceps.

"Get her out of here," he said to the captain, nodding at me.

His voice was light and airy, a complete opposite of his words. He jabbed the blade of his sword into the floor, straightening his fencing glove while looking directly at me.

"That's hardly the way to greet a lady," I replied, folding my arms across my chest.

"Forgive me, but my anger is not directed toward you, milady," he said sincerely. He pointed his sword at Adrian. "You made this mess. You clean it up. I already told you that I want no part of this."

Adrian shrugged with one shoulder. "I can't really take her back now, can I? Half the city would be after me."

"You should have thought about that beforehand. That's your problem, Adrian. You never think through your idiotic plans."

"My plans have results."

"They have casualties."

The swordsman's eyes pierced through Adrian. Adrian looked away for a second, seemingly to regain his composure.

"You have any other bright ideas then, Henrik?" Adrian asked. "Or would you like to give up and go home now? I'm sure it would be easy for us to pick up another job…"

He didn't finish the sentence, but it seemed he didn't have to. A wave of pain fluttered across the swordsman's face for a brief moment before he shook his head sharply. Not saying another word, he hung his sword on the wall.

"Allow me to properly introduce you, princess," Adrian said to me. "This is Henrik, my first mate and older brother, who is constantly disappointed in me."

"I don't blame him," I replied. "I've known you for twenty minutes, and I don't have high hopes for you either."

Adrian shoved his tongue in his cheek, turning back to his brother. "Well, she's awake now. Can you do it?"

Henrik sighed in irritation and shook his head.

"Only on a full moon," he said. "I told you this already."

"Isn't it all the same? A moon is a moon. It's almost full. Maybe the spirits can't tell the difference."

"And this is why the spirits don't like you."

I couldn't hold in my laughter. "Spirits? What exactly are we discussing here? Ghosts? Fairies?"

They looked at me with cold eyes, then at each other.

Henrik nodded to me, but spoke to Adrian. "She doesn't believe in magic?"

Adrian shrugged. "So far it's the only thing we have in common."

Henrik sucked air through his teeth and nodded slowly. He approached me, grabbing my arm and looking at it from my elbow to my wrist, the same way Adrian had earlier. The difference was that Adrian had looked at my skin like he wanted to devour it. Henrik looked at my arm as if he was a doctor examining it for surgery.

Henrik eventually spoke. "I suppose it doesn't matter whether or not you believe, Mademoiselle…?"

"Esmeralda."

"Mademoiselle Esmeralda," he finished. "Your blood will point us to the Eros either way."

He dropped my hand and looked me over with disinterest. How rude. I straightened my hair in pride.

"So when is the full moon again?" Adrian asked with a yawn.

"Six days," Henrik replied.

Adrian threw back his head and groaned. "So I gotta entertain this thing for a whole week?"

"Your problem, little brother. Not mine."

Henrik pulled a dagger from his pocket, gold on the handle and rusted red on the blade. He looked around the room, stopping when he found a sharpener on the floor next to his scattered books.

"Are you going to go back to swashbuckling ghosts?" Adrian asked as Henrik began to sharpen the knife.

"You know, you're far too relaxed, *Captain*."

Henrik said the title like a swear word.

Adrian only shrugged. "I don't need to stress when you do that enough for both of us." He turned to me. "Come on, Princess Blood. I have a job for you to do for the next week until we slit you open."

I stepped back and folded my arms. "And what makes you think that I'll work for you *or* allow you slit me open? Have you lost your mind?"

"Need I remind you that you're on a boat surrounded by men who are at my command?" He tucked a finger under my chin, forcing me to look up at him. "Don't take my good looks and charming humor at face value. I'm capable of a lot more than you think."

I pulled away. "You only seem capable of impatience and narcissism."

"I could say the same for you, dollface."

"The difference is," I said, "you need my blood and I don't need you at all. So who's at the disadvantage here?"

He stared blankly as I raised a pointed eyebrow. Henrik snorted, licking his lips as if he were trying to wipe away his smile.

Adrian narrowed his eyes at his brother, then turned back to me and gripped both of my wrists again. I winced at the surprise, but, again, it wasn't painful. His hands were unusually warm; his long fingers coiled around my delicate wrists like vines. He leaned in close to my face, pulling his lips back into a smile. I refused to back away, not wanting to give him the satisfaction of the upper hand.

He took it as a challenge, inviting himself closer until his lips almost touched mine.

"Don't be too proud of yourself," he said. "I need you alive, but I don't need you to be happy about it. I can torture you in ways you couldn't dream."

I stared into his eyes. Yes, he meant what he said, but at the same time, somehow I knew he was more harmless than he let on. It must have had something to do with both being captain and having such a tough older brother. That's what I assumed, anyway. I had a gift of reading people, after all, strangers and acquaintances alike.

I leaned to his ear, if for nothing more but to get his lips away from mine.

"I don't think there's any worse torture than listening to you run your mouth for the next week," I replied.

"You know, I'm beginning to like her," Henrik said off to the side.

Adrian growled from his ribs.

"Listen closely, Princess Blood," Adrian muttered. "If you don't want me to go back to your precious broken home and give your father a world of more trouble, I suggest you obey me."

My heart suddenly shattered. Father. I had been so caught up in being kidnapped that I hadn't even thought about how he must have been feeling now, his wife dead and his daughter gone. He must have spent the night without sleep, his head in his hands, just like the day of Mother's funeral.

I had to get back to him. I couldn't let him live that pain twice.

"That's better," Adrian hissed. "There's the submission I was looking for."

"If I help you," I said, "will you let me go back to my father?"

He nodded. "As soon as the Eros is in my hand, you can go back to your father and your fancy suitor, and live happily ever after."

My fiancé? How did he know?

Wait. Jacques. Jacques saw Adrian take me from the balcony. There was no doubt that he had reported it to Father and his friends. As men of the king's navy, they would come for me.

There was hope for my rescue, but I had to survive.

"What are you going to do with her for the next six days?" Henrik asked flatly.

"I'm going to put her to work," Adrian replied. A wide grin decorated his face. "And I have the perfect job for her to do."

CHAPTER 5

FIRST JOB

"Don't get any ideas," Adrian said, arms crossed.

I wasn't sure who he was actually talking to until the cook replied.

"And what ideas would I get?" Luc asked, his fiery hair twirling around his face like a hurricane. "I have to say, I have many ideas, and you'll need to tell me what category not to have ideas in. I have many ideas regarding poetry and soliloquy, introspective and morality, the weather and sea. Or perhaps you'd like me to avoid thoughts about purpose and truths —"

"Everything," Adrian sighed, pinching the bridge of his nose. "Please just don't have any thoughts."

"What an insane way to live!" Luc cried with a shout, clutching his hand to his chest and sinking against the kitchen counter in despair.

"The irony of you speaking about insanity…" Adrian muttered under his breath. He parted his lips with disinterest and turned back to me. "You're his problem now. Or he's your problem. One of the two."

He turned to go up the stairs. I pulled him back by his sleeve.

"You can't leave me here with him!" I said.

He looked down at my hand on him and smirked, seduction glittering behind his eyelashes. "Would you rather come with me?"

I swallowed with disgust and detached myself from his sleeve. He bounced an eyebrow at me and went up the stairs, leaving me alone with the colorfully robed man sobbing over his counter of dry bread.

I pursed my lips.

"He's gone," I muttered. "You can drop the act."

Luc instantly straightened, putting on a dashing smile, wrapping one arm around his waist, and resting his chin on the opposite hand.

"So observant," he said coolly.

I smirked. "Messing with the captain's head, are you?"

"Messing with the captain's head is one of my simple pleasures," Luc replied. "Along with sunsets on the sea, a glass of rum with an intimate partner, or a slow song full of regret."

I stepped forward, looking at the arrangement of breads and fruits around the kitchen. Soup boiled in a pot nearly the same height as my knees, the sharp spices of cumin and chili powder hitting my nose.

I leaned against the counter on my elbow, taking in Luc's facial expressions. Though they were dramatic, they were genuine; they were as wild as his clothes and seemingly as dangerous as the knives beside him.

"Also…" He stepped in closer to meet me, a razor-sharp smile on his lips. "I enjoy observing beautiful women to see what dark secrets they hold."

He studied me like a painting, his eyes darting around my face frantically like he was looking for a secret code on a map. He swooped into my personal space, his face in the same breath of air as my own.

"You smell like the sea," he commented.

"I've been on a boat all night," I replied. "And I live next to the shore."

He touched the sleeve of my dress. "Your family is wealthy."

"Used to be."

"You find me attractive."

He raised his eyebrow and bit his lip. I wasn't impressed, even though he was trying very hard to impress me.

"Not especially," I replied honestly.

He held his smile, regardless. "Not even a little?"

His voice raised slightly, attempting to sound charming.

I shook my head at him. "I'm afraid not."

His bright green eyes sparkled with interest and surprise. "How fascinating…"

"So what will I be doing here?" I asked, stepping back. "It doesn't look like there's much you haven't already covered."

He took a deep breath, puffing out his chest with pride. "It doesn't seem like much, but this kitchen is critical to the morale of the men. Nothing lifts a man's soul like coming back to a hot meal after a day of stealing and killing."

I froze, scrunching my nose. "That's not what you really do, is it?"

"Me? No. Gentle as a fish, I am. I leave all that to the captain and his men."

"What do they steal?"

"What *don't* they steal? Money, food, ships, people…" He directed the last word at me with his finger. "That's what pirates do."

I shifted my weight, my neck chilled. Pirates. Yes, Adrian had referred to himself as such earlier, hadn't he?

I had heard of them, but I had never met them before. And now to be kidnapped by them…

I sighed. Luc cocked his head at me.

"Would you like to share your thoughts?" he asked.

"Why would I trust you with them?" I replied.

"I didn't say a word about trust, little dove," he said. "I just asked if you wanted to share. You don't share a cake with a friend because you trust them with your secrets. You do it because it's simply better than eating alone."

He leaned against the counter, the wild look in his eyes still there. Yet somehow, there was a warmth and patience in them. He was simultaneously the child who refused to stop playing on the beach and the old man looking out on the sea with wisdom.

"I miss my father," I admitted, not knowing why. "I can't imagine what he must be thinking…"

Luc nodded and clicked his tongue. "He's probably devastated. But don't look so depressed. The captain doesn't seem interested in harming you. Not truly, even though he'll probably threaten it. And the first mate would throw him overboard if he tried."

"Henrik?" I asked with a disbelieving laugh. "Why would Henrik defend me?"

"Henrik *is* a man of high honor. He's not the friendliest, as you've probably seen, but he's more pure-hearted than the captain. I dare say the first mate hates this voyage as much as you do."

I wiggled my nose at the thought. Henrik had made an interesting first impression to say the least. Swords in the wall, talk of spirits and slitting my arm in half…and yet, he spoke like a complete gentleman, with an obvious distaste for his brother's ideas.

How curious.

"Are you ready for your work then?" Luc sang.

"What do you want me to do, exactly?"

"Plenty, but we hardly know each other."

"I beg your pardon?"

"In the meantime," he continued, without repeating, "I would like you to wash your hands and put on your best smile. You're a waitress to the crew now, little dove. My personal assistant, and my new favorite slave."

***

There was no mercy.

Luc was quite the dramatic individual, but he was strict in his work, commanding me to clean the kitchen, cut vegetables, and collect eggs from the chickens on board. Honestly, I didn't know how the chickens weren't seasick. The only reason I had any sea legs at all was because Father took me out on ships when I was little.

I had always loved the ocean and the sea. I loved looking at it from our balcony with Mother and Father, while Father told old navy stories and Mother acted them out to make us both laugh. The sea would always remind me of home. And, somehow simultaneously, it would always remind me of how broken my family was now.

"Storm coming in," Luc mentioned casually a few days later as I brought him chicken eggs. "Get those baby yolks somewhere secure."

"A storm?" I asked, slightly nervous.

Even with my experiences at sea, I had never been through a storm before.

"A mild one, perhaps. But enough to put everything on lockdown. Don't worry your feathers, little dove. Even if you fell overboard, you'd bob right up."

He flicked his wrist with a smile, as if that would be enough to comfort me.

"Meanwhile," he continued, "I need you to get on deck and serve lunch. The men are waiting, and I didn't make this soup just so it could tip over when the storm comes in."

Whisking the basket of eggs out of my hand, he grabbed the top of my head and spun me around, shoving me forward. With a scowl, I complied, going to the stove to ladle soup for the men.

The men ate in shifts. Half ate at one time, and then the other half ate after them. This meant that I had the displeasure of dealing with Captain Adrian one hour, and First Mate Henrik the next.

Today, Henrik ate first.

He didn't even acknowledge me as I set down the soup in front of him. He was deep into a book, also ignoring the men around him, who didn't seem interested in him either.

There were graphs and charts on the page he was reading, along with the header, *History of the Winged Islands.*

"Swashbuckler and scholar, eh?" I asked without thinking.

He raised his head, his lips flat, but his large eyes piercing through me.

I cleared my throat. "You know, my father served in the navy near the islands. I always wanted to visit them, but I didn't have the chance. Is that where we're going?"

He pursed his lips. "We go wherever your blood tells us to go."

"Yes, I was thinking about this, and I was thinking, do you really need my *blood?* Can't you just take a lock of hair or spit, or something less—"

"The spirits demand blood. I don't make the rules."

"Yes, but you're a pirate. Can't you break rules?"

He slammed his hand on the table, jumping to his feet to meet me in the eyes.

"Never call me a pirate!" he growled in my face. "I have never once betrayed my king!"

Stunned, I could only stare at him, his eyes filled to the brim with anger and resentment. They were honest; however, his tone and words reminded me of my father's own loyalty to the king. A sense of guilt washed over me, seeing his patriotism.

"Forgive me," I said meekly. "I hadn't realized."

His face paled, his eyelashes fluttering rapidly.

"No, that was inappropriate of me," he said, shaking his head. "I shouldn't have raised my voice at a lady in such a way. None of this is your doing. I…"

He stammered, trailing off as his face contorted into a thousand emotions. I opened my mouth to reply, but before I could say a word he gave a bow, not making any further eye contact as he scrambled to pick up his book and walk off. I only stared, unsure of what had just happened.

One of the men at the table chuckled. "You poked the volcano."

I came out of my daze and focused on the man who spoke. "What do you mean?"

"One wrong word and—*pow.*" He made an explosion gesture over his head. "Be careful, Miss. Many a man has lost a digit or two by the first mate."

He wiggled his fingers for emphasis. I squeezed my hands into fists, confirming that all my fingers were still there.

Luc had called Henrik honorable, and yet, the crew seemed to have an opposite opinion. Even Adrian seemed to have mixed feelings about his brother.

Adrian, on the other hand, seemed practically useless. He was good at managing the crew and keeping them in line, but he had no input on how to do things on a ship that needed to be done. He was like a boy playing with a toy boat, enjoying the adventure and avoiding all of the work.

Adrian had threatened me, but all of his threats proved empty. From the sound of it, Henrik didn't have the same methods.

One brother pretended to have power. The other actually did.

So why was Adrian the captain and not Henrik?

FOUR DAYS

CHAPTER 6

SUFFERING

"Oh, Miss Hostage," Adrian sang, waving his hand back and forth as if it were a bell. "My soup is a bit cold."

I sighed, going back to the table with a hand on my hip. Adrian only smiled, ignoring my obvious annoyance.

"And a moment ago it was too salty, and a few moments before that it was too soggy," I replied. "You're a sailor. Not a king. Just drink it down."

He gave a fake pout. "Ahh, but how can I be a captain if I have no strength? I need a hot meal to keep myself going."

"Then don't be captain," I said over my shoulder as I handed soup to the rest of the crew. "See if I care."

His tone dropped an octave lower, suddenly serious. "Maybe I wasn't clear when I said that I was *captain*."

I turned to meet his eyes. Even though he was leaning back in his seat like a man of leisure and grace, his eyes looked at me like a man who would love to slit my throat open just to watch me bleed.

Which may have been the case four days from now.

For Father's sake, I clenched my teeth, put on a fake smile, and nodded.

"As you wish, *Captain*," I said, adding quickly under my breath, "Captain Jackass."

I returned to the kitchen, leaning against the counter and looking at Luc.

"His Royal Highness would like hotter soup now," I said flatly.

Luc growled. "Is he trying to punish you or me at this point? I don't appreciate the extra work, you know."

"You think I'm enjoying it? I've been kidnapped by pirates and sentenced to kitchen duties before having my body sliced open to find some, what, magical stone that controls fish? Shall we trade places?"

I huffed, sprawling across the counter in emotional exhaustion. I could feel Luc's eyes on me as I watched his hand on the ladle, stirring the soup.

"You don't believe in the powers of the spirit realm," he commented, not a question.

I gave a lazy shrug. "I always enjoyed the myths and fairy tales my mother told me. Father always talked about his life on the sea as if it were a magic carpet ride. But…"

He raised his eyebrows. "But?"

"But then Mother died. Slowly. Painfully. She told stories to keep her spirits up as her own soul left her. None of those stories could save her, and none of them could put together the pieces of my father's heart."

There was a pause.

"It's not your responsibility, you know," Luc said.

"What?"

"To keep your father together."

I straightened to look at him, swallowing my frustration back down my throat.

"Your father grieves because it's part of life," Luc

continued, his eyes—deep as the sea—looking straight through me as he spoke. "But in his grief, he also remembers beautiful things that he wouldn't change for the world. His strength comes from that. He's broken, yes. But he's not fragile, my dove. And there's nothing you can do to put the broken pieces together. That's his own journey."

I clasped my shaking hands into fists.

"What do you know about my father?" I threw back. "Or my family? He's lost everything."

"At some point, we all do."

"You don't know the way he's suffered—"

"Life is full of suffering," he said far too apathetically. "The objective is to accept it and become stronger."

I rolled my eyes with a bitter laugh. "Is that it then? It's as easy as just picking up your knees and marching on?"

"The alternative is sinking to the bottom and suffocating."

I saw red. The nerves in my body suddenly vibrated in frustration.

"How can you say such things without any idea of what we've been through?" I asked. "My family has suffered gravely in the last few years. You shouldn't speak of moving on so casually to someone who has suffered deeply. It's far too cruel."

Luc dropped his ladle, stepping forward and caging me between himself and the kitchen counter with both of his hands. He towered above me, getting my full attention with his deep, swirling eyes. There was a powerful energy coming from him that commanded me completely still.

"Would you like to hear a story about suffering?" he asked in a low voice. "I know a good one."

My jaw clamped shut. He continued.

"I know a bittersweet tale of a boy who grew up as an orphan in the capital city," he said. "He had no family of any sort, and the headmaster of the orphanage beat him so hard that he often blacked out from the pain. He ran away from the orphanage as a teenager, hoping to find a new life. And he did."

He leaned in more, the silk of his robe dancing across my feet as the soup beside us simmered.

"He found a girl of his own age, beautiful and kind," he continued. "Her family took him in, feeding him and hiding him away from the authorities that wished to drag him back to the wretched hellhole he grew up in.

"That girl grew up to be a woman with dreams and aspirations like his, and he couldn't help but fall madly in love with her. In his obsessive love, he asked her to marry him. She agreed. A week before their wedding, he came home to find out that she had been killed in an accident."

My heart stopped. For a moment, I couldn't decide who was more invested in this story: me or Luc.

He took a soft breath through his nose. "Her parents lost their only daughter, and all they were left with was a useless orphan son. In their grief, they abandoned him, and he was alone once again.

"Even now, he is completely alone in his journey. But his pain doesn't hurt him anymore. The memories of his deepest loves keep him alive. And because he learned what great treasure was, he can continue with nothing and still be content. Which is good, because do you know what he does now?"

I shook my head. He leaned into my ear, his breath

fanning the side of my face.

"He makes salty, cold soup for crooked men who like to play pirate."

He pulled back, ladling a new bowl of soup and handing it to me.

"Take this to the captain," he commanded, snapping back into his usual whimsical tone. "Tell him one more complaint about it, and I'll throw him over the side of the ship myself."

His eyes didn't meet mine. He only put his head back over his soup in concentration. My mouth dry and without words, I turned to go back up the stairs.

"Oh, and Esmeralda?" he called.

I turned to face him, but he was still staring at the soup pot.

"Don't worry about your father," he said. "I'll get you home. You have my word."

He turned his back on me as he dabbed the corner of his eye with his knuckle.

I walked mindlessly up the stairs and to the table. I could hear the muttering of the men next to me, but they sounded distant, their voices muddled with the sounds of the waves.

That story wasn't true, was it? I didn't want to accept it. Had a man as vibrant and wild as Luc really…?

"Hey, Princess Blood! Over here!"

I turned back to the sound of the captain's voice, realizing I had completely passed the table. Adrian raised an eyebrow at me, silently asking me what I was doing. I scowled at him in return, storming back to the table and dropping his soup on the table in front of him. It splattered on his shirt. He jumped back with an irritated yelp.

"What are you doing?" he asked, wiping the soup off

his shirt.

I put my hands on both my hips. "Stop asking Luc to remake your food. If you want to torture me, just do it. But stop making him work harder because you want to show off your power like some childish prince."

I was about to walk away, but Adrian's arm shot out to stop me. He stood from his seat, the men going silent as they watched.

"Why the sudden defense for my staff?" he asked, stepping in closer. "Here I thought you weren't an easy woman, but I suppose even the great Princess Blood can't resist the cook's charm—"

"Get your mind out of the mud," I shot back. "I have no affection for any of you. I'm only complying with your ridiculous requests for my father's sake."

"Then I suggest you learn to hold that tongue of yours. He's not any safer when you open your mouth."

I felt my blood rushing in ways it never had before.

"Go near my father," I growled, "and I'll cut you open myself, *Captain*."

I stepped forward to pass him, but he grabbed me and pulled me back, his teeth bared.

"I think you need to cool off, princess."

With that, he reached for his mug of beer and dumped it on my head. I screamed as it ran into my eyes and down my lips, it's stench completely nauseating. He raised the empty glass in a cheer, smiling as if we were old friends making a toast. The men at the table chuckled in amusement at my expense, some even whistling.

With a growl, I turned on my heel and left, going down the stairs to one of the ship lavatories.

I looked in the broken mirror, my hair and face

covered in beer and dirt. I reached down for some water—as brown as the beer itself—and rubbed it against my face.

A bath. All I wanted was a bath.

And for my clothes not to be soiled and torn.

For my hair to have the beautiful shine it always had.

And for my father to be happy as he once was.

But I didn't have any of those things. And for the first time in my life, I had no way to control it. On land, I had the world at my fingertips and my family in my arms.

And now…nothing.

A few tears landed in the barrel of dirtied water. I watched them, my eyes so blurry that it looked like rays of light were sprouting and sinking to the bottom.

Before my sight could clear, a voice struck out behind me, low and far too suggestive.

"I can help you with that wet dress if you'd like."

I looked over my shoulder, to a face I had seen around a few times but never paid much attention to. There were too many men on this ship that wanted the attention of the sole female on the ship, and it was nearly impossible to keep them all straight. He was a full head taller than I, with a twisted beard and crooked teeth. The scent of alcohol became even stronger as the unnamed man stepped in closer, his eyes glittering in ways that made the hair on my neck freeze.

"It must be difficult to be on this ship all alone," he continued. "Surrounded by careless men like the captain."

My stomach soured as his eyes drifted over me. I had a feeling he wasn't much better than the man he was bad-mouthing. Wait, no. He was worse. Adrian was childish and moronic, but he never made me feel like I was in danger.

I couldn't say the same for this man.

I swallowed my disgust, trying to stay diplomatic.

"I appreciate your, uh, consideration," I said, "but I won't be needing your assistance with anything. Please leave."

He shrugged as he crept closer. "Why? There's a lot we haven't learned about each other. You probably don't even know my name, right? Should I introduce myself?"

The way he said it indicated that it wasn't his name that he was offering.

"That won't be necessary," I said firmly. "I'm leaving. Let me pass."

He held his arms out to block me. "Not so fast. Not until I get to know you a little better. Don't you want a friend on board?"

"I need to return to Luc. It's been nice chatting with you."

I tried to bolt past him, but he stepped in and grabbed me. I screamed for him to let me go, but he didn't listen. Instead, he pinned me between himself and the wall. I felt his hands in my hair, and I had a feeling that he wasn't trying to get the beer out of it.

"Thomas!" a voice commanded above us.

Suddenly, there was space and fresh air, my attacker now three steps away from me and bending on one knee to someone at the top of the stairs.

Henrik.

CHAPTER 7

HONOR

Henrik towered atop the stairs, his shadow pouring down them as he stepped down into the room. Once he reached the bottom of the staircase, he glanced at me and then turned back to his subordinate, his eyes narrowing.

"Perhaps I wasn't clear enough when I told you that I only allow men of honor on this ship," Henrik said, his eyes black in anger even though his voice was even. "Do I need to remind you of my rules?"

The man shook his head, still on his knees not daring to look up. "No, sir."

The man curled his fingers under him. As he did, I realized he was missing his middle and ring finger.

"Get up," Henrik commanded. "If I see you within five feet of this woman, I'll be putting you to work with nothing but your right hand."

The man gave a nod and stumbled to his feet, racing back up the stairs. Henrik's eyes followed him, then slid back to me. I was still against the wall, processing everything that had just happened.

Henrik had a casual air about him as he walked toward me, and his soft energy made my shoulders relax.

It wasn't that Henrik was warm or comforting by any means, but something in his presence assured me that he meant me no harm.

He stepped in front of me, looking over my damp hair and soiled dress. I hated him seeing me in such a manner. I hated that anyone saw me like this.

"Your brother poured beer on me," I said quietly, answering his unspoken question.

Henrik gave a short sigh. "Sounds like something the idiot would do."

He looked me over again, as if he was trying to solve some kind of mystery. He could at least have waited to stare when I was properly groomed and dressed.

"You don't know how to fight back, do you?" he asked suddenly.

I burst into laughter. "What kind of question is that? You could at least have asked me if I was all right or if I—"

He suddenly put a hand at my throat, shoving me against the wall. I froze.

Scowling, he dropped his hand.

"Not even a reaction," he muttered. "How inconvenient."

He put his hands in his pockets, chewing his lip thoughtfully.

"Inconvenient!" I threw back. "Being kidnapped is inconvenient enough! If there were some prerequisites you wished I had met, you should have thought about that before—"

He held up a hand. "You're on a ship full of men who are looking for ways to satisfy their greed, selfishness, and empty pockets. Do you think you can survive this place with your quick words alone?"

I shut my mouth tight, narrowing my eyes at him.

He pressed his lips together, nodding to himself. "After dinner."

"What?"

"Come to my room after dinner," he said. "I'm going to teach you how to use something sharper than that tongue of yours."

***

I went to Henrik after dinner.

I wasn't going to. I didn't want to see his face any more than he wanted to see mine. But the one face I *especially* didn't want to see was Adrian's. He wouldn't apologize for his actions, and he would probably just torture me more if given the chance.

The sea was getting rougher, as Luc had predicted. The storm hadn't hit yet, but it wasn't too far off; the wind whipped my hair around into my face as I went from the kitchen to Henrik's room. I was still in my beer-soaked dress since I hadn't a change of clothes on this ship. My hair was in shambles, and so I ran my fingers through it frantically, trying to straighten it.

Oh, what was the point? There was no one to impress on this ship. Why did it matter that I was put together? Everything else was falling apart, why not fall apart with it?

I didn't realize I was standing mindlessly in front of Henrik's door until Henrik threw it open, startling me.

He looked at me quizzically. "You came."

"You told me to."

"I didn't expect you to obey."

"I didn't expect to get trapped on a ship with a bunch of psychos looking for a magic stone. Shit happens."

I threw a hand over my mouth, annoyed at my sudden outburst of emotion. I never had outbursts like that. It wasn't ladylike. And I was nothing if I wasn't a damn charming lady.

A smirk pulled at Henrik's lips, and he motioned for me to come inside.

I walked in, noticing the piles of books scattered around his desk. Walking in further, I noticed a collection of knives, swords, and strange boxes filled with ingredients I saw in doctor offices. I hadn't noticed these things the first time Adrian showed me to Henrik's room.

"Books, weapons, and medicine?" I asked. "Who are you, really?"

Henrik looked over his shoulder as he went toward a pair of swords. "You wouldn't like it if I told you."

"I don't like much of anything these days. Humor me."

He picked up two swords, walking back to me.

"I think the question is who are *you* ?" he replied. "A descendant of one of the Guardians, and yet doesn't believe in magic? I would think that your family would be swimming in it."

I shrugged. "My mother liked fairy tales, but that's all they were."

Henrik must have heard the pain in my voice, because he paused for a long moment before continuing.

"I wasn't much of a believer in the beginning either," he said. "My uncle claimed to have connections to the spirit world. We all thought he was crazy. I certainly did. That was until…"

He paused for a moment, looking as if he was deciding whether or not to continue.

"Before what?" I encouraged.

He sighed. "Before the spirit world started talking to me."

I raised my eyebrows at him as he bounced the swords in his hands, looking at the handles.

"First it was hallucinations," he said. "Then vivid dreams. Voices of the dead. My uncle taught me how to read stars to predict the future, and I thought it was a useless party trick…until it started working."

I cocked my head to the side. "You're an astrologer."

He sighed with a nod. "An astrologer and an alchemist, thanks to my uncle. I did my best to run from it. Astrology is not a proper pastime for a naval officer."

My heart skipped a beat. "You're navy?"

He winced as if I had just jabbed him. "I *was.*"

He held out a sword to me. I reached for it, not sure of why I was taking it.

"You're giving your hostage a sword?" I asked. "Seems counterproductive."

"To be perfectly clear, I did not kidnap you," he said, suddenly defensive. "I had no idea that my brother was even planning it until he showed up with you, unconscious. Had I known that he was planning such a terrible thing, I wouldn't have allowed it."

The cold tone in his voice convinced me that he was telling the truth.

"You could let me go home, you know," I said.

He took a deep breath, letting it out slowly. His eyes met mine, a deep and exhausted pain in them.

"I wish it were that simple," he replied.

Thunder ripped across the sky. I jumped, holding the sword to my chest.

Henrik looked up as if he could see it through the ceiling. "The storm is coming in. Come on. I need to teach you basic defense before it arrives."

"Defense?" my head was swirling with too much information now. "Why would I need to learn that? Why are you offering in the first place?"

"Because I don't want anyone spilling your blood before I do."

He said it so flatly, he must have been telling the truth. Did he have to be so casual about cutting me open? It was eerie.

"So let's begin the first lesson," he said. "How to hold a sword. Pay close attention. I'm not trying to cut you open."

He gave a quick ironic smile.

"Yet," he added.

CHAPTER 8

BEFORE THE STORM

Holding a sword was harder than I remembered. Father always kept a sharp rapier on his wall as a toast to his glory days in the navy. Henrik's sword was incredibly similar, which gave me some comfort. It was almost as if I was a five-year-old girl again, Father telling me how to parry and strike, a laugh on his face, proud of his only daughter being as tough as the men of his ship.

Only I wasn't on his ship.

And I wasn't as tough as I thought I was.

And Henrik was anything but proud of me.

"I suppose I shouldn't have expected you to be naturally talented in this field," he said, seemingly half to himself. "You've probably never lifted your arm longer than it takes to wave for a maid."

I gritted my teeth. "You certainly have a lot of opinions."

"Am I wrong?"

My eyes dropped to the ground as I tried to catch my breath.

"All you taught me was how to hold it and wave it around in the air," I threw back, changing the subject. "You taught me nothing useful at all."

"Holding it in the air and waving it around is the basic foundation of sword fighting, you know."

He smirked. I frowned.

"Forget it," I finally replied. "If you're just going to insult me, I don't need your instruction."

I tossed the sword at his feet and crossed my sore arms. He slipped a foot under the sword, bouncing it up in the air and catching it. He leaned it up against the wall and walked back toward me.

"You'll take my instruction," he commanded, "because I might not be able to save you when things go south."

"Then make sure nothing goes south," I replied, shrugging.

We shared a brief smile.

Suddenly, the ship lurched to the side, knocking us both off our feet. I flew onto Henrik's bed, and he stumbled forward, landing on top of me. I instinctively shut my eyes as the ship rebalanced itself, Henrik pinning his elbows on either side of me to keep us both steady.

When it had calmed, I opened my eyes and huffed out a shaky breath, realizing how close he was to my face.

I gave a charming smile.

"Perhaps this was all a ruse to get me alone?" I asked, raising my voice slightly to make it sound more innocent despite the content of my words.

His eyes changed. It was such a small shift, but it was enough for me to see I shouldn't have spoken so thoughtlessly. Even more so when his fingers brushed my shoulders. I froze again.

"H-Henrik?" I asked.

He then shook his head sharply, pulling away from me and coming back to his feet. He didn't make any eye contact as he turned away and checked on the belongings that had slid off his desk.

"That's enough for the night," he said, his ears turning pink as he picked things up off the floor and threw them back on the desk. "You should return to your roo—"

He stopped, realizing.

"You mean Adrian's room," I finished.

He huffed, licking his lips. "That's right. You sleep in his bed, don't you?"

I tsked. "The monster makes me sleep on the floor. Then he purposely sticks his foot in my face to wake me up in the morning."

Henrik snorted, pressing his lips together to swallow an obvious smile.

"He's probably waiting for you," Henrik finally said after clearing his throat. "And the storm is coming. You should get back to your room."

"Can't I just—"

"No."

He paused, sucking his lip for a second and shaking his head.

"What I mean is…" he began. "I'm a…and you can't… "

He trailed off, looking completely lost at how to answer. I sighed, sliding off the bed.

"I understand. I'll go back." I gave a slight curtsey before going to the door. "Thank you for the lesson."

"Esmeralda, wait."

I turned toward him.

He avoided my eyes for a moment before speaking. "If…if my brother tries anything, please inform me."

"Tries…?"

He narrowed his eyes, and I caught his meaning.

"And come back tomorrow," he continued. "I still have a lot to teach you."

"Can you teach me how to get revenge on your brother for the beer stains in my dress?"

His lips pulled to the side. "It'll be our first lesson."

***

The wind beat against my face as I went back up the deck. Men were yelling to each other as they went from one side of the ship to the other. My nerves shook. Was the storm going to be bad? Perhaps the ship would topple over in the middle of the storm, and we'd all fall into the ocean and drown. Or perhaps I'd be left behind to save myself, only to get trapped and go down with the ship. Or perhaps Adrian would throw me overboard to save his men. Whatever the outcome, it was far too unsettling.

I ran to my room, shutting the door behind me with a slam.

Then I remembered why I had wanted to stay in Henrik's room in the first place.

Adrian looked up from his desk, glaring through thin glasses. He took them off and threw them on the desk next to his papers, leaning back in the chair to analyze me. I frowned back.

"You're late," he said.

"I didn't realize I had a curfew."

"You got better places to be?"

"Anywhere away from you is fine by me."

He gave a long, *long* sigh.

"I wonder if Henrik knows a way to silence you until the next full moon," he said, coming to his feet and stepping toward me.

I stepped back, scowling, not answering. (Besides, I knew that if Henrik knew a way, he would have used it on someone already.)

Adrian continued more in my space, eyebrows matting as he looked at my face.

"Where were you?" he asked. "And why are you so out of breath?"

I wasn't going to tell him about Henrik's lesson. If I had told Adrian that Henrik was teaching my sword fighting, he would probably ask me to demonstrate something.

"Shouldn't you be out on the deck with the others, Captain?" I asked instead.

He rolled his eyes. "My men don't need me for a pithy drizzle. We're not in any real danger."

The ship lurched sideways again, knocking me to the floor. Adrian towered above me, raising an eyebrow.

"You're quite unbalanced," he commented.

I tried to return to my feet, but my ankle folded under me, shooting pain into my leg. It wasn't half as painful as my embarrassment, however. I still smelled like beer and kitchen smoke, my hair was sticky, and my dress was starting to tear. I put my finger through one of the holes in my dress. Instead of wearing this expensive thing only to have it ruined by pirates, I could have sold it to help my father.

I didn't even know we were hurting so badly. I had no idea that my father was suffering alone.

"Are you just going to stay down there?" Adrian taunted.

I bit hard on my lip. He couldn't see me cry. That was the last thing he could do.

He grabbed my arm and pulled me up to my feet. I dropped my head down so he couldn't see my eyes, but it didn't last long. He reached over and turned my chin up to face him. I couldn't see his expression through my tears, but I felt his hand soften against my jaw before it dropped.

It was silent for a long moment.

"These clothes are terrible for working in, aren't they?" he asked, his voice unusually soft.

I dabbed my eyes with my sleeve as he stepped away to a chest in the corner, opening it and pulling out a large navy blue dress shirt, a belt, and some slacks. He handed them to me.

"They're not the latest fashion," he said, "but they're clean, anyway."

He held my gaze, the whites of his eyes soft and innocent. He did nothing but breathe as I reached out for them, my fingers grazing his as I took them.

"Thank you," I whispered.

He nodded. "Happy birthday."

I burst into laughter, the irony and idiocy hitting me at once. When I couldn't stop laughing, he laughed with me, almost like a boy instead of the feared captain of the ship.

A terrible rumble ripped through my chest and made the windows shudder. I yelped, dropping the clothes in my hands and jumping into Adrian's chest. He scoffed, but I felt one strong arm wrap around me, holding me steady.

"It's just thunder, Princess Blood."

I wanted to let go of his shirt out of pride, but I couldn't.

"I've never been on sea during a storm," I said. "Are we going to be okay?"

"No one dies on my ship."

"What if we get thrown off?"

"I'll come get you."

I leaned back, looking into his eyes. He was smirking like a boy who liked to pull girls' pigtails and show them worms, but the way his arms were wrapped around my waist was anything but boyish.

"We still need to cut you open, right?" he added.

I shoved him away, remembering myself. I looked down at my arm.

"I'm not going to kill you, you know," he said. "It's just a cut."

I rubbed my arm. It was already aching.

"What are you going to do with this stone of yours once you find it?" I asked.

He shrugged. "Get a lot of money."

My mouth gaped. "That's your master plan for the most powerful stone in mythology?"

He pursed his lips and nodded.

"You're using me for a get-rich-quick scheme?"

"Hey, I wouldn't call it *quick*," he returned. "First, I had to get a crew, then I had to steal a ship, and then I had to find the descendant of one of the Guardians of the Eros and kidnap her…I've been busy. This has been a lot of work."

"You're ridiculous."

"You're high maintenance. We're even."

"I'm high maintenance? You're the one—"

Thunder boomed again, sending me to my ankles. I swung my arms over my head to protect myself. Adrian snorted and laughed from above.

"I guess there's no other option," he muttered. "I'm going to have to keep you close to me tonight."

CHAPTER 9

LESSONS

I awoke to the smell of the sea. It was fresh and clean, the salt cleansing my mind of all stress and fear. This was the reason I slept with my bedroom window open. The scent of the sea was always the cure for anything that made my heart ache.

Mother's death.

Father's failing business.

My betrothal to a total stranger twice my age.

The thoughts tumbled through my mind, but only stayed for a moment, the smell of the sea soothing my aching heart.

I squeezed my pillow.

It'll be okay, Mother. I'll keep our family together now that you're gone. I won't let us fall apart.

My pillow sighed.

I gasped, eyes shooting open. I sat up, my head spinning from the sudden shift in position as I looked behind me. Adrian looked up at me, half awake, his eyes still heavy.

"Morning, Princess Blood," he croaked. "Did you enjoy sleeping in my bed last night?"

I gasped a second time, wondering how I could have forgotten that I was kidnapped and staying in a room with a pirate.

Well, a lot had happened in a few days.

Wait…why was I in Adrian's bed and not on the floor?

Memories of the previous night hit me like a tidal wave. There was a storm. Thunder, lightning, and then I—

Oh no…

I turned my face away and tried to straighten my hair.

"How dare you try to take advantage of an honest lady, Captain."

Even I couldn't deny the crack in my voice as I said it.

He chuckled. The bed shifted, and suddenly his chin was against my shoulder.

"First," he said deep in my ear in a low, groggy voice, "I'm no honest gentleman. Second, *you* came onto *me* last night."

I threw my head back to scold him, not realizing how close he was. I turned away quickly, cheeks burning.

"I-I-I did no such thing," I insisted.

"You don't remember?" he teased. "How scared you were during the storm? How you jumped into my bed and gripped onto my shirt, begging me to protect you?"

I swallowed and shook my head.

"You held on so tight to me all night," he continued. "I'm sure there's fingernail dents in my neck still. Why don't you look for me?"

I slithered out of bed, not looking at him. "You're full of stories."

"Not to mention all the dirty little things you say in your sleep…"

I picked up the belt Adrian had given me yesterday and fastened it around my waist, the coolness of his shirt next to my skin. I tried to ignore how much I now smelled like him, as well as the coy look he was giving me from his bed.

"I'm going to help Luc with breakfast," I said, storming out the door.

I slammed it behind me, still dizzy as I tried to scrub the memory of last night out of my head.

"Don't leave me, please. I'm so scared."

"I've got you, princess."

"Hold me…just for a little bit. Until it stops."

I inwardly groaned, drowning in embarrassment.

How could I throw myself at him like that? Even if I was half asleep at the time and thought it was a dream…

Oh God. What else had I said in my sleep?

I arrived at the kitchen, vaguely aware of Luc humming and bobbing around the kitchen.

"Good morning, my queen!" Luc said, nearly dancing across the kitchen as he cooked breakfast. "How did you sleep last night? It was a beautiful storm, was it not?"

I finally let out an unladylike groan. "Let's not talk about last night, please."

"You don't feel energized and alive?" he asked. "I always feel great after a good storm."

I had to admit, I felt a bit lighter than I had yesterday afternoon. I slept really well. Mainly because of Adri—

No. No, that wasn't the reason.

Luc pranced toward me, his bright and vibrant robes swirling around him. He smiled, his teeth like pearls. He took my hands in his, bringing them to his chest.

"I was thinking about you last night," he said.

I blinked at his sudden confession. "What?"

"I want us to be friends, my dove," he said. "I heard you give the captain an earful yesterday on my behalf. I was quite touched. I think you and I would make a good team. What do you say?"

I sighed, giving a weak smile. "I wouldn't mind having a friend in this place, honestly."

His warmth radiated as he smiled even brighter.

"I thought as much!" he sang. "You and I are kindred spirits, dove. I'm sure of it."

He bounced back to his counter, munching on a stale piece of celery, his hands dancing around the vegetables and knives. It was hard to believe Luc had ever suffered, the way he always glided and danced through his daily tasks. How had he healed? What were his secrets?

"Be a dove and get the eggs from the chickens, could you?" he sang. "I think this calls for a special soup of mine."

I laughed as he danced around the kitchen while he spoke. If working included colleagues like Luc, then maybe I could get a decent job to help Father.

If they ever let me off this ship, that is.

I spent the entire day with Luc, helping him prepare breakfast, lunch, and dinner for the crew. He taught me some tricks of cooking for the men, even teaching me to chop the ingredients.

"You're holding the knife wrong," he said.

"I'm holding the handle," I threw back. "How else do you hold it?"

"Like you're in love with it, dove. Like this."

His fingers wrapped around mine, slipping them around the knife in a new manner. He smiled over my shoulder, his airy scent tickling my nose.

"There," he whispered. "Isn't this much better?"

I shrugged apathetically, looking at the new way my fingers were torqued around the handle.

"It's not as comfortable as before," I returned.

He lingered there for a moment, pursing his lips. I looked back at him, waiting for him to say something. He flipped over my wrist, putting two fingers against it.

"Your heart isn't racing," he commented.

I raised an eyebrow. "Should it be?"

"Of course! I'm an incredibly desirable man with my hand on yours. You should be weak in the knees. I'm insulted at this lack of response."

I laughed, pulling my hand away. "Don't you have more important things to concern yourself with, Chef?"

He scratched at the faint stubble on his chin, not answering.

"How did you become part of the crew here, anyway?" I asked.

He shrugged. "I worked odd jobs in restaurants. Some restaurants were for more…*colorful* crowds than the others. I heard Adrian was hiring for his ship, and I jumped at the chance."

"Did you know Adrian before this voyage?"

"Only by reputation. Surely you heard about the fires at the courthouse and the hijacked food carriages?"

"*That* was his doing?" I gasped.

Luc nodded nonchalantly. "Among other things."

There had been multiple shortages of supplies across the country due to groups of thieves ambushing traders on their routes. The courthouse fire was the grandest talk of the town right after Mother had passed. The authorities struggled to find any suspects of the damages that had injured nearly half a dozen people, deemed a terrorist attack by someone who was clearly against the king himself.

"And despite all that," I said, "you decided to work for Adrian anyway?"

Luc opened his mouth to answer, but a loud cheer came from above the kitchen. He shut his mouth again, laughing to himself.

"A story for another time, it appears," he said, reaching over and preparing the trays for me to take. "The men are ready to eat. Take this food on up, dove. The last thing we want are hungry men bound for hell."

***

"Better," Henrik said after our fourth lesson. "You're sharper today."

I smiled at the compliment, handing him back his sword. I felt more powerful during this lesson, and I was happy that Henrik noticed it as well.

"This is where you're supposed to say that it's because I'm an excellent teacher," he said after some silence.

"I wouldn't want to ruin your humility," I replied.

He chuckled, putting the swords away. As he mounted them back to the wall, I was reminded of Father. How was Father now? Was he still healthy? Did he have hope at my return?

My smile faded, and I sat in the chair next to Henrik's desk, tracing the maps on the pages of his books.

"What's wrong?" he asked after a moment.

I sighed. "You know, I'm not sure what's worse: being kidnapped, or the life I have to return to once I'm set free."

I leaned my chin against my hand, looking down at the books. The map in front of me was the same islands

Henrik had been looking at before: the Winged Islands. The ones that Father had promised to show me before Mother died. He could probably never show them to me now.

"You know my family is completely broke," I said.

Henrik hesitated. "Aye."

"Did you know I was betrothed?"

I could nearly feel Henrik's shock behind me. "What?"

"I don't know him," I admitted. "He's an old colleague of my father's, from the navy. I'm sure he's very honorable, but when I go back, I…"

I couldn't finish the sentence. Henrik's bootsteps came closer until he was standing right in front of me, his presence lingering over me like seafoam. His jaw was tight, his eyes shifting into something deeper than before.

"You said you were in the navy too, didn't you?" I asked, wanting to avoid his possible questions. "What happened? Why are you on this ship now looking for the Eros? A mission for the king?"

He flattened his lips as if he wasn't meant to tell me. To my surprise, he began to answer.

"Something like that," he said. "The truth is—"

"So here you are," a third voice said. "I wondered where you kept disappearing to."

We both turned to Adrian in the doorway, eating an apple as he stared at both of us. Henrik straightened while I rolled my eyes.

"Can you knock?" Henrik asked.

Adrian shrugged. "It's my ship. I'm the *captain*, remember?"

There was a low growl from Henrik's throat, barely audible. Adrian approached us, still chewing on his apple.

"I didn't think you'd be so hospitable, Henrik," he said. "You never show any of these types of courtesies to the men on this ship."

"She's your captive. Not mine."

Something in my chest fluttered as Henrik said it, as if he was protecting me instead of keeping me against my will.

"That's true," Adrian agreed. "She *is* my hostage. So why does she keep coming to *your* room?"

He looked around the room, his eyes stopping at the swords on the wall. He narrowed his eyes.

"You're teaching her sword fighting," Adrian said, answering his own question. "Why?"

Henrik stepped forward. "Because the moment we cut her open—"

"Please stop saying it that way," I interjected.

"The spirit world is going to open up with her," Henrik finished. "It's best to be prepared."

My heart sank into my stomach. No one told me about the opening of the spirit world. This week had been busy enough already.

Adrian only laughed. "What? Are we going to get attacked by demons and angels, sea monsters or fairies? Don't be crazy."

"I'm not crazy," Henrik huffed. "And no, it won't be what you expect, but there is still a great power in the waters that you don't understand—"

Adrian interrupted, "The only reason I agreed to all this nonsense was for the Eros. I agreed to all your voodoo methods until this point, but we're reaching a new level of psychotic."

Henrik's face went red, his eyes deepening to a dark void. It was such a subtle shift, but something that probably happened often.

"You still think I'm crazy, don't you?" he asked. "Even after everything?"

Adrian shrugged. "You're family. It doesn't matter much to me if you're crazy or not. But you're going to end up like Uncle Leo at this rate, muttering insane babel—"

Henrik took the apple out of Adrian's hand and threw it against the wall. It splattered, the pieces hitting the ground around Adrian's feet.

"He wasn't crazy because he could speak to spirits!" Henrik threw back. "He was crazy because no one believed that he could!"

I came to my feet, the sudden urge to calm the tension in the room. "Gentlemen, gentlemen. Let's not forget that *I'm* the one getting sliced the day after tomorrow. I'd rather you both keep your wits about you if you insist on this."

I had no reason to say such things, of course, but if these two were really planning to cut me open, I didn't want them to be so emotional as they did so.

I touched Henrik's shoulder. He softened at my touch, looking over his shoulder at me. There was a pain in his eyes I hadn't seen before, mixed with the obvious anger I had seen often.

Adrian leaned over and grabbed my hand. His grip was harsh, as was his voice, as he pulled me away from Henrik.

"I'll be taking my hostage back to her room now," Adrian said. "One of us has to do this right. And your voodoo better come through, older brother, or else you'll be the same stain on the family crest that Uncle Leo is."

Henrik's eyes blazed as Adrian dragged me out of his room, and despite how hard I struggled, Adrian only held on tighter.

"What on earth is wrong with you?' I yelled as he dragged me back to his room. "What's the problem with me spending time with Henrik?"

He pulled me forward to face him. "The problem, Princess Blood, is that you're a hostage. You're not a guest. You don't teach a hostage how to fight back. You teach a hostage to submit."

As he said the word, he shut the door and shoved me against it, leaning his face close to mine. I tried to break free, but he only pushed me up against the door harder.

"Listen to me," he said in a low growl. "You are not one of my men. I'm not here to protect you, care for you, or do any form of worship. I just need you to bleed out for me, and if you can't remember that, I might take more blood than necessary just so you don't forget my authority here."

"What authority?" I threw back. "I've never once seen you act as captain. All you do is play pirate captain like a child. There's not an ounce of maturity in you that could sustain the responsibilities of being a captain! Henrik is more of a captain than you'll ever be."

His grip tightened. I winced. All the other times Adrian had gripped me like this, it had been playful. Henrik's name, however, seemed to have hit a piece of his spirit that was off-limits.

"It doesn't matter who you think is more qualified," he growled in my face. "I own this ship. I own this crew. I own the moon, the stars, and the sea—and now, I own you."

His head dipped down further toward mine, his nose grazing my cheek. I turned my head away, my heart pounding in my throat.

"Don't you dare," I breathed out.

For a breath, he was still in my space, hesitating, his breath close to my neck. He then suddenly released me, stepping back to look me in the eyes.

"You've made a mistake in comparing me to him, princess," Adrian said, licking his bottom lip. "Now I'll show you just what kind of pirate captain I can *really* be."

ONE DAY

CHAPTER 10

STORIES

"Think of it as your belated birthday party."

Adrian smirked as he motioned to all the men sitting around the tables, already getting into a heavy amount of drinking for the evening.

I frowned. "A party? For me? You said I wasn't a guest on this ship."

"You're not. Which is why you won't be celebrating with us. You'll be getting more alcohol for my crew."

He kicked me in the rear with his hard boot. I grunted, turning and kicking him in the hip in return. My kick wasn't nearly as strong as his, but I wasn't going to show that I knew that. By his smirk, I could tell that he already knew how weak I was in comparison.

For now.

I wished I was spending time with Henrik that evening, just to learn how to stab Adrian, if necessary.

"I think you're too comfortable with me," Adrian said, chuckling, motioning to where I had just kicked him. "Should I show you your place—"

"Oh, enough! I'll get your stupid alcohol. Just stop bragging about your position."

His tongue grazed the bottom of his lip as he popped his eyebrow. "Is there another position you'd like me to talk about?"

I threw my hands up in disgust and turned my back on him. I could hear him laughing as I left to go to the kitchen.

"His royal captain demands more alcohol," I told Luc.

"It sounds like a party!" Luc said with some enthusiasm. "It must be because of the ceremony tomorrow."

I shuddered. "You all say it so casually. As if cutting me open means nothing to any of you. I expected you to care a little bit, Luc."

He chuckled, holding up my arm. He slid a fingernail down the vein that started at the wrist and went to my elbow.

"It's a harmless cut," he said gently.

"That's a foolish combination of words."

"It's sincerely not dangerous. They'll take a small silver dagger, made of pearl and black ocean stone, and put a tiny nick in your arm. Right here." He tapped on the meaty part of my arm between my wrist and elbow. "Henrik will say a few words, you'll drip some blood on a candle, and the candle will explode and open up the spirit world."

I stiffened.

"You want to say that last part again?"

He shook his head at me as if he were calming an anxious child. "You're a hostage, dove, but you're not in any real danger. I'll protect you. You have my word."

"Why don't you protect me by preventing me from getting cut open and opening up the spirit realm? I'd rather not do either one, you know."

He took both my hands and shook them warmly. "I wish I could, dove. I really do."

"Why can't—"

He shoved two large bottles of alcohol into my arms.

"Take this up to the captain," he said with a smile. "Let him drink his fill tonight. He may not have the chance to drink properly after tomorrow night."

Luc turned me around and shoved me back up the stairs.

"Why does everyone keep forcing me to walk back and forth from the kitchen?" I complained. "Just tell me to go. I can walk. Both you and the captain, I swear…"

I muttered to myself as I went back up the stairs, handing out the bottles of alcohol. The men took it eagerly, thanking me and bantering as they filled their cups to the brim.

"Always good to see a bottle of rum and a pair of beautiful eyes," one of the crew said to me, raising his bottle in thanks.

"Enough of your nonsense, Christian," I replied.

"I prefer the rum," another said with a cackle, nodding at me bitterly. "It doesn't have a pair of lips to tell me to pick up my laundry."

"Or to point out the way you smell," I added with a twisted face.

The men at the table chuckled in response.

"Esmeralda!" Adrian barked from the other side of the table. "Come here."

I rolled my eyes and put a hand on my hip as I walked over to him, awaiting another one of his orders. He waved two fingers at me to come closer. I didn't. He waved two fingers again, sharper. I huffed, walking over to meet him.

"Can I help you?" I asked, standing next to him.

He grabbed my arm and pulled me into his lap, wrapping an arm around me. I squirmed, annoyed at the arrogant grin on his face.

"What are you doing!" I yelled in his face. "Let me go at once!"

"You still have a submission problem," he replied, not releasing me. "You're going to sit here until you understand how that works."

The men laughed as Adrian wrapped a second arm around me, bringing me in close to him.

"Atta boy, Captain!"

"Show her who's boss!"

"Lucky bastard has all the fun!"

I put a hand in his face, pushing his greasy smile away from me.

"Have some manners!" I growled.

He pulled my hand away, his arrogant smile now replaced by an irritated scowl.

"Why don't you be a good girl and feed me those dried pieces of fruit on the table?"

He twisted my wrist slightly, making me wince and hiss. His fingertips digging into my back were a second warning.

I reached back to the table and picked up the fruit, cringing as I stuck a piece in his mouth. He chewed happily—like a juvenile calf chewing grass—making me more and more uncomfortable with each bite.

"Childish scoundrel," I muttered in his face.

"High-maintenance *debutante*," he replied.

The men continued to laugh. I looked over my

shoulder, realizing that Henrik was sitting at the table not too far off from where we were. He looked at both Adrian and me then glared, the anger starting to cloud his eyes once more as his hand tightened around his glass.

Adrian put a finger to my chin and forced me to look at him.

"Eyes over here, princess. I want to watch you hate me as you do this."

"You're a terrible and vile human be—"

Luc's voice rang out above the crowd. "Gentlemen! Allow me to be your entertainment tonight!"

He practically sang it as he said it, jumping up on the table and using it as a walkway to greet the men. He skillfully danced along the dishes and cups, not knocking a single morsel of food from its plate.

"I have a wondrous tale of adventure and intrigue," he said, "and a little romance, if it tickles your fancy. Would the captain be ever so gracious to allow my tale?"

Adrian shrugged and nodded. Luc looked at me and winked.

"Then listen closely, dear men of the sea! For among the five great seas is a terrible curse!"

The men buzzed with laughter and intrigue.

"What kind of curse?" one man shouted out to appease the storyteller.

"I'm glad you asked, good sir. Glad you asked! You need to know many things about our dear waters if you ever hope to survive them."

Luc sank down to his ankles, his robe brushing the plates of fruit and dried bread. He held his hands out as he began his story.

"Once the sea was guarded by spirits of the air and water, a harmony of beautiful protection and fair travel for the sailors that wished to find their own way."

The table went silent. Even Adrian didn't seem as interested in torturing me for the moment, his eyes glued to Luc.

"The spirits blessed the sailors," Luc continued, "hoping to see the humans thrive and live peacefully, in a way that brought harmony to the spirit and human realms. And for many—nay, hundreds—of years, the spirit realm and the human realm were one in the same."

I glanced at Henrik, who was leaning forward on his elbows in interest.

"But!" Luc cried out, "the humans became greedy and arrogant. They thought they were greater than the spirits. 'They serve us!' they cried. 'We are the masters of them! Look how they worship us!' Their hearts became proud and cold, demanding from the spirits things that were not theirs.

"As time progressed, the spirits became more and more angry. 'Look at these men!' they said. 'They worship themselves so that they choose to abandon their families, betray their kings, and torment the spirit world with their boasting! We shall create demons to patrol the waters, destroying those who would bring impurity to the sea.' And thus, the sirens were born."

Adrian chuckled. "Sirens? Those half-fish people?"

Luc clicked his tongue in dissatisfaction. "Those are *merfolk*, my dear captain. They existed long before the curse, and yes, they were turned into spirit creatures of the sea. Sirens, however, were creatures born of the air. They bore wings and flew over the sea, finding sailors of black hearts to bring to their deaths. Whoever escaped the sirens were killed by the merfolk. Whoever escaped the merfolk were plucked out of the sky by sirens."

Something in my stomach churned. The idea of killing men—evil or not—made everything within me shudder with fear. How could someone kill so easily? Were there really men so far from redemption?

"And under what conditions did the sirens and merfolk decide who would be destroyed and who wouldn't?" Henrik asked, breaking his silence at the table.

Luc put a finger to his nose with a smile. "I should have known you'd ask the philosophical questions, my dear first mate. To find the men of black hearts, a siren only has to look deep into the eyes of his victim. From that he can see every pure or black-hearted desire."

Luc's eyes rested on mine for a long moment, the light of the moon picking up his green irises in a breathtaking glow. It wasn't until he looked away that I remembered to inhale.

"A load of bullshit," Adrian said with a laugh. "Is there a man so pure? If sirens existed, they would have swept half these bastards off my ship."

The men laughed in agreement. Luc curled his fingers against his own chin thoughtfully.

"You may not laugh so much when the spirit world is opened once again," he warned.

Adrian grunted as he rolled his head back. "You and Henrik must spend too much time together. You both go on about the same things."

Henrik said nothing, his expression cold.

"You'd do well to respect the spirit world, Captain," Luc said, his voice serious despite the playful glow in his smile. "Just because you pay no mind to them doesn't mean they won't search your heart."

Adrian shrugged, uninterested. "I have no concerns for my morality."

Henrik was the one to laugh at this statement. "No truer words spoken."

With a stone gaze, Henrik threw back the rest of his drink and stood from the table. He waved his hand in dismissal at the rest of the table, then abandoned the party to return to his room.

Adrian watched him leave, an uncomfortable swallow sliding down his throat. I saw a flicker of something in his face. Pain?

He turned to face me, his eyes meeting mine. As if he could see me trying to read him, he hardened his face and his grip.

"You wanna stare closer, princess?"

He leaned in, and I shoved him away, standing to my feet. He watched me with a straight face, his shoulders and jaw tense.

"Let's get back to the party," he said to the others, raising his glass in a toast. "To our blackened and useless hearts, gentlemen!"

The men cheered and they all drank, Adrian's eyes sliding back toward his brother.

***

Adrian was a heavy sleeper when he was drunk. He snored with his mouth wide open, tempting me to drop something in it just to watch him choke.

On the other hand, he looked like a child; not like the fearless captain of a ship who spent none of his time commandeering and all of his time trying to prove that he was better than everyone else. No, there was something so innocent about his vulnerability in this moment.

But I was going to strangle him if he didn't stop snoring.

Deciding to let him live, I left the room and went out on the deck. The ocean was calm and deep, black in the moonlight. Something about the sight of it instantly soothed my soul despite the situation.

Tomorrow they would cut me. Luc and Henrik were sure it would open up the spirit world. What did that mean?

Just thinking about the possibilities, my entire nervous system vibrated, bringing goose bumps to my skin.

"You'll catch a cold," a voice said behind me.

I turned to see Henrik, who looked as if he had just woken up himself. His hair was floating around his face from the ocean wind, reminding me of cotton candy at the town fair. He removed his outer robe and stepped forward, wrapping it around me.

"Such a gentleman," I commented as he wrapped my shoulders. "You're not a very good kidnapper, you know."

He smiled as he looked into my eyes. "You're not my hostage."

After a heartbeat he looked away, leaning against the rail of the ship and looking up into the sky.

"Why are you out here?" he asked.

"Your brother snores like a dying horse when he's drunk."

Henrik snorted and laughed. "I haven't heard it said in quite those words, but yes, now that you mention it." He then stiffened. "Did he try anything on you?"

I shook my head. "He passed out as soon as he got

into his room."

Henrik nodded, satisfied. "He's not a terrible person, really. Truly. He's just incredibly naive and has no sense of good and evil. He sees a goal and he goes for it. He doesn't think about the consequences."

I leaned over the rail, looking at Henrik's face instead of up at the stars with him. From the side, his nose was straight and proper, much like Henrik himself; his cheekbones high on firm on his rectangular face. It amazed me how his face reflected his character, and I wondered which one had been shaped first. He caught my gaze, looking back at me with confusion.

"What?" he asked.

"Why are you two *really* at odds with each other?" I asked. "Every time you stand in the same room together, I feel like someone is going to get stabbed."

He laughed, leaning back and continuing to look at the sky. "It's that obvious, is it? Yes, we have some bad blood between us. We want the same thing, but we have very different views on how to get it."

"What do you want?"

He didn't answer right away, the wind blowing through his hair as if to encourage him to share his thoughts.

"We both want the Eros," he said after a moment.

"You as well?" I asked, surprised.

"Aye," he said. "Myself as well. And unfortunately, you're the only one who can make that happen. I wish I was able to ask you for your assistance properly, but it seems I'm too late now."

"Adrian said it was for money, but I have a feeling that it's not the same for you."

Henrik laughed. "That's where you're wrong. I'm in it for the money as well."

I raised my eyebrows in confusion. "What do you mean? I can believe that Adrian would want a get-rich-quick lifestyle, but that's not who you are at all."

He swallowed, looking at me as if he was deciding whether or not to tell me anything further.

"Tell me?" I asked sweetly, trying to encourage him.

He puffed out some air before running his fingers through his hair. "Our mother is sick."

The words hit me in the chest. Hard.

"And our father," Henrik continued, "is unable to work to help her. His arm was crushed in a carriage accident, and no one will hire a cripple. I was working in the navy to share the financial burden, but my crew never felt comfortable with me. The king was always wary of my…talents."

He looked at his hands.

"They thought you were a shaman, didn't they?" I asked.

He nodded. "They said I'd bring the devil on the king eventually. They said it like it was a joke, but I always knew it wasn't. It took me years to prove my worth as a navy officer. But then…"

He stopped, shaking his head like he had water in his ears. "Forget it. Why am I telling you all this? It's not important."

He held his head, starting to walk away. I grabbed him and pulled him back.

"Of course it is," you replied. "I get it now. You were released from the navy because they didn't trust your gifts. But if you find the Eros…"

He nodded to himself. "I can prove I'm not insane.

I can present it to the king and perhaps get my job back. If I don't..."

His eyes drifted with his words, down to my hand on his arm, and suddenly my fingertips burned. I slowly released him and held fast to his jacket around my shoulders instead.

"Henrik, you've shown me kindness in this situation, and I want to return the favor."

His eyebrows matted. "What do you mean?"

I took off the coat he lent me and handed it back to him. He took it like it was a foreign object he had never seen before.

"I'll help you," I said.

He dropped the jacket. "What?"

"It'll save your mother, won't it? And your reputation with the king?"

He picked his jacket up off the floor. "Yes, I suppose…but…why would that concern you? We stole you, Esmeralda. You're in danger because of us."

I looked up at the stars, the ones I had wished on so many times. If I had had any chance to save my mother from her death, I would have sold my soul for it. But I knew it wasn't possible. She was gone. I couldn't save my mother anymore, but maybe I could save someone else's.

"It concerns me more than you think," I said. "Whatever you need, I'll give you. Just tell me what to do."

REDEMPTION DAY

CHAPTER 11

OPENING

I was shaking by sundown.

"You're going to cut yourself open before the ceremony if you keep trying to chop vegetables like that," Luc said, noticing my hands.

I dropped the knife, holding my face in my hands. If I shut my eyes tight enough, I was back in my room, waking up in my bed next to the oceanside. I would wake up to Father's blueberry crepes for Sunday brunch, then curl up with Mother on the sofa with our embroidery and talk about the current art exhibits in town.

Warm hands suddenly covered my own, pulling them away from my face.

"Open your eyes, little dove," Luc coaxed.

I bit my lip. "I don't think I can."

His thumbs grazed my eyes, the calluses on his fingers somehow soothing. He said nothing until I finally felt brave enough to open my eyes and look at the gentle smile on his face.

"Don't be so nervous, dove," he said. "I promised to protect you, didn't I?"

I swallowed, mouth dry. "What's going to happen?"

"To you? Nothing."

"But Henrik said that the spirit world would open. What does that even mean? You and Henrik both—"

"Understand that reality is more than it seems," Luc finished. His hands tightened around mine. "Henrik has been called by the spirit world for some time. He knows what he's doing."

"And you?" I asked. "What connection do you have?"

His eyes shimmered again, like the sun reflecting off the waves.

"When I lost my fiancée, I wondered if I could ever find her again," he said. "In the depths of my grief, I searched for a path to the afterlife to find a way to hear her speak one last time. I saw fortune tellers and psychics, priests and hypnotists."

He stopped, licking his bottom lip. My heart pounded.

"Did you hear from her?" I asked, holding my breath.

He gave a light and empty smile, shaking his head.

"The dead are dead. They have their own realm, separated by bodies that can't reach us here." He raised his head a bit higher. "But, at the same time, I learned that there was a different world than our own. A world desperate to be connected again. Drowned out by man's own ideas of morality and purpose, the spirit world has been lost and exiled. Do you know what happens when it's connected again?"

I shook my head. He leaned forward, so close that I could smell the scent of rum and lime on his breath against my cheek.

"Redemption," he whispered.

Something made my blood run hot as he said it. The

word was familiar, like a form of nostalgia.

"Am I interrupting?" a voice asked from the stairway.

I turned to Adrian's frown. Luc took a step back, putting his hands in his pockets and giving a nod of acknowledgment.

"It's rare to see you in my kitchen, Captain," Luc said. "What's the honor?"

"Supply check," Adrian said. "There's a port three days east. I need to know if we need to stop."

Luc nodded. "We will."

Adrian raised an eyebrow. "You're sure?"

"It will be a much longer journey than you anticipate, Captain." A mischievous grin hid in the corners of Luc's lips. "Also, you'll need to stop by the blacksmith, perhaps, and pick up something to protect yourself from the demons of the spiritual realm."

Adrian laughed and rolled his eyes. He held up his hands. "These have served me well enough."

He came forward, reaching out and grabbing me by the arm.

"You don't have to drag me everywhere," I scolded as he started to pull me to the door. "All you have to do is ask like a gentleman—"

"Where's the fun in that?" he returned.

He looked over his shoulder to Luc.

"She won't be able to help you this evening," Adrian said. "She needs to be prepared."

Luc gave a salute. He wasn't emotionally distraught enough, honestly.

I thought you said you'd protect me? I asked him with a look.

He only looked straight at me and smiled.

Adrian dragged me back up the stairs, taking me toward Henrik's room. He stopped just before the door, pushing me up against the wall, as he tended to do when he was annoyed about something and couldn't figure out how to use words properly.

"Fancy meeting you here," I said with a sigh. "There's nothing intimidating about this position, you know."

"Do you want to tell me what you're doing?" he asked.

"Ballet rehearsal."

"I'm serious, Esmeralda," he said. "Why is it when I find you with Luc, you're always—"

He stopped, visibly gritting his teeth. I looked down at our feet, which were so close together that they were nearly on top of each other.

"As close as you and I are now?" I returned.

He didn't answer, unintentionally agreeing to my question.

"And why does that bother you, Captain?" I asked.

I searched his eyes as he remained silent. It took less than a moment to understand.

The captain was jealous?

I couldn't help but smile. How entertaining.

"Does it bother you?" I teased. "That I'm so close to another man on your ship?"

I didn't think he would be able to come any closer, but he proved me wrong. His feet were nearly up against the wall with mine. I had never seen a look so serious on his face, the usual childish charm completely evaporated.

"Don't tempt me, woman," he whispered. "I'm already out of patience."

He stood against me for a breath, until the door

opened beside us. Henrik stepped out, looking between the two of us. His face was flat, completely void of all emotion. He crossed his arms over his chest.

Adrian took a step back and then grabbed my hand and pushed me toward Henrik.

"Get her ready," Adrian growled. "Let's get this over with."

***

The moon started to rise over the ship. It was full and white, sending light over the deck as Henrik drew circles with white chalk around us.

"What is it for?" I asked.

"It protects the ship," he said, not looking up. "And you."

I shuddered. "Am I in danger?"

To this, he stopped, lifting his eyes to meet mine. "We all are."

Adrian's boots echoed over the deck as he appeared on the scene. He looked over the chalk markings.

"You're going to clean all this up, right?" he asked. "I don't want this staining the wood."

Henrik rolled his eyes. "You should be worried about more important things."

"This is important. This ship is a loan."

"It's stolen."

Adrian waved his hand apathetically. "Logistics."

Adrian looked over at me, as I sat quietly in the middle of a triple circle of chalk, an unlit candle three feet from my ankles.

"You're finally being submissive?" he asked.

I shrugged and folded my arms in annoyance.

"Henrik acts like a gentleman and treats me with utmost respect. Your life would be much more fruitful if you did the same."

He swallowed roughly. I didn't know why he was so angry about the critique.

"How do you know this is going to work?" Adrian asked Henrik while glaring at me.

"Does it matter?" Henrik returned. "You haven't believed anything I said about the spirits since I first spoke with them. I don't need your interest now."

"By the way," Adrian said, ignoring his brother's bitterness, "I heard you told the crew to prepare for battle. They all have weapons at the ready and keep watching the horizon. What ghost story did you tell them to get them all spooked? You're supposed to be second in command. I don't want you abusing your power."

Henrik slammed his chalk on the ground, breaking it in half. "Which one of us has abused his power, Adrian?"

It went silent, with only Henrik's breathing and the waves filling up the void.

"Forget it," Adrian said, huffing. "Just finish up."

He went toward the edge of the ship and sat against the rail, turning his back on the both of us.

Henrik exhaled slowly, putting his hand through his hair. He came and kneeled in front of me, pulling out a dagger. It was just as Luc had said: a silver dagger made with a black stone and a pearl handle.

"It's beautiful," I said, not thinking.

He stopped in surprise, then quickly smiled. "For such a proper lady, you have a strange interest in sharp objects."

"I've never seen a design like that. Where did you get

it?"

"Black market. It's the only place to buy items related to magic." He gave a sarcastic smile. "Regular markets don't serve the *insane.*"

His energy turned cold and heavy. I couldn't help but put a hand on his.

"I don't think you're crazy," I said.

His hand shifted under mine, but he didn't pull away. "You believe me?"

I nodded.

"Why?"

I thought for a moment. "I don't know...but something in my gut tells me that everything you say is true."

"Why aren't you afraid, then?"

I leaned forward, trying to make sure Adrian didn't hear me.

"Believe it or not," I said, "I'm always afraid."

His energy softened, a trace of warmth filling in his eyes.

"Henrik," I whispered, half desperate. "Will you protect me?"

He swallowed, his hand slowly retracting from mine and coming up to my face. He tucked a stray hair behind my ear, his touch soft and endearing.

"Of course I'll protect you," he said. "Anything you ask, Esmeralda."

He blinked twice, shutting his eyes hard and pulling away. He held his head—just as he had the previous night—and shook it.

"Are you all right?" I asked. "You've been doing that quite often recently. Do you get headaches?"

He looked down at his hand with the dagger, then back up at me. His eyes narrowed, the warmth in them replaced with confusion. His hand tightened on the dagger.

"Who are you?" he whispered in an accusation.

I didn't have a chance to ask what he meant.

"It's almost time," a third voice cut in.

We both looked up to Luc, his expression surprisingly grim. The moon held itself high above his head, the ocean breeze swirling his hair against his face.

Henrik nodded at him. "Came to watch?"

Luc's lips puckered. "Something like that."

Luc's eyes rested on me.

Henrik turned back to me, taking a pack of matches out of his pocket. He lit the candle at my ankles, the flame holding strong despite the breeze around us.

I swallowed.

Henrik reached his hand out. He invited my hand, not taking it by force like Adrian would have. I looked to Luc, who only nodded. With his encouragement and no other options, I reached out and took Henrik's warm hand. He pulled my arm straight over the candle, the flame licking the bottom of my arm.

"Forgive me, mademoiselle," he whispered to me.

With one long last glance, Henrik said something under his breath, raised the knife, and sliced the blade across my arm.

CHAPTER 12

MERGED

I winced. The cut stung and ached, the blood slowly pushing through the slice of my arm. It trickled down toward the candle.

It fell.

One drop.

Two drops.

Three drops.

When I breathed out, the ship rattled.

Thunder split the sky in half, so loud that my ribs shook. I couldn't hold back a scream, the candle exploding into a pillar of fire in front of me. I was yanked backwards, a body suddenly covering mine.

I could hear voices yelling in chaos around me, but they were weak compared to the thunder that was still rolling above us. I was pinned, unable to look up at the sky.

Instead, I looked over my shoulder to see who was on top of me.

Luc smiled down at me, petting my hair in reassurance.

"I'm here, little dove. Don't worry."

"What's happening?" I asked.

He looked up at the sky, grinning.

"Redemption," he said.

Suddenly, there was a long, low gasp in the air. It turned into a chorus of gasps, becoming louder and louder, as if the gods of the sea were trying to suck the air out of the sky. Luc's warm hands brushed against my hair as he shushed me and commanded I stay calm. I could barely hear him over the gasping sounds and the pounding of my heart in my ears.

"What the hell is that?" I heard Adrian cry out.

I looked at the thick pillar of fire, where the candle used to be. Now, there were teal and gray gusts of smoke swirling around the flames, winding tighter and tighter until it choked out the flames completely. The flames burst even higher in the air, breaking through the clouds. Henrik grabbed Adrian by the neck and threw him down, his eyes shifting to me quickly and then to Luc. He nodded to me, as if he was trying to console me, but then turned his attention back to the pillar of teal, gray, and fire.

The tower of fire touched the tip of the sky, splitting it in half with white light. The ship lurched underneath us, and I couldn't help but scream again, the jolt bringing air back to my lungs. Luc tightened his grip around me, his ocean scent releasing some tension in my nerves.

The gasps turned into the sounds of birds, as if hundreds of birds were in the air at once. The light in the sky began to melt and drip, and before the light fell into the water, it turned into wings and flew over the ship.

"What are they?" I asked Luc.

He looked down at me with the smile of a boy on Christmas day.

"The sirens," he said, laughing.

The wings burst into light and fire, then morphed and stretched until they resembled something relating to a human shape. They were like angels, or perhaps human butterflies, transforming from teal wisps to human flesh and raven feathers. It was hard to look away from them as they swarmed the ship.

"Devil blood…" they whispered in unison, their voices shaking the air.

One of them flew straight at Luc and me. I could only watch, seeing its face slowly change from pure fire to the form of a human skull.

But before it could reach us, it hissed and drew back. I recognized Henrik's boots in front of us.

"Release!" he yelled.

Suddenly, there was a cry from the men and the sound of leather snapping. Luc covered me completely. I couldn't make out what was happening. All I heard was hissing, battle cries, and later…the sound of silence.

Luc's breath was ragged on top of me, but when the silence had fully taken over and the ship had calmed, he slid off.

He slumped back, breathing heavily as he curled up in pain.

"Luc!" I cried, holding him steady. "What happened?"

"One of the bastards got me," he whispered, his eyes rolling to the back of his head.

He passed out cold on the deck. I cried for Henrik, who came to our side and ordered the men to take Luc down to his room. My hand slid from Luc's grasp as they took him.

"He protected me," I muttered to myself, eyes tearing from guilt.

Henrik's hands came to my shoulders. "Are you all right?"

"Yes, but Luc—"

"I'll take care of him. I promise."

Henrik's eyes softened. My hands shook.

Someone groaned next to us. "I'm fine, thanks for asking."

Adrian rolled his tongue across his lip as he came to his feet and glared at both of us.

"What was all that then?" he asked Henrik.

Henrik helped me to my feet as he spoke to Adrian. "The spirit realm."

"I got that, smartass. But what *was* that?"

"Sirens," I said mindlessly.

"And what was it you threw at them?" Adrian asked Henrik, not seeming to hear me.

"Stones soaked in holy water," Henrik replied. "The combination of natural earth and something connected to the spirit realm burns them."

"So they're not dead?" Adrian asked.

Henrik shook his head. "They're depleted of energy, probably. They'll come back, though. Sirens are called to declare the hearts of men good or evil, remember?"

I started to shake, my nerves taking over again. It felt like my soul was trying to separate from my body, just as my mind had separated from reality. I felt Henrik's arms wrap around me.

"What's wrong with her?" Adrian asked, his voice seeming far away.

"She's in shock, you idiot."

My gaze met Adrian's. He stared into my soul, jaw firm. I could see him, but I couldn't say anything or even move.

"Take her back to my room," he commanded. "Watch her until I return from checking on the rest of the men. Get ready to prepare more of those stones and water. I refuse to go down so easily, from a demon, fairy, or otherwise."

"Captain!" a voice called from the crow's nest. "Look starboard!"

Adrian turned his head, looking out onto the horizon. When he stopped, I gasped, seeing what the commotion was about.

In the far distance was a red beam, shooting up from the ocean to the sky, turning into a blood red star.

Adrian smiled. "The Eros."

CHAPTER 13

AID

Henrik walked me back to Adrian's room, gently helping me to sit on the sofa. I couldn't help but look at my arm, the blood now dry against it. Henrik followed my eyes. He knelt down and brushed his shirt against the blood, flicking it away.

"It really worked," I said.

Henrik let out a chuckle. "You said you believed me."

"I believed you. I just don't believe what I saw."

Henrik stopped and looked up at me, breaking into a giddy smile and laughing.

"What's so funny?" I asked, never seeing him in such a state.

"Oh, it's fantastic!" he cried, rocking back onto the ground. "Now they know I'm not crazy! They all saw it from themselves, didn't they?"

He threw his head back and laughed, as if he was releasing the tension from every nerve in his body. He was half hysteric, this new side of him making me unsure of how to react.

When he finished laughing, which was some time, he stopped to stare at me with gratitude, tears streaming down his face from laughter.

"Thank you, Esmeralda," he said. "Because of you, my name won't be stained any longer."

My heart pounded as he smiled, but my joy in his praise was short-lived.

"But now…" I started.

I didn't know how to finish. Henrik caught my meaning and nodded solemnly.

"Yes," he said. "The spirit world is now reopened."

"What closed it in the first place? What happens now? Will they come after us again? Will they go after other sailors at sea? What about the navy?"

Henrik waited until I finished asking questions, but shook his head. "I don't have the answers to everything. I just know that our worlds were separated for a time, and now they are reconnected again. Now there's nothing holding back the sirens and merfolk from judging the sea again."

"Is it only the sea they judge?"

Henrik nodded. "From what I understand. I was once told that the spirits don't destroy men on land— men on land destroy each other. The sirens and merfolk wait until men are secluded. Then they strike."

I swallowed. If a siren was to look into my soul, what would they see?

Also, what would happen to the men on the ship? To Luc? To Adrian? To Henrik?

Henrik stood, sitting next to me on the sofa and folding his hands in his lap. He leaned forward, resting his elbows on his knees and staring at the wall in thought.

"This will be a terrible shock for the people who disregarded the warnings all these years," he eventually said. "We can only hope those in spiritual positions can lead them in the right direction."

The emotional distance between his face and his words was painful. I rested a hand on his. His fingers wrapped around mine as he hung his head. We sat together, hand in hand, in complete silence as the weight of the new world weighed on both of us.

Adrian threw the door open, looking at us both. His eyes rested on our hands linked together. Under Adrian's intense gaze, I started to pull my hand back, but Henrik held it fast.

Adrian rolled his tongue against his lip.

"We had a few injuries," Adrian reported. "I'll need you to look at them. You have the most experience with this kind of thing."

"And Luc?" I asked eagerly.

Adrian's eyes flicked over to me and he nodded softly. "He seems stable."

Henrik nodded, squeezing my hand before coming to his feet and getting ready to leave. Adrian grabbed his arm before he got all the way out the door.

"I'm sorry," Adrian said, his voice saturated in earnestness.

Henrik stopped, but didn't look at him, only nodding before he left again. I saw the pain in Adrian's eyes once more as Henrik stepped out.

Adrian then came to me, looking down at me with some type of sincerity. I had never seen such concern in his eyes before.

"Are you all right?" he asked, with no mockery in his tone.

I nodded. I came to my feet to meet him, but stumbled, my legs still weak from the stress. Adrian caught me before I hit the ground, laughing softly.

"Henrik was right," he said. "You're pretty weak."

I gritted my teeth and began to open my mouth to reply, but he swept me into his arms off the ground before I had a chance. He smiled as he held me bridal style, the corners of his mouth gently teasing me.

"I'll just have to be your strength then," he whispered.

He carried me to the bed, sitting me down on it and standing over me with a smirk. When he turned his head away, I noticed the blood dripping from his elbow to his wrist. I reached out and grabbed his shirt.

"You're bleeding," I said.

Adrian followed my eyes to his cuts and shrugged. "I guess we're even then."

I pulled him back and rolled up his sleeve, finding the source of the cut at his bicep.

"How did you get cut?" I asked.

"Not sure. A lot was happening." He laughed. "Why do you look so worried? I've been sliced deeper than this."

I looked to his nightstand, reaching for the wrap bandage there. I had been using it for my blisters from Henrik's sword training, but now it had a different purpose.

I pulled hard on Adrian's arm to make him sit next to me. He grunted.

"I'm fine, princess…"

"Shut up before I change my mind."

I wrapped his arm, ignoring how strong his gaze on me was. The soft sound of the air going in and out of his chest made my heart pound, wondering what words he was conjuring.

"What's gotten into you?" he asked. "You refuse to even stand in the same room as me if you can help it. Suddenly, you want to tend my wounds? What's the game?"

I scoffed, sealing the wrap. "No game. I was only trying to help."

"Why? Because of my brother?"

I looked at him, confused. "What are you talking about?"

"Don't play the fool, princess. I've seen the way he looks at you. The way you're always together." He nearly growled it as he said it. "Are you trying to be nice to me to gain his affections?"

I laughed in his face. "First you accuse me of being too close to Luc, and now Henrik? Honestly, Captain, if I wanted *Henrik's* affections, I wouldn't need to be nice to *you*. This is only kindness. You'd know that if you'd ever try being a decent person."

He pinched my chin, bringing my face up to meet his. He was closer than he should have been, his breath fanning my lips in a way that made my lungs freeze. His eyes drifted over my face before he gave a pained smile.

"I hate how innocent you are," he whispered. "It makes me feel like a demon."

He let go, pulling back. I exhaled, swallowing my heartbeat.

"Besides, you already have a suitor, don't you?" he asked as I finished up the dressing. "That tall, honorable-looking creature that met us on the balcony?"

"I don't have a suitor," I countered. "I have a—"

I stopped. Adrian raised an eyebrow at me, waiting for me to continue. I swallowed my words.

"Don't tell me..." Adrian said, showing his teeth as he gritted them together. "You're betrothed?"

My head snapped up. "How did you know?"

He paused, his eyes darkening.

"I didn't." He rolled his tongue against his cheek. "I was making a joke. I thought I was, anyway."

He stood and stepped away from the bed toward the mirror. I held my knees as he looked at the wrap around his arm in the reflection.

"What now?" I asked to break the silence.

"A bath, maybe."

"I meant about the Eros."

HIs eyes met mine in the mirror. "You saw the red star. We follow it. Wherever it leads. For however long it takes."

"And your promise?"

"What promise?" he asked coldly.

I stood from the bed, stepping toward him. "To take me back to my father."

He smirked and shrugged. "Is the Eros in my hand? Once I have it, you can go back to your father. Maybe."

"Then at least let me send word to him—"

"Out of the question."

I grabbed his arm, desperation pouring from my throat. "Please, Adrian…"

The captain stopped, looking at my hand gripping his arm.

"I'm all he has left," I whispered.

Adrian's eyes darted around the room for a moment before he shook me off. Without a word, he walked to the other side of the room and opened the drawer to his desk. He handed me a piece of blank paper.

"Write it in your own hand then," he said. "But leave out names and locations. Tell him you are well, and nothing else."

Overcome with relief, I wrapped my arms around his neck and hugged him. He grunted in annoyance, but it wasn't long before an arm snaked around my waist in return.

"You better keep your distance, princess," he said in my ear. "Before I lose my senses to you completely."

CHAPTER 14

TRANSPARENT

I awoke to boots stomping across the floor.

My eyes fluttered open, Adrian's blurry room coming into view. There was a light breeze as he walked past the bed, the scent of rum and cinnamon waking me further, my eyes clearing.

Adrian removed his jacket and sat at his desk, pulling out his glasses to take a look at a pile of maps. He pulled out his compass, taking notes in a small journal. I stayed silent, unmoving, wanting to observe him longer without him knowing.

I had never seen him so focused. With the earnest focus in his eyes, it was hard to believe this was the same cocky, devil-may-care criminal who kidnapped me.

My arm ached as I stretched out. The cut in it wasn't deep, but it stung, a terrible reminder of the things I had witnessed the night before.

"You're awake," Adrian said.

I sat up slowly, realizing I was in his bed again. I looked at the bedsheets, dazed.

"Did we—?" I started.

Adrian lifted his eyes to mine, palming the compass in his hand. He shook his head. "You slept alone. Don't get used to sleeping in my bed, though, Princess Blood. You're still not my guest."

His eyes turned downward, and I suddenly saw the dark circles under them.

"You didn't sleep?" I asked, sliding off the bed.

He gave a bitter laugh, writing more notes in his journal. "I saw demons fall from the sky and attack my men. You think I could sleep after that?"

He scribbled his notes more aggressively. I stood up and approached his desk, looking over his shoulder at his notes. He spread his hand over the page, blocking my view.

"Keep away from my journals, princess. The information in them doesn't concern you."

I frowned. "I was just curious. No need to bite my head off."

There was a frustrated aura around him, something heavy and hopeless.

"What's wrong?" I asked.

"Nothing."

"You're lying."

"I'm not."

I put a hand on his shoulder. "Adrian…"

He stood, shaking off my hand and walking to the other side of the room to his shelves, his back toward me. "Don't say my name like that. Shouldn't you be getting breakfast ready or something?"

I gasped, a hand flying to my face as I remembered the events of the day before fully.

"Luc! Is he all right?"

Adrian shrugged. "Go see for yourself."

I ran to the door, swinging it open. I turned my head back one more time to Adrian, watching him violently flipping pages in his book at his shelf, his lips muttering silent words to themselves.

I tapped on the door frame for his attention. "I asked if you were all right too, you know."

He shut his book, his head rolling over his shoulder to look at me.

"Don't worry about me," he muttered. "We're not *arranged* to care for one another."

I glanced at his bedsheets, eyes narrowing.

"Not *arranged* to care, huh?" I asked. "Is that why you took care of me last night?"

He stopped, putting a hand on his bookshelf and dropping his head. He then looked at me with one eye narrowed as if he was trying to solve a mystery.

"I'm not suited to take care of anyone, princess. Don't forget it."

He turned his back on me, going back to his desk.

With nothing to say, I left him to his brooding, rushing down the stairs to find Luc in the infirmary. Out of habit of having perfect manners, I knocked on the door first.

"Come in," a hoarse voice returned.

I threw open the door at the weak sound of his voice. He was lying on his bunk, wrapped tight in blankets, only his head and arms exposed. He turned his head toward me and gave a weak smile.

"Little dove, is that you?" he asked.

I went to his side, sitting on the bed and looking into his deep green eyes, dull and faded in the dim light of the room.

"Do you feel any better?" I asked. "Are you in pain?"

He gave a weak smile. "You know, even though we've only known each other for such a short time, I feel like I've known you forever. Kindred spirits, you and I."

He reached out for my hand and I gave it to him, alarmed at how cold his hands were.

"Luc?" I asked, concerned.

"Ah, what a time it's been on the sea!" he sighed. "I should have liked to sail with you forever. That kitchen… it's been so lonely. I never realized until now."

His eyes searched mine, a faded look on his face.

"Promise me that you'll take care of the men," he said. "And yourself."

He coughed, giving a jagged breath.

"What's wrong?" I asked.

He winced. "Siren poison. I'm afraid I've been cut deeply."

"What! What do you mean? I'll get Henrik—"

I stood from the bed and started to leave, but Luc pulled me back.

"There's nothing he can do," he said. "We tried. It's too late."

He gave a sorrowful smile, grasping my fingertips.

"I wish I could keep my promise," he said, coughing again. "But I don't know how much time I have. Can I have one last request?"

I nodded. "Yes, but don't call it your last."

He held his arms out. "Give me a hug goodbye? I shall miss your arms, little dove."

I turned my head away in thought, then turned back to him and nodded. I leaned down on the bed and wrapped my arms around him, letting his warm embrace engulf me. His hands rested on the small of my back as his lips brushed against my ear.

"I hope we meet in the next life, my dove."

I nodded. "As do I…but first I'm going to send you to hell where you belong."

I reached for a pillow and smothered his face with it, standing up with an exasperated grunt. He pulled the pillow off, laughing.

I gripped my hands into fists. "If you dare fake your death again, so help me, Luc, I'll really make you spew your last words!"

He rested his arms behind his head with a wide grin. "I really can't fool you, can I?"

"You're no better than the captain, honestly."

He faked a look of shock. "How dare you! I'm far more charming and pure."

"You're both liars who play with other people's emotions."

His smile faded a bit. "Yes…I suppose that's true."

He watched me as I folded my arms in annoyance.

"When will you return to work?" I asked.

He shrugged. "Maybe tomorrow. I'm enjoying the day off. You're welcome to stay with me, if you'd like."

He pulled me down on the bed with him, wrapping an arm around me in a playful hug. I rolled my eyes at him.

"And just what do you think you're doing?" I asked.

"Seducing you," he said hollowly.

He lifted a finger to my face, gently dragging it down my cheek. I raised an eyebrow at him, questioning the way he was ridiculously biting his lip. He stopped, reaching for my wrist. He put two fingers against my pulse. His eyebrows matted, but then relaxed as he broke into a devious smile.

"Why do you keep doing that?" I asked, pulling away and looking at my wrist.

He stared at me for a long moment. "You really have no idea, do you?"

"That's why I'm asking."

"No, not the pulse."

He held my gaze, his eyes suddenly burning through mine. Something in the color of his eyes trapped me like a rush of cold water, and I suddenly jolted from the gaze like I needed fresh air.

"I have to run the kitchen," I said. "I should be going back."

He let me stand to my feet, watching me as I straightened my hair and dress.

"I'm curious to know why you're determined to feed a crew that's holding you hostage," Luc asked. "Has a nerve of sympathy pinched you? Or affection, perhaps?"

I stopped. Luc sat upright, his elbow against his knee.

"The crew has been rather attentive to you," he continued. "Rather odd considering they kidnapped you. Even stranger considering that women aboard pirate ships is incredible bad luck."

I shrugged, straightening my spine. "I'm simply a likable person."

"Yeesss." He drug out the word in a thoughtful hiss. "The first mate and captain seem to think so as well."

I stayed silent, not knowing how to answer.

"You know," he said, tapping his chin with his finger, "I don't know what I find more amusing: the fact that the captain and his first mate are both fighting over you, or the fact that you have no idea why they're doing it."

I laughed. "Fighting over— Ha! You've lost your mind."

"You haven't noticed? The way the captain insists on keeping you to himself in his own chambers? The way the first mate stares at you across the table with a longing look in his eyes? Don't tell me you hadn't noticed."

It would have been a lie to say I hadn't noticed anything at all in the way the crew treated me. Adrian was constantly upset whenever I spent time with Luc or Henrik, and Henrik had been mostly level-headed but far too kind for a man with so much to lose. I had never felt like a prisoner at all, honestly.

"Oh, little dove," Luc said, grinning. "You truly have no idea what power you own, do you?"

"I've simply inherited my mother's charm and my father's warmth," I said. "It attracts many people to me, and it always has. But I would hardly say that Adrian or Henrik has romantic feelings for me."

He leaned back, chuckling darkly. "Romantic isn't the word I was thinking of."

"What other word would you use?"

"Something a bit more…tainted, perhaps?"

Luc's eyes darkened, suggestive in nature. Heat crawled up my neck.

"What a foolish conversation," I said. "I'll be in the kitchen doing *your* job if you care to feel guilty enough to do something about it."

Feeling awkward and flushed, I went toward the door, putting my hand on the knob.

"I wouldn't trust those two brothers," Luc called out. "When the tides turn, so will they. Don't forget that."

I turned back, raising an eyebrow at him. "And why should I trust your words? Couldn't you be the same?"

His eyes glittered at me from across the room. He stretched out on the bed, a power and a peace coming from his smile.

"I could," he replied. "But we both know that if I was lying to you, you could tell."

CHAPTER 15

HAPPINESS

Four weeks.

We had been to two ports for supplies since then. To my relief, Adrian sent my letter to Father from the first port, but I assumed he wouldn't allow me to send word again. I didn't know how long it would take us to reach the little red star we were following, but Henrik assured me that we were getting close to our destination. With his knowledge of the spirit realm, he spent his time making plenty of defenses guarding us from danger.

Adrian reluctantly allowed me to take sword lessons from Henrik in the evenings, Luc convincing him that the sirens could come again at any moment to take the crew members from the ship. Adrian eventually caved, and Henrik taught me and a few of the men on board. But Adrian was adamant that I never step foot in Henrik's room alone.

"You're being ridiculous," I said to Adrian, reaching up and pulling a wiry hair from his chin.

He hissed, swatting my hand away. "My ship, my rules."

"Stop being afraid of Henrik. His link to the spirits is a gift, not something to be feared."

Adrian held his forehead in disbelief. "How much has he brainwashed you? Fine, I admit that he has some kind of voodoo. I'm a big enough man to admit it. But I'm not going to give him the opportunity to put you in the middle of more demon ambushes."

"Why, if I didn't know any better," I said with a teasing smile, "I'd say that you cared about me, Captain."

He stepped forward, leaning down to invade my space with his, as he always did. His eyes were powerful and playful as he looked down at my lips and smiled.

"I do care…" he said. "Without you, I come back broke."

I rolled my eyes, shoving him away. He grabbed my hand and pulled me back to his side.

"I mean it," he said sternly. "If there's even a hint of the spirit world coming after you, you make sure to get out of there."

His fingers dug into my skin. By the way he held his breath, I could tell that the weeks of silence from the spirit world was making him more and more on edge. I relaxed my muscles, hoping he would do the same.

"Maybe you should lean on your older brother, Captain," I suggested.

His eyelids fluttered, an ironic laugh breaking his lips. "That's one thing I can't do."

He let me go, not making eye contact as he walked back to his desk full of maps. I sighed, not understanding his secrets, but understanding that they were weighing him down. If the things Henrik had said were true, Adrian was doing these things to save his family. The responsibility of that was clear on both brothers' shoulders, even if the captain pretended to be unaffected.

But how could anyone be unaffected when it came to their mother's life?

It was like reliving my past all over again. The pain I felt for them ran deep even though it shouldn't have.

Luc's words still rang in my ears after all this time.

"When the tides turn, so will they."

I didn't want to believe it, but there was no reason not to. Henrik and Adrian needed the Eros. That was all. They had no use for me, and if I returned to Father, it was a risk for them. Even if I didn't intend to turn them in to the authorities, there was the possibility that I could. They knew that.

But, to be fair, what reason did I have to trust Luc? He was a stranger, as much as anyone else on the crew.

But he had protected me from the sirens when the world split open.

Then again, so did Henrik. And in his own way, so did Adrian.

Even after so many weeks, I couldn't stop my thoughts from spinning in circles.

Attempting to push my thoughts aside, I left the room to help Luc in the kitchen.

"You're late," Luc said as I entered the kitchen, not looking up from his soup pot.

I rolled my eyes. "His royal captain wished to remind me of how evil his honorable brother was."

Luc chuckled. "So the captain is still trying to keep you for himself then?"

"I swear, I've never met a man so grown and yet so childish. You'd think he'd be tired of such games at his age."

I put on my apron, catching Luc's eyes as he looked me up and down.

"Are you sure they're just games?" he asked solemnly.

Between his glare and his question, it was suddenly quite difficult for me to tie the strings of my apron behind my back.

"Why of course they're…I mean, you can't really think…. Honestly, Luc, you're full of so many stories."

I grunted, unable to make the tie. In two steps, Luc had his hands on my shoulders, spinning me so my back was facing him. He tied my apron behind my back, leaning his voice next to my ear as he spoke.

"He's only a man, little dove," he said. "And men can resist their demons for only so long."

He snapped the apron strings and waited for me to turn around to face him. His lips were silent, but his eyes were quite loud, singing a warning to be cautious.

I swallowed. "He's never touched me behind closed doors."

I don't know why I felt the need to say such a thing.

Luc's eyebrow popped up. "But he's thought about it. And so has his honorable brother."

Luc wiped his hands on his apron, walking over to the side of the counter and leaning against it. His eyes rolled back in thought.

"Perhaps the problem isn't so much that they've thought it," he muttered, so low I thought it might be to only himself. "The bigger problem is that you don't acknowledge it."

"Just because I've been to both of their rooms—"

"Frequently and regularly—" he interrupted.

"Doesn't mean they have such…improper thoughts."

"Ha! You think mankind is so innocent?"

"They could be."

He laughed, dropping his head back to look at the ceiling. "Oh, little dove…you have no idea how incredible it is for you to have such an idea."

"Why would they have such ideas at a time like this?" I asked, something feeling unsettled in my chest as I did so. "They have more important things to think about. The sirens, for example."

Luc threw vegetables in the soup pot but didn't say anything. The spoon clanged against the pot sides. I hated the silence.

"Why do you think they haven't come back?" I asked.

Luc scratched his chin, shutting his eyes. He went quiet for so long that I thought he might have missed my question completely.

"I heard from a psychic many moons ago that creatures of the spirit world are very patient," he finally said. "It would gain the sirens nothing to judge the world so quickly. After all, their main objective is to save it."

"So that's it then? We just sit on the ship, get ambushed again, and they drag us to hell?"

He chuckled. "Only the ones who deserve it."

"I can't imagine anyone deserving such a thing."

I tried to steady my hands as I chopped. I must have done a poor job, because it wasn't long until Luc's hand rested on top of mine to stop me. His fingers curled under my chin and forced me to face him. His eyes searched mine before his face softened into a reassuring smile.

"I highly doubt you'll be the one to burn, little dove," he said. "Rest your heart."

I swallowed roughly, my stomach twisting. "And if the people I care about burn?"

He was silent for a moment, his fingers rubbing my jaw.

"To correct the evils of the world, the first step is to acknowledge that it comes with a cost," he said. "And the second step? That's accepting that the cost is always worse than you ever imagined."

*****

I wiped the sweat from my neck, smiling.

"That's enough for today, men," Henrik barked. "Return to your stations."

I bounced my sword in my hand, its weight now familiar and comfortable in my palm. I couldn't believe that it had only been a few months since I could barely hold my arms up for a single lesson, and now I nearly didn't want to let go of the sword at all.

The men dispersed to their stations as Henrik approached me. He noticed my smile and returned it.

"Your speed has improved," he said. "And your form was much stronger this time around."

I handed Henrik back his sword and smiled.

"I think I'm starting to really enjoy it," I replied.

He nodded, pleased, then extended a handkerchief to me.

"No need," I declined politely. "My sleeve will do just fine."

I wiped my brow with my sleeve, the sweat staining it. When it came to sword fighting, I wasn't as good as the others, but I wasn't bothered by it. I felt my muscles strengthening, along with my mind. Even if I couldn't keep up with the others, I could do something for myself for the first time in years. I wasn't doing something to benefit my father. It wasn't something to benefit my family. It was something for me. And it was freeing.

"I didn't know you could smile so wide," he teased. "And while learning fencing, nonetheless."

"Wait until I *win* a fight," I replied.

He chuckled. A thought seemed to suddenly strike him, and he turned his head over his shoulder to look at the red star in the sky once more.

"How much longer?" I asked.

He sighed. "I don't know. It seems to get farther and farther away from us. I worry—"

He stopped. I put a hand on his arm.

"Was she bad when you left?"

He shook his head.

"Her pain was just beginning," he said. "We can only hope that she's still fighting until we arrive back home."

"And then what will you do?"

He looked confused. "What do you mean?"

"When you have the Eros, will you give it to the king? Save your family? Allow me to return to my father? Everything resets?"

He looked at me for a long moment. "Is that what you want? A complete reset?"

I thought about it for a minute.

"I don't know," I finally said. "Of course, I want to return to my father. I hate being away from his side."

"And your…"

He stopped, not finishing his sentence. I could swear that his face had turned pink as he looked down.

"My fiancé?" I finished, impressed he had remembered it even though I only mentioned it once or twice. "I've known him for ten minutes. I'm not sure how I could miss him."

I looked out on the water, the waves slowly drifting in the moonlight, lapping against the side of the boat.

"What is it?" Henrik asked softly.

I took a deep breath. "I was starting to become fond of it."

"What?"

"The sea."

Henrik's eyebrows lifted. "You're not sick of sailing?"

I shook my head with a smile. "I think this is the most at peace I've felt in a while. There are no businessmen to impress, no standards I have to meet. It's just me and the ocean, and any adventure I should want."

Henrik stepped in closer, but I kept my eyes on the water.

"Do you want to stay with us?" he asked.

I turned toward him. He didn't back down, looking down into my eyes as he waited for my answer.

The problem was that I didn't know what it was.

"Henrik!" a voice shouted from the crow's nest. "We have trouble!"

Henrik turned toward the sea just as the shadow of a ship floated into the moonlight, fire burning from torches on the deck.

Henrik growled.

"What is it?" I asked.

"A signal," Henrik replied. "We're being attacked."

CHAPTER 16

RESCUE

"Prepare cannons!" Henrik yelled.

The men went to their stations, unsheathing their swords in anticipation. In organized chaos, everyone went to their posts preparing for the worst. There was one face I didn't see, however. One that *should* have been leading the crew.

I rushed to Adrian's room, throwing the door open. He looked up from his desk, raising an eyebrow.

"What in th—"

"Get your ass out here and be captain!" I yelled.

He grunted and stood from his desk. "You really don't have—"

"We're being attacked," Henrik boomed over my shoulder, making me jump. "Pirates."

"Pirates?" I asked. "Aren't you—"

I stopped, remembering Henrik's response to the word *pirate* the last time I had used it.

"*Real* pirates," Henrik replied after I had stopped myself. "The kind of no honor and no mercy."

He looked at Adrian, his eyes burning.

"Then let's go defend your precious king," Adrian snarled back. "And the ship I stole from him."

Adrian grabbed a knife and headed toward the door.

"Taking a knife to a sword fight?" Henrik asked as we followed him.

Adrian turned, opening his coat pocket to reveal a pistol and a small collection of throwing knives.

"These are all I need," he replied.

Adrian rushed onto the deck, the wind whipping through his hair as his eyes darkened. Henrik and I followed, looking at the ship as it came closer and closer to ours.

"It's going to hit us!" I cried.

"That's the idea," Henrik replied flatly.

"Don't let them see you bleed, gentlemen!" Adrian commanded, flicking his knife with his wrist. "Give them the proper welcome. Allow no survivors. Understand?"

The crew cheered. Henrik stood silent beside me, watching his brother.

It seemed the self-proclaimed pirate captain could, in fact, be serious. It also seemed that when he was, it was deadly.

Adrian took off toward the bow, jumping onto the ledge as he watched the enemy ship. The ship wasn't quick, but it was sailing straight toward us, its sails looming as tall as ours in the moonlight.

Not looking away from the ship, Adrian pointed straight at me.

"Get her someplace safe," he commanded.

Henrik grabbed my arm, but I stopped him.

"What are you doing?" I asked. "Let me stay with you. I can help, can't I?"

Henrik hesitated, staring at me blankly.

"Get her out of here!" Adrian commanded again.

Henrik shook his head as if there was water in it, then pulled at my arm again.

"You're too valuable," he whispered, taking me down to the kitchen.

He pulled me down the steps, shoving me at Luc. Luc invited me with open arms into a hug as I collided into him.

"Come to visit me during off hours?" he asked playfully, his arms wrapped around me.

"Pirate attack," Henrik said.

"Ah, then am I to play bodyguard? How adorable."

Henrik tightened his jaw, glancing once between us and then heading back up toward the stairs. Luc smiled at me.

"Time to hide," he said, motioning to the storage room.

"You're far too calm about this, Luc."

"It would be foolish to be anything else in this moment."

He shoved me into the storage room, and we crouched together with the hens. Luc pulled a large kitchen knife from his robe, palming it as he watched the door.

"Luc…?" I asked, suddenly feeling my blood rush frantically through me.

"Don't worry, little dove," he replied. "I promised to protect you, didn't I?"

"I didn't realize you could fight."

He looked back at me and smirked, his teeth shining like pearls.

"I wasn't always a cook, you know."

Crash.

The ship swerved hard, and I was thrown off my feet and into the wild, noisy hens. I swatted them away as they flapped their wings and squawked.

"What was that?" I asked.

"They're here," Luc sang quietly.

There were cries of war as the sound of boots rained down above us. I was glued to the floor, unable to move from my spot, unable to breathe. Luc continued to palm the knife while watching the stairs, his eyes darting around the ceiling as the boots thundered above us.

"This is going to get messy, dove," he said. "If anything happens, I want you to cut your way out until you make it to safety. And when all else fails, abandon ship."

"Abandon…you mean jump into the ocean?"

He nodded.

"It's pitch black! There could be sharks!"

"The sharks are already on the ship," he replied. "Besides, the water will protect you."

"How on earth would the ocean protect me?"

A cry from the kitchen stopped Luc from continuing. He jumped out of the room, shutting the door behind him and locking me in. I stood to go to the door, hearing nothing but grunts outside of it.

There was a cry.

Then silence.

My mouth was too dry to say anything, my heart pounding harder than the boots above me.

I reached for the door.

It swung open before I could touch it. A face I had never seen before was on the other side.

"Ah!" the man yelled in satisfaction. "Here you are."

I stepped back as he stepped forward.

"Stay back," I commanded, voice cracking.

"Wait, now," he replied. "I'm not here to harm you."

I suddenly recalled the crew member with missing fingers that had cornered me months before, and the space in the storage room began to shrink. There was no reason this man wouldn't attempt something similar. My skin crawled.

I took another step back, looking at the slit between him and the door. There was a blue-and-teal robe laying across the ground.

"Luc!" I cried, stepping forward to get to him.

The man stepped between us. "I need you to come with me."

"The hell I will!"

I reached back and took some eggs from the hen's nest, pegging him in the face with it. He cried and stumbled back, trying to get the oozing yolk out of his eye. I grabbed the sword from his hand pointing it at him while he was distracted.

"Step back!" I commanded.

He raised his hands as he stepped backward. "Listen—"

"No! Step back and get away from him!"

He did as he was told. I turned toward Luc, my sword still pointed at the stranger. I walked backward until I was at Luc's side. Luc was panting, but his eyes were blinking.

"Are you all right?" I asked.

He gave a breathy laugh. "I am now. Who knew you'd be my rescuer, little dove?"

He waved his fingers at me, motioning for the sword. I handed it to him, and he came back to his feet to face the man once more.

"I'm afraid I can't let you take her," Luc said coolly. "She means too much to me."

My heart fluttered at his words.

"She means a lot more to my employer," the man returned.

Employer?

Before I could ask any questions, Luc's hand struck out and grabbed my wrist.

"Get off the ship," he whispered.

"What?"

I heard, but I didn't understand.

"Don't let them take you," he said, his voice more urgent. "Get off the ship."

"Luc—"

"Go!"

His command had never been so strong. All I could do was obey.

I ran up the stairs, Luc close behind me, his back facing mine as he pointed his sword at the pirate below. At the top of the stairs, I held my breath again.

Bodies were littered across the deck, blood staining almost every floorboard. The sight was horrific, but the smell of iron and blood was much worse. I barely had enough time to be nauseous when two men barreled toward us, swords drawn. Luc jumped in front of me, quickly slicing both of them open. He held his arm out to guard me, sword raised.

"Keep going!" Luc said, backing me toward the tail of the ship, away from the fight.

Cannons fired. I threw my hands above my head, throwing myself to the ground in fear as the ship lurched from side to side. My limbs shook as my covered my head. Luc pulled me back to my feet, consoling me as he pulled me farther down the ship.

More men came for us both as we made our way toward the back of the ship. Luc kicked his boot into one attacker and sliced him, then elbowed the other in the face and sent him over the boat into the water.

The men swarmed us, Luc still standing in front of me as a guard. No one moved in immediately as they slowly backed us into the corner.

"Give us the girl," one of them commanded.

"You don't want to do this," Luc replied, his voice in a nonchalant sing-song as always.

My back hit the rail of the ship, the black water directly below me.

"Luc…" I said.

"Do you trust me, dove?" he said over his shoulder.

"Of course, but—"

With a single move, he turned and shoved me off the side of the ship.

The water hit hard, sucking me down into the black sea. I came to the surface for a quick burst of air, before the waves pulled me down once more. I opened my eyes, searching the surface until I saw moonlight.

Fingers wrapped around my ankles.

I was pulled down farther, unable to kick back to the surface. Fear struck my throat. The fingers released.

Suddenly, two pearls were floating in front of me.

No, not pearls. Eyes.

White eyes made of pearls.

They blinked, a sudden shimmer surrounding it. It looked like scales of a fish as it glistened, but fingers came to its face like a human.

It reached for me. I screamed, the water engulfing the sound.

The creature grabbed my face with what might have been hands, silently demanding that I look at it. I could only stare in horror. It, in turn, blinked. Then a black hole opened in the scales. A mouth?

I was launched back to the surface. The water split apart as I broke through. I became weightless, high above the ocean. I flew past one of the top sails, gasping for air as I plummeted back down to the water in a scream.

I hit the water harder than the first time, opening my eyes to be greeted by the creature once more. It blinked, cocking its head to the side.

The water split, another body landing beside us. There was a hiss in the water, and the creature of glittering scales turned to dust, shimmering like stars as its remnants surrounded me. Another hand grabbed me, bringing me back to the surface.

I found myself caught in someone's arms, his hard grip around me familiar.

"I told you I'd come get you," Captain Adrian said proudly.

He moved the wet hair out of my face, a warm smile coming to his lips.

"No one takes my hostage, hostage," he said.

I wrapped my arms around his neck, shivering. "Adrian. What was that…?"

"I'm no expert on the spirit realm, but considering it combusted from this holy stone knife I made last week, I'm guessing it's a siren."

"Aren't sirens the ones with wings?"

He shrugged. "Whatever. Let's get you back on deck before I have to stab anything else."

He grabbed hold of a rope hanging off the side of the ship and smiled as we were pulled back onboard. The crew pulled us up, cheering as we both landed on the deck together. Adrian laughed and flashed me a smile, and I couldn't help but flash one in return.

Maybe he wasn't so bad.

He came to his feet, helping me up. With his usual arrogance, he turned back to the ship, which had now gone quiet.

He stepped forward to a line of men with their arms twisted behind their backs, many of them bleeding. All of them kept a defiant look on their faces, not daring to show any weakness to the captain.

"Now," he said. "Which one of you dared to lead an attack on my ship?"

"I did," a familiar dark voice said.

I followed the voice, gasping when I saw its owner.

Jacques de Villiers.

CHAPTER 17

REUNITED

Jacques gave a lopsided grin as his eyes met mine. I automatically reached up and fixed my hair in response.

"Ah, I remember you," Adrian said, waving his knife haphazardly in Jacques's face. "You're the lover, right? Did you come for your future bride?"

I could tell Jacques was laughing even though there was no sound coming from his parted lips.

"Fascinating theory," Jacques replied flatly.

Adrian turned back to me, wetting his lips and holding his dagger tight. Even though he was smiling, there was a hollowness in his eyes I hadn't seen before.

"The fool must truly love you, princess," Adrian said. "It would be a shame if I had to cut his heart out."

I padded across the deck with bare, wet feet. "Adrian, please—"

"Give me a reason not to kill him."

Adrian waited, eyes drilling a hole through me. He probably expected some disgusting romantic line—that I loved Jacques and couldn't live without him, or some nonsense—but the truth was I was terrified of Jacques. He stared at me like a demon, no compassion or affection of any sort.

And I definitely wasn't going to say, *Because he's my future stepson.* I'd rather get my own throat cut than to die from that kind of embarrassment.

"You want the Eros, don't you?" I asked. "Think of him as insurance. With him as your prisoner, you can command me to do whatever you wish."

Adrian looked at me as if I had eaten bugs in front of him. The confusion on his face morphed into disbelief, a laugh escaping his lips with the roll of his eyes.

"You shouldn't give me those kinds of ideas, princess," he said, stepping in closer. "You have no idea what I'll ask you to do."

He leaned down, his eyes scanning my body for a quick moment before he straightened and cleared his throat. I puffed out some air, frowning at Jacques for the situation he had now put me in.

"Very well," Adrian said. "Take them to the brig. We'll decide what to do with them later."

Adrian didn't look at me as he walked away. I could feel a sharpness around him, as if he were wearing daggers as a shield to keep anyone from coming close. As he walked off, I glanced at Henrik, whose eyes had gone dark and heavy. He glanced between Jacques and me, taking in a breath before stepping forward and ordering the men to continue their orders.

The men forced Jacques and his crew forward with their hands tied behind their backs, down into the brig below. Jacques's eyes caught mine for a brief moment as they took him down, a knowing smirk still across his face.

That smirk was something to be afraid of. I knew it. What I didn't know was *why.*

***

I didn't speak to anyone until evening the next day. By then, the clothes Adrian had lent me had been washed and dried out in the sun, along with some other clothes from those who had perished the night before.

The dead men of the enemy were stripped bare and thrown overboard, while the dead men of Adrian's ship were kept clothed before being thrown into a water grave with the others. I knew some of the men who had been killed in battle, and to think I'd never see them on the ship again was an eerie, echoing type of pain.

I could even still smell their blood when I stepped on the deck. I could still see the floorboards stained deep with it, even though every floorboard had been deeply scrubbed.

Death. I hated it. I hated how much it took from me. I hated how much it took from others.

At the thought, my knees went weak and I had to hold on to Adrian's bookshelves for support. I barely heard his footsteps come toward me, vaguely remembering that he was in the room.

"Hey," he whispered, taking a gentle hold on my elbow and shoulder. "What's wrong?"

I blinked but couldn't face him. Instead, I started to shudder. Suddenly, Adrian's arms were around me, holding me up instead of the bookshelves.

"It took you longer to go into shock this time," he said, a hint of amusement at the edge of his voice. "I suppose that means you're stronger?"

His warmth and his cologne were oddly comforting, and I leaned into it.

Just for a minute… Just until I can get my bearings…

"I'm sorry," Adrian said over the top of my head. "I'm not good at these sorts of things."

Finding the strength to speak, I opened my mouth. "You're not doing poorly at the moment," I whispered.

He gave a light laugh. "That might be the only time I hear you say that."

I leaned back to look at him, trying to search his face for an answer to a question I hadn't formed yet. He only stared back, a softness in the corners of his hollow and heavy eyes.

"Are you all right?" I was the only thing I could ask.

His eyes widened. "Why are you asking me that?"

"You lost some of your men yesterday. Aren't you in pain?"

He paused, staring at me. With a swallow, he found his words again. "My men knew the stakes," he said. "We will move forward, holding them in highest honor."

There was not a single emotion in his voice as he said it, but his eyes showed his guilt and regret as clear as sunlight. I patted his arms in comfort, wishing I knew what to say. He slipped out of my embrace, still holding me firmly by the elbows to keep me steady.

"You really are too innocent," he muttered, not looking at me. He sighed, pulling me back toward the chair to help me to sit down. Without a word he stepped away and poured a drink, coming back with the glass and handing it to me. I took a sip, realizing it was straight rum this time. No water.

"Are you trying to get a lady drunk?" I teased, the alcohol returning my humor to me.

He shrugged with a weak smile. "Let me know if you need anything else."

He took two steps before I spoke.

"Wait," I said.

Adrian turned to face me. I looked him in the eyes.

"Let me speak with him," I said.

He tsked and looked up at the ceiling in disbelief. He shook his head sharply.

"Why the hell would I allow some secret rendezvous?" he asked.

"It's not a rendezvous," I replied, half tempted to tell him the truth. I didn't know what would be worse: Adrian thinking I was going to marry that gargoyle, or Adrian finding out that I was going to marry the gargoyle's father.

"I want to ask about my father," I continued. "I need to know he's well."

Adrian seemed to think it over for a moment, staring at the wall in front of him.

"You can escort me if you're that paranoid about it," I added, getting frustrated. "Please, Adrian…"

He sighed, a look of defeat washing over his face as he rubbed the heel of his palm into his forehead. He stepped toward the door, half growling over his shoulder.

"Start walking, princess."

I followed him down to the brig. The stench of sweat and metal was strong, along with a few sour fragrances I didn't want to ask about.

"Hello, and welcome aboard the *Quetzalcoatl*," Adrian said in a condescending tone, waving to all the prisoners. "Thank you for choosing to sail with us. Should you need any amenities or facilities, please feel free to daydream of the happy little life you had before you made the mistake of coming aboard my ship."

He hissed the last words out, muttering to himself as he walked further down the cells.

"First flying demons, water spirits, pirates…what next? Leviathan?"

I shuddered, hoping that wasn't a real creature.

Adrian turned back to me and waved his hand at a cell in the back as we approached it.

"Visitor, lover boy," Adrian muttered, leaning against the bars.

Jacques looked up from where he was sitting. As I approached, he laughed and rolled his eyes. There were patches of blood on his clothes, his hair slick and greasy from his time on the sea. He looked animalistic compared to the night we first met. The only thing that was the same about him was the devilish look in his eyes, as if he were going to take me to hell with him.

"Were you injured?" I asked, looking at the blood on his sleeves.

He raised an eyebrow as he held my gaze. "You're concerned?"

He then glanced between Adrian and me, narrowing his eyes.

"I wanted to thank you for coming for me—" I started.

"Don't bother. I wouldn't have to if you hadn't been foolish enough to get taken in the first place."

I huffed, my mood shifting and appreciation suddenly depleting.

"You didn't let me finish," I replied. "I said I wanted to thank you…and I would have if you had done your job properly."

Adrian snorted.

Jacques glared at me. "Why are you down here, exactly?"

I gripped my pants, hands sweating. "My father… how is he?"

Jacques scoffed, leaning his head back against the wall and closing his eyes as if I was the most boring person in the room.

"He's gone a bit mad," he said. "His temper has reached an unhealthy height. Your letter calmed him down some, but there are many who think he's going to put himself in the grave with his outbursts."

"Outbursts?" I asked. "My father doesn't have outbursts. He's the most level-headed person I know."

"Not when his daughter's been kidnapped by pirates, he isn't."

Jacques opened his eyes again, looking again between Adrian and me.

"Although…" Jacques added, drawing out the word. "It would have proved useful in your letter to let him know how comfortable you are among the company of thieves."

"What do you mean?"

Jacques looked me over intensely, as if his eyes were burning the clothes off my body.

"You're wearing a man's clothes," he said. "By the style, I would say they're his."

Jacques nodded at Adrian. Adrian only shrugged with a smirk.

I huffed. "That's not your concern."

"I think we both know it is."

Jacques stared hard, his eyes going right through mine. It was as intimidating as it was captivating. I was nearly entranced by it until Adrian's hands came around each side of me, trapping me between him and the bars.

I felt him over my shoulder as he spoke to Jacques.

"You should probably also know that she stays in my room," Adrian said. "Usually in my bed. With me."

I turned around, putting a hand on his chest to stop him. "Adrian, please…"

"What?" Adrian asked. "Afraid what the truth will cost you?"

He stared at me, challenging me. It pissed me off.

"Step back," I hissed at him.

His cockiness dropped off his face as he stepped back.

"Go stand at the entrance," I commanded. "This conversation is difficult enough without your comments."

He huffed, stepping back slowly to return to the entrance. I was grateful that he didn't fight me on it like he usually would.

Jacques stood, coming to meet me at the bars. I took a step back.

"Quite bold, aren't you?" Jacques taunted. "Charming even the captain himself into your bed."

"First of all, it's *his* bed, and I sleep on the floor. Second off, you have a lot of nerve to assume such a thing."

He sighed. "I should have known this is something a woman like you would do."

"A woman *like me*?" I spat back. "Care to elaborate?"

He shrugged but didn't answer.

"Well, if I'm so horrid," I continued, "why are you here?"

"My father sent me to retrieve you."

His words were cold and empty, same as his eyes. I swallowed, trying to keep my composure.

"Is he well?" I asked.

Jacques chuckled, a sharp look in his eyes. "Of course. I'll tell him of your concern next time I see him. I'm sure he'll be touched."

He said each word with such poison that I thought his saliva could melt the bars between us. I stepped back just in case it could. Jacques stepped back as well, creating even more distance between us. He stared, not saying a word. It unnerved me, my heart speeding up as I started to sweat.

"I don't want to speak with so many ears listening," I finally said. "We'll continue this later."

"Later, there will be far more ears listening," he said, chuckling, "I guarantee it."

I glanced at him for a long moment, trying to process his words. Another riddle of his, no doubt. Such a strange man.

I walked back toward the stairs where Adrian was waiting.

"He seems charming," Adrian teased.

I huffed and went back to the deck, rubbing my face with my hands in frustration. The salty air whipped against my skin, the red light of the Eros mocking me as I stared into the unknown.

Adrian came up beside me, shoving his hands in his pockets and looking out onto the Eros alongside me.

"You two have an unusual relationship," Adrian commented.

I sighed. "You don't know the half of it."

"You're actually planning on marrying him?"

I turned to him, opening my mouth to say something, then shutting it again. It was like my soul shut down every time I even thought of the words. I couldn't bring them past my lips.

He sighed, chewing his bottom lip and shaking his head to himself. He stared out onto the water, his eyes getting heavy along with his shoulders.

"We're nearly to the Eros," he said flatly. "Once we arrive and the stone is in my hand, you can take your husband and live whatever life you choose."

The words were a promise of freedom, but they were so sharp that it felt more like an attack than a reward. Before I could ask any questions, Adrian spun on his heel and went back to his room, slamming the door shut behind him.

CHAPTER 18

WAITER

"I can't believe you threw me overboard, Luc."

Now that I had recovered from Jacques's attack on the ship and the deaths that had followed from it, I felt revitalized enough to yell at Luc in the way he deserved.

Luc stopped stirring the soup as he looked over at me, pulling his lips to the side.

"I told you that you were perfectly safe, didn't I?" he replied, not as guilty as I wanted him to be. "You bobbed right up. Just like I said."

"I didn't bob up! I was thrown in the air! By some—"

I stopped. I hadn't told anyone what I had seen in the water. I had spent the last few days processing all the events that had unfolded since Jacques's attack on the ship, and quite frankly, I had no idea how to tell anyone what I had seen.

"Luc," I said, tugging on his sleeve. "I saw something. Something in the water that day."

He put down his spoon, turning to face me with focused eyes. "What was it?"

I ticked my head back and forth as I tried to remember. "It was some sort of spirit. Some sort of water creature made of…what? Bubbles and pearls?"

Luc smiled. "The merfolk. They're back in the water."

"Merfolk? Aren't they supposed to be fish?"

"In full form, yes."

He said it like I was supposed to know the difference between *full form* and whatever the alternative to that was.

"So what does that mean?" I asked.

He chuckled darkly and went back to his soup. "It means all the bad eggs need to stay on board."

I grabbed his sleeve and shook it. "I'm serious, Luc."

"So am I."

"Why didn't it attack me?" I asked. "Well, it did throw me up in the air once, for no apparent reason, but it mostly just stared at me. I thought it was supposed to drag me down into hell?"

Luc wiped his hands on his apron, looking deeply into his pot. He licked his lips, turning his head over to look at me again, his eyes narrowed.

"What is it?" I asked, unnerved by his gaze.

With a breath, he shook his head and moved on to one of the counters to slice some carrots.

"Nothing," he said. "The fact is, if a merfolk looked at you and didn't try to take you, it means you have nothing to worry about."

"Take me? Take me where?"

"If a siren or a merfolk declares you evil, they will take you to the Den of Sirens to be tried."

I was genuinely confused. "A trial? The spirit world has such a thing?"

"The spirit world is hardly so disorganized. There's always a system of balances."

I held my head, the information hurting my brain. "This is too much to understand this early in the morning."

"Then take this soup up to the first morning shift. They've been waiting awhile."

I grabbed the bowls and put them on the tray, resting it against my hip as I looked at Luc one last time. He knew I was staring at him — I could tell by his unusual stiff posture — but he didn't seem interested in looking back at me. Not having the time to address the issue, I sighed loud enough to let him know I wasn't done with this conversation, then went up the steps.

The crew was quieter these days than they had usually been. It seemed to be a reflection of both Adrian and Henrik, who had turned quiet since we were attacked by Jacques and his crew. Part of Jacques's crew had already surrendered and accepted to become part of Adrian's crew, which I was told was normal for captured ships even though I thought the disloyalty was rather pathetic.

Henrik was on the first shift this time, and he barely acknowledged me as I set his food on the table. He had never been so silent with me, even when we had first met.

I stood over him as I put down the soup, waiting for him to acknowledge me. He didn't. I cleared my throat, but he still wouldn't look at me.

"How have you been?" I asked, my voice weakly breaking the silence between us.

He looked up at me, his eyes a mix of innocence and bitterness in a way I hadn't seen before. I swallowed as he held my gaze, but he broke our eye contact with an ironic laugh.

"I've been busy," he replied flatly.

"I've barely spoken to you in five days," I said. "You haven't come to the deck at midnight like you used to."

He pulled his soup to his mouth. "Mind your own interests."

I opened my mouth to reply to Henrik's cold comment, but someone spoke before I could.

"Who put a scorpion in your bed?" Adrian asked, walking to the table. "You spent the last few months training her in sword fighting behind my back, and now you want to act like this?"

Henrik huffed, drinking more of his soup. Adrian looked at me with a half smile.

"Take Luc with you today to feed the prisoners," Adrian commanded me. "Henrik and I have other important business to attend to."

"Do we?" Henrik asked. "I wasn't aware of anything."

Adrian pointed over his shoulder to the glowing red light that was moving toward us.

"We should reach that light within the next week," Adrian said. "I want to discuss the preparations for landing with you."

I put a hand on my hip. "You almost sound like a real captain."

"That's because I *am* a real captain, princess."

He gave a weak smile and winked.

Henrik chuckled darkly. "You want my help now?"

"As much as I've studied, I know I don't have the knowledge you have," Adrian replied. "I'm not good with books. You know that."

Henrik stood from the table. "So now I'm supposed to save your ass? Like I've been doing for our entire lives?"

"I need you to teach me. This spirit world nonsense doesn't make any sense to me on paper, but I know you can teach me what I need to know."

Henrik ran his hand through his hair, his wild, bitter smile taking over his face once more. He shook his head to himself. Adrian swallowed, his jaw ticking as he faced the rest of the men.

"We're drawing close to the Eros, gentlemen," Adrian announced. "Make sure to be ready for anything. Listen to Henrik's instructions from here on out. Whatever he tells you to do, I want your full cooperation. Is that understood?"

The men *aye*'d and went back to their breakfast. Henrik stared at Adrian with skepticism, the tension between them sweeping through the air with the sea wind once again.

"I'm asking for your help," Adrian said in a low voice to Henrik. "I have no one else to depend on."

Henrik licked his bottom lip, a twisted frown across his face. "And whose fault is that?"

Without another word, Henrik walked off, leaving Adrian to shove his hands in his pockets and stare at the light of the Eros.

***

The prisoners found it odd that we would feed them, and to be honest, I found it strange as well. It wasn't that I was a professional pirate or understood their codes by any means, but at the same time, I was sure that prisoners weren't supposed to be treated as equals, especially since they had attacked our ship.

But it was Adrian's orders to keep them alive.

He was acting so strange these days.

"You make a single complaint and I'll let you starve for the next two days," Luc warned as he slid the soup through a hole at the bottom of the bars. "I have no patience for whiners."

The men took their soup quietly, and Luc nodded toward the back.

"Let's go see this infamous fiancé of yours," he said.

I sighed. "He's not my fiancé. Who told you that, anyway?"

He shrugged. "There isn't much to do aboard a ship besides clean and gossip. If he's not your fiancé then who is he?"

Even telling Luc about the situation made me uncomfortable. I liked Luc and respected him as my boss. But between Henrik's and Adrian's flip in personalities the past couple of weeks, Luc was my only source of stability. I couldn't tell him the truth and risk losing his friendship.

"He works for my fiancé," was the best I could come up with.

Luc clicked his tongue and nodded. "I see, I see. Your fiancé must be rich to have the ability to send someone after you. But it also seems a bit cowardly, don't you think?"

"He's not cowardly, he's just…"

Old. He was old.

I inwardly cringed, stopping the conversation by knocking on Jacques's cell bars to get his attention. His eyes were closed, his head leaned back against the cell wall. He looked apathetic as always as he slowly opened his eyes and looked over at me.

"Are you hungry?" I asked, trying to start a conversation.

He chuckled darkly in return. "That's a very *motherly* question to ask."

I cringed. Jacques didn't speak much, but when he did, it was like the devil stabbing me in the heart.

Luc came up behind me, taking the soup from my hand and sliding it under the bars.

"Esmeralda has the heart of both a mother and a goddess," he said matter-of-factly.

Jacques gave a twisted smile.

"That's…*convenient*," he replied.

Jacques stood, walking toward us as if he was going to get the soup, but instead, passing it completely. He stepped in closer to us, leaning against the bars and eyeing us both.

"You're all sailing toward the Eros," he said. "Isn't that right?"

I nodded cautiously. He gave a genuine smile this time, throwing me off balance.

"That's also very convenient," he said.

"How are you familiar with the Eros?" Luc asked. "It's not a popular mythology."

"It's not unpopular either," Jacques replied. "Also, it's hard to miss the sky opening over the sea with a red glow. People talk."

"What have they been saying on land?"

Jacques shrugged.

Luc stepped up closer to the cell, asking again, his voice changing into the playful sing-song he did when he met hard-headed people.

"You should answer questions when asked, shouldn't you?" Luc asked.

Jacques leaned forward, not even blinking. "I don't have to explain anything to *you*, do I?"

Luc stared at Jacques for a long moment. With a hiss, Luc jumped back from the bars, putting a hand between Jacques and me, as if to protect me from a wild beast.

"You're..." Luc started, but didn't finish.

Jacques gave a single nod.

"Why are you here?" Luc asked.

"Why do you think?"

Silence passed between them, confusing me even more.

I tapped Luc on the shoulder. "Gentlemen?"

"Don't worry," Jacques said to Luc, ignoring me completely as he always did. "I'm not in any rush. There's plenty of time."

Jacques picked up the bowl of soup, bringing it to his lips with a smile. He sipped it, sucking it and making a face.

"A little salty," Jacques said with a twisted grin.

Luc stood, seemingly frozen.

"You're dismissed," Jacques finally said.

Luc stepped back more, grabbing my hand and dragging me back up to the deck. The wind blew his hair around like a hurricane, his breath shallowing.

"Luc, what's—"

He grabbed my shoulders. "Don't go down there again."

I blinked. "What? Why?"

"Do you trust me, little dove?" he asked, taking my hands and putting them against his face.

I nodded mindlessly, confused at his wild expression.

"Then trust me when I say that you need to stay away from him."

He opened his mouth to say something else, but shut it.

"Luc, why—?"

He shook his head and stepped away before I could say anything else. With the pained and berserk look in his eyes, I couldn't even form a question.

I had seen Luc be many things. This was the first time I had ever seen him afraid.

CHAPTER 19

CONFESSIONS

I pounded on Henrik's door.

He was actively avoiding me, and I couldn't understand why. He had spent weeks training me with a sword, meeting me on the deck at night to comfort me, and joking with me at the table during meals. But after taking Jacques and the crew captive, he had been completely cold, seemingly angry. He never stayed in the same room as me for a long period of time, and I couldn't get a read on what he was feeling or why.

So I decided to beat it out of him.

Knock, knock, knock.

He opened the door, his eyes hollow as he stared at me.

"What do you want?" he asked coldly.

"To talk to you," I replied.

"I'm busy now," he said, starting to close the door. "Come back when—"

I kicked the door back open, smacking him in the face with it. He stumbled back, holding his eye and hissing.

"When I say we need to talk," I said firmly, "I mean that we're talking *right now*."

He rubbed his face as I came into his room, shutting the door behind us. I crossed my arms and leaned against it, letting him know that I had no intention of leaving. He sighed, shifting his weight to one foot.

"What's wrong with you these days?" I asked. "You're brushing me off. And your brother. And half the crew some days. You're always brooding in your room."

"I do not brood."

"You definitely brood."

I gave him a small smile, hoping he would do the same. He didn't. He turned to his desk instead, papers and books scattered across and beside it. His room was always a mess, but this was frantic. He went to his desk and shut some of the books, piling one on top of the other. From where I stood it looked like he was chewing on his tongue, as if the words were sitting there but he couldn't spit them out.

I stepped forward. "Please tell me what you're thinking."

He turned his head toward me, his eyes suddenly filled with sorrow, a stark contrast to the hollow shells they were before.

"Henrik?" I asked again.

"I opened the spirit world," he blurted out. "I wanted so badly to clear my reputation that I didn't care about the consequences. And now…now I'm faced with too many things I wasn't prepared for."

I helped him straighten the books on his table. "You know more about the spirit world than most people. You have a power I've never seen before."

"The connection between the spirit world and the human world, I understood," he replied, putting his books on the bookshelf. "I understood that I could manipulate it and wield some of its power, but I didn't understand the creatures that lived within that world. They could judge every man on this ship, and their deaths would be on my hands. Who knows what else I've—"

He was shaking by the time he finished. I stepped forward, taking his hands in mine to steady them. The pain in his face made my heart sink.

"You mended something that was once severed," I said.

"Maybe it wasn't meant to be mended."

"You did nothing wrong—"

"I hurt you!" He grabbed my arm, showing me the faded scar across it. "I cut you open and let you bleed for the sake of my reputation and my family's finances! How much more blood will be on my hands now that the spirit world is opened?"

He inhaled through his teeth, like it was crushing him to even breathe.

"You asked why I hadn't been coming to the deck at night," he said. "It's because I'm an astrologer. I can read the stars and tell you what the future holds. I don't think… I don't think I can go out at night, look at the stars, and handle knowing all the damage I've done. All the damage that is coming now because of me."

He dropped his head, holding it with one hand as he caught his breath. Not knowing what else to do, I stepped forward and wrapped my arms around his neck, holding him close to me.

I had no power of the spiritual realm. This was all I could offer him.

His arms eventually returned the gesture and embraced me, holding me against him as he buried his head in my shoulder. I rubbed his back, hoping it would soothe him.

Minutes passed, each one somehow becoming more uncomfortable than the next. He pulled back, his bloodshot eyes not meeting mine.

"You should go," he croaked. "Your fiancé wouldn't like you in another man's room."

I huffed. "Henrik…it's not what you think. I'm not betrothed to him."

"You told me you were engaged."

"Don't you remember? I told you my fiancé is twice my age."

"Yes, well it seems he found the fountain of youth."

I sighed, leaning against the wall. "Jacques is not my fiancé. He's…he's my fiancé's son."

I said the last part so quietly that I was sure Henrik didn't hear it until he snapped his face toward me.

"Tell me I didn't hear what I think I heard," he said.

"His father, my real fiancé, has a knee injury, if I remember correctly. I'm guessing he sent Jacques to retrieve me for his sake."

Henrik's eyes fluttered shut as he sighed and ran his hands through his hair. He paused there for a moment, holding his head, looking up at me with complete confusion.

"You mean, all this time, I thought—" He groaned. "I should have realized. I mean, I didn't even think…"

I shrugged. "You had a lot to think about."

There was an awkward pause.

"So if he's the son of your fiancé," Henrik started, "then that would make him your—"

I covered his mouth with one hand. "Don't say it. I hate it too much for you to say it."

I could feel him smile behind my hand. I dropped it, staring at the ground.

"I owe you an apology, Esmeralda," Henrik said after a moment. "In my own self-absorption, I failed to act like a gentleman."

I stepped forward and patted his chest with my hand in reassurance. "No, no. I didn't realize how much pain you were in. If I had known, I would have—"

Henrik's hand wrapped around mine, his stare taking the words from my lips. The soft pads of his fingertips rubbed against my knuckles, sending fire through my arm and into the pit of my stomach. He stepped closer. I couldn't move, struck by the intense gaze in his eyes as he looked around the edges of my face, stopping at my lips.

"I don't know what I find more entertaining…the fact that those two brothers are fighting over you, or the fact that you don't know why they're doing it."

Gasping, I stepped back. Henrik's eyes widened in surprise.

"Sorry," I said. "I just remembered something Luc wanted me to do. He'll be furious if I forget. Forgive me this once?"

He exhaled, nodding. "Of course. If anyone should be asking for forgiveness, it should be me."

I shook my head. "Let's call ourselves even, then."

Patting his hand, I stepped back and ran out the door, my heart racing in my chest as I shut it behind me.

Henrik's touch…it had been so gentle, yet powerful. There was so much affection in the way he looked at me.

Was Luc right? Did Henrik really…?

I dropped my head, a wave of shame flooding through my veins.

Henrik couldn't love me. No one could. And I could never have the luxury of loving someone. I already belonged to Jacques's father. I couldn't go back on my word.

If I did, my family would fall apart…and I couldn't handle that again.

CHAPTER 20

CONSEQUENCES

"Never forget the magic of everyday life, Esmeralda …it's the weapon we use against everyday darkness."

I watched the moon reflect in the water as the salty summer wind bit my nose, my mother's words echoing in my mind.

Magic.

In the past, I believed in it. I believed in fairy tales about princes, dragons, and happy endings. I considered myself a member of the royal family; my father and mother the king and queen of the city, their parties and socials our grand masquerades.

But in the end, no prince could save the princess from an incurable disease.

We never even learned the name of the disease either. The doctors did all they could—as did my father's finances—but neither could save my mother. My father lost the childhood sweetheart he had loved since he was ten years old, left with a single daughter too unskilled to help him.

The moon hovered next to the red glow of the Eros star, taunting me. Here, I could see magic. I knew it existed. I knew the fairy tales were true. And yet…at the same time, it was like the sky was saying, *"Yes, magic does exist, but it doesn't want to save you."*

Was there a way to save my family? Was there a way my weak hands could put everything back together?

If that kind of magic existed, I would do anything.

The sea air suddenly felt cold and unwelcoming. With one last wish, I went back to my room, forgetting that it was, in fact, Adrian's room.

Why did I keep forgetting that?

Adrian was at his desk, scribbling in his notebook. He closed it as soon as I walked in, then peered over his glasses at me.

"You were out late," he said.

With his scowl and disapproving look through his glasses, I couldn't hold back my laughter.

"You look just like my father when you say it like that," I said.

He smirked, putting his journal in his desk drawer. "Considering how much you admire your father, I'll take it as a compliment."

"It was."

We shared a small smile, the tension in my shoulders ebbing. He took off his glasses, leaning back in his chair.

"Were you with Henrik?" he asked.

The tension in my shoulders returned. Feeling the blood rushing to my cheeks, I gave a small nod. He took a long breath. Nodding to himself, he stood from his desk and put his hands in his pockets and wandered around the room, stopping at his mirror. He straightened his outer shirt.

"Henrik's…Henrik's a good man," he said. "You don't have to hide your meetings from me. You have my approval."

I put my hands up in confusion. "What are you talking about?"

"I've seen the way he looks at you. It's obvious considering how much time you spend together."

"That's not—"

"I have to say, I'm impressed." He turned from the mirror and faced me, taking one slow step after the other to meet me in the middle of the room. "You can choose between an honorable naval officer or a rich, civilized aristocrat. It must be exhausting to have so many good options."

I gritted my teeth. "You've made too many assumptions, Adrian."

He pinched my chin between his fingers, bringing it up as he stepped in closer, his eyes hard and intense.

"Oh?" he asked, his breath fanning over my face. "Should I steal you away then?"

I swallowed. With a long breath he leaned in, his natural scent tempting me to close my eyes. Instead, I pulled back, putting a hand on his shoulder to stop him. With a hollow smile and an empty laugh, he pulled back.

"I figured you wouldn't bother with a demon like me," he whispered.

He released his hold on my face, stepping back to take off his outer shirt. Throwing it to the side of the room, he crawled onto his bed, lying with his head on his arm as he looked at the ceiling. The silence was deep and suffocating, his aura tormented as if he were a little boy who just had a nightmare.

I stepped forward and sat next to him on the bed. "I don't think you're a demon."

He rolled his eyes. "You know nothing about me."

"I've heard some of the terrible things you've done. It doesn't change my mind."

"What have you heard?"

I thought about it. "The courthouse fires. I heard that they were your doing."

He smiled. "My best work, honestly."

"And I know you've started riots in the city."

"Not as successful as I had hoped."

"Let's not forget that you kidnapped me."

He cocked his head to look at me, something sincere reflecting in his eyes as he looked me over.

"Can't say I regret it, either," he said.

I broke eye contact, worried he could see the blood rushing to my face. He sighed.

"Did you hear that I got Henrik fired?" he asked.

I raised my head again to look at him. "What?"

"I got Henrik fired," Adrian said again. "I knew that Henrik was on probation for his voodoo methods. He was under the king's watchful eye, constantly monitored and analyzed. Yet Henrik pledged his allegiance to the dirtbag. Loyal and respectful to a fault. I hated it.

"When the doctor told us Mother was ill and gave us the estimate for her treatments, I lost it. My reputation was trash and I knew I could never get a job. I could never be a respectable officer like Henrik. So I did what I do best: destroy things. The courthouse fire, that was a salute to the king who overcharged his citizens on medical expenses and who also treated my brother like a dog."

There was a heartbeat of silence.

"But when they found out who did it, and who I was, they sacked Henrik immediately." His eyes glossed over as he stared at the ceiling. "He never once yelled at me for it. He never once acted like he knew it was my fault. He continued to act like my honorable older brother, looking after me when I didn't deserve it."

He gave another long exhale, not blinking. I patted his arm to show my sympathy.

"You have a choice to be honorable every time you inhale," I told him. "If you want to pay Henrik back, become someone your brother can be proud of."

He scoffed. "It's too late for that."

I looked up at him. "It's never too late for that. If it was too late, you wouldn't have saved me from the merfolk that day. You wouldn't be taking care of the crew. You wouldn't be pursuing the Eros to save your family."

Adrian held my gaze, his eyes piercing into mine. He licked his lips and turned his head away, nudging me away from him.

"Get on the floor, princess. Stop coming on to me so hard."

I huffed, punching him in the side. "Who's coming on to you, you arrogant mule?"

"Ow! Do you intend to be this violent with your future husband? The aristocrats will eat you alive for this sort of behavior."

"Then let them!" I huffed. "They've already spread every other rumor they can think of."

He laughed mockingly. "Is living at the top of the food chain so cutthroat?"

"People love it when others fail, regardless of social class." I sighed. "But especially if it's a higher class than them."

There was a heartbeat of silence.

"My mother died a few years ago," I said. "The aristocrats helped us then. The lower class only laughed at our loss, as if my father's bank account somehow erased the pain of losing my mother. But then, Father started losing his business and is now losing everything else. That's why…that's why I agreed to marry."

Adrian seemed to process this information for a moment, dropping his head. "You're not in love with him then?"

I shook my head, laughing even though it was incredibly painful. "It seems you and I are both after stones for money."

I held up my left hand and wiggled the ring finger to show what I meant. He watched, shutting his eyes for a brief moment and exhaling.

"Is it so easy then?" he asked. "Marrying someone you don't love for money?"

I chewed my lip. "It's a horrible feeling."

"Then don't do it."

I laughed and rolled my eyes at him. "Your answer to saving your family is by kidnapping and stealing, yet you want to tell me not to marry unless it's for love? What a ridiculous irony."

"The difference is I *enjoy* kidnapping and stealing. You're miserable. Who's the one making the bad decisions?"

"Then maybe when this is all said and done, I'll just steal the Eros from you and sell it myself," I teased.

He sat up, leaning in to meet my eyes. I froze.

"I have nothing to lose, princess," he said softly. "I'll gladly accept that challenge, but I don't have faith that you'll beat me."

172

He held my gaze, challenging me. I huffed, sliding off the bed.

"You're so bloody condescending!" I snapped at him.

He smiled. "It's part of my charm."

"One day you'll be very sorry that you underestimated me."

"I look forward to it," he said with a laugh.

His eyes were playful, showing that, once again, he didn't think seriously of me at all. It was humiliating to even speak of my arrangement and marriage, and to have him tease me in such a way was unbearable.

"I don't think you're in any position to lecture me on moral decisions, Captain," I hissed.

He shrugged. "Then make your own poor decisions and suffer for it. It's not my business is it?"

He lay on his back and then turned over, not facing me. I huffed again, clenching my jaw.

I couldn't believe it. Was he making fun of me? What right did he have? *He* was the one doing things illegally, breaking laws and risking the imbalance of the spiritual and physical realms with his pursuits. At least my arrangement was honest.

I gripped my clothes, trying to get my hands to stop shaking.

I wasn't immoral. I wasn't.

I would marry a good, stable man of high reputation. He would take care of me and my family. We wouldn't suffer at the hands of others like we had before, and my husband would do what he could to keep our family together.

Wouldn't he?

Or was I fooling myself into thinking that my arranged marriage would bring me any happiness at all? What if it was all a lie?

The questions bounced around in my head until they were too much to bear.

But I knew exactly who would know the answers.

CHAPTER 21

PURE

I stepped quietly down the stairs, trying not to wake the prisoners.

It wasn't like they could attack me or anything. The most they would do is make a bunch of noise and get me in trouble. Luc and Adrian would scold me for my recklessness. That was all.

Regardless of the circumstances, I couldn't keep my questions to myself anymore. I needed to know more about this man I was arranged to marry. It wasn't that I wanted this bloody marriage; however, I wasn't taught any real trades and only had a basic knowledge of arts and culture. Most of my time was spent with my father or with his colleagues, talking business. I didn't mind it, and I could probably be fairly good at it, but what business could I take part in? Father had already lost his. Had I known sooner, I would have asked to become part of the trade to help him, but he had never indicated anything was amiss, and I had never thought to ask.

Marrying a complete stranger was the only way I wouldn't be completely useless to my father. He had already lost so much… I couldn't sit around and wait for him to lose even more.

I came to Jacques's cell, peering in between the bars. He was asleep, his legs bent in a strange position and his face turned away from me toward the wall.

I gently tapped on the cell bar. He didn't move. Deciding he must have been a heavy sleeper, I tapped again, whispering his name. Even in the dark, I could tell that he wasn't even flinching, no movements despite how much noise I was beginning to make.

"Jacques?" I whispered, "Are you alive?"

No movement. Looking around, I picked up a broken piece of wood and pegged him in the back with it. He still didn't stir. A warning flag flashed through my mind. Was he ill? Did he get sick down here? I hadn't come down in days and anything could have happened. And if anything happened to him, then his father…

I reached for the key on the wall and unlocked the door, closing it behind me. I went to Jacques's side, touching his shoulder.

"Jacques?" I asked again, nudging him. "Are you all right?"

I yelped as I was suddenly slammed against the wall behind me, two hands pressing my shoulders hard into the stone. Jacques's eyes were cold, even when a small grin curled on his lips.

"You fell for the oldest trick in the book," he teased. "You really have no sense, do you?"

I tried to shove him off, but he held fast, staring at me as if he was trying to analyze my existence. His eyes dropped to the key that was now on the floor next to us.

"Are you going to escape now?" I asked, trying to stay calm.

He chuckled. "I could. But then where would I go? I don't have a ship, and I don't care too much to take over this one, honestly."

I shifted under the weight of his hands against my shoulders. "Aren't you taking me back?"

His head cocked to the side as he looked at me. "Who said I was here for you at all?"

"But…your father…you said…"

"I said that my father sent me to retrieve you. I never said I intended to do it."

I furrowed my brows at him.

"What?" he asked. "Did you think I really cared whether you lived or not? We don't know each other. I have no attachments to you. Even less so with you at my father's heel."

He dropped his hands, taunting me with his smirk.

"I am not at your father's heel," I threw back. "I wasn't even told who I was arranged to until after our dance."

"Ah, that explains it then."

"Explains what?"

"The way you looked at me when we first met," Jacques said. "So…hopeful."

I could feel myself flush. I turned my head down.

"But then you realized you were arranged to marry my father and decided that was better, yes? Money is quite the hot commodity these days."

"I don't care about your money. I care about my father."

"Which requires money. Don't try to spin it, dear *mother*. A gold digger always has a legitimate reason, but that doesn't change who they are."

"Do not call me *mother*," I said, disgusted, "and I am no gold digger."

"You agreed to marry my father for financial stability, yes?"

I opened my mouth to reply, then shut it again.

"You're no different than the other women who have tried the same," he said. "You're all horrifically boring at this point."

"Then why are you here?"

He stared at me, as if the answer would appear in the air without him opening his mouth to say it. After a few breaths, I understood.

"You came for the Eros, didn't you?" I said.

His head dipped to the side as he smiled. "So you can read me that easily, can you?"

"It's not hard to determine what you want now that I know it isn't me."

I paused, stuttering, realizing that it had come out entirely different than I had wanted it to.

He chuckled darkly. "Is that your problem? You wished for me to come after you?"

"Of course not!"

"Maybe I was wrong about your intentions. It seems you have desires I wasn't aware of."

"What are you talking about?"

He leaned closer, his dark eyes even more bottomless in the light of the cell. "I could offer you a choice, I suppose. Do you want to become my stepmother, or do you want to become *mine?*"

I shoved him off, coming to my feet. "You disgusting rat! I have no interest in you or your stupid mind games. I have met plenty of aristocratic gentlemen—dull to the absolute core—and wouldn't even agree to marriage if it weren't for my father. It was only by his recommendation that I agreed to this betrothal."

"And why would you agree to help him?" He came to his feet to face me. "How can you have no bitter feelings? Your father sold you."

"My father gave me an option. If I had refused him outright, he would have changed his mind."

"Then why didn't you refuse?" He scoffed, curling his upper lip. "You really are a gold digger."

I turned to face him, taking a step in. "Aren't you as well?"

He didn't say anything, but his eyes burned.

"Whether it's a woman searching for a husband," I continued, "or a man searching for buried treasure, isn't it the same?"

He stepped in close to me. "So if I were the rich man, would you come to me instead of my father?"

He was trying to bait me—get some kind of power over me—and I didn't appreciate it. I shrugged with one shoulder, batting my eyelashes innocently.

"I can't imagine you to be rich, Jacques. Therefore, I've never considered you."

He grabbed my wrist and spun me back to him, his eyes filled to the brim with frustration and aggression.

"You have no idea who you're speaking to," he growled. "I possess things far more powerful than money. Mark my words. You'll regret your carelessness, dear mother."

"Stop calling me that!" I replied. "And what does it matter what you have to offer? I've already been *sold*, remember?"

Saying the words myself made my heart waver. I bit my bottom lip, trying to steady it. Long silence passed between us. I could feel Jacques watching me, even though I wasn't meeting his eyes.

"Is…is he kind?" I asked.

I heard his breath. "What?"

I looked up. "Your father. Is he kind?"

He held my gaze, no words coming through his lips. He looked away.

"You're more pure than I anticipated," he replied bitterly. "It makes you far more irritating."

I laughed ironically. "Adrian said the same thing. I didn't realize you two had so much in common."

Jacques returned to face me, narrowing his eyes. It took him two full breaths to speak.

"You actually care about the crew on this ship, don't you?" he asked.

I ignored him, leaning over to pick up the fallen key. Gripping it in my hand, I walked over to the door, and shut it behind me to lock Jacques back in his cell. When I turned to him, he only smiled, walking forward to lean against the bars.

"That's a mistake, dear mother," he said. "You should never fall for a sailor until he's been rightly judged."

I rolled my eyes. "I haven't fallen for anyone."

He laughed through his nose as I began to walk away.

"Be careful what you get attached to," he called after me. "You never know when it will be taken from you."

CHAPTER 22

SUGGESTIONS

We traveled for three more days, closing in on the source of the red light. Everyone on the ship was on edge, including myself. I didn't know why, but I felt something in me vibrating. The tremors in my spirit seemed to increase the closer we became.

When night had fallen, I came up to the deck, looking out at the red star that was nearly touching us. We would reach it within the next day, according to Adrian. I wasn't sure how I felt about it.

What would we find when we reached it? And how could everything change once we had it? The spiritual world had come alive again. Wouldn't that mean that humanity would be judged?

What would happen when they came to judge me?

"You're here."

I turned to the sound of Henrik's voice, met by his warm smile. He seemed hesitant while coming forward to meet me, even though I knew he was glad for my company. And I was sure that he knew I was always pleased to meet him.

"Can't sleep?" he asked.

I nodded. "You too?"

He nodded, pointing to the star. "I didn't think we'd really make it. But now that we have, I feel incredibly unprepared for it."

He stood next to me by the rail. His fingers twitched as he leaned against it, looking up at the star.

"How difficult can it be?" I asked. "Is there more to it than stealing a rock and leaving?"

"The Eros is the cornerstone of the spiritual world," he said. "I hardly doubt it's sitting on a bed of flowers, unprotected."

I nodded solemnly. "It's a good thing you taught me how to fight then."

He chuckled. "Are you ready for it?"

"I don't have much choice in the matter. But whatever you decide, I trust you."

He looked me over for a moment.

"And what will you do once we find the Eros and go home?" he asked.

I shrugged. "We might die in the process and then I won't have to worry about it."

"I'm serious."

"As am I."

Silence took over for a moment. He reached out and took my hand in his, his touch warm and inviting. Chills ran up my arm as he turned to face me, his eyes determined.

"You know I'll protect you," he said. "Whatever happens on the other side of that star, I won't leave you."

I gave him a warm smile. "I have no doubts."

He chewed on his bottom lip, seeming to build up the courage to say something else. I waited.

"You said you loved the sea. And sailing. That you hadn't tired of it. Is that still true?"

"Well…yes, it is."

"Is it safe to assume that you haven't grown sick of us yet either? I mean, despite the circumstances?"

"You mean, despite the fact that I was kidnapped?" I gave an ironic smile. "To be honest, this is the most comfortable I've felt since my mother passed."

He stepped in closer, still holding my hand in his. His eyes searched mine, and I could only look back, entranced by their glow in the moonlight.

"I want you to stay with us, Esmeralda," he whispered. He swallowed. "With me."

My lips parted in surprise, no sound coming from them even though I tried.

"Stay with me," he pleaded. "I'll take care of you. You have my word."

I finally found my voice. "What are you saying? Why are you suddenly—"

"I'm in love with you."

I heard the words, but they struggled to process. As I searched my mind for how to respond, Henrik took both my hands in his and looked at me with such sincerity that I lost my thoughts a second time.

"I tried to ignore it," Henrik continued, stroking my knuckles with his thumb, "but it feels impossible to keep to myself anymore. Not when we're this close to the unknown. Not when death could find us at any moment. I'm obsessed with you, Esmeralda. I have the ability to read the stars and tell the future, but it means nothing to me if you aren't in it."

His confession was so passionate and overwhelming that I had to take a step back.

"Henrik," I breathed out, "I absolutely adore you, but this is a lot for me to take in… I'm not sure what answer I can give you."

"Say you'll stay with me."

He gently pulled me back toward him, leaning down to meet his lips to mine. Before they touched, I put a hand on his shoulder, stepping away as my heart pounded, sank, and clenched all at the same time.

"I'm sorry, I can't. It wouldn't be an honest answer," I replied, a hand on my chest to calm my heart. "My father has probably already announced my engagement. If I go back on it now, then his reputation will be—"

"What's more important then?" Henrik asked, voice on edge. "Your father's reputation or your happiness?"

"How can I be happy with my family in ruins?"

"Are you saying I would stain your family name?"

My eyes widened. "Of course not. Please, Henrik, listen—"

"Unless you want to marry the old man," Henrik continued. "Perhaps he's richer than I gave him credit for. Or you find his son more interesting. Don't look so surprised. I saw you sneak down to meet him the other night."

"Henrik—"

"Or maybe sleeping in my brother's bed every night has swayed your affections?"

Suddenly my head swarmed. "Are you insane? How can you say that?"

"It's natural, isn't it? When you spend that much time with someone?" He stepped closer to me. "Maybe you're interested in a fling here before going back to your rich husband?"

"What's wrong with you? You're never like thi—"

He grabbed my hand again, this time, with force.

"I won't let go of you that easily," he said. "Not to my brother, not to a rich officer, not to anyone. I don't care about the consequences."

I had never truly been afraid of Henrik, until now. The way he looked at me was predatory and dominant, not at all like the man I knew him as.

"This isn't like you," I squeaked out. "You're not like this. Stop. Please."

Henrik's hand tightened around my wrist as he opened his mouth to speak, but someone else spoke before he did.

"Let her go, dearest first mate."

The moonlight struck Luc's eyes harshly, even though his voice was soft and sweet. Henrik stepped back, eyeing him.

"This doesn't concern you," Henrik replied.

Luc's voice remained in his flippant sing-song manner as he took heavy steps forward.

"But you'll be a better man with some beauty sleep," Luc replied with a cheerful tone. "You can't win the lady's heart with such a brute force, you know."

Henrik's hand loosened around my wrist, his eyes seeming to gloss over. He shook his head, as if his headache had returned, then looked back at Luc.

"What are you saying?" Henrik asked Luc.

"Tell the lady good night," Luc replied, his voice still sweet. "She'll only respond to a gentleman, you know. And a gentleman doesn't stay up past curfew."

Henrik paused, seeming to process the words. He swayed forward a little, then cleared his throat. He turned to me, his eyes now completely blank instead of intense and possessive as they had been only a moment before.

Henrik's eyes narrowed. "This is—"

"Oh, first mate," Luc sang again. "You don't want to do this at all, do you?"

Henrik paused, his hand fully dropping from my wrist.

"Tell the lady good night," Luc commanded.

"Forgive me," Henrik said. "But I must retire early."

He gave a short bow before turning on his heel and walking past Luc. When he was out of sight, Luc took three long strides to meet me.

"Are you all right, little dove?" he asked.

I stepped away from him, unable to understand what I had just seen.

"Luc, what was that?"

Luc blinked innocently. "What's what?"

"How did you get Henrik to leave like that? It was incredibly…unnatural."

Luc licked his bottom lip, looking over his shoulder. He turned back to me, eyes narrowing on my wrist. He lifted up my arm, tracing the marks that Henrik had left on it.

"Did Henrik say he was in love with you?" Luc asked.

I blinked. "Yes, but how did…"

"Did Adrian? Or any of the other men on the ship?"

"That seems a little obsessive." I tsked.

He put two fingers to my wrist. "Your heart is racing."

"Under the circumstances, I don't find it inappropriate."

His lips twitched. "What if I told you I loved you?"

He put an arm around my waist and pulled me in, staring hard at me. I could tell by his eyes that he was only teasing me again, and I didn't appreciate the joke. I pushed him away.

"Stop playing around, Luc. It isn't funny."

"What if I was being sincere?" he asked. "Couldn't you love a man like me?"

He sweetened his voice as he smiled innocently at me, but I still didn't like this teasing.

"That innocent act won't work on me," I said. "So stop."

"What if I do this?"

He leaned in and kissed my temple, his lips lingering as he breathed close to my ear.

"What about now?" he whispered darkly.

I stepped back a little, confused. "Luc…"

He reached for my hand, flipping it over and putting two fingers to my wrist again. He smiled, a breathy chuckle leaving his lips.

"Your pulse *slowed*," he said. "That settles it then."

I retracted my hand. "Why are you so obsessed with my pulse? Do you really think a sweet voice and a friendly kiss would be enough to make my heart race?"

"It would," he replied, "if you were human."

He held my gaze, not blinking, not wavering. His eyes narrowed slightly.

I laughed.

"What on earth are you talking about?" I asked, backing away from him.

"Your pulse doesn't race for me," he said, stepping forward to follow me. "You don't react to my sweeter tones. You don't listen to my commands like the rest of the crew does. The only reason you wouldn't respond to me is if we were of the same world."

I was even more confused than before. "What?"

He leaned down to my ear.

"The truth is, I'm a siren, little dove," he whispered. "And so are you."

CHAPTER 23

SIRENS

"A siren?" I asked, holding back my laughter. "You? And I?"

Luc pouted his lips as he looked to the side. "Why is it hard to believe? Is it because I'm a man? I realize that in the mythology sirens are usually women, but that's rather sexist, I must say."

I shook my head at him. "It's impossible."

"You saw the sky split open with a pillar of fire, and you still think there are things that are impossible?"

I looked into his glowing eyes, an unmistakable power in them, no irony to be found in any of the edges. I swallowed, trying to hold on to my disbelief.

"Haven't you ever noticed the way others fawn over you?" Luc asked. "How they bow to your whim? Laugh at all your jokes? How you can see their true emotions the longer you look at them? I admit, you haven't harnessed your powers well. They're unfocused. With some training, we can fix that."

"Powers?" I scoffed. "Training? It's too late, and I'm too tired for jokes, Luc."

"And I'm not laughing, Esmeralda," he replied, his tone more serious than I was used to. "But I understand your resistance. I didn't believe it at first either, but it's true. We're both from the spirit world. I knew it the moment your heart didn't race for me."

I swallowed, trying to find my words. "What does my heartbeat have to do with anything?"

"We can manipulate anyone, little dove," he said. "People fall at their feet for us. Their heart races. Their palms sweat. They get obsessive and possessive, yet they don't know why they do it. Our charm captures them regardless of whether or not they want to be captured. You could ask any man on this boat to marry you, and they'd do it. All you have to do is raise your voice a little. *Just like this.*"

He made his last sentence sweet, raising the note of his tone and turning it into a small melody, as he did often. He smiled as I connected his meaning.

I shook my head, starting to step away.

"No. No!" I said. "You're a terrible storyteller, and I won't have you insulting me in such a manner."

I tried to walk away, but Luc pulled me back, his lips flat. "You know as well as I do that if I was lying, you could tell."

Words failed to form. The look in his eyes was so serious, so intense that I thought it could break me. Even though it was completely ridiculous, I knew he believed it full-heartedly.

"But...the sirens on the ship..." I started. "They looked completely different."

"We're incarnates," he replied coolly. "We have human bodies, but siren souls. The sirens we saw that day were the first stage: pure. Pure sirens and merfolk have no body shape. Like the merfolk you saw when I threw you overboard. Then there are the full-formed sirens, those who have wings. We're the third form: cursed incarnates."

"Cursed?"

"Full-formed sirens are given the task of judging the human world. Should they abuse such power, they are put on trial, same as the humans. Sirens who have been found guilty of power abuse are…executed in a sense. Their souls are embedded into human bodies—over and over again—with no recollection of the past."

I took a few minutes to process, looking for the flaw in his argument.

"If we don't remember our past," I asked, head spinning, "then how do you know we're sirens?"

He chewed his lip for a moment before speaking. "When I was searching for my fiancée in the spirit world, I met with dozens of fortune tellers and astrologers who spoke of spiritual creatures. One of the fortune tellers tried to read my fortune to tell me about my past life. She couldn't. She said something was blocking her from reading my past. It was a first for her. I didn't think anything of it, but she felt it was incredibly important.

After a month, she tracked me down and told me that there was something about me that wasn't of this world. She told me of the sirens and spirits that forgot their homes. I laughed at her. I thought she was just adding salt to my open wounds. To be a spirit creature and not find the spirit of the woman I loved was just insulting. Then she convinced me to try the powers of a siren. You see, even in our cursed forms we can't lose it completely. We have charmspeak and the ability to see everyone's true self."

I swallowed, trying to put all the pieces together. I didn't want to believe it. It didn't make any sense. A siren?

With the ability to charmspeak? Was that why my father's business partners always praised me? How I knew which aristocrats and politicians Father should work with and which ones were scoundrels? Was it the reason I was always the center of a party or the first to be asked to a social event by the gentlemen in town?

Was it the reason Henrik had suddenly become so angry and possessive only moments ago?

"I know you're scared," Luc said, gently tucking my hair behind my ear. "I'm here to help you."

I looked into his soft eyes, the realization hitting me.

"You've been charmspeaking everyone on the ship," I said. "That's why they listen so closely to your stories. That's why they don't reprimand you for your behavior. That's how you controlled Henrik just now."

He smiled wide. "*Oui.* But you've been doing it yourself without realizing. Henrik's been affected by your powers. So has Adrian. Their thoughts are so easy to see, even without me reading their minds."

"Wait...what? You can't mean— You can *see* their thoughts?"

He nodded. "It's a power of a siren. We judge good and evil. Both of which start in the human mind."

"But surely you can't see..."

I trailed off, realizing.

I had always been good at reading people.

Luc stepped forward, his eyes glued to mine.

"I can see everything," he said. "Humans and sirens, alike. I can see every dream and desire you've ever had. Does that frighten you? Or does that thrill you?"

I lost my breath, drowning in the seriousness of his eyes. Only when he blinked did I feel myself come up for air, nearly gasping.

"You can't know those things," I said defiantly. "You can't expect me to believe all this so easily—"

"You can't fix your family, Esmeralda."

I stopped. "What?"

He held my gaze. "Marrying a complete stranger won't cure the pain you and your father are facing. It won't make your family whole again."

My stomach clenched as he held my face in his hands.

"You couldn't save your mother," he continued, "so now you're trying to save your father in order not to feel the same guilt all over again."

My eyes started to water, but I gritted my teeth. "You're—"

"You can't help what you are, you know. You can't help your love of the sea, your understanding that the world is more than what it seems, and your desire to help others before judgment sweeps them away."

I dipped my head as tears dropped. Luc pulled my face up, forcing me to look at him.

"You believed your mother's fairy tales because they were real," he said softly. "And you keep trying to save your family because you've been designed to save people."

He stroked my hair, a look of pity on his face. I hated it. I hated Luc looking at me with such pity. I blinked away my tears, my stomach knotting with panic and irritation.

"You're ridiculous," I said. "I've never once been angry with you, Luc, but this—"

"Try it on me, then," he replied, coming into my space. "Just once. Look at me and tell me what I want. Go ahead."

I tried to turn my head away, but he grabbed my chin and directed my eyes toward his.

"Look at me," he commanded.

My breath stilled. I gazed at him, getting lost in his desperate eyes completely. Then a thought struck me. It was strong and undoubtable, like a fact from a history book.

"You want to be reunited with the others," I said.

He dropped his hands and nodded with a sad smile.

"I was born an orphan," he said. "My fiancée is dead. I don't have anyone anymore. But if an incarnate proves themselves, they can get their wings back. They can become their full-form selves once again. And I can become part of something that makes all this suffering worthwhile. You noticed that the sirens never returned after that night, yes?"

I nodded weakly.

"Because there are two sirens *already on* the ship," he said. "They won't come after the crew for judgment as long as we're here."

I suddenly remembered something.

"But what about the time they first appeared? They attacked you, didn't they?"

Luc shook his head. "My wounds weren't from the sirens. My wounds were from Henrik."

He held up his shirt, turning around for me to see his back. There was a red welt in his skin.

The holy stones.

"Spiritual defenses work on incarnates too," he said, dropping his shirt and turning back to face me. "It's a rather bothersome drawback."

I leaned against the railing, processing the information. Luc was a siren. I knew it. Everything in me knew it was true. I couldn't explain why or how.

"Where are the others?" I asked. "How will you reunite with them?"

"The Eros," Luc said.

"What?"

Luc pointed to the star, squinting one eye with a smile.

"The Eros can be found under that star," Luc said, "in the Den of Sirens. Our home, Esmeralda."

CHAPTER 24

SURPRISES

It wasn't hard to feign illness.

Luc's words spun through my head all night, stealing all of my sleep, and I couldn't bring myself out of bed to help him in the kitchen the next morning. My stomach knotted at the idea of seeing both him and Henrik after what had happened last night.

Adrian allowed me to stay in his room for the day, a wave of concern washing over his eyebrows as he checked my temperature.

"Should I have Henrik look at you?" he asked.

I shook my head forcefully. "Please don't. It's something of the…feminine nature."

He held his hands up in surrender and took a step back. The lie was embarrassing, but the truth was insane.

"I won't ask any more questions then," he said.

He left the room, and I curled up under my blankets on the floor, wishing I could wake up to another reality. Being kidnapped was bad enough, but a siren? How could I be? I could accept Luc being a siren, but if I were a siren, I would know something like that, wouldn't I? Wouldn't I have some sort of clue?

And what was an incarnate? Did that mean I had died in a previous life only to live again in another body? That this body wasn't mine?

I looked at my fingers and wiggled them. This was my body. It had to be. I had never known another body. If I was an incarnate, did that mean I had stolen a baby's body?

A sudden chill ran through me. What a terrible idea.

But there was no denying what I had seen. Luc had controlled Henrik with his voice. The anger I saw in Henrik melted far too quickly for it to be natural. And not to mention the way that Luc interacted with the men on ship. No matter what trouble he got himself into with the crew or the captain, he always had that smile on his face, his voice sweet and melodic no matter the circumstances.

I saw the welt on his back. It was undoubtedly the shape of the stones Henrik kept on ship for the sirens.

Luc was definitely a siren. I accepted that. I wasn't afraid of it either, even though I probably should have been. Luc, however, had been nothing but kind to me. He had also been through so much pain. He was dear to me, no matter who or what he was.

But so was Henrik. And if I was honest, so was Adrian. So were half the men on this ship.

Except Jacques. I really didn't like him.

I sat up, remembering him. Luc was afraid of Jacques, but he never told me why. Was it something to do with the sirens? Something to do with the spiritual world? Or had they simply met before in another circumstance?

I didn't have the strength to get out of bed and find out. But I knew one thing: Jacques and Luc had a secret between them.

***

I spent the entire day in bed. Night fell and no one had come to visit me the entire day, thankfully. I couldn't face anyone. But after an entire day of thinking, I had no conclusions about anything. I only had questions, and I couldn't handle it anymore.

I threw off the covers and stepped over to Adrian's bookshelves. Adrian wasn't back yet, still preparing for our arrival to the Eros. He had been out late for the past few days, and if he was going to stay out as late as he normally did, it would be a few hours before he arrived. It gave me time.

Adrian had been borrowing books from Henrik's room about mythological creatures of the spiritual realm. He must have had some books lying about that would confirm or deny this incarnate nonsense.

I could believe Luc was a siren. Fine. But I couldn't be a siren. I couldn't accept that this body wasn't mine or that I had some sort of power to manipulate people.

I searched through the shelves, finding books about star alignment, religious traditions, and historical accounts of sightings and interactions with fortune tellers and astrologers. There were maps and myths and stories, but nothing about incarnates. Barely any mention of sirens or merfolk, for that matter.

Everything in Adrian's shelves were unsatisfying, so I went to his desk. There were piles of books and papers here (that had not slidden off despite how rocky the seas became some days), and with how much Adrian was studying recently, it was bound to have something important.

I went through the stacks, only finding more history on explorers and maps. I wasn't skilled at map reading, however, so I had no idea what I was looking at. Most of the things on Adrian's desk were about navigation and sailing, not about mythological creatures or whether or not I was one.

With a frustrated grunt, I threw one of the books back on the desk, only to topple over the pile of books next to it. They spilled on the ground, papers flying out of them. I swore to myself.

"Adrian is going to kill me," I whispered.

I leaned over to pick them up and stack them back on the desk. A small black book lay face down on the floor with its pages crumpled, so I opened it up to smooth them back out before closing the book.

It was a journal. Despite my ethics, I found myself looking at the pages as I smoothed them out. Adrian's handwriting was messy and nearly impossible to read. How could he read his own notes? I'd never seen someone with such poor penmanship.

I stopped, the next page stealing the breath from my lungs. It wasn't writing at all, but a drawing. It was a woman, sitting on a bed with her knees tucked in at her side, her hair matted and falling over one shoulder. Her long-sleeved blouse hung off her shoulder, her collarbone accenting a small jeweled necklace. I looked closely at the design of the necklace and gasped, my hand coming to my throat.

I flipped through a few more pages, the same woman sketched on multiple pages. One leaning over the side of a ship, another picture of her making soup over the stove, and yet another picture of her sleeping. My heart pounded harder with each page.

It was me.

"I told you to stay out of my things."

I dropped the notebook. I was so lost in its pages that I hadn't even heard Adrian open the door. He licked his lips before shutting the door behind him, taking slow steps toward me.

"It looks like you saw something you weren't supposed to," he said, his voice low.

His voice was cool, his face emotionless as he came to me. I stepped back, more afraid of his emotionless demeanor than his angry one. If he had yelled or teased, it would have been more comfortable than the serious stare he was giving me.

He leaned over, picking up the notebook and tossing it on the desk.

"I didn't mean to," I started. "It fell off the desk, and I went to pick it up—"

He leaned against the desk, trapping me between his arms. I looked away when his face came in close to mine, but he ducked down to meet my eyes anyway.

"Don't act shy on me now, princess," he whispered.

"W-what are you doing?" I asked.

His eyes darted down to the notebook. "You saw my drawings."

I scratched at my collarbone, feigning innocence. "You can draw?"

He smirked with a small ironic laugh, bringing his hand up to move a strand of my hair from my face. A chill shot down my neck as his fingertips grazed my skin, the air becoming too thick to swallow.

"You know you're beautiful, don't you?" he asked as if he didn't expect me to answer. "There are many beautiful women, of course. They always know it. They make it a point to smooth out their hair and straighten their clothes…same as you. You aristocrats are all alike."

His fingers moved to my cheek, his eyes soft and vulnerable. He was never like this. He was never so completely open.

"The problem is," he continued, "beautiful women have no idea when they're breathtaking. They know when they feel beautiful, but they have no idea when a man can't take his eyes off them."

He stood straight, looking down into my eyes. I could hardly breathe.

"What are you saying?" I asked, my mouth dry.

He laughed, looking at the floor for a brief moment before looking back up.

"Come on, princess," he said. "You can't sleep in a man's bed and expect him to feel nothing."

I looked away. Henrik had said the exact same thing, hadn't he? He accused me of having a fling with Adrian, while Adrian was…

Oh no.

"I don't know what I find more entertaining…the fact that those two brothers are fighting over you, or the fact that you don't know why they're doing it."

That's what Luc meant.

If I was a siren, then were Adrian and Henrik *enchanted?*

My thoughts were interrupted as Adrian's lips brushed against mine. His feathery kiss grazed my lips, catching me completely off guard. He leaned back to look at me, his eyes warning that he would try it again. I pulled back, stepping away from the desk so he couldn't trap me against it again.

"Adrian..." I started, voice shaking. "We can't do this."

He took a step toward me. "Why? Because of your fiancé? Or because of Henrik?"

"Not because of any of that. I—"

"Please don't deny me, Esmeralda," he whispered desperately, my name sounding incredibly sweet on his lips. "It's already too difficult to live with this obsession."

Obsession. That was the word Henrik had used as well. Right before Luc made him leave.

And if I was a siren, I could do the same thing.

And if I wasn't, then I could prove it here and now.

"Stop, Adrian," I said, raising the tone of my voice into something sweet.

He stopped despite the way that my voice shook as I spoke. But that didn't prove anything. He could have done that just because he was confused. I tried to calm my nerves and speak again.

"Esmeralda..."

"Do you want..." I swallowed, readjusting my voice into a melody like Luc did. "Do you want me to be yours?"

He nodded, his eyes drifting up and down my body.

"Then you have to do something for me," I said.

He nodded.

"I... I-I need you to dance."

He raised an eyebrow. "Pardon?"

I cleared my throat. "If you want me, you should properly dance as good gentlemen do."

He seemed to consider it for a moment, looking up at the ceiling. He took a step forward and then to the side, shaking his head as he narrowed his eyes in thought.

He was trying to do…a waltz?

I swallowed. This wasn't true. It couldn't be.

"You also need to sing," I added.

He stopped, suddenly annoyed. "What do you mean, sing?"

"I want a gentleman who can sing and dance."

We stared at each other for a moment. He seemed too stunned to do anything at all. I breathed out in relief. Of course the captain of a pirate ship wouldn't sing and dance on my command. I couldn't be a siren. That was proof enou—

"I only know a few songs," Adrian said. "But if that's what gets you to come to me…"

He started to waltz again, his breathy voice forcing out a random sea shanty I didn't know the words to. When he lost his balance while dancing, so did I.

Captain Adrian—the same captain who had kidnapped me, forced me to feed him, and demanded that I obey his every command—was now singing for me while stumbling around like a fool.

I gasped and put a hand over my mouth, stepping back.

It couldn't be true. I shook my head to myself. No, it couldn't be.

Knock, knock, knock.

Adrian stopped, a clarity coming back to his eyes. Were they glazed over before? I hadn't even noticed.

He signaled me to wait as he answered the door, one of the crew members on the other side.

"What's wrong?" Adrian asked.

"We need you to come to the first mate's quarters right away," the man said. "Something's happened to Henrik."

Adrian nearly flew out the door, and I ran to follow. Did something happen to Henrik because of what Luc had done?

Or what I had done?

I ran out the door, only to be greeted by shouts and drawn swords.

"What the hell is this?" I heard Adrian yell above the cries.

Coming toward them, I stopped just outside of a circle of men. Henrik was on his knees in the center of the circle, Adrian quickly being brought to his own. I felt my arms being twisted behind me, until a voice called out for them to stop.

"The girl is with us," Luc's voice said behind me. "Release her."

The man behind me released and quickly apologized as Luc stepped forward into the circle. He clasped his hands behind his back, looking down at the captain and first mate, who were now on their knees in front of all their men.

Luc only smiled.

"To answer your question," Luc said, "this, my dear captain, is called a mutiny."

CHAPTER 25

BETRAYAL

"Tie them up, please," Luc sang with a smile.

He turned toward me, the noonday sun catching the glimmer in his eye. At the sight of Henrik and Adrian being forced to their knees so ropes could bind their wrists, I rushed to meet him, grabbing his sleeve.

"Luc? Luc, what are you doing?" I asked.

He gently took my hand as his lips pursed together.

"I'm sorry, little dove," he said with sincerity. "But this is necessary."

"Mutiny? Necessary?"

He nodded solemnly. "It time for the souls of men to be judged once more. It's my duty…and yours."

I looked over the men of the ship, fear wrapping tightly around my throat.

"This can't be proper judgment!" I yelled after him.

"Judgment will come at the Den of Sirens," Luc replied, not turning back to look at me. "I hope you'll consider your position in this equation, little dove."

My eyes stopped on Henrik, who had double the men trying to restrain him and get him to stay on his knees.

"I won't yield!" Henrik yelled.

Luc approached him, waving his hands back and forth as if there were a melody.

"Easy, dear first mate," Luc sang. "You're not cooperating."

Henrik blinked hard, shaking his head. He glared at Luc.

"Why do you resist more than the others?" Luc asked. He looked up at the men holding Henrik back, switching his voice to his regular sing-song manner. "Get him back to his knees, men."

Henrik was shoved forcefully to his knees.

"Resist?" Henrik echoed. "You expect this ship just to submit because you smile when you command our imprisonment? I assure you, there's no amount of charm—"

Henrik stopped, his mouth still open. His eyes widened.

"Charm," he said. "Charmspeak. You're…"

His eyes shifted from Luc to me.

"You're both sirens," Henrik said quietly, almost to himself. "You've been manipulating our thoughts and emotions this whole time. You two planned it from the beginning, didn't you?"

"No!" I yelled, coming forward to meet Henrik. I crouched in front of him, raising his face to meet mine. "I didn't plan this at all! I know barely anything about it! Please believe me. You should know better than anyone what it's like to have a power you don't understand."

His eyes searched mine with no affection in them.

"Stop speaking," he said. "I can't believe anything you say now. Or anything you once said."

Luc pulled me back to my feet and away from Henrik.

"Wait, please, Luc. Tell them that I didn't know—"

Luc wrapped an arm around my shoulders, pulling me close so that his lips were resting on my ear.

"It won't matter, dove," Luc whispered. "We're the enemy now. I have to keep the enchantment going. If I don't, they'll kill us both."

"They wouldn't—"

I looked back at Henrik and Adrian, their eyes dark and focused. It was the same look I had seen when Jacques had stormed the ship. Blood-thirsty. Cutthroat. Merciless.

Suddenly, I couldn't breathe.

"It's part of the enchantment," Luc said. "The affection they've given you isn't real."

I turned to face him, clenching my fists.

"And my affections for them?" I asked. "Were those also fake?'

He reached up and gently moved a strand of hair from my eyes, the deepest look of pity across his face.

"No," he said softly. "Your feelings are real. And that's the price we pay for our power."

"So you sirens came to sentence the entire crew to hell?" Henrik yelled out.

"No," Luc snarled. He gripped hard to his knife, stepping forward and pointing it between Adrian's eyes. "I came onboard to judge the captain."

Even though Adrian was on his knees with a dagger a breath from his face, he held his head steady and high, no emotion upon it.

"Your sins have gone on long enough," Luc told Adrian.

Adrian shrugged. "Not sure what you're talking about."

"The spiritual world sees and knows all," Luc replied, "but if you need evidence, I have some ready for you: the courthouse fires."

"Is it the spiritual realm's job to make sure we pay our taxes?"

"A woman died in those fires," Luc said, ignoring Adrian's comment, "You killed her. The week before her wedding."

A memory struck me.

"And in his obsessive love, he asked her to marry him. She agreed. A week before their wedding, he came home to find out that she had been killed in an accident."

I gasped, throwing my hands over my mouth.

Adrian laughed and rolled his eyes. "From what I read in the papers, there were no deaths that day. What are you talking about?"

Luc's hands visibly shook. He clenched them together.

"Her name was Maria," Luc replied. "She was twenty-three years old and dreamed of owning her own jewelry store. She liked summer roses and winter skies. She died, and you're the one who killed her."

Adrian's eyes went blank, confusion settling against his forehead. I could tell by the look in his eyes that he wasn't faking it.

He had no idea.

"You'll all be taken to the Den of Sirens to be tried," Luc continued. "Should your hearts be deemed pure, you'll be released to live your lives. Should your hearts be deemed a tool of the devil, then we'll send you back to him. And *you*," he added, pointing his shaking dagger at Adrian, "will be the first I put on the execution block."

Luc started to turn away, but I grabbed him by both shoulders, trying to catch up with my thoughts.

"Luc, you can't really mean to kill them."

"And why not?" he replied. "It's our job as sirens to pass judgment, regardless of the consequences. Do you not understand the importance of balancing good and evil?"

"Barely! I haven't understood any of this! Luc, I don't even think Adrian knows what happened. Look at him—"

"It doesn't matter what he knows," Luc replied coldly. "A man pays for his sins whether or not he is aware of them."

"I can't agree to let them die like this!"

"Those are the rules, little siren," a new voice said. "You need to get used to them."

I turned to the sound of the newest voice in the conversation, my throat constricting further as I took a step back.

Jacques smirked as he came forward to meet us. Luc grabbed my arm, throwing me behind his back and putting a block between Jacques and me. Jacques only chuckled.

"That's adorable," Jacques told Luc, "but you know it won't help you."

"How did you get out?" Luc asked.

"It's not exactly high-level security around here," Jacques replied, waving his hand nonchalantly. "I've been kept in worse prisons. I could have gotten out days ago, but we weren't at the Eros yet."

Jacques smiled as he looked at the burning star.

"You've made my job much easier, Luc," he said. "I'll remember that."

"Job?" I echoed. "Luc, is he a siren too?"

Luc hesitated, then shook his head. "Remember how I said that there is a balance between this world and the spiritual world? That everything is organized?"

Jacques turned his head toward us, fully attentive to what Luc was saying.

"Yes…" I replied.

Luc swallowed. "This man…is a Judge of the spiritual realm."

Jacques gave a single nod, starting to unbutton the top of his shirt.

"Let me explain it to you this way, dear mother," Jacques said, as he continued to unbutton his shirt. "You understand that sirens judge humanity, yes?"

Before I could answer, he opened his shirt, revealing his chest decorated in circular Celtic patterns. They were dark—nearly black—and deep, as if they had been burned into his skin. Luc grabbed my hand at the sight of it, his hands sweating in mine. Jacques quickly smiled at our hands together, then pursed his lips.

"The sirens judge mankind," Jacques said, stepping forward, "and I judge the sirens. I decide whether you get your wings, or whether you're sentenced to an eternity of endless reincarnation for your sins."

Jacques looked up at the glowing red star with a smile.

"And thanks to you, Luc," he said, pointing in the distance. "I now get to judge the *entire* Den of Sirens."

CHAPTER 26

PATHS

"You can stop trying to protect her," Jacques said to Luc. "We both know it won't protect either one of you from the Trials."

Luc's shoulders dropped, but I could still see the tension in them. Jacques waved to his own men, who were now also free from their cells, and gave them orders to continue sailing toward the light. He then turned back to us.

"The Siren King will be very pleased at your delivery, Luc, I'm sure," Jacques said, nodding to Adrian and Henrik. "Especially so soon after the spiritual and physical realms have been united."

Luc swallowed, but said nothing.

"That will work in your favor to get your wings back," Jacques said.

"Wings?" I asked.

Jacques then turned to me. "Yes. The end of your cursed state. That's your goal as well, I take it?"

I had no idea what anyone was talking about, but I was tired of Jacques accusing me of wanting things.

"I only wish to return to my father," I said.

He chuckled softly to himself. "Oh, Esmeralda. You really have no idea, do you? There are only two choices for you. You can become a fully winged eternal siren once again, or be reborn into another useless human body after this life."

He stepped forward, looking down into my eyes. Luc stepped in protectively, but it wasn't necessary. I wasn't afraid of Jacques. I had no reason to be.

"I have a hard time believing you don't want your real power back," Jacques said to me after a moment. "I can already tell by your face that your soul has been through many lives to get to this current one."

"And what is that supposed to mean, exactly?"

I honestly had no idea what it meant, but it felt insulting.

"Your soul is pure," he replied with an irritated sigh. "Which means that your soul has worked over a long period of time to redeem itself."

"Can you see why we were sentenced to reincarnation?" Luc asked Jacques warily.

"I could. With the right tools and a little of your blood, I can read your pasts easily."

"What is it with you people and bloodletting?" I asked.

Luc only chewed his lip and nodded, taking a step back. Jacques eyed him for a moment and then nodded to Henrik and Adrian.

"Finish giving the orders to your…followers," Jacques told Luc, "then take to the helm. I assume you can steer?"

Luc nodded respectfully.

"And do you know where the Den of Sirens is?" Jacques asked.

"I have a general idea," Luc replied.

"Perfect. I know the *exact* location," Jacques replied. "We should get there easily then."

Jacques turned on his heel to command his men while Luc turned to walk to his position at the helm. I stood, confused for a moment, wondering who I should follow, and yet not wanting to follow either one.

"Put them in the brig," Luc ordered his men, pointing to Henrik and Adrian.

"You'll pay for this, Luc!" Henrik swore, breaking his silence. He winced as he shook his head. "Siren or not, I'll make sure you pay for this betrayal."

The men started to drag Henrik and Adrian off. Adrian didn't look at me, but Henrik did. I had never seen his eyes so cold and vengeful. I wanted to go to him and explain, but Luc pulled me back before I could even take a step forward.

"You need to stay away from them, little dove," he said softly. "The veil is gone now."

"What will happen to them? Why the sudden mutiny? And what was Jacques talking about…wings? Luc, please…"

His eyes drifted toward the light of the Eros. With a shake of his head, he turned to leave. "I need to get to the helm," he said.

I followed, close at his heels. "If you want me to trust you, you need to give me answers. Now."

Luc stopped and turned around, hesitating before opening his mouth to say something. He didn't get the chance to, however.

"I need you at the helm, Luc," Jacques said behind us. "Sail portside."

Luc nodded and left me without any answers.

Jacques eyed me for a moment. "You seem to have a lot of questions," he said. "I thought you knew all this."

I shook my head at him, everything suddenly spinning. "How many times do I have to say that I don't understand?"

He was quiet for a moment before exhaling slowly from his nostrils.

"A cursed siren who purifies their soul and redeems themselves can return to their full form as a winged siren."

I blinked at him.

"Should the king of the sirens find it favorable, you will be tried as pure or impure. Pure sirens who have redeemed themselves will return to their true form, should they wish. Impure sirens return back into their curse as humans."

He stepped forward, towering over me as the red light of the Eros lit up his face.

"But that decision is partly mine," he said darkly. "I can free you from your curse, or I can sentence you to it."

I sighed.

"Stop trying to be so intimidating," I returned. "If that's true, it's not like I can remember the reincarnation, right? So if I die, I forget everything again and start over?"

Jacques rolled his tongue over his teeth, but he didn't answer.

"I'm not sure how I can be afraid of you," I said, "when I'm not sure what there is to be afraid of."

"Then I guess you'll just have to see it for yourself."

He pointed behind me. I turned and looked over my shoulder to a rock cavern towering in the water, the red glow bursting from the center of the ceiling. I had never seen such a cavern above the water—as if Aladdin's cave was floating on the surface.

Jacques ordered Luc to go straight into its mouth. The sounds of the ship echoed against the walls as the tips of the sails scraped the top of the cavern. As we went deeper, the sunlight was replaced with a furious red glow, its waving patterns on the walls and ceiling sparkling like gems were hiding in the crevices. Despite the red glow around us, it was somehow difficult to see ahead. I leaned forward to look, but there was only darkness.

Then the sea stopped.

I heard a voice shout my name right before the ship tipped forward, sliding into the darkness below.

Cold air burst against my skin, and I felt my feet lift off the ground, right before two arms wrapped around my waist and pulled me back down on the ship. The ship plummeted further then crashed against the water again, the sea spitting large waves into the boat and soaking me through. When the ship straightened and evened out, I rolled over to see the man who had rescued me from falling into the abyss.

It was a drenched and furious Jacques.

"Why the hell would you get so close to the edge?" he scolded me. "Did you even have the notion to step back from the edge of a waterfall?"

He held up his drenched clothes and groaned.

"Well, then next time keep your grubby hands to yourself and let me fall overboard!" I scoffed, coming to my feet. "No one asked you to help anyway, *Your Honor.*"

He threw a few curses at my back as I walked away, trying to wring the water out of my clothes. Was there anything worse than soggy, cold clothes? Hardly.

Except maybe finding out your friends hated you and that you may have been assisting them to their doom. That was possibly good competition.

"Are you all right, dove?" Luc yelled after me from the helm.

I walked up to meet him, as he steered the ship. "No," I replied. "I'm not all right at all."

It was silent for a moment.

"I know it's still a lot to swallow," Luc said, "but I didn't lie to you about who you are. And now we can join our family. Our *real* family."

My eyes narrowed at him. "My father and mother are my real family."

"And Maria and her family were mine," Luc replied. "I remember the feeling of it. But they're gone now. This is our true family, Esmeralda. Our bodies may be human, but our souls belong to the sirens."

"So what do you want me to do then? Just abandon my father?"

He shook his head strongly. "No. I would never ask you to do that, but you have to realize that you are far more powerful than you ever thought. What are you going to do with this knowledge? Go back to your arranged marriage and live a miserable life? Or use your power to create a balance in the world again?"

He stared at me for a long moment, then turned his eyes back on the sea. I took a deep breath, not knowing how to answer.

I couldn't leave my father behind. I wasn't going to abandon him. I wasn't going to let his heart break like that.

Not again.

The glow continued to flow through the caverns, and Jacques shouted orders to Luc and the other men as we maneuvered through the crevices of the caverns. It was like an underwater maze, the boat hitting and scraping the sides as we got deeper and deeper. The cool air of the cave steadied my nerves, and for some reason, it felt like I was breathing slower and deeper than I had in my entire life. Blood streamed through me with ease and regeneration.

After some time of sailing, the cavern opened up even more, stretching long patterns of ruby glitter across the ceiling like night stars. I could only look up in awe as we pulled up next to a long slab of marble stone, perfect to hold a ship in place.

"Is this…a dock?" I asked.

But no one answered. Jacques was too busy looking at the ceiling to say a word. I almost jabbed him to ask him more questions, but when I heard the fluttering, I stopped too.

The ceiling was dark compared to the rest of the caves. I thought that the light should have reflected off the cavern ceiling, but it only seemed to get absorbed in the shadows.

Then the shadows moved.

CHAPTER 27

THE DEN OF SIRENS

The shadows fluttered and split apart, falling down from the ceiling and swooping across the ship. I screamed and ducked down as the wind picked up over us. Jacques didn't seem perturbed whatsoever and held his ground despite the shadows swarming around him. He popped an eyebrow as the figures landed on the ship, standing straight to reveal a swarm of men and women with large, dark wings.

Sirens?

"Quite an entrance," Jacques said, monotone.

"Why have you come to the Den of Sirens?" one of the male sirens asked, stepping forward.

Jacques lifted up his shirt slightly to show the Celtic designs across his ribs. The sirens all took a step back, a sudden serious shift in the atmosphere.

"Where is your king?" Jacques asked.

There was another pause.

"We will take you to him," the siren said with a bow.

Jacques waved for Luc and me to come forward.

"These are incarnates," Jacques told them. "They're with me."

It was odd to hear those words coming from Jacques's lips. It made it sound like he was in charge of me somehow, and I didn't like the idea of it. But it was the first time he had actually tried to keep me close instead of insulting me or attempting to feed me to the sharks, so I took it gracefully.

What I couldn't take gracefully, however, was the reaction of the sirens.

When the male siren's eyes met mine, his jaw slackened and he took a step back. The others did similarly after him, all of them staring at me with wide eyes.

"It can't be..." the male siren said.

"She's returned?" another whispered in the back.

"Even after the last time..."

"How many times...?"

I couldn't understand all of their mutterings. I had never gotten such a rude welcoming in all my life, and that was including my meeting with Adrian.

Jacques turned his head over his shoulder to look at me, one eye narrowing.

"Intriguing," he said as he looked at me. "It seems you have a reputation here."

I motioned to the caves around us. "How is that possible? I've never been here before."

"That you remember," Jacques replied. "You forget that sirens are born here. It can't be your first time."

I looked around the caves, digging deep into my memories for anything remotely familiar. But no, I was positive I was seeing all of this for the first time. I had never been here before.

"Take us to the king immediately," Jacques commanded the sirens. "And there are human men in the brig awaiting trials. Take them to Purgatory."

Something in my stomach clenched. I stepped forward to object, but Jacques only shot me a terrifying look of disapproval. Before I could speak, however, Luc gently grabbed my arm and gave me a reassuring smile.

"They won't harm them," Luc said. "Not until after the Trials."

I gritted my teeth. "Not that it matters to you either way."

I ripped away from Luc's hold and followed the other sirens, keeping my head high. Who cared if I was a cursed incarnate? Not that I fully believed that anyway. Whatever I was, or wasn't, I knew this: I was still the same dignified lady I was before I had ever gotten on this ship. My father was still grander than any king. And no matter what happened here, I would return to my family.

Two sirens led in front, while the others flanked us at the side and back. Other sirens stayed back on the ship, and it looked as if they were collecting up the crew and bringing them down to the cavern.

I looked over my shoulder as long as I could, not seeing a glimpse of Henrik or Adrian. I wanted to speak to them. I wanted to tell them everything I had found out in such a short time. I wanted to tell them that I never planned to hurt them.

But Luc had told me that I was their enemy. Would they really try to kill me? Did they really feel nothing at all toward me without me charming them?

The sirens led us from the ship into the caverns that stretched long and wide in the darkness. The caverns only became darker and deeper, and there were moments when I couldn't even see my hand in front of my face. The sirens in the lead commanded us to follow their voice, and I did, trying not to stumble across the slick ground beneath us. Regardless, I didn't feel afraid in the slightest. In fact, I felt more at peace than I ever had. It was like a warm Sunday morning breakfast with my parents, a nostalgic comfort as we walked on the cool ground and breathed in the clean, fresh wind that caressed our skin.

After one final dark tunnel, the caverns opened up again to a massive dome, with a ceiling higher than any building I had ever seen. There were sirens flying slowly around the edges, their dark wings in full spread. It was impossible not to watch them soar, the graceful way they fluttered on the wind.

Suddenly, the skin between my shoulder blades ached.

I caught Luc's glance at the sirens flying above us as we walked, his jaw slacked in complete awe.

They then brought us to a hallway that looked like it was made of glass. It shimmered and glowed the further we walked, to a room made of what looked like ruby glass. The floor was made of dark stone, stretching across a rosy lake in long strips like a spiderweb. On the far side of the room was a staircase leading up to a grand throne that must have been ten feet high, a man sitting on the throne looking tiny in comparison, with one elbow on his knee. As we got closer, I realized that there were two more figures, one on his right and one on his left.

The man on the throne had glowing alabaster skin, rich copper tones seeping from the shadows. His eyes were sharp, somehow full of darkness and light at the same time. His long hair was straight and white—not the muddled white of an aged man, but instead, a pure white that reflected light much like the moon. The man on his right had a bright round face and clear eyes, a warm smile across his face. The man on the left was the polar opposite, a long oval face, his eyes as dark and clouded as his scowl.

The man on the throne stood as we approached, nodding to the men who had led us in.

"We've brought a Judge and two incarnates, Your Majesty," one of the sirens said, bowing.

The Siren King.

The king gave a nod to our leads, and they left. Jacques stepped forward, not showing any formal respect at all.

"King Melchior," Jacques said. "It's been some time."

The king gave a warm smile before nodding briefly. "It's good to see that you are still well, Jacques."

"Well, it looks like our schedules are now disrupted," the emotionless man on the left of the king said.

"Yes, but how wonderful to have guests again!" the man on the right replied.

"And who might you be?" the king asked us, not paying attention to the two beside him that had just spoken.

"These are two of your own," Jacques replied for us. "In the human realm, they go by Luc and Esmeralda. They're incarnates that have delivered a ship of humans to you now that the worlds have reopened."

Luc gave a bow when the king met his eyes, and I gave a much-practiced curtsey when he met mine. I was a lady, after all.

"Incarnates!" the man on the right of the king said, clapping excitedly. "It's such a rare treat to find humans who realize their true souls."

The man on the left scoffed. "Incarnates who were condemned for a reason. Let's not forget that they were sentenced to eternal punishment."

"It has been some time since the Judges have come to us," the Siren King said, nodding thoughtfully. "I assume you wish to complete the trials as quickly as possible? You always do."

Jacques ran his tongue against his cheek, not answering. The king gave a warm chuckle in reply and stood. He turned to us.

"Please, allow me to offer you a place to stay until the Trials are complete," he said.

"But my father—" I started.

I quickly threw my hand over my mouth. I hadn't meant to say it out loud, but for some reason, I suddenly found it too easy to speak my thoughts.

"Forgive me, Your Majesty," I added. "I hadn't meant to speak out of turn."

He cocked his head to the side, looking oddly amused. "Is that so?"

"I am, however, concerned about my father's well-being."

He took a few steps forward, not speaking at first. He then nodded again, the color in his face glowing.

"Yes, you are not the first incarnate to have a family they love and wish to return to," he said. "I'm not offended."

He stepped down further, coming closer to look more intently at me. I felt nervous under his gaze, yet at the same time, felt completely safe. As he looked at me, I really could see both darkness and light in his eyes, perfectly balanced, sparkling as he looked at me. After a few moments, he gave another warm smile.

"Your Trials will be tomorrow," the king said. "If your Trial goes well, you can choose between staying with us or returning to your family."

The king then turned to Luc. "And you? Do you wish to return to your family?"

Luc bowed his head, the light leaving his eyes. "I have no home to return to, Your Majesty."

The king nodded. "Yes, that is common too. Then this shall be your home."

Luc chewed his bottom lip as he took a deep breath.

Home. That was probably a word Luc hadn't heard in a long time. Part of me wished to see him finally find a place to rest his heart, but on the other hand, I was still hurt by his actions.

"Come with us," the king said, motioning to his right- and left-hand men. "We will show you to your *wings.*"

He chuckled, putting emphasis on his last word and looking to his right- and left-hand men for a reaction.

His right-hand man clapped. "A play on words! Wings of a siren and wings of a building. How entertaining!"

"A pun?" his cold-looking left-hand man said. "You have a better sense of humor than this, Your Majesty."

"Oh, lighten up, Hugo," the right-hand man said. "It never hurts to laugh at a joke."

"You're right, Vito," the left-hand man replied. "I laugh at you all the time."

"Exact— Hey, wait…"

The king shook his head with a smile and motioned for us to follow him.

The caves were a deep and beautiful maze, the caverns stretching high as if they were the sky themselves. Sirens flew above us, fluttering from one hole in the ceiling to the next, as if they had their own floor that humans could never touch. It reminded me of bird nests high in the tree branches, unattainable by the critters on the ground.

"These caverns are quite large," the king said as we followed him. "You'll get lost easily if you don't know your way. The incarnates and sirens stay on this side of the caverns. The humans stay across the way."

He pointed across a large chasm to another maze of caverns. As he pointed, a line of people walked across, each man tied to the man in front of him.

At the front was Adrian. At the end was Henrik.

I stepped forward automatically, only to have Jacques grab my arm and pull me back.

"You can't fly yet," he said flatly. "So don't try to jump across any holes in the ground like a fool. Especially for humans about to get tried."

I glared at him, but quickly turned back to watch Adrian and Henrik as they were taken deep into the caverns opposite of us, disappearing into the darkness.

"How will they be tried?" I asked, almost whispering.

"The way everyone else is tried here," Jacques replied. "With blood."

CHAPTER 28

ROOM

"You can both stay here until the trial tomorrow," the king said, nodding to Vito to open the large crystal door in front of us.

Vito happily opened it up, revealing a single dormitory room with four stone bunk beds that jutted out of the walls like shelves. Each bed had a red blanket and single pillow, along with a folded pair of black robes I had seen the other sirens wearing. The room was completely empty otherwise.

"Welcome to the most boring room in the caverns, incarnates," Hugo said, monotone.

"Yes," Vito agreed, "but once the Trials are over and you get your wings, you can get upgraded to a wonderful single suite!"

"Unless you're found guilty and sentenced again to eternal reincarnation," Hugo added.

I turned around to face the king.

"Can you tell me about the Trials?" I asked. "It's a blood trial, isn't it? Is it the same ritual Henrik did on me the first time? Because even though it wasn't that bad, it was still quite uncomfortable—"

The king raised his hand to stop me, matting his eyebrows. "What do you mean, the first time? Who's Henrik?"

I looked at Luc and Jacques momentarily. Jacques had one eye squinted, as if he was somehow suspicious and confused at the same time. Luc chewed his lip and turned his head away before I could see his full expression.

"H-he's the first mate of the ship, Your Majesty," I replied, suddenly nervous. "The reason I was brought aboard the ship was to point them toward the Eros. They slit my arm to open the spiritual world and take them to…well, here."

I showed him the faint scar on my arm from where Henrik had cut me open so many months ago. The king touched my arm with a soft, gentle hand, looking at the mark with alarm. He motioned for Jacques to come and look as well.

"What do you see?" the king asked him.

Jacques stared at my arm for a long moment, eventually shaking his head.

"Nothing," he said. "Her blood has been sacrificed, but I can't see any of her marks until after the Trials in the spiritual realm."

I stared at both of them blankly. "Um…I'm sorry?"

Jacques ignored me and raised his head to turn to Luc.

"Luc," he commanded. "Explain this to me."

Luc gave a calculated exhale, licking his lips before speaking.

"Captain Adrian's heart was set on finding the Eros," Luc said. "And his brother, Henrik, is an astrologer who figured out that the way to reopen the spiritual world again was to sacrifice the blood of a descendant of one of the Guardians."

I still didn't understand some of that, but I didn't interrupt.

"The Guardians were released from their duties nearly three hundred years ago," the king said. "That must have been quite a task to track down."

Luc glanced at me before shaking his head. "It wasn't difficult. I already had found Esmeralda by the time we started to set sail."

I blinked at him, not understanding. "What do you mean…*you* found me?"

He paused, starting to speak, but pausing again before he actually did so.

"I was the one who traced your lineage," Luc said. "I knew the spiritual realm had been divided for too long, and I wanted to help put it together again. So I tracked you down and gave that information to the captain as insurance to be brought aboard with the rest of the crew."

"Clever," Jacques commented. "I'm sure your charmspeak helped as well?"

Luc nodded. "I was able to convince them not to hurt Esmeralda for her blood, but I hadn't expected the captain to take her hostage. I suppose I should have stayed with him for the mission, but how could a cook ask to tag alongside the captain? When they brought her aboard, I was able to convince Adrian to make Esmeralda my assistant, so at least I could keep my eye on her."

I was hearing the words, but nothing was processing.

"I didn't realize she was an incarnate right away," Luc continued. "Not until she refused to respond to my charmspeak. Henrik resisted at first, too—due to his background in astrology and alchemy, I suppose—so I thought it was simply another challenge for my power."

"Get to the point," Jacques said. "What's the deal with this scar?"

"It isn't difficult," Hugo interjected, causing us all to face him. "Her human body is a bloodline descendant of one of the Guardians, while her spirit is an incarnate of one of our sirens."

"What a fantastically miraculous coincidence!" Vito added.

"Miraculous indeed," the king agreed, smiling in satisfaction. "If it wasn't for Luc, you might have never known who you were, Esmeralda."

I glanced at Luc, but he looked away.

"Also," Jacques added, "the spiritual and human realm would have been severed for much longer than it was."

"Both are winning points for Luc," Vito beamed.

"But have no benefit to Esmeralda," Hugo added.

The king stepped forward. "As far as I'm concerned, both of you sacrificed for the redemption of the spiritual and physical realms. Maybe you weren't aware of it, but it is still so. That will not go unnoticed in your trial tomorrow."

The word brought me back to my original question.

"What happens at the Trials?" I asked.

The king smiled, instantly calming my racing heart. "We take a drop of every siren's blood, and then mix it with mine. The blood will decide if you are pure or tainted. Should you be pure, you'll be considered for your wings once again. Should you be found tainted…"

"You'll vanish from this existence immediately," Hugo finished.

"But you don't have to pack anything for the next life, at least!" Vito said happily.

"Wait," I interrupted. "Vanish?"

The king nodded, this time looking more solemn. "Tainted reincarnated sirens are returned to their curse and born into another human body immediately."

"Then I won't…" I shook my head at him. "You can't take me away from my father, Your Majesty. Please…"

He brought his hands and gently touched my shoulders. "I understand your concern, Esmeralda, but I ask that you trust me."

How could I? I had never met the man. Still, something in me wanted to trust him despite the situation. It was something in his voice, or his familiar demeanor, but I couldn't put my finger on why the king felt so familiar to me.

"I don't think she'll be cursed," Jacques said, seemingly to no one. "I can already tell that she's been through a long purifying process."

"A professional Judge!" Vito said with a clap. "Such experience!"

"It means that he's cursed a lot of sirens," Hugo added.

Jacques didn't reply. He only looked off to the side of the room.

"I'll have your meals brought to you," the king said to us. "Please take this time as a cleansing period before your trial."

"And the human crew?" I asked. "What will happen to them?"

"They will be tried after the sirens," the king said. "After all, I can't have tainted sirens judging humanity. That wouldn't be helpful."

"And if they're guilty? The, uh, humans, I mean?"

Hugo made a fireworks gesture with a popping sound.

"They don't feel a thing though," Vito added.

I felt like my heart had stopped. The king gave an empty half smile.

"It seems cruel, I know," he said. "But remember this: the balance of good and evil in both realms is far too important. If I don't judge them, the humans destroy each other. There would be nothing left of that world at all should they go unpunished for their deeds."

"But to destroy them in such a way…"

"They have a chance to repent," the king replied. "They always have the option. But a hardened heart cannot be redeemed. It doesn't want to be."

He motioned back to the beds.

"It's late," he said warmly. "Get some rest. I will come tomorrow to fill you in on the other details."

He gave Luc a pat on the shoulder and nodded to him, turning on his heel to leave with his men. Jacques lingered a moment longer, meeting my eyes and then following the king.

I slumped onto the closest bed.

Vanish? Those who were deemed tainted or whatever would just vanish? How could that be true? Did that mean I would never see my father again if I were ruled as tainted? Would Adrian or Henrik simply disappear before my eyes, never to be seen again? Would their parents also never see them return home?

A hand came to my shoulder. "Don't panic, little dove."

I snapped out of my thoughts, throwing Luc's hand off of me. "Don't call me that anymore."

"Listen, I—"

"You lied to me!" I said, standing from the bed. "You never told me about your plans, or who you were, or what I was. Maybe if I had known sooner…"

I stopped, looking at my hands. Luc grabbed both of them.

"I'm a siren, Esmeralda," he said. "When I realized this, I knew I had a bigger purpose. I had to bring in the humans to be tried. That was my responsibility. You, however, had no idea of this burden. I couldn't give it to you so quickly."

"So you simply sent away people that I cared about to their deaths?"

"I cared about some of them too, you know."

"But not Adrian. You're happy to watch him die."

Luc swallowed, not looking away from my eyes.

"Yes," he replied.

I tried to pull my hands away from his, but he didn't allow it.

"If someone killed your father," he asked, "wouldn't you feel the same?"

I didn't want to answer the question, but I couldn't help but feel convicted.

"Perhaps…" I replied bitterly. "Perhaps I would have been vengeful as well. But what about Henrik? He's innocent."

"He's an alchemist who performed deadly assaults on behalf of the king," Luc replied with a scoff. "I wouldn't bet on it."

"Deadly assaults?"

"What do you think people in the navy do for the king?" Luc asked. "They siege pirate ships to capture and kill the crew. It never occurred to you?"

I turned my head away. Henrik wouldn't, I mean, he couldn't…

But then I remembered the day Henrik saved me from that vile attacker—the one with two missing fingers.

Luc dropped my hands, stepping back.

"I didn't want to hurt you, little dove," he said sincerely. "Truly. Of anyone I've met since Maria's death, you're the only one who has—"

He sighed, cutting himself off. He shook his head and ran his hand through his hair, staring at the ground.

"I suppose it doesn't matter now," he said. "But just know that I truly consider you a friend, no matter what you feel about me at the moment. Should we both get our wings, I hope that I can have your forgiveness. And if one of us is cursed, even more so."

He lay on the bed across from me, looking up at nothing as I sat across from him. I wanted to forgive him, but for some reason, I couldn't.

Even if one of us was destined to disappear tomorrow.

CHAPTER 29

BAD MATCH

I couldn't sleep. It seemed logical considering my doom would be sealed the next day.

I watched Luc as he slept soundly, breathing heavily as he gave way to dreams. I wondered how long it had been since he slept somewhere that felt like home. This place seemed to soothe him. I could see it.

And I also knew that it soothed him because this place soothed me, too. The amount of peace I felt in this place was alarming.

I stepped out of the room, wandering into the caverns. I wasn't worried about getting lost; for some reason, I didn't feel afraid of many things here. I felt afraid for my trial and the crew's fates, but in everything else, I felt nothing.

The air here was cool and refreshing, and every ache in my body seemed to release. With such a healing feeling, I wanted to stay here forever.

But guilt nagged the back of my mind at the idea of it.

I didn't know how long I had wandered through the caves, but no one stopped me or accused me of trespassing. In fact, no one had been speaking to me at all except for the king. Whenever a siren and I crossed paths, they went the other direction, head down, refusing to make eye contact. The more it happened, the more concerned I became, not knowing how I could offend so many sirens I had never met before.

The caves now were still and quiet, the only sounds breaking the silence being the rushing brooks that ran down the caverns.

I followed the path of one of the brook branches, ending up in a strange room that had a bluish-white glow. The brook streamed into a large pool, the steam from the hot water rising to caress my face.

"Is this…a hot spring?" I asked myself.

I touched the pool with the back of my hand, the water warm and inviting. I agreed to its invitation, slipping off my shoes and dipping my toes in. Somehow, I knew this wasn't against the rules. Somehow I knew this was completely common and accepted here, but I didn't question why I knew such a thing. I wiggled my toes under the water, sighing with a smile as the heat coated my legs in warmth.

"Is that all it takes for you to be happy?" a voice asked.

I gasped and turned to the voice, irritated to find Jacques sitting on the other side of the pool, fully immersed in the water. He was topless, the water surrounding the bottoms of his ribs as he sipped a glass of wine. "I didn't realize you were here," I said.

He chuckled. "So I noticed."

There was a glow that rose out of the water, hitting Jacques's skin and bringing a strange power to the dark, patterned circles across his chest and shoulder. He cocked his head to the side as he looked at me.

"Do you like what you see, Mother?"

I made a sour face at him. "I told you to quit calling me that."

He chuckled, bringing his wine glass to his lips. "That's one way to dodge my question."

I couldn't help but stare at the patterns across his skin.

"Did they burn those into you?" I asked, unable to hold in my curiosity.

He nodded as he swallowed. "Burning the skin is the only way to release the demons."

I blinked. "Demons?"

"Judges are humans who were once possessed by demons."

I snorted. "Are you sure you're not still possessed *now?*"

He swished his wine in his cheek with a distasteful look at me as he set the wine glass down next to him.

"So you're human?" I asked.

He laughed. "More than you are. Both my body and soul are human still, but I now have some special abilities thanks to my demonic residue."

He said it casually, as if he had explained it to many people before, but the glow in his eyes made it clear that he didn't take the situation lightly.

"Are you in any sort of pain?" I asked.

His eyelids fluttered as he laughed again. "Hardly."

"How did you become possessed?"

"My mother was an astrologer. A lousy one. She accidentally summoned demons while trying to speak to the dead, and one of them took my body for a while."

"How terrifying!" I said, genuinely shivering. "How can you say such a thing so casually?"

"It doesn't matter now," he said with a shrug. "The demon is gone, and so is my mother."

I sighed, stomach sinking. I had figured that Jacques's mother was dead. Bastard sons were rarely claimed by their fathers unless there was no other living family. Not only for the way it badly reflected on the status of the family, but also because women scorned by rich men were almost criminal in their revenge, demanding payment or material possessions. At least, that's what I had heard from Lina.

There was a sudden ache as I missed her, along with my own mother.

"I'm sorry," I said to Jacques sympathetically.

"Don't be," he replied with a cold edge to his voice. "I'm not."

He met my eyes. His stare made my breath freeze, goose bumps rippling across my skin from my ankles to my ears.

"W-what are your powers, exactly?" I asked. "Can you read minds?"

He shook his head sharply. "I can see many things most humans can't. I can see the auras of both humans and the spiritual realm creatures. Which means I can see the emotions of those creatures, as well as whether they are becoming tainted or pure."

It took me a moment to process what those might all mean.

"Is that why you called me pure that one night?"

He paused, as if remembering the night I came to him in his cell. He then nodded.

"Also," he added, "once your blood has been sacrificed in this realm, I can read your soul's history on your arm."

He pointed to the flesh of his forearm. I remembered the king and him staring at my arm only hours earlier, and it made a little more sense, yet not entirely.

Jacques stretched his arms back out in the tub, and I was glad he couldn't read my mind. Before I was able to stop myself, all I could think about was touching the marks across his skin. I wondered what they would feel like—if they were smooth like the rest of his glowing skin, or if they were rough and jagged like the look in his eyes.

"But," he suddenly said, breaking me from my thoughts, "I don't need to be a siren to read your mind, Esmeralda. Your thoughts are quite obvious."

He stood from his seat and came closer, and I scooted back from the edge of the pool I wasn't able to come to my feet before he smiled and grabbed my foot, pulling me back toward the edge of the pool. His wet fingers wrapped around my ankles, pulling my calves deep into the water. He looked into my eyes, an arrogant smile dancing across his lips.

"Everything you're thinking about," he whispered, "is easy to read."

I shivered as his fingers curled around my ankles, brushing the bottoms of my calves under the water. Everything in my head screamed to pull back and run out of there as fast as possible, but the mischievous look in his eyes had me frozen in my spot.

He smiled devilishly.

"It would be quite dangerous, you know," he said. "A reincarnated siren and a Judge."

As I processed his meaning, he continued.

"I've had a few…offers from both incarnates and fully winged sirens. The problem is that my job is to sentence them to an eternal curse should they betray the spiritual realm. Otherwise, I'm the one who has to pay for their crimes."

His fingers crept higher up my legs under the water, and it robbed me of my will to fight back.

"You would…pay their crimes?" I asked, distracted by his fingers.

"Yes. I would be cursed eternally just as the sirens are if I failed to judge righteously. Just as you'll be condemned should you neglect your duties as a siren."

I couldn't hold back a gasp as his fingers brushed behind my knees. I jumped and pulled back, putting my hands against his arms to signal him to stop. The arrogance on his face didn't change, but his fingers fell back to my feet.

"You're quite sensitive," he said with a chuckle. "Are you…untouched?"

I shifted uncomfortably. "I don't know how that's any of your business."

"I assumed with your powers, you'd have a collection of men at your disposal," he said. "I'm intrigued why a female siren in need of financial stability wouldn't seduce any rich man she came across."

"Just because I have some sort of charm does not make me any less of a dignified lady, sir."

He laughed even harder. "A dignified lady? Why is that so important?"

I swallowed, trying to collect my thoughts. His fingers lingered near my feet but didn't touch me, and I felt my thoughts clear as I spoke.

"Because when I act respectable," I said, "it gives honor to my father."

He rolled his eyes. "And why are you so obsessed with honoring your mortal father? Does it have benefits?"

I paused, catching a trace of bitterness in his eyes. Yes, Jacques was a bastard, whose parentage had caused him more grief than reward. He wouldn't understand. So I chose my words carefully.

"Because if I honor my father, then others will too," I said. "And should my father be seen as an honorable man, perhaps it will eventually produce more good men just like him."

He met my eyes for a moment. With a bitter scoff, he stepped back, pushing his hair back with his wet fingers.

"You're frustrating, you know that?" Jacques asked. "All the power in the world and you choose to help a human for no reason."

"He gave everything for me," I replied. "It seems fair that I give what I have for him."

A thought then struck me, suddenly making me ill.

"But, what if…"

"What if what?"

I met Jacques's eyes.

"What if my father was charmed? If my powers affect humans, then maybe…maybe he never truly loved me."

Jacques was silent for a moment. I broke away from his stare as my eyes teared. I waited for him to tell me that I was a crybaby and that it was just the way things were. I don't know why I had said anything aloud in the first place. It wouldn't mean anything to him anyway.

"I can tell when the humans are enchanted by you," Jacques finally said. "I can see auras that come off their bodies, much like the way steam comes off the water in these springs. Those under your enchantment have a certain aura. The stronger your charm, the stronger the aura. The crew on the pirate ship? Completely entranced and charmed with you. The captain and his first mate, especially. Your father, however…"

He stopped, wetting his hair with his fingers again.

"My father?" I asked, wiping away a threatening tear.

"His aura is changed, slightly, but it's not as strong as the others."

I sniffled. "What does that mean?"

Jacques held my gaze. "It means that he's barely enchanted by you at all. Not as a siren, anyway. From what I've seen and heard of your father, I believe that he's simply enamored with his daughter for the fact that she's his daughter."

A new set of tears filled my eyes, and I couldn't help but smile.

"Thank you, Jacques," I said.

He curled his lip. "I wasn't attempting to console you. I am, however, bound to the truth regardless of the circumstances."

He pressed his lips together and looked away.

"You should go to bed," he said. "You have an important day tomorrow."

"I don't think I can sleep," I said honestly. "If I disappear tomorrow, I'll never get to tell my father goodbye. That's worse to me than any curse."

There was a long silence between us. I didn't dare look up at Jacques as I pulled my feet out of the water and shook them dry. With a heavy heart I stood, but before I could take two steps, Jacques called out for me.

"Esmeralda," he said firmly.

I turned to meet him.

"You're far too irritatingly pure," he said.

I laughed painfully. "Yes, you've said that."

"That's why I don't think you have to worry. As much as I'd like you to be an impure, twisted incarnate, doomed to another life of reincarnation, I can't seem to find fault in you."

He reached back and grabbed his glass, drinking the last of the wine.

"But we'll see the final results after the Trial," he added. "After all, none of us truly know where we'll end up tomorrow."

CHAPTER 30

TRIALS

K nock.
    Knock.
Knock.

Luc and I looked at each other, neither one of us opening the door. It felt foolish to invite in the people who wanted to doom our souls to an eternity of cursed wandering.

Luc eventually swallowed and stepped forward to open the door of the small dormitory we had been allowed to stay in, the two sirens standing on the other side stone-faced and somehow paler than normal.

It then occurred to me: they were probably to be trialed as well.

"The Trials will begin soon," one of them said. "We've been asked to retrieve you."

The siren eyed me, his frown deepening. The second one didn't look at me at all. While the Siren King seemed to have warm emotions toward me, the sirens themselves appeared to have the stark opposite. I shifted uncomfortably.

"Where is the king?" I asked.

"He's preparing to perform his duties at the Trial," the siren returned flatly. "You can see him at the court."

I nodded thoughtlessly, following close behind Luc as we walked to our doom.

My hands started to build sweat as we walked farther and farther into the caverns, not a word between any of us as we walked. The fear was putting us all on edge. Something in me wanted to break the silence, if only for my own benefit.

"Tell me a story, Luc," I whispered.

Luc's eyes widened for a moment before he swallowed, his nerves showing more than my own. Maybe he was simply confused that I was speaking to him at all, after all the things I had said to him last night.

"Is this really the time?" he asked.

"It may be the only time left," I replied.

He paused. After a moment, he reached back and squeezed my hand, pulling me forward to walk with him.

"There once was a beautiful enchantress who lived in a golden castle," he started. "She was loved by all—far and near—praised for her beauty and magic.

"Then one day, while she was walking to the market, she was cornered by a terrible thief. 'Give me your greatest possession,' he said. So she offered him money. He refused, asking again for her most precious possession. She offered him jewels and again, he refused. 'What is it that you want?' she asked. 'I cannot think of a single thing more precious than my money and jewels.'"

Luc then gripped my hand, pulling me in closer to him.

"'I want the most precious thing of all,' the thief replied. 'Your heart.'"

Luc stared right at me as he said it, making my breath still as my stomach sank.

"But she couldn't give him her heart," Luc continued. "For his hands were too dirty to hold it properly."

"Luc…"

"And so the thief was left with nothing, unable to have what he wanted most because his hands were too dirty to hold it, and because even a thief knows he can never obtain a lady's heart unless she gives it willingly."

I squeezed his hand, trying not to cry. He gave an empty smile, stopping us both so he could rub his thumb against my cheek.

"Don't worry, little dove," he said. "Whatever happens to us, remember that your friendship brought me great joy for a time."

I squeezed his hand once more. "Me too."

"Over here," the siren in front of us said.

We stepped forward, following the sirens into the inner court. The caverns stretched high and wide around us, light reflecting off the obsidian ceilings due to the deep, clear pool in the middle of the room. I knew immediately that this pool was more than a hot spring. I could feel the energy coming from it, but I couldn't decide if it was something to be feared or embraced.

The room was full of sirens—hundreds of them, possibly—all standing in the coliseum seats around the pool. Fear gripped my throat as I looked around us, wondering what would become of those here who would be found guilty.

King Melchior appeared, moving toward the center of the lake. He walked directly on the water, and I realized that the pool was not deep at all but simply an illusion. Unless King Melchior was floating? But how? He hadn't wings like the others.

Jacques stood next to the king in the water, his shirt completely off with his Celtic circles exposed and glowing. There were four more men—men from Jacques's crew—all with the same marks. I recognized them as the prisoners I used to feed after the ambush.

So Jacques really had planned to come to the Den of Sirens from the beginning. He wasn't coming for me at all.

His eyes caught mine as if he had heard me, but I dipped my head.

We were then stopped by Hugo and Vito. They held out their hands to us.

"Give us your hand," they said at the same time, although their tones were completely different.

Luc and I, as well as the two sirens with us, held out our hands. Hugo and Vito pricked the fingers with a small piece of metal, and I was thankful that it was far less painful than what Henrik had done. Red blood came from Luc's and my fingers. Teal blood came from the sirens' hands in front of us.

"It's been so long since I've seen red blood!" Vito said in delight. "What a beautiful shade!"

"And the red fire that will consume the guilty will be just as beautiful," Hugo said flatly.

"Ah, why do you have to scare everyone?"

"It's only the truth."

"Why not be a little more optimistic?"

"Optimism doesn't save you. Only truth does."

"Yes, but hope carries you through the harshest truths."

The four of us left Hugo and Vito to argue as we were ushered to rows in the front. I switched between watching the blood flow from my finger to the king standing on the pool in front of us. I wished I could speak with him again before judgment. He seemed so warm and inviting, but I didn't have the chance to speak with him as much as I wanted.

I then realized I wouldn't have the chance to speak to Adrian or Henrik either. I couldn't apologize. I couldn't explain myself. I couldn't tell them what they meant to me.

But according to Luc, it wouldn't make any difference anyway.

"Everyone is here," the king announced.

The room went silent.

"After more than a few hundred human years, the spirit world and the human world have been united once again," King Melchior continued. "This means that the tasks of the sirens are hereby reinstated. But the judgment of the humans cannot be entrusted to those who have strayed from good or from truth. So today you will all be trialed."

The silence felt like a sucked breath. The king gave a sad smile.

"If you have faithfully followed in your purpose," he said gently, "with your heart turned toward truth and good over evil, then you shall remain here. If, however, your hearts have turned toward evil, and your purpose has become selfish and destructive, you will be cursed as a human until you have redeemed yourself. But you will always be welcome to return."

His eyes landed on me and Luc.

"No matter how many times it takes," he said with a smile.

The sirens looked over to us. I straightened, trying to look as dignified as possible, regardless of how uncomfortable I truly was.

The king pointed to Jacques and the other Judges on the sides of the pool. They nodded, stepping forward into a five-point star around the king. The king then brought out a knife, the blade reflecting the light from the water as he cut across his own hand, Jacques and the others doing the same directly after. All five of them held their hands out over the pool, until blood dripped down their hands and into the pool below.

The blood dropped, and the water rippled. As the ripples webbed across the water, the pool turned from red to gray to teal, the colors swirling and spinning until the water began to rise up like a geyser.

I reached out for Luc. He took my hand, holding it firm in his.

The water then formed into long, twisting lines like snakes, striking out at the audience. I screamed and ducked, feeling something wrap around my wrist like a wet and unbreakable spiderweb. I tried to pull my hand away, but it held tight, a thin line of red and teal running from my hand to the pool of the king.

Screams echoed off the walls, and I looked back for a moment, only to see sirens around us burst into flames. Their wings were the first to disintegrate in the flames, the shadows of their bodies following right after. In a moment, the fire and the heat vanished, their seats instantly empty.

It stopped as soon as it began. The light and water turned back to white. Gasps and wails filled the hall as sirens were now realizing who had disappeared.

I looked next to me to Luc, who was wide-eyed and breathless, but still next to me.

We were both still here.

In fear, relief, and sorrow, I wrapped my arms around him. He didn't say anything and held me close, rubbing my back after a moment.

I looked over my shoulder to Jacques and King Melchior. Jacques quickly came to the king's side right before King Melchior's knees gave way under him.

"My own…" I heard the king say painfully. "It never hurts less."

The king's skin was pale with grief, his rich alabaster tone faded, the white in his hair darkening. Jacques supported the king until the other Judges came to assist, and they carried him to a throne off to the side of the room. Hugo and Vito stood on each of his sides, their heads bowed in respectful grief.

I felt myself shake. Luc held me close, trying to settle my nerves.

Even though the sirens around us had been strangers to me, they *felt* like people I had once known. I wanted to grieve them deeply, but I didn't understand why. Something in me was tearing. Like my mind was a thin piece of paper and there were holes in it with light seeping through.

"Don't be afraid, little dove," Luc whispered in my ear. "It's good news. This means you can choose to go home to your father."

I looked up at him, still shaking. "Really?"

He nodded, moving the hair out of my face. "I promised to get you home safely, didn't I?"

His warm smile nearly made all my hatred of him disappear.

"You're both still here," a familiar voice cut in.

We turned to see Jacques, who was still shirtless. I turned my head away quickly, embarrassed.

"Don't act so shy, Esmeralda," Jacques said with a chuckle. "You've seen me undressed before."

I glared at him from the corner of my eye.

"Can you tell us what happens to the two of us now?" Luc asked.

"You've both been deemed pure," Jacques said. "As incarnates, that leaves one final task. It's time to decide whether or not you get your wings."

CHAPTER 31

PASTS

We met with the king later that evening. At least, I assumed it was evening, since there was no way to tell time in the Den of Sirens.

There was a solemn air in the den, as if the walls themselves knew there had been a great loss. When I stopped and looked at the caverns above, I could hear snippets of sirens grieving their lost companions, and I had to fight the urge to cry as well. I didn't know why, but I wanted to grieve with them. Also, I didn't know why it had never occurred to me that the spiritual world would feel grief.

Luc and I were escorted to the throne room. The rosy lake in the center of the room gave a beautiful soft glow to the room, but it didn't hide the pain of the people in it. The king was still pale when we came to meet him. Despite his obvious pain, he greeted us with a warm smile.

"You're both still with us," the king said to Luc and myself. "That means your curse is lifted. You can return to us, if you both wish."

The king stood but wobbled, off-balance. Hugo and Vito both grabbed one of his arms, holding him up as he steadied himself.

"This is hardly the time to celebrate," Hugo muttered with a sigh. "We should be grieving our losses."

"Yes, perhaps," Vito said, calmer than usual, "but we also need to give our people some joy in such a dark time."

King Melchior raised his hands to tell both his men to stand back. They did as commanded, and he stepped forward toward Luc and myself. Part of me wanted to reach out and hug him, but logically, it didn't seem appropriate.

"Jacques," King Melchior called behind us. "Can you come and tell us about their curses?"

Jacques stepped out of the shadows in the corner of the room, pursing his lips.

"You say it like you don't already know," he said.

The king cheekily smiled in response. "I never said the information was for *me*."

Jacques acknowledged the king with a nod, then made his way over to us. He came to me first, grabbing my arm and sliding my shirt sleeve up my elbow. The sensation of his fingers sliding up my skin made me flinch, and I pulled my arm back.

"What are you doing?" I accused.

He puffed out some air. "Reading your history. It's written on your arm."

I looked at my skin. There was nothing there.

"No, it isn't," I replied, suddenly nervous.

"You can't see it," Jacques said. "Only I can."

He stared at me, holding out his hand so I would give him my arm again. I shook my head, not wanting to give in so easily.

"Read Luc first," I said with a scowl.

He dropped his hand in annoyance, but then gave an amused smile. "Have it your way."

I rubbed my arm, chewing my lip as Jacques approached Luc. Luc was far less anxious than I, allowing Jacques to life his sleeve to look at his arm.

"Hmm…" Jacques hummed. "Interesting."

"What does the reading say?" King Melchior asked.

"He's lived about seven lives," Jacques said. "Most of them were short, too short to redeem himself fully. But it seems his suffering has cleansed his sins."

"And what sins would they be?" the king asked.

Jacques met Luc's eyes, waiting for a moment as if Luc was going to object. He didn't.

"Adultery," Jacques said casually. "Luc was found guilty of stealing at least half a dozen human women from their husbands."

I choked. "You mean that he—"

"It can't be true," Luc replied, pulling back his arm and searching it. "I would never steal another man's wife. Not after my—"

He stopped, swallowing hard again. The king stepped forward, putting a hand on his shoulder and speaking softly.

"Your cleansed spirit wouldn't be able to understand your tainted one," the king said. "Once you've been purified, your old sins will repulse you."

"He's suffered a great loss," Jacques added. "Multiple times across multiple lives. Whatever sins he committed, he paid for them."

The words sank into our ears, but they seemed to hit Luc's the hardest.

"Maria…" he whispered, his eyes glossing into the most sorrowful I had ever seen them. "Forgive me. It was my sins that killed you."

The king brought his hand to Luc's hair much in the way my father did when I was in pain.

"Your sins have been paid for," the king said. "Now it's your choice on what to do with your freedom."

Luc nodded. He turned his head away, wiping his thumb under his eyes and clearing his throat.

"I would like to find my home," Luc said.

The king's face was firm. "You understand the weight of your responsibilities? If you accept your wings, you must return to the skies, weighing the souls of man as you once did. You can be tried and cursed again at any time."

Luc nodded. "I understand."

The king lifted Luc's head, looking straight into his eyes for a few moments. He smiled warmly, nodding.

"Yes, your heart is true," King Melchior said. He turned back to Jacques. "Shall we give him his wings?"

Jacques looked him over for a moment. "He's been purified, and he helped reconnect the spiritual and physical worlds together. I have no objections."

I stepped back automatically as Luc followed Jacques to the center of the rose lake in the middle of the throne room. They walked along the thin bridges of dark stone that stretched across it until they were in the direct center, the water rippling below them.

Jacques motioned for Luc to stay still on the platform, leaving him to go to the throne. Luc stood still over the water. My heart pounded in my chest as we waited.

Vito and Hugo stepped away from the throne, taking new places on the sides of the room. The king stood at his throne, waiting for Jacques to stand beside him before speaking.

"You've done well, Luc," the king said. "Or...should I call you Rhys once again?"

With that, the throne split in two, a red glow bursting from the crevices. The glow twisted in the air—much like the teal strands in the courthouse did—and swarmed around the lake in a deep mist. The water rose from the lake and twisted with it, creating a breathtaking rosy wave that towered Luc on both sides. I saw him flinch right before the water swallowed him completely, wrapping around him like a cocoon.

The water split into multiple sections, twisting and weaving until it created rose-colored wings on Luc's back. They fluttered, sending water scattering across the lake; then they dripped, more and more until the remnants turned into the shape of feathers. Luc fell to the ground, sitting up and breathing roughly as the wings burst into full expansion.

They were absolutely breathtaking to look at. They were dark, but sparkled like stars, equally darkness and light.

The throne then closed on itself, becoming whole once again. The king helped Luc to his feet and brought him away from the lake back to the throne.

Luc looked back at his wings, a smile bursting across his face as an excited cry left his lips. He twirled with his wings like an old friend, and they fluttered in return, lifting him clear off the ground.

I could only stare. I couldn't even breathe.

"I remember!" Luc said. "I remember everything now. All the lives I've lived…I remember."

He turned back to the king, gratefulness spilling out of his eyes. He bowed on one knee, holding King Melchior's hand.

"Your Majesty," he said as if he had known the king since childhood. "Forgive me for my actions against you."

The king laughed, stroking Luc's head in adoration. "It's good to have you home again, Rhys."

Rhys.

Luc's true name was Rhys.

I then realized that somewhere in that rosy lake was my true name as well.

Something in me split in two completely. There were two separate griefs: wishing to see my father at home again, and realizing that I had a home here too.

Jacques grabbed me as I started to faint, holding me up by my arms.

"Passing out is a little dramatic, don't you think?" he asked.

I met his gaze. Even though his voice and face were stoic, I knew he was teasing me. He brought me up to my feet again, holding me steady.

"Do you believe now?" Jacques asked. "Do you realize the weight of everything?"

I swallowed, looking at Luc. His joy as he stood next to the king broke my spirit. I wanted that joy. Something in me was thirsting for it more than anything. But I also couldn't abandon my father.

"I feel it," I replied. "I can't even describe to myself, but I know I'm meant to be here somehow. I felt it when those sirens were cursed. I felt it the moment we stepped into the den."

"But...?" Jacques prompted.

"But...I miss my father still. If I never returned home, he would be so broken. Regardless of my desire to be here, I still love him."

"Idiot," he said, "who told you that you had to love your father less?"

I couldn't read his eyes as he said it. Perhaps it was another unintentional way to console me. He held out his hand again. I glanced over his shoulder at Luc, who was still speaking with the king. King Melchior turned to look at me, then smiled and nodded to encourage me.

I swallowed. Jacques held out his hand once more.

"Come on," he said. "You're next."

I inched my arm toward Jacques. He took hold of my wrist, with a firm but considerate grip, flipping my arm over to read. His eyebrows matted, and his pause was far too long for me to remain comfortable.

"What is it?" I asked.

"You said your human body was a descendant of one of the Guardians, was it?"

"So I've been told."

"Then…do these names mean anything to you: Alain, Juanell, Neva, Silvan?"

My mouth gaped. "Neva. Neva was my great-great-grandmother."

His eyes met mine with a grave expression. His eyelids fluttered as he exhaled through his nose.

"Can you see her charge, Jacques?" the king asked.

"I can," Jacques replied, still staring at me.

He paused again, his firm grip on my wrist slipping.

"These are the names of four of the Guardians of the Eros," Jacques replied. "The four Guardians that you killed over two hundred years ago, Esmeralda."

CHAPTER 32

CURSES

I stumbled back, not understanding what Jacques was saying.

"Killed?" I repeated. "That's impossible. I could never…"

"Your pure soul wouldn't understand your tainted soul," Jacques said, repeating the king's words. "As you've suffered, your morality has purified. The woman standing in front of us wouldn't be capable of the same sins."

I couldn't fully understand his meaning, but my mind was too frazzled to understand much at all.

"It would explain your human obsession to protect your family," Jacques continued. "Just as Luc's adulterous soul would be obsessed with romantic love."

I looked at Luc, who now looked like a complete stranger. It wasn't just the wings. There was something about him that was now somehow mature and battle-scarred, as if all the lives he once lived had caught up to him. Something flickered in his eyes as he looked at me, his mouth gaping as if he had just seen me swallow a bee. I couldn't understand why he was suddenly looking at me in such a way.

I didn't have a chance to ask.

"But your sins have been cleansed," Jacques said, squeezing my arm to get my attention. "And you have a decision to make."

I glanced at the platform in the middle of the lake where Luc had received his wings. It was somehow drawing me in, a clueless moth to an eternal flame.

"I can't," I managed to whisper out.

His eyebrow bounced, unamused. "I had a feeling you'd say that."

"It's just too much information at once," I replied. "I don't understand what's happening…"

"If she waits too long, she may slip into the next life still cursed," Hugo commented.

"Yes, but to make any decision in haste could be tragic for all of us," Vito replied.

King Melchior stepped forward, approaching both Jacques and myself.

"Esmeralda…" he said gently, "come with me for a moment."

He held out his elbow, nodding for me to accept the invitation. I took his arm mindlessly, wrapping my fingers around his biceps. The touch was warm and nostalgic, like a childhood blanket wrapped around my shoulders.

Hugo and Vito followed behind us as Luc and Jacques stayed in the throne room. The king led me into the maze of halls, taking one slow deliberate step after the other. Vito and Hugo stayed ten feet behind us, walking in unison.

"I know you, don't I?" I asked, looking up at King Melchior.

His lips pulled to the side in a fake, confused smile. "What makes you ask that?"

"Because Luc spoke to you as if he knew you. And when I touch your arm, I feel like I should know you too."

The king paused for a long moment before answering.

"I know all my people," he said, "from the moment they came into existence, and even in every human body they reincarnate to. We knew each other once, yes. And should you take your wings again, you will recognize me."

I swallowed, sighing. "I feel like I'm split in two, Your Majesty. I can't understand any of this."

He stopped, turning to face me with a warmth in his eyes I felt was unearned.

"I won't force you to return to us," he said gently. "I won't force you in any direction. Our den is missing one without you, but I understand that your human home is missing one as well."

I swallowed and nodded. "You've been very good to me, Your Majesty. But my father has been good to me too. I don't know if I could live for an eternity knowing I abandoned him."

He gave an amused smile.

"You are not the first to have such anguish," he said, "and you won't be the last. It's difficult to let go of the only life you've ever known for a life you know nothing about."

I was at a loss for words, overwhelmed by both his kindness and his wisdom.

"Take your time," he said. "Should you desire your wings, all you need to do is ask. But remember that should you pass away in your human body in this life, you'll be sent to another human body immediately, with no recollection of any of this."

Something pained my heart to hear such a thing, yet I wasn't sure why. I only knew of this place since yesterday. How could I be so homesick for it when I hadn't known it?

"Your Majesty?" I asked. "Do you think I could find this place again if I passed into the next life?"

He laughed. It was the first time I had ever heard him truly laugh, and I didn't understand why he was so tickled at the question.

"My dear, you don't remember a thing at all," he said, "but let me tell you a secret: this is the third time you've found us."

***

The king and I walked around the hallways a little more, the paleness in his skin alarming me. There were deep shadows behind his eyes, and I knew that even though he was happy to see Luc and myself return to the den, he had still lost more sirens than he had gained. I insisted he rest—for whatever benefit it might have had to the king of the sirens—and Hugo and Vito took the king back to his room.

I wandered around, somewhat in the direction of my own room, the room for incarnates. Now that Luc was a siren again, I would be in the room alone, and I wasn't sure how I felt about it.

Something fluttered overhead.

I looked up, just as Luc soared over me and landed only three feet in front of me. His physical form was thin before, but now it was classically masculine, his muscles rigid and defined like a statue of Hercules or a painting of a Roman gladiator. His wings expanded twice the length of his arms, yet he seemed completely in control of them as if he had owned them the entire time.

There was a shyness in his eyes, however; one I was not accustomed to seeing.

"You refused your wings?" he asked, his voice softer than normal.

I wrapped my arms around myself and nodded. "For now."

"Will you ever…?"

I shrugged. "I don't know."

He chewed his lip, looking around the room as if he were trying to find his words in the rafters.

"You don't remember me then," he said.

I cocked my head to the side. "What do you mean? I haven't forgotten you."

"No," he said with a laugh. "I mean, from the life we had before."

He held my gaze.

"We knew each other once, yes. And should you take your wings again, you will recognize me."

If I knew the king at one time, did that also mean…?

"I wondered why I was instantly drawn to you the moment I saw you," Luc said. "In all honesty, I thought it was love at first sight, since I had never experienced anything quite like it before. I often heard older people talking about how they met their true love and felt as if they knew each other for a lifetime."

My heart fluttered at his words, and I couldn't help but rub the goose bumps on my arms.

"When I realized you were a siren, I dismissed the love-at-first-sight notion," Luc continued. "I decided it was because we were both from the same world, and that was why I was drawn to you. But now that I remember all my lives—every reincarnation I've ever had—I realize the truth."

He hopped forward, a playful smile bursting across his face. The sudden change in emotions baffled me despite Luc's consistent inconsistent nature. To add in more confusion, he swung his arms out wide and then wrapped me in a hug, his wings expanded out next to us.

"We were friends here, you and I," he said in my ear. "From the time we were pure sirens, barely having a body to call our own."

He leaned back to look at me, the stars practically dancing in his eyes.

"There were five of us: you and me, Liwei, Sophie, and Renaldo." He pointed to the ceiling. "We used to play hide-and-seek in the upper catacombs. And we'd go to the surface and see who could skip rocks across the ocean furthest. Liwei's record was 642 skips."

His wings fluttered, and he held me close as our feet came off the ground. I gripped on to his arms.

"Luc…"

"I know you don't remember any of this, Ast— um, Esmeralda," he whispered. "But I wish you did. I wish you could remember what it was like to live together here…before we all chose our dark paths and were cursed for our sins."

His lips flattened, and he pressed them together. My heart sank.

"They're…gone?" I asked, not sure why my heart was breaking.

Luc brought my feet back to the ground.

"Renaldo was cursed first," he explained. "And then you. Sophie, Liwei, and I tried to find you both for a time, and then I was caught, and I don't know what happened to anyone after that."

Before I could catch his facial expression, he leaned his forehead on my shoulder.

"I don't want to look for you again," he said softly. "I've spent too much time searching for people who can never come back to me."

I wrapped my arms around his back, the soft feathers of his wings brushing against my hands. His embrace became strong, almost desperate.

"Please come back to us," he said in my ear. "Please come back home."

I lost all the words in my throat, pain and confusion taking over my entire body. The pieces of me that were hanging on by a thread were now completely shredded.

What could I do?

Someone cleared their throat.

Luc and I turned to Jacques, his eyes somehow hollow and blazing at the same time. He glanced between us, a bitter smile across his face.

"Forgive me for interrupting a sweet reunion," Jacques taunted.

I scowled at him. "What do you want?"

He put his hands in his pockets and stepped forward. "I came to tell Luc to be at the courthouse tomorrow afternoon. You can come too if you want, Esmeralda, but you'll be absolutely useless as an incarnate."

"She could ask for her wings by then," Luc replied defensively. "Then she would be able to participate."

"I'm sorry, but have you really known this woman your entire life?" Jacques returned. "Even I know she won't agree to her wings until she's seen her father. How can you be so oblivious?"

"I've known her longer than you've been alive, so I suggest you take your opinions and—"

"Enough!" I said, annoyed with their childish argument. When had Luc become so argumentative with Jacques anyhow? "Just what on earth is happening tomorrow that we need to come to the courthouse for? Didn't we already have our trials?"

Jacques's eyes met with mine. "You did. The humans didn't."

My mouth went dry. "You mean tomorrow—"

"Yes," Jacques said, monotone. "So if you want to say goodbye to your star-crossed crew members, I suggest you do it by tomorrow. They might not exist by sundown."

CHAPTER 33

DEMONS

I wish I could have seen the stars from the Den of Sirens. I needed something to wish on.

It was the second night that I had short, dreamless sleep. I sat on the edge of my bed, alone, wondering what I should do.

If I rejected my wings, I could go home to Father as an incarnate. From what I had been told, I might forget the den completely once I was out of its parameters, depending on what the Siren King decided. Not all who came to the den remembered it once they left.

Or if I asked for my wings, I would have to abandon my current life completely. I would have to take on the responsibility of judging humanity, sorting the good from the evil. I would have to possibly sentence men to die, ripping them away from their families and futures. And I would have to leave my father. He would age alone, without a soul to help him.

But, additionally, if I *had* my wings, perhaps I would have had some power to save the crew from their fate.

Shaking, I jumped from my bed and started toward the courthouse. The trial was not for another few hours, but

I couldn't stand the sight of my bedroom walls anymore. Maybe if I went early I could find the king and…

A gentle hand tugged on my arm. In my sleepless daze, I lost my balance but someone caught me before I fell completely.

"Esmeralda?" Luc asked, his eyes full of concern. "What's wrong?"

The shaking only increased. Luc rubbed my arms as if he was trying to warm me up.

"Esmeralda?" he asked again.

"I can't stand it, Luc," I admitted. "I can't stand being powerless and powerful at the same time."

"What are you talking about?"

I swallowed, trying to put my thoughts together. "If I get my wings, I lose my father. If I reject my wings, I lose Henrik and Adrian."

His eyes turned bitter in a moment, but his touch remained gentle. He brought his hand to my face, dusting stray strands of hair from my forehead.

"The crew is damned whether or not you have your wings," he muttered. "You can't change their fates."

"But I would have the power to try."

"No," he said firmly. "Every human heart must decide its own fate: to be cursed or to be saved. The sirens judge their hearts, but we don't affect the outcome. If we were to tamper with the results, we would be cursed again."

The tension in my muscles released, as if they had given up along with my spirit. Luc held me with sympathy, even though I knew he didn't feel the same way I did.

"I know you hate them," I said.

"I do. And so should you. They kidnapped you—"

"I know."

"They threatened your life, your father's life, and used you for their own benefit."

"Yes, I know."

"They were planning to use you to steal the Eros and get money. And you're still crazy enough to want and protect them? Why are you being so ridiculous?"

"Because I can see their hearts!" I yelled back. "And so can you!"

Luc huffed and turned his head away.

"You know that Henrik and Adrian were only trying to save their parents."

"That doesn't excuse their behavior."

"Yes, but you can't be a siren and pretend you don't see the good in them. You can't pretend to not see Henrik's guilt or Adrian's protectiveness—"

"And you can't pretend that *some* good means the same as *not* evil!"

He huffed again, this time through his nose.

"I know you care for them," he said sternly. "I get it. Fine. But your feelings are making you forget who they are. They're both murderers, Esmeralda. They're law-breakers, kidnappers, and traitors to the spiritual realm. They have to pay for their sins, no matter how you feel about them. Just like we paid for ours. You understand that, don't you? You understand why your affections can't be more important than their justice, right?"

I took a deep breath, as if I hadn't been breathing for hours. There was silence between us, his words settling in my chest. I couldn't speak against them. I had no argument.

I only had a request.

"Can I at least say goodbye to them?" I asked.

Luc's face hardened, and he looked down at his feet. He swallowed then looked back up, meeting my eyes.

"It's only because I lost you hundreds of years ago that I agree to this," he finally said. "I don't want to reunite after all this time only to have you hate me."

***

I sat in the court for what felt like hours before the crew was brought in. It was empty and cold, and it wasn't until only a few minutes before the Trials that the sirens started to come into court. When they saw Luc and me they stopped; or perhaps it would be more appropriate to say that they stopped when they saw Luc, ignoring me completely. A few of them smiled and waved to him, while others just nodded in acknowledgment.

"They all know you?" I said.

"Of course. They recognized both of us as soon as we arrived here."

I folded my arms. "They sure didn't act like it. They look over me like I don't exist at all."

Luc licked his lips and looked down, but didn't say anything.

The doors opened. Everyone came to their feet.

Adrian's crew.

Through the open doors, the sirens came in, in pairs, two guards for each human. The humans were stopped at the door, and their fingers were pricked, just as mine and Luc's had been for our trials. The difference was, the king and Judges were not at the lake as they had been before. This time, there were designated sirens standing in the lake, ready for the trial.

I recognized every human face as it came in, but my heart stopped at the fourth face to be brought in.

Adrian.

Despite Luc's alarmed voice behind me, I raced over, meeting Adrian just after his finger had been pricked. He blinked at me a few times as if he wasn't really seeing me.

"I think I must be dreaming again," he muttered with a smile.

I stepped forward, bringing my hands to his face.

"Adrian," I asked. "Are you hurt?"

His skin felt cool and healthy, too healthy to suddenly die in minutes should he have been found guilty.

He only smiled and shook his head. "It hasn't been all that bad. The food here is better than Luc's cooking, if I'm honest—"

"Stop joking," I interrupted. "Don't you understand how serious this is?"

His eyes flashed for a brief moment before softening.

"Yes," he said. "Which is exactly why I need to keep my sense of humor. I wouldn't want you to remember me in any other way, princess."

I chewed hard on my lip, trying to keep it steady. "I don't want you to—"

"Don't think about it. I already told you that I was a demon. It's only fitting to be sent where I belong."

He held my gaze, meaning every word of it. He didn't seem remorseful or afraid, and I was angry because *I* was.

I opened my mouth to say something, but a furious scream echoed across the courthouse.

Henrik was drug in through the door. He pulled back so hard that the sirens almost fell over him. His hair and eyes were wild, his clothes seeming to hang off his bones. He looked nothing like the gentleman I knew only days ago.

Adrian sighed. "It seems my brother is on his way to hell with me."

"What happened to him?"

Adrian shrugged. "He's always had a temper, but since being brought here, he's snapped completely."

As they brought him closer, I ran to meet him. His nostrils flared as I approached. Before I could even say his name, he was growling at me.

"Get away from me, siren!" he yelled, spitting at my feet.

I jumped back. He huffed, out of breath, as if he had fought the entire way to the courthouse. Judging by how exhausted his siren handlers were, he probably had.

"Henrik?" I asked. "What on earth—?"

"Shut up!" he barked. "I'm sick of the sounds of you bloody sirens. Stop trying to get inside my head! You won't have me!"

I stepped back further, not understanding his rage. He wasn't like this at all. I hadn't known him long, but even in our few months together I knew this wasn't him. Or was Henrik like this all along and I just never knew it?

"Ignore him," Adrian said to me. "He's lost his mind. Same as Uncle Leo. He went into the same fits of rage right before he died."

I shuddered at the idea of Henrik suffering the same fate. "Henrik's not usually like this…is he?"

Adrian's eyes dimmed. "Not until recently."

I tried to meet Henrik again, pulling my shoulders back. Henrik looked at me with contempt, nearly foaming at the mouth as he huffed.

"Henrik," I said sternly. "I know the honorable gentleman I met on that ship is still in there. Please let me speak to him. I don't want to part like this."

His eyes flickered, a flash of sorrow filling up his irises before disappearing. He narrowed his eyes, rage filling them again.

"Save your sentiments," he spat out. "Your words are poison. I don't want to hear any of them."

His siren handlers took this as their cue to leave, and they started to drag Henrik off to the edge of the lake. I could only watch, all the words I was wanting to say drying up in my mouth completely.

"I'll take a goodbye," Adrian said gently beside me.

I turned to him, taking a step forward.

"I'm sorry…" I began.

"For what?" he asked. "You haven't done anything wrong. *I'm* the criminal, remember?"

"Even so, I didn't want it to end like this."

A heartbeat passed.

"You know," Adrian said, "I was only supposed to come for your blood."

"What?"

He smiled dreamily.

"The night of your party," he said. "I was supposed to collect your blood in a bottle and take it back to the ship. But the moment I saw you, I wanted you for myself."

I swallowed as my stomach fluttered.

"If you're a siren, that explains why I was put under your spell so quickly," he continued, "but make no mistake: even if I lose my life in the next few minutes, I won't regret having you by my side for as long as I did."

Losing all my breath at the sincerity in his eyes, I could only breathe out his name.

"Adrian…"

A disgusted grunt echoed beside us. I jumped as I saw Jacques. How long had he been standing there?

"This aura is incredible," Jacques grumbled, looking between us. "Somehow your siren hold on him is stronger than last time. Either you're incredibly careless with your powers, Esmeralda, or you truly enjoy this little pirate captain's affections."

Adrian gave Jacques a playful grin as he shrugged.

"Get him to the edge of the lake," Jacques told Adrian's handlers. "I can't stand looking at his face anymore."

"Can I at least have a last word?" Adrian asked. "You can have your shot at her once I die, mate."

Jacques rolled his eyes and gave a wave with the back of his hand. Adrian leaned into my ear, his soft musk tickling my nose as his breath fanned against my skin.

"Even if you don't remember me fondly," he whispered, "at least remember how warm it felt sleeping next to me."

He leaned back, a proud smile on his lips just before the sirens tugged him away to the middle of the court. I wanted to follow, but Jacques raised his hand up to stop me.

"You're staying with me during the trials," he commanded. "No more running off."

"You're not part of the trial?"

He shook his head sharply. "I judge sirens. The sirens judge humans. I get a break this time around."

He pulled me into the rows of seats with the other sirens that had come to watch. I scanned behind me, looking for Luc. He was a few rows back, his eyes narrowed, completely focused on the lake in front of him.

I didn't have to read his soul to know that he was waiting for Adrian's death.

"Did you say your goodbyes?" Jacques asked, nonchalant.

I sighed. "I tried. Adrian accepted my goodbye. Henrik refused to speak to me at all."

King Melchior came through the doors, Vito and Hugo beside him. Everyone in the stands stood as the king walked in, and we all bowed as he went to his throne. He stared at the human crew in front of him, nodding to the sirens standing on the lake.

"Your souls will be judged today," the king said to the crew. "Should they be true and pure, you will return to your homes with no recollection of this place. Should your souls be cursed and evil, you will be sentenced to the afterlife."

To this, Henrik gave a twisted laugh.

"You think you really have the power to get rid of us all, Your Majesty?" Henrik asked. "There isn't a king alive that can't be dethroned."

King Melchior paused at this, then turned his head away as if he hadn't heard it.

"You may begin," he told the sirens.

The sirens held up their knives, ready to cut their skin. Jacques laughed beside me.

"I thought the first mate was the honorable one?" he asked me, scratching his chin. "It seems like the fool wants to burn in hell."

"I don't understand why he's like this," I said. "He's never been so angry or twisted. It seems like the closer we got the Eros, the worse he became."

The sirens cut the men's hands, the blood dripping into the water. Jacques stiffened.

"Wait…" he said, spinning to me. "You said he was an astrologer, didn't you?"

"Yes, that's right…"

"*Shit.*"

Jacques jumped from his seat and ran forward, just as the throne split in two. The red light burst through the cracks.

The light of the Eros.

There was a high-pitched wail, something gut-ripping and inhumane, and it took me a moment to realize that Henrik was the one to make the sound. He ripped from the sirens and sprinted toward the light. Jacques knocked him to the ground before he could make it. Teal snakes burst out of the lake as they had the day of our own trial, and the crew screamed in terror right before a majority disappeared in bright explosions.

The guilty. The guilty had been sent to the afterlife.

As my eyes cleared from the light of the explosion, I saw that the teal snakes had wrapped around Henrik completely, sealing him closed like a caterpillar in a cocoon. Another one of the Judges and a few sirens had gathered around him, holding him to the ground as a bright light swarmed him.

Before I could even breathe out, the light that was supposed to sentence him to death turned black, blazing like dark fire around his body. His eyes turned yellow as he made the high-pitched wail once more. The sound was so terrifying that I fell out of my seat onto my knees.

What was happening?

The teal spiderwebs disappeared, the throne shutting once again. The red light disappeared, and most of the humans were now gone.

One of them, however, wasted no time to break free of the sirens and run toward Henrik.

"What's happening to him?" Adrian yelled, just as two sirens pulled him back.

Adrian…was still alive?

Jacques put up a hand to signal Adrian to stay. "Don't come closer!"

"Answer me!" Adrian screamed.

I came to my feet, shaking as I tried to run forward to meet them. I couldn't make it, my feet folding beneath me. I hit the ground, body shaking.

"Are you all right, Esmeralda?" Luc asked, coming up behind me and taking my arm. "Are you hurt?"

I gripped on to the top of his robe. "What's happened? Why is Henrik wrapped in black light?"

Luc huffed as he looked over his shoulder.

"Luc?"

"He can't be sentenced," Luc answered. "We can't sentence those who have lost control of their souls."

The words didn't make any sense. "What are you saying?"

Luc clenched his jaw and released it before answering.

"Henrik has lost his humanity," Luc said. "He's demon possessed."

CHAPTER 34

HELPERS

"This is unfortunate," King Melchior said, leaning his chin on his hand as he sat on his throne.

Luc and I, as well as Jacques and one of the other Judges, had been called to the throne room after the trials to discuss Henrik's fate. Adrian and the remaining guiltless crew had been released, free to return home by the ship they had been brought in with.

Once they left the den, Luc told me, the entire crew would forget everything that had happened here.

Did that mean that they would forget me? Or Luc? Or about the Eros entirely? I didn't know. Luc refused to answer when I asked, which definitely meant I wouldn't like the answer in one way or another.

Regrettably, I wasn't able to speak to Adrian or Henrik in the chaos. Henrik had been taken by the Judges and other sirens before I could even get close to him, and Adrian had followed them. The king had dismissed everyone else in the court immediately to attend to the situation, and then after some time, he called everyone into a meeting to discuss the next step.

I wrung my hands together.

"Increase the guards around the throne room," King Melchior ordered Hugo. "As well as the hallways. Put the sirens on emergency shifts until we can extract the demon from the boy."

"How could we not see that Henrik was demon possessed?" I asked. "Shouldn't it have been obvious?"

Jacques shook his head. "Demon possession is rare, for starters. Only a small percentage of those who deal with the dark arts get possessed. The host—in this case, Henrik—has to be weak and vulnerable for the possession. That's why demons usually go after children, not adults."

Jacques's eyes dimmed for a moment. He blinked before I could catch the meaning of it.

"The pure sirens knew," Luc said. "When the spiritual world was reconnected, they called for demon blood. As an incarnate, I thought they were talking about evil humans. It never even occurred to me that one of the crew members was possessed."

"It's quite impossible to tell," the king assured Luc. "It isn't until they get close to the Eros that their greed takes over."

"The demons start to slip up and show themselves," Jacques said. "You said that Henrik resisted your charmspeak, correct?"

Luc nodded.

"That means that the boy has a stronger resistance to the spiritual realm," the king said. "Demons also use charmspeak. If Henrik resisted you, then he most likely resisted the demon possessing him as well. He's probably still resisting."

"But we can't be too cautious," Hugo added. "A human can only fight demons for so long."

"Yes, but this boy is stronger against demons than the others," Vito said. "As long as he continues to fight against the demon, we can extract it."

The other Judge that came with us nudged Jacques, who had been lost in thought.

"You'll help him, Jacques. Won't you?" the other Judge asked. "You extracted my demon. As well as Zosar's and George's."

Jacques looked at the Judge from the corner of his eye, then back into nothing.

"If he's fighting against the demon, I can extract it," Jacques replied eventually. "If he has accepted his demon, it's another story."

"Why would Henrik accept a demon?" I asked.

"Demons offer power," Jacques replied. "The kind of power humans thirst for more than anything. Some accept their demons because they want to hold power over the people around them. Some accept because they don't have any purpose in their current lives. Some accept because they believe they don't have a way to survive otherwise."

"You were the last one," King Melchior added, nodding at Jacques with a warm smile. "I still haven't forgotten that teenage gang leader who tried to kill me. Twice."

Jacques rolled his eyes and grunted.

"I'm sorry, did you just say *gang leader*?" I asked.

Jacques waved his hand dismissively, changing the subject. "I can stay and try to extract the demon. It might take some time. The question is, what are we going to do with Esmeralda?"

Everyone looked at me. I jumped at the sudden attention.

"Me?" I asked.

"Yes, you," Jacques replied. "Without your wings, it's dangerous for you here with a demon on the loose."

"I can protect her," Luc objected.

Jacques turned around to face him. "Then protect her by taking her home. I don't want her back on Adrian's ship for the next three months—"

"I wouldn't mind it," a voice chimed in.

We turned around to see Adrian behind us, smirking in satisfaction.

"How the hell did he get in here?" Hugo asked.

"How did we not notice him?" Vito asked.

Adrian smiled and stepped forward. Luc's wings flew open, and he flew in front of Adrian, the ground shaking as he landed. Adrian only chuckled.

"Easy, Feathers," Adrian said nonchalantly. "I'm not here to harm your king."

I couldn't see Luc's face, but I could see the anger in his shoulders.

"That's enough, Rhys," King Melchior said calmly. "Let me speak to him."

Luc hesitated, but stepped to the side. He, however, kept a murderous eye on Adrian as Adrian walked past us and straight for the king.

"You noticed I was here right away, didn't you?" Adrian asked the king.

King Melchior gave a quick smile and leaned forward in his seat.

"I wanted to see when you would chime in," the king said. "You're quite bold to sneak into the throne room of the Siren King. If your heart wasn't already declared pure, I would have put an end to you immediately."

King Melchior said it casually, but it didn't feel like an empty threat. Regardless, Adrian stepped forward, ignoring everyone except the king.

"I came on behalf of my brother," he said. "I won't go home without him."

"A very noble captain, indeed," Vito said.

"Yet somehow disrespectful at the same time," Hugo added.

"We are discussing how to help your brother now," King Melchior told Adrian. "The suffering of humanity affects the spiritual realm quite deeply, you know."

Adrian's jaw ticked as if he didn't know how to respond to a king. Maybe he didn't.

"You want to protect your brother," King Melchior continued. "I understand."

"But I don't, Your Majesty," Luc interjected, coming forward. "When I found him, his heart was black. I saw it with my own eyes. How could he not be sentenced with the others?"

King Melchior cocked his head at Adrian and stood. With powerful steps, he came down from his throne and stepped forward to stand directly in front of Adrian. Adrian froze to his spot as the king stared deep past his eyes, perhaps directly into his soul.

"Yes…" the king said after some time. "This boy had a dark soul at one point. But that's no longer the case. Even the humans can become purified should they find the right path."

"I'm not sure what path he could have found," Luc said. "The day he hired me, his heart was black. He went from arsonist to murderer, from murderer to kidnapper, from kidnapper to traitor. His plan this entire time was to steal our most treasured artifact. How could he find a way to purity?"

"Why don't we let him tell us?" The king cocked his head again, smiling at Adrian. "Just what changed your mind between the sea and the Den of Sirens?"

Adrian stayed silent, his back to us. The king's eyes shot to me.

"Oh…so that's it then," the king said, his eyes now on me. "To find purity, you had to see it first."

Jacques stepped forward, grabbing Adrian's forearm and pulling up the sleeve.

Adrian stepped back, raising his other hand up. "I'm flattered, mate, but I'm afraid I'm only interested in women."

Jacques grunted and yanked on Adrian's arm again to read it. Wait – could he read the past of humans as well? Humans weren't reincarnated, so why?

Jacques slapped a hand to his forehead, pulling his hair back with one hand in frustration.

"That explains why your aura around Esmeralda is so strong," Jacques muttered.

"You couldn't see that before?" Luc asked.

"I can see auras and I can see the past, but not *at the same time*," Jacques threw back. "Blood had to be sacrificed before I could see his life paths."

"Life paths?" I asked. "Humans have them as well?"

Jacques nodded. "How else do you think they're judged?"

"I still don't even understand how someone's entire past can be written on their arm."

"With very tiny lettering," Jacques said flatly.

"But how did he become purified?" Luc snapped. "What does Ast— uh, Esmeralda have to do with it?"

The king stepped between Adrian and me, glancing at us both.

"The human heart is influenced rather easily," the king explained. "Since their hearts are mixed—darkness and light—they can be swayed in either direction when they see something pure or something evil. Those with a truly evil heart will despise purity. But there are those who have not been lost to their darkness completely, and they see the darkness in themselves once they come in contact with something pure."

Suddenly, Adrian's words echoed in my head.

I hate being around you… it makes me feel like a demon.

I looked at Adrian, who didn't seem half as confused as I was.

"It seems that you, my dear, became this boy's mirror," King Melchior said. "The darkness in his heart changed because of you."

CHAPTER 35

REFUSAL

"I'm not leaving," Adrian said, his arms crossed as he leaned against the hallway wall. "You heard what the king said."

Jacques rubbed his hand over his face and groaned. Looking at him now, he had somehow aged ten years in the last twenty minutes.

Before sending us out of the throne room, the king had made the decision to let Adrian and the others stay three days to prepare for departure. Adrian was allowed to visit Henrik during that time, just as long as he didn't interfere with Jacques's work.

I was relieved. Luc and Jacques, however, were not.

"Too many humans in the Den of Sirens will end badly," Jacques said. "Especially if they're pirates."

"Haven't my men been deemed pure?" Adrian replied with a shrug. "Isn't that the verdict of the spiritual realm?"

"You're still a risk."

Adrian licked his bottom lip with a smile.

"Let's be honest, mate," he said. "You just don't want me making a pass at Esmeralda."

Adrian reached out and tickled a finger under Jacques's chin. Jacques swatted his hand away with a furious grunt.

"Your feelings for her aren't real, you idiot!" Jacques replied. "You're under a spell."

My stomach sank slightly at the truth, but Adrian didn't seem affected. His eyes met mine, the mischievous twinkle in them dark and inviting.

"Isn't all love a spell?" Adrian replied softly.

My heart fluttered.

Luc stepped in between us, his wings half extended to separate me from Adrian.

"She won't be anywhere near you," Luc said coldly. "I'll make sure of that."

I reached up and touched the top of his wings to calm him. "Luc…"

"You're allowed to stay here for a few days," Jacques reminded Adrian. "But for the sake of your brother, don't cause us any problems."

The playfulness in Adrian's eyes suddenly dimmed.

"What will it take to heal my brother?" he asked.

"Nothing that you can do," Jacques said. "Only a Judge can extract a demon, and you are not one. Tend to your men and prepare them for departure. That is your duty."

Adrian's face remained blank. I wanted to reach over and comfort him. I could see the world on his shoulders: parents succumbed to illness, the majority of his crew lost to the underworld, and his brother tormented by demons.

How could he still stand after all that?

"These sirens will take you and your men to your quarters," Jacques said, pointing to the sirens standing in the hallway with us. "Even though you have been found pure, that doesn't mean the Den of Sirens will tolerate any form of rebellion."

Jacques's eyes met mine, his jaw suddenly clenching.

"Luc— Rhys, or whatever your name is, take Esmeralda with you," Jacques continued. "Make sure she stays away from them."

I stepped forward. "Now, wait a moment—"

"With pleasure," Luc growled, turning around and grabbing my arm.

I pulled back.

"Luc, this isn't nec—"

He pulled me in, scooping me up into his arms and bursting into the air. I screamed in surprise, the ground suddenly thirty feet below me. I gripped on to Luc's neck as he flew us around the den toward the upper suites made for the sirens.

I didn't have any breath in my lungs to scold him; I was too distracted by the sights of the den from above. It was a completely different world up here. I never realized the floor glittered like glass, the rocks and stone chiseled into abstract art on the ground below. The air was warm and welcoming, relaxing my muscles even though everything in my mind was so tense.

Luc flew straight into one of the suites, sliding in through the curtain that blocked the door.

Luc's suite was more human than I envisioned. Random piles of books, knick-knacks, and toys were littered around the table and floor. There was an unmade bed in the corner—made of stone as the ones in the guest room had been—and a recess in the wall to hang clothes. There was only natural light, if it could be called that. There were no windows, but the light of the den outside the suite leaked inside and rippled against the wall like small waves.

Why did this place feel so familiar?

"Don't try to run off," Luc warned. "The drop from here is deadly for you."

I turned back to Luc, huffing. "This is hardly necessary. Adrian would never—"

"Would never what?" Luc threw back, cutting me off. "Hurt you? Kidnap you, hand you over to his brother as a type of sacrifice to the spiritual realm, and then threaten you and your family for money? *That* Adrian?"

He licked his lips as if his anger had dried them out. I looked down at my feet.

"You were never this naive," he said. "If you only had your wings, then you'd remember. You'd remember how evil humans really are."

I stared at him for a long moment.

"And us?" I asked. "Were we much different?"

This time, he went silent, watching the lights as they reflected from the floor below into his room.

"No," he said eventually. "We were just as evil."

He stepped forward, lost in thought as he came forward to meet me.

"But you..." he continued, "you can't remember evil. You've been purified so much that you can't even see it anymore. And that's dangerous. You can't fight against evil if you never see it. And if you don't fight it, it will consume you."

I couldn't help but think of Henrik. I wondered how he felt with a demon controlling his mind and spirit to the point of insanity. Was he aware of it? Or was he gone forever? What if Jacques couldn't save him?

I ran my tongue over my teeth, trying to think of an answer. "I understand it. But Adrian was trialed and declared pure—"

"Only from your spell on him. As soon as that spell breaks, he'll go back to the way he was."

Luc turned his back on me, seemingly distracted by the lights on the ceiling once more. It was silent between us for a few moments.

"And your vengeance?" I asked. "Does it not also have the danger of consuming you?"

He didn't answer right away, his eyes glued to the lights around him.

"I loved her…" he said eventually. "Even as a siren, I remember how much I loved Maria as a man. How can I look her killer in the eye and not do anything? How can I let him walk free?"

I stepped over to him, leaning my forehead against his back and wrapping my arms around him from behind. His wings stayed folded in his back, their soft, dark feathers brushing against my face. His breath was shallow. Even just touching him I could sense how heavy his heart was.

"If you don't cure the rage in you," I said, "you'll end up cursed again."

He gave a breathy laugh. "Maybe it would be worth it. Just to see him pay for his sins properly."

I squeezed him harder. "You don't mean that. The way your face lit up once you had your wings and remembered who you were—"

"That was before Maria's murderer was set free. That was before I realized…before I realized that you wouldn't come back to us."

I leaned back, suddenly filled with guilt. Luc turned to face me, pain and anger mixed in his eyes. I stared into them until I could see everything he was thinking, even if it was an invasion of privacy.

He wanted family. He wanted a home. But he felt alone everywhere.

How painful were his lives before this last one?

While staring into his eyes I forgot he could read me as well. I only realized when his lips pulled to the side in knowing.

"You can't save everyone, little dove," he said. "You don't even have the wings to save yourself."

He started to walk away, but I jumped in front of him and put my hands up to block him.

"Promise me, Luc," I said. "Promise me that you won't go after Adrian and do something you shouldn't."

He held my gaze for a long moment.

"Promise me the same," he replied.

I swallowed, my throat dry. He took in a deep breath and nodded.

"I guess neither one of us can make that promise," he said.

***

I couldn't tell if it was day or night, but my body eventually wore itself out with thinking, and I ended up falling asleep on Luc's bed. When I woke up, I couldn't determine how long I was asleep, but it took a long while for my eyes to readjust to the lights of the cavern. I blinked and rubbed my eyes repeatedly, positive that I was wrong about what I was seeing.

But my eyes weren't playing tricks on me.

Luc was gone.

CHAPTER 36

FALLING

I jumped from the bed, heart in my throat.

"Luc?" I called out.

There was no answer besides the rippling blue lights of the den. Panic rushed through all of my senses, my heart racing as fast as my mind.

Had Luc really gone after Adrian? What would he do? Would he get himself cursed again? I could feel my heart physically break at the thought of Luc lost to another curse.

I raced to the entrance, pulling back the curtain and looking down. It gave me instant vertigo. The drop below warped and twisted in the shadows, the ground below an unmeasurable distance. Stepping back from the ledge, the skin between my shoulders started to fiercely ache, as if my skin knew it once had wings that would carry me safely to the bottom.

But I didn't have wings. I was human. And if I dropped to my death, I would go to another body, never to see anyone here again.

"Hello?" I called out into the den, the sound echoing off the walls. "Is anyone out there?"

Complete silence.

"Luc?" I called out into the drop below. "Are you out there? Can you hear me?"

Nothing.

"Can anyone hear me? There is a lady in need of some assistance!"

Even that resulted in no response. I huffed and threw aside the curtain, looking around the room. There were no other exits, only a window in the ceiling. Could I crawl out the top and climb down the side?

I looked around the room for something to climb up to the window. There was nothing but books and clothes and toys…

Crunch.

I jumped back to look down at whatever I had stepped on. It was a toy man, wrapped in strings. Picking him up to look for any damage I may have caused, I realized his tangled strings led to a parachute hanging off his back. With an energetic gasp, I untangled the strings to look at his parachute. It was not incredibly complicated: a square cloth with four strings.

Could it work?

I pulled down the curtains and their ropes, laying out the little man so I could copy his parachute. Tearing small holes in the corners of the curtain, I laced the rope through and met the ropes in the middle. I couldn't help but applaud myself. It was almost an exact replica.

Then reality struck. I wasn't a toy man, I was a real person, and there was a lot to lose if this didn't work.

I grabbed the toy and took him to the entrance, looking into the drop below.

"I expect nothing but the best out of you, good sir," I said to him. "Luc and Adrian's fate depends on you."

With a salute, I dropped him over the side.

He slowly fluttered down to the bottom of the den.

Slowly…

Slowly…

Gliding down for what seemed like a real eternity before hitting the bottom. There wasn't a noise or alarming signal from where I stood, so I took it as a sign.

I picked up my own parachute, wrapping the ropes around my waist and legs like the toy man's parachute. With each sailor's knot that my father and Henrik had taught me, my heart ached more and more.

Henrik…Adrian…Luc…my father…

It felt like each rope of my parachute represented each person I wanted to help but couldn't.

My stomach clenched with the last knot. I walked closer and closer to the entrance, the pain between my shoulders almost screaming at me. I told it to quiet down, ignoring its throbbing protests.

If I had my wings, I could save them.

But if I had my wings, then my father…

I exhaled, looking down. The ground warped and swirled once again, like a black marble whirlpool. I sat on the edge of the ledge of the entrance, my feet dangling off the side.

"This is your last chance to help a damsel in distress!" I called out to the den. "I'm going to jump if you don't answer me!"

The threat seemed to fall on deaf ears. Or reluctant ears. I was well aware that the sirens acted distant from me for some reason. At first, I thought it was the human thing, but the sirens weren't even so aloof when it came to Henrik, and he had a demon in him. It was *me* they were avoiding. Was Luc avoiding me too? No, no. That thought had no merit. Luc was protective, not wary. And if he knew I was thinking about jumping from this place, he would lose his mind.

I sighed, the realization of how bad an idea this really was. I couldn't risk leaving Luc alone. I would just have to yell into the caverns until someone answered. But away from the edge.

I slid back, putting one hand on the ground to come up to my feet.

There was pain as my ankle rolled. And then the floor was gone. And then I was screaming.

Air rushed through my clothes and hair as I plummeted down toward the marble floor below. I reached for the ropes still attached to my arms and legs, trying to straighten myself. There was a sudden tug on the ropes as the parachute opened up. My fall slowed—the parachute was actually working!—but I was still falling too fast for my liking.

Heart in my throat, I looked up at the parachute to see that it was fully opened.

But one of the corners was ripping.

I pulled on the opposite side as if that would take the pressure off the corner, but it was an illogical idea. The parachute tipped sideways, pulling me along with it.

And the corner ripped.

"Luc!" I screamed with everything in me.

I squeezed by eyes shut right before I plummeted to the bottom. I screamed as the air rushed out of my lungs, suffocating me.

With a gasp, the plummeting stopped.

And two arms wrapped around me tighter than I had ever known.

"You have *no idea* how much trouble you're in, woman," a voice barked in my ear.

Gasping for air, I opened my eyes to Jacques's furious expression.

"Jacques?" I asked, panting from the fall. "Why? How did you…?

He placed me on my shaking feet, his eyebrows matting in furious confusion as he looked at my back. I had to steady myself on his arms, the adrenaline taking all the strength out of my legs.

"Did you make a parachute?" he asked. "Of all the *stupid* things you're willing to do—"

I looked up at Luc's room.

"How the hell did you catch me from here?" I interrupted. "How did your arms not snap in half?"

I yelped as he gripped my waist and hoisted me up into the air. It was incredibly effortless for him. I felt like a cat instead of a person.

He gave me a blank stare, but I could see the pride in his eyes.

"I told you," he huffed. "Demon residue."

He placed me back on the ground, starting to untie the knots in the ropes around my legs.

"Demons provide super-human strength," he explained. "It doesn't fully leave, even when the demon does. Now, explain to me why you decided to drop out of the sky and risk your soul's reincarnation."

"I know you won't believe me—"

"I will, probably. At this point, I wouldn't put anything past you—"

"It was an accident."

"Yes, I can see how building a parachute could happen by chance."

"No, no. The parachute was on purpose, but the falling was accidental."

"And *why* did you make a parachute?"

"Luc's gone."

"I don't see why that's alarming enough to drop to your death."

"He threatened to go after Adrian."

"Slightly more alarming, I suppose." He pulled the ropes from my legs and waist and stood straight, scratching his chin. "What is Luc's obsession with Adrian anyway?"

"Adrian killed Luc's fiancée."

Jacques stopped scratching his face. "That explains a lot then."

I grabbed his arm. "He'll be cursed again, Jacques —"

"So you decided to risk your life to stop him?"

"What was I supposed to do? Stay still?"

"Maybe if you stayed still once in a while, you wouldn't be in half the situations—" He stopped, clenching his jaw. "Never mind it. It doesn't matter right now. Let's go find him."

Jacques grabbed my hand tight, pulling me with him. I looked down as he interlaced his fingers in mine, then raised an eyebrow at him. He understood the question.

"I don't trust you out of my sight," he said. "You need a leash."

He squeezed my hand, the warmth from it canceling out the coldness of his tone.

"The prison is close to here," Jacques said. "Adrian was there the last time I checked. If he isn't, we'll go to the king."

"How's Henrik doing?" I asked.

A heartbeat of silence passed.

"Not good," Jacques replied. "But don't go getting any ideas about it."

"Why? What's wrong with him?"

Jacques exhaled through his nose, pulling me forward next to him.

"Henrik has submitted to his demon," Jacques replied. "He's not fighting him. But even if he wanted to fight back, it would be too difficult. Demons feed on power, and being this close to the source of spiritual power has made the demon too hard to fight. We have to get Henrik away from the Eros."

"What exactly is the Eros?" I asked. "I still don't quite understand it. I understand that it's powerful, but nothing else."

He tugged on my hand again as we took the path to the prison. "The Eros is the freedom of the spiritual world. Before the Eros was created, the spiritual world was at the command of the Siren King. He could use his power to command any creature in the realm to do as he willed. However, the king found this to be a burden more than a blessing."

"So he gave up his power? Wouldn't that cause more chaos in the realm?"

Jacques shook his head. "There were two major problems before the Eros. Well, in the king's eyes, anyway. One, the creatures of the spiritual realm would do his will, but they wouldn't do anything *without* his will. They were empty soldiers with no life in them. And second, well, have you seen the way that the Siren King feels about the creatures of the spiritual realm?"

I thought of the day that the sirens were judged. The way King Melchior fell to his knees in pain at the loss. The warm, gentle look in his eyes when he looked at Luc and myself.

"He loves them quite deeply, doesn't he?" I asked.

Jacques nodded. "Just as you were afraid that your siren charms were controlling the people you love most, the king couldn't stomach the same pain. So he locked his powers into the Eros, kept deeply hidden in his throne. As long as it's in the throne, the spiritual realm has freewill. The will to do good or evil, the will to be loyal soldiers who return the love of their commander."

Silence passed between us again as we started down the prison stairs.

"Did you really try to kill the king?" I asked.

"Yes. Twice."

"Because of your demon?"

"Yes."

"You were young when you were possessed, weren't you?"

He paused on the stairs, turning to look back at me. Something painful flickered in his eyes, but he didn't let it stay there.

"I was eleven," he finally said. "I was possessed for ten years. Tragic backstory. Et cetera, et cetera. But don't dig too much into it. The details of my past are not important anymore."

He started down the stairs again, but I tugged him back.

"I think they're important," I said.

He laughed. "And why is that? Because we're going to be *family*?"

"No," I said, gripping his hand. "Because I care about what happened to you. Simply as a person, Jacques."

He searched my face for a moment, and I couldn't decide if he was thinking about opening up to me or throwing me down the stairs. He blinked and looked away before I could read his eyes.

"Don't look into my soul, siren," he said. "My suffering isn't for you to know. My suffering is so I could become strong enough to do what I do now."

Jacques tugged on my hand to lead me farther down the stairs. His hand was now softer than it was before.

The dungeon was still as cool and calm as the rest of the den, but there seemed to be a darkness here that I couldn't explain. It wasn't because we were deeper into the caves, although that may have been part of it. It had nothing to do with lights.

Instead, it felt like someone was putting pressure on my soul.

We reached the bottom, the cells stretching out in front of us. There were more cells than I thought there would be in a spirit realm, and I wondered why there were so many. How many humans did they judge here?

One of the other Judges approached us, nodding at Jacques. He opened his mouth to say something, but his eyes dropped to our hands clasped together and he stopped. Jacques cleared his throat and let go of my hand.

"Have you seen the pirate captain?" Jacques asked.

The Judge shook his head. "Not since earlier today. You came just in time though. George is having a mental breakdown."

"What?" Jacques asked. "Why?"

"The first mate's demon started tearing into him,"

the Judge explained. "Fed on every painful childhood memory George had until he snapped."

Jacques sighed. "Yes, they love to do that. All right, let me check on him."

Jacques looked at me and gave a long, irritated breath.

"It's too dangerous for you to come with me," he said. He looked up the stairs. "It's too dangerous for me to let you go back up."

He pointed at the last step.

"Stay here," he said. "Don't move from this spot. Not up, not down, not sideways, nothing."

"I don't think it's possible for me to move sideways, really—"

"You'd find a way if it irritated me enough. Now, stay here and don't move until I come back."

I huffed, folding my arms and sitting down on the last step. Jacques glared at me one more time in warning, then followed his men down the prison hallway. When they were out of sight, I sighed and put my head in my hands.

Please, Luc... Please let go of your anger... You're the only true friend I have...

I prayed the same words over and over until a voice interrupted my thoughts.

"Sssiren..."

I shot my head up at the twisted whisper echoing down the hall. I swallowed.

"Jacques?" I called.

"Helpless little sssiren..." the whisper said.

The voice was nowhere and everywhere at once. I stood, not understanding where it was coming from. The top of the stairs? The cells?

"Losssing everyone you care about…nothing you can do…"

It felt like the voice was closer this time, about to swallow me whole.

Then there was a hiss, a deep, intimate hiss right in my ear like a summer mosquito. I swatted it away from my ear, but it only got stronger.

"Jacques!" I yelled again, running down the hall and away from the hiss to find him. "Jacques where are you?"

The cells turned into a maze, stretching further and further in front of me. I continued to call for Jacques, but my voice was lost against the whispers echoing down the hall.

"Don't be ssscared, sssiren…it will all be over soon…"

I lost my breath from both running and from fear, tripping down the hallways until I reached a dead end. I needed to go back to the stairs. I should have gone up, not gone into—

I turned around, gasping.

Henrik's disheveled figure leaned against the prison bars, his arms hanging on them, his eyes watching me with a warped sense of delight.

It wasn't Henrik.

I could tell by his yellow eyes that it wasn't.

"Hello, *sssiren*," he said, grinning as he watched me. "I've been waiting for you."

CHAPTER 37

TAME

Every bit of my skin crawled as Henrik eyed me. There was something sharp in his eyes and teeth, as if he was ready to tear me apart piece by piece.

"Henrik?" I struggled to ask.

His grin widened.

"If *that'sss* what you want to call me," he replied, his voice deep and strangled.

The lights of the den flickered across his face in a way that was hard to catch the thoughts behind his eyes. I stepped closer, trying to read him. He chuckled, cocking his head to the side.

"Sorry, *sssiren*," he said. "You can't read me like the *humansss*."

"Who are you?"

"My name *isssn't* important," he returned. "*Besidesss*, I'd rather talk about you."

His eyes raked over me for a long moment. I shivered.

"You're very lovely," he finally said. "You're *obviousssly* a woman of high *statusss* and well-grooming. Even if you didn't charm him, I could *undersssstand* why Henrik would want power over you."

I stepped forward, suddenly angry at both the gull of the demon saying such a thing about Henrik.

"How long have you been possessing him?" I asked.

He shrugged. "I've been around for a while. I found him right after he *lossst hisss* job in the navy. When he was the most *powerlesss.* The *weakessst.*"

"You're wrong. Henrik isn't weak."

He threw his head back and made a screeching laugh, causing me to step back in fear once again.

"I have his *sssoul,*" the demon replied. "I beg to differ."

Some part of me knew that he only had Henrik's body, not his soul, but I lost my voice to object.

"It was quite the *tasssk* to get his *sssoul,* though, I'll admit." He ran his fingers through his hair. "He fought me for *monthsss.* Until you, that is, the moment he found out you were a *sssiren…*"

The demon snapped his fingers.

"He handed over his *sssoul* to me in a moment."

I clenched my teeth, trying to keep them from chattering against each other. It wasn't cold, but my blood suddenly felt like it was freezing in my veins.

"You won't have him," I threw back. "We'll find a way to get rid of you—"

"Henrik *hasss* to want that first," the demon replied. "*Ssso* far, he *hasss* no *interessst* in letting go of the power I can give him. And if he *triesss…*"

The demon took a step back.

"I'll kill him," he finished.

As if a strong wind had blown through the den, Henrik was sent flying off his feet and into the wall behind him. I couldn't tell if the crack against the wall was the stone or his bones, but I could tell that the painful cry from his lips was no longer the demon.

"Henrik!" I screamed, reaching for the key to the cell.

I unlocked the door, swinging open the door and rushing to his side as he lay curled up in pain. He slowly straightened out, sitting up against the wall. His demon smiled back at me.

"You're brave, *sssiren*," he said. "I'll give you that."

"I want to speak to him," I demanded.

"Oh?" he asked, laughing. "And who are you to command me, *sssiren*?"

He wrapped a strong hand around my neck, pulling me toward him. As he pulled me in I could see yellow flicker across his eyes like candle flames.

"You know I can *crusssh* your throat in the blink of an eye, don't you?" he asked, wetting his lips.

I grabbed hold of his arm, unable to break his grip.

"But you won't," I returned. "Not with Henrik's soul in there. He won't let you hurt me."

The demon laughed. "You're so *sssure*? You don't know him at all, do you?"

"I can see him in ways you can't, demon."

The demon cocked his head to the side, a small smile peaking from the corner of his lips.

"All right," he said. "You want to *ssspeak* to him? You can. But it won't go the way you plan, *sssiren*."

His hand released my throat as his eyes flickered once more. The look in his eyes suddenly hollowed, emptying until I could read the thoughts behind them once more.

Henrik.

Henrik took a moment to look around the cell, then back up at me. His eyes hardened.

"Hen—"

"You shouldn't be here," he said coldly.

"Henrik?" I asked again, grabbing his hand. "Henrik is that you? Don't worry. Jacques will help you. He can get rid of the demon—"

"And why should I get rid of him?" he barked back. "So I can be controlled by creatures like you?"

Henrik came to his feet, grunting in pain. I put a hand to his shoulder, but he swatted it away.

"Get out," he commanded. "There's no telling what we'll do to you."

"You won't hurt me. You won't let him—"

"Won't I?" he asked, squaring his shoulders at me. "Shouldn't I have a way to protect myself from your power?"

He stared at me for a long moment, and I could see the brokenness in his eyes. I could hardly breathe seeing how much I had hurt him.

"I had no idea what I was," I said, almost in a whisper. "I care about you, Henrik. Truly. You've always been so strong and kind—"

"And where did my kindness get me?" he hissed back. "Kicked out of the navy? A laughingstock to the king himself? The inability to help my own family? I've been possessed by both a demon and a siren… *Hasss* my *kindnesss* led to anything profitable?"

His eyes flickered yellow once more, but he grabbed his head and grunted.

"Fight him," I said, coming to his side. "Don't let him take over…please…"

His hand struck out for my wrist, grabbing me and pulling me toward him. He stared deep into my eyes, the desperation and bitterness swirling in his dark, velvet eyes.

"If I get rid of him," he whispered, "will you come to me?"

My heart completely froze as he stared at me, his lips parting as he breathed heavily in pain. Before I could speak, however, he shut his eyes and threw himself back against the wall, this time holding his head with both his hands.

"No!" he yelled. "I won't!"

My feet froze to the ground, not knowing what to do.

"We'll get rid of him," I said. "We'll get rid of the demon so you can—"

He straightened. "Why? So you can *possesss* me?"

He reached out and gripped my wrists, spinning me around and forcing me against the wall. He stepped in closer, the bitterness in his eyes mingled tight with a twisted pride.

The demon was taking back over.

"Stop," I said. "Don't—"

"Do you want to *possesss* me too?" he asked. "You want my *sssoul* to play with?"

I shook my head at him. "Please let me explain—"

"You can take me too, then," he hissed. "I'm tired of fighting. Against this demon, against my family, against you… I don't have the strength anymore."

His grip tightened until it felt like my wrists would snap in half. His eyes flickered yellow again, his teeth sharpening as I looked at them.

His lips pressed hard against mine. I could feel his desperation though his kiss, intensifying the more his mind slipped. It then switched, his kiss going from possessive to apologetic, and with a gasp, he pulled back.

"Save me," he pleaded against my lips.

Suddenly, Henrik was ripped away from me. He flew back, hitting the ground. With a grunt, Jacques threw a hard punch across Henrik's face, keeping him down.

"Goddamned demons," Jacques cursed.

I stood frozen against the wall as the Judges came in to restrain Henrik before he could get back to his feet. Jacques wrapped an arm around me and led me out of the cell. I heard the cell slam behind us as Henrik's demon screeched down the hallway. The sound made me shake, knocking the strength out of my knees. Jacques grabbed me, bringing me back to my feet and holding him tight against him.

"Are you all right?" he asked.

I leaned against his shoulder, burying my head in it. Jacques brought a soft hand to my shoulder as he held me.

"Let's get you out of here," he said. "The demon can still mess with your mind as long as you're down here."

Holding me up, Jacques led me out of the dungeons and helped me up the stairs as my head spun. When we reached the top, my knees nearly went out again. Jacques held my elbows, not letting me fall.

"I should have told you to wait at the top of the stairs," he muttered. "I didn't think he could scent you—"

"You're not going to yell at me?" I asked.

"No," he said softly. "Demons are good at tricking people. It's not your fault this time."

He gave a shadow of a smile.

"Besides, I already understand your thinking," he continued. "You thought because you helped Adrian that you could help Henrik as well, didn't you?"

I sheepishly nodded.

"You're not hard to figure out. Knowing this, I shouldn't have left you alone. I apologize."

His tone was sincere. I exhaled.

"I was trying to find you, but I got lost and I ended up at the cell…and I thought…"

He brought a hand to my head and patted it. He then tilted my chin to look up at him.

"When a man is possessed with demons," Jacques said sternly, "it's not your job to tame them. It's his. Understand?"

The realization hurt, but I felt some relief in the reprimand. I nodded.

Jacques's thumb came to my lips and wiped them gently. "Are you really all right?"

I swallowed, his touch more comforting than I anticipated. "Yes. Thanks to you. For someone who really doesn't like me, you keep saving me. Thank you, Jacques."

He turned his head away from me.

"You're welcome," he said. "Come on. We should go see the king."

***

When we arrived at the throne room, the king was already preoccupied, with two men on their knees in front of him.

Luc and Adrian.

The king stood in front of them both, his eyes dark.

"Do you both understand?" the king asked, his voice cold and rigid.

They both slowly nodded, their eyes on the ground.

Jacques scoffed. "It looks like the king found them before we did," he said. "That works out."

I breathed in relief, seeing that they were both alive and unharmed. I took a step forward to greet them, but Jacques grabbed my arm and pulled me back.

"Let the king finish his work," he said blankly. "Let's go."

I wanted to object, but Jacques pulled me from the throne room before I could say a word. He took me down the hall to the large fountain, gesturing for me to take a seat.

"We can wait here," he said.

He didn't sit next to me. He only stood, watching the door. Silence passed between us. I could feel how tense he was even though he wasn't saying a word.

"What's wrong?" I asked.

He grumbled but didn't say anything understandable at first.

"You'll stay with me from now on," he eventually commanded.

My head spun for a brief moment while I tried to understand his words.

He looked down at me. "Luc was supposed to protect you per my command and he failed to do so. I'm not letting you go back to his room just so you can parachute out the door again."

"Honestly, do you really think I would—"

He raised a pointed eyebrow at me. I slumped.

"Yes, well, I suppose you know me better than that, don't you?" I replied.

"You're not so hard to figure out, Esmeralda. For better or worse, you simply follow the path that you think leads to a happy ending. Unfortunately, the world is too dark for that."

His words shook my heart, breaking it a little more.

My back started to ache once again.

The doors of the throne room opened, and Luc stepped outside.

"Luc!" Jacques commanded, harsher than I had ever heard him speak before.

Luc froze, meeting his gaze. Jacques wagged two fingers to call him over. Luc hesitated until he saw me, concern matting his eyebrows across his face. He jogged over to me.

"Esmeralda," Luc huffed out. "How did you—"

"She was your responsibility, Luc," Jacques said, cutting him off. "I gave you a direct order. Because of your reckless behavior, she jumped from your room."

"Fell," I corrected.

"If I hadn't been there, she could be dead," Jacques continued. "Do you understand the weight of your actions?"

Luc took in the words for a moment, and all I could do was shamefully bite my lip. Before I could read the expression forming in Luc's face, Jacques stepped between us.

"She'll stay in my room from now on," Jacques continued. "I can't trust her to you any longer."

I stood to touch Jacques's arm. "That's not—"

He turned to me and silenced me with a single glare.

"I will make sure you are protected properly until I can return you to your father," he said. "My job is to keep both sides balanced."

I tugged on his shirt. "I never agreed to this."

"I never gave you the option to agree. I'm not leaving you with an unstable siren or a smitten pirate. You're staying with me. End of discussion."

He opened his mouth to continue, but the king's voice echoed into the hallway.

"Jacques, I'd like to speak with you."

Jacques looked between us and the door to the throne room, unable to decide who to answer. He shook a finger at me instead, pointing to the ground in order to tell me to stay put. He turned and went into the throne room before I could object.

"Is what he said true?" Luc asked, suddenly angry. "Did you actually jump? You could have died! If something happened to you, I would have never seen you again!"

"I was terrified of the same thing!"

His shoulders dropped, his wings seeming to flutter sadly. He dropped his eyes.

"You're the only one who likes me without some bloody curse," I continued. "You're the one I trust the most out of everyone. What was I supposed to do if you were cursed again, hmm?"

His eyes met mine, the gaze in them full of grief and regret. "I didn't think I was so important to you."

I tried to form my words.

"You know," I started, "I spent my entire life around businessmen who wanted a piece of my father's fortune, and women who wanted to find a fault in our family to gossip about. Everything to those types of people becomes a power game. So I hid myself in my family and rarely made friends outside of them in fear that they would try to find fault in my family."

Luc only looked at me, his eyes soft.

"You were the first friend I made on that ship," I continued. "And maybe even the first friend I ever had, if we're both from this eternal world. How can I lose you?"

He raised his hand to my face, brushing a thumb against my cheek. With a sigh he pulled me in, wrapping me in both his arms and his wings. He leaned his head on top of mine and held me tight.

"Forgive me, little dove," he whispered. "I was so used to being left behind that I didn't even realize you cared about me as much as you did."

I laughed. "You idiot. You said you could see every desire I ever had. You couldn't see my desire to keep you with me?"

His arms tightened around me, and he held me for a few moments longer before looking into my eyes. I let him, wanting him to see how much he meant to me. When he smiled, I could tell that he found the answer he was looking for.

"Are you sure you're all right?" Luc asked.

I stiffened, remembering Jacques asking me the same exact question right after Henrik's demon had attacked me.

Please...save me...

"Esmeralda?" Luc asked. "What is it?"

I winced, the same pain coming to my shoulder blades again. It was now pulsating, throbbing for relief.

"The longer I'm here," I said, "the more I feel my wings."

"You *feel* them? What do you mean?"

"My skin knows that something else belongs there. The longer I'm here, the more it hurts."

Luc rubbed my back as if it could soothe it. Looking at his wings, I knew that it wouldn't.

"Jacques said I was too pure," I said. "That I can't even see evil anymore. Is it because I don't have my wings that my perspective is so...limited?"

Luc seemed lost in thought for a moment then eventually nodded. "From the way you've been purified, you can only see good. It's not a terrible thing, but it's limiting. Same with anyone who can only see evil."

"Do humans like that exist?"

"All kinds of humans exist. That's only two of them."

Luc's wings fluttered, and I couldn't help but reach out and touch them. Their feathers were as soft as cat's fur and as delicate as cotton candy. I couldn't help but run my fingers through his feathers, watching them gracefully catch in the breeze.

"Esmeralda?" Luc asked.

"I think I know what I want, Luc," I said, meeting his concerned gaze. "There's no point in pretending. I want my wings."

CHAPTER 38

GONE

I t was the third day.

Adrian and the others were supposed to be departing from the Den of Sirens for good. I hadn't spoken to him in this entire time, Jacques keeping his promise of keeping us separated. But it hadn't stopped me from worrying about Adrian. How was he? How heavy was his heart? How did he feel about leaving Henrik behind?

And…would I ever see him again?

I hadn't seen or even asked about Henrik since the day I met his demon. I didn't know what questions to ask Jacques, and I didn't know if I could even be any help.

Not in this form, anyway.

I took a deep breath. I knew my decision. I had been avoiding the topic since I had started staying in Jacques's room. Jacques had either been physically absent—watching over the other Judges and Henrik—or he had been emotionally absent, lost in his own thoughts as night fell.

But now it was time to tell him.

I waited for him to return from his afternoon shift of watching Henrik.

"Is he the same?" I asked Jacques.

Jacques took a deep breath, nodding his head. "It's too hard to reach him. The demon has too much power. Once Adrian's ship has been out to sea for a day, we'll take Henrik out to sea as well. We'll extract the demon when we're out at sea."

I nodded thoughtfully. "I wonder how Adrian feels about that idea."

"He doesn't know it." He waved a pointed finger at me. "And don't go blabbering it to him either."

"How can I when you won't let me see him? It's hard to tell him anything, quite frankly."

"It's for your protection. You have a way of being reckless."

I folded my arms, tipping my chin up at him. "It's part of my charm."

"It gives me a headache."

He rubbed the back of his head, the usual dark circles under his eyes darker than before. He sat on one of the benches in his room, leaning his head against the wall and shutting his eyes with a long sigh. I almost felt guilty for being stubborn with him for the past couple of days, knowing how hard he was working to help Henrik. But I also knew that he was too worn down to fight with me, and I could use that to my advantage.

"Will you let me see Adrian off?" I asked.

Jacques opened his eyes slowly to stare at me. He hesitated for a moment, his fingers curling into loose fists.

"Give me one good reason," he said.

"Because it will be the last time I ever see him."

Jacques chuckled. "Giving up the pirate captain then? I'm rather surprised, I must say. I thought as soon as you got back home you'd throw off the engagement and go after him. With the spell you have over him, he'd definitely come looking for you. You're telling me that doesn't tempt you?"

He stood up again, walking over to his bed to strip and change shirts. I had seen him shirtless so many times since we met that I didn't even feel awkward about it anymore. Instead, I gripped my hands in my clothes, stepping toward Jacques's back and summoning up my courage.

"I'm giving up everyone," I said. "I've decided to get my wings, Jacques."

He stopped halfway through buttoning up his clean shirt to turn back and face me. I tried not to cower under his gaze, despite how intimidating it was. It wasn't that he was angry. But he was serious. More serious than I had ever seen him.

And that was saying something, considering he was quite serious most of the time.

"What did you say?" he asked, voice low.

"I said I want my wings," I replied. "The longer I'm here, the more I know I belong here."

He stepped forward to meet me. "You know what this means, then? You have to give up everything, Esmeralda. Your father, your friends, your previous life completely—"

"Yes, I understand it. And I hate it. I hate leaving my father, but what else can I do? I feel like no matter what world I live in, I'll be missing a piece of me. My heart aches no matter which path I choose."

"And what makes you think your wings will fulfill your ache?"

I shook my head and shrugged. "I don't know. I just know that the world feels so terribly small now. If I go back to my life before, I'll always feel claustrophobic."

He spent some time processing the words, and I didn't rush him. The silence was making my heart pound and making my decision waver. He finished buttoning his shirt, then slowly exhaled through his nose, not looking at me.

"Then…" Jacques said finally, breaking the silence. "You have two options. When I return to your father I can tell him that I never found you, or I can tell him that you're dead."

Now my heart was pounding so hard that it was making me shake.

"What do you mean?" I asked. "Are those the only two options?"

He looked at the ground for a moment longer, then finally rose up to meet my eyes.

"You have to understand something, Esmeralda," he said. "When you get your wings, you become a full spiritual creature again. Your soul will separate from this body. And since your body is dependent on your soul…"

He allowed me to finish the sentence by myself.

I slowly lowered myself on the bench, trying to understand. I looked at my hands, the lines in my palms deeper than normal.

"They won't remember me," I said.

He grunted in objection. "They won't *recognize* you. There's a difference."

"But how? That doesn't make sense. When Luc got his wings, I recognized him still. We all do."

"Because we're still in the Den of Sirens," he said. "Nothing is completely hidden here. But the moment you leave…"

My hands shook. The moment I left this place, I'd lose my true identity, my original family, the king, and Luc. But if I stayed, then my father…

"If nothing is hidden here," I said, "then shouldn't I have recognized the king when we first arrived?"

He exhaled with an exhausted hiss.

"First, the king hid himself from you purposely. He can break the rules as he pleases. Second, as an incarnate, you're between worlds, and the rules bend differently." He sat down next to me. "You can't recognize the sirens, but they recognize you. If you get your wings you'll recognize them again, but the human world won't recognize you anymore."

I leaned over my knees, resting my elbows against them as my heart sank in my chest.

"Is that why they stay away from me?" I asked.

"Who?"

"The sirens."

He tsked. "Noticed that, did you?"

I nodded. He was silent. But only for a brief, peaceful moment.

"You were a murderer here," he said flatly. "It makes sense that they would keep their distance until you've been cleansed and given your wings back, at the very least."

I sighed, exasperated. "There's that optimistic honesty, once again."

"Do you prefer me to lie to you?"

My shoulders slumped. "No. I'm quite grateful for your honesty, actually."

A thought struck me.

"What about you?" I asked Jacques suddenly. "You travel between worlds. When I become a siren, will you forget me as well?"

His lips twitched, but he neither smiled nor frowned.

"My soul has been tainted by my demon," he said. "Because of that I can never be purely human again, regardless of my mortality. So the answer is no, I won't forget you."

I held my head in my hands, groaning. "There are too many rules."

"That happens when the spiritual crosses with the physical. Each realm has their own rules, and when they cross there are even more complications."

"You never told me any of this before. When we were in the court and Luc got his wings, you never mentioned that my own father wouldn't recognize me."

"Because I already knew your love for your father. And in knowing that, I already knew you'd reject your wings."

I scoffed and folded my arms. "I really hate how you act like you know me so well."

"It's not an act when I'm right."

He gave a teasing smile, looking away as soon as I caught it.

"I won't pretend to understand your attachment to your family," he continued. "And it's not important for me to understand it, so I won't bother. But with these things in mind, do you still want to go through with this?"

I hesitated. He caught it.

"Okay then," he said. "Well, if you still want your wings before we leave with Henrik out to sea, I'll take you to the king to have the ceremony finalized. Otherwise, I'm taking you home. Understand?"

I scoffed. "I'm not sure why you keep calling me *mother* when you're the one who's so damn bossy."

He chuckled. "Be nice to me. Or else I'll change my mind about you seeing off the pirate king."

I sat up straight. "You mean—?

He stood up with another long, annoyed sigh.

"Let's go see off this pirate captain of yours," Jacques said. "You can say your final words. Again."

***

The *Quetzalcoatl* looked like a ghost ship.

Perhaps in some ways it was, considering half the crew had been sent to the afterlife. There was no doubt that Adrian's heart weighed heavily from the loss. I saw the guilty, sorrowful look in his eyes when Jacques's crew had attacked the ship and killed some of his men.

That was probably why Jacques had no intentions to see Adrian off personally. Jacques had only walked me to the exit of the den, stopping right before the entryway.

"Say your goodbyes and come straight back," Jacques said, motioning toward the ship. "If you take off again, I'm not saving you this time."

Even though he was serious, I couldn't help but smile.

"You know," I replied, "when we first met you said I'd keep my distance once I found out who you were. Now that I've learned, *you're* the one who hasn't stayed away from *me*."

His eyes narrowed as I gave him a smug laugh, but he didn't say anything.

I turned to walk out of the den, the entrance now blocked by a couple sirens. It seemed that they didn't want the pirates coming back in. I passed by them and went to the ship.

Even though the ship was grander than I had remembered it, that wasn't the first thing that caught my eye.

He was.

Adrian had one leg up on the rail of the ship, leaning against it on his elbows as he stared off into the den. There was no doubt in my mind that Adrian was trying to think of a way to sneak in. He was so focused that he didn't see me staring at him from down below.

He didn't see me board the ship.

He didn't even see me when I came to stand beside him.

"Don't get cocky," I said next to him.

He jumped and turned to me.

"Just because you succeeded in sneaking in once doesn't mean you can succeed again," I added.

A breathy laugh escaped his lips.
"If I didn't know any better," he said. "I'd say you were my conscience."

He smiled but it was hollow. I couldn't think of a reply when I saw the ache in his soul like that. He turned his head back toward the den, the faint wind picking up locks of his hair and twisting it around his eyes.

I had seen him like that many times. It had never affected me, not until now, realizing that this was the last time I'd see it.

And that this would be the last time he'd see *me*.

I wished there was something I could give him. But all I could do was offer him some peace.

"I'll look after him," I said.

Adrian looked at me for a moment, then looked down at his shoes.

"I know you will," he said with a nod. "Henrik's better off here than with me, anyway. I didn't even notice that anything was wrong. He started slipping, same as our uncle, and I thought it was nothing more than his bitterness toward me. Had I known the reality, perhaps…well, I don't know, but maybe…"

He trailed off, without finishing a complete thought. I already understood his turmoil and put my hand on top of his.

"It's not your fault," I said firmly.

He flipped his palm over and squeezed my hand, giving a small but genuine smile.

"Is there any chance we'll cross paths when this is over?" he asked.

His hair caught the wind again as he stared at me. It was a genuine question—a vulnerable one—and I wanted to answer in a way that gave him hope.

But I couldn't.

I looked at the entrance of the den, remembering what Jacques has said about getting my wings. Adrian wouldn't know my face even if he saw me. This would be the last time we ever saw each other as we fully were. Perhaps he never even saw me as I was. He was under a spell, wasn't he?

He squeezed my hand for an answer, and I stumbled over my words for a bit until I could find them.

"I'm needed elsewhere," I finally said. "But for what it's worth, know that I thought about it."

He took a deep breath as he took both my hands in his, holding them thoughtfully.

"You were quite the adventure, princess," he said. "I can't think of another that will measure up to you."

He raised the back of my hand to his lips and kissed it softly. I tried to smile through my embarrassment.

"Yes, well…" I muttered, blushing. "I'm sure there are plenty of women who will curse you as well."

He caught the joke and laughed, interlacing his fingers in mine as he swung our hands together. There was a boyish playfulness in his eyes, one I had never truly seen before. It was no longer the arrogant, prideful smirk of the captain of the *Quetzalcoatl*. It was the pure, enchanting smile of a man.

There were a few surprised murmurs that made both Adrian and I turn our heads.

Boarding the ship was the King of Sirens himself, along with Hugo and Vito, a cool disposition on all of their faces as they stood tall among pirates.

Adrian nodded his head in respect.

King Melchior smiled and approached us, while Vito nodded to all the pirates. Hugo ignored them completely.

"Did you come to make sure we'd leave?" Adrian asked the king.

The king looked around and shrugged. "I didn't think you'd trick me. But you couldn't even if you wanted to, honestly."

The king smiled at him. Adrian sheepishly scratched his ear.

"I brought you extra supplies," the king said, motioning to the sirens flying above us.

The sirens landed on the ship, leaving piles of spices, food, and wine on the deck.

"And also," the king said, waving Vito forward, "for your family."

Vito brought out a smooth, wooden box. He slowly opened it to reveal a box of multicolored gems, each one looking more expensive and delicate than the one next to it. Adrian took a deep breath, nodding.

"This is enough, I assume?" the king asked.

Adrian gave a short laugh of disbelief and bit his lip. "More than a sinner like me deserves, to be sure."

King Melchior waved for Vito to close the box. Vito did as he was told, then handed it to Adrian. Adrian had to release my hand to take the box, and my hand suddenly felt cold without him.

"This is your last chance to live with honor, Captain," the king said. "Remember that."

Adrian didn't answer, only bowing his head in acknowledgment.

"We will send your brother back home once he's cured," the king continued. "How long that will be will depend on him. I can't guarantee the time."

"I'll think of something to tell my parents," Adrian said. "They wouldn't believe the truth if I told them."

"Most people don't. But I warn you, the human realm and this realm are connected, but they are not one. There are details you will forget."

The king smiled.

"In fact, you'll probably forget me telling you that you'll forget," he added.

The king's smile disappeared.

His smile suddenly shifted to an open mouth of terror and pain as he threw a hand to his chest, doubling over as he screamed. Vito and Hugo rushed in and grabbed him before he could fall to the ground. He was pale, losing color faster and faster by the second until he was almost gray.

"What's happening?" Adrian asked, nearly throwing the box of jewels aside and coming to the king's aid.

"This has never happened before!" Vito said, holding tight to the king's arm. "Your Majesty, what—"

King Melchior grabbed Vito's arm, gritting his teeth.

"The Eros…" King Melchior forced out. "Get to the Eros. Now."

CHAPTER 39

UNITED

We carried the king to his room as he paled further and further.

The moment the king had collapsed on the ship, Jacques took off for the throne room to find the culprit. Adrian helped Vito and Hugo with carrying the king, and I followed them close behind to assist in any way that I could.

They lay him on his bed—a large slab of stone decorated with deep carvings filled with teal light—and I came to his side to take his hand and check his forehead. When he smirked at me, I realized my foolishness for checking the temperature of the spiritual world king like he was a frail, old man.

Adrian came and stood beside me, resting a hand on my shoulder but keeping his eyes on the king.

"What can I do, Your Majesty?" he asked.

The king turned his head toward Adrian with a warm glow.

"The right thing," the king replied softly.

Vito patted his chest. "We should go to the throne room and help! Jacques will need reinforcements!"

Hugo shook his head with a complete poker face. "What good is the right and left hand of the king if they are not at his right and left hand?"

Vito muttered nervously to himself as he switched his weight from one leg to the other, back and forth, back and forth. Hugo, on the other hand, became a full general.

"Call for alarm," Hugo said to the other sirens that had followed us to the king's room. "Get sirens to guard the throne room, the hallway, outside the king's door, and the prison. Make contact with Jacques and provide any reinforcements he may need. Emergency code: red. Highest priority. Go."

Most of the sirens left to follow orders. Some lingered, worried about the king's condition. As they crowded Hugo and Vito with questions, one siren pushed through, breathing heavily.

Luc.

"Your Majesty?" Luc called, coming forward to his bed. "What happened? I saw them carry you—"

He stopped, eyes narrowing at Adrian.

"You!" Luc called, jumping at us, whipping his wings in fury.

I let go of the king's hand and jumped between Luc and Adrian, holding out my arms to block them from each other. My arms were tiny compared to Luc's wings, but I didn't back down.

"It wasn't him!" I said.

"Then why—"

"Rhys," the king whispered out.

Luc's fury fell from his face, and he went to the king's side. He bowed in respect.

"Remember…" the king continued, "remember the gift I have given you."

Luc's shoulders dropped, along with his eyes.

"Yes, Your Majesty," he said. "I will remember."

"Gift?" I asked.

Luc looked at me for a moment but didn't answer. He didn't have the chance to.

"It's gone!" Jacques announced, storming into the room. "The Eros has been taken from the throne."

There were gasps and murmurs by the sirens standing by, Luc clenching his fists. Vito gripped his hair. Even Hugo paled. Adrian and I, however, were confused.

"What does that mean?" Adrian asked.

"It means that whoever has it can control the spiritual world," Luc said.

"Which means it's going to be difficult to catch the bastard," Jacques added. "If any of the sirens get close to him, he can command them at will as long as he possesses the stone. The Judges aren't affected by it, however…" He swallowed. "Two of my men are dead now."

The room went silent. Adrian licked his bottom lip, looking down.

"It was my brother, wasn't it?" he asked.

Jacques didn't show any emotion as he nodded. "It seems his demon is in full control now."

Adrian narrowed his eyes in pain. There was a wave of silence. After a moment, he licked his lips, an ironic smile coming to them.

"You said the Eros controls sirens, correct?" Adrian asked.

Jacques nodded. "That's right."

"What about humans?"

"It doesn't have any effects on humans or demons. That's why Judges can—"

Jacques stopped, looking blankly at Adrian. Adrian popped his eyebrow, a full smile coming to his face.

"I have half of a pirate crew trained to take treasure, mate," Adrian said. "If you need backup, all you have to do is ask."

Jacques gave a long sigh, looking off to the doorway and nodding.

"It seems we have no other options. You realize the possible outcomes, don't you?"

Adrian nodded, his fingers reaching for his sword. He unsheathed it slightly, a sharp clink echoing as he jammed it back in the scabbard.

"Yes…" Adrian replied solemnly. "I understand it."

Jacques looked at the king and then back to Adrian.

"Then let's go," he said. "The sooner the better."

Jacques pointed at me as if he knew that I was getting ready to step forward.

"*You* stay with the king," Jacques said. He pointed to Luc as well. "Both of you. The stone affects you, even as an incarnate. I won't allow what happened last time…"

He trailed off, seeming to not want to finish the sentence. He swallowed, instead, and with a shake of his head he started to walk toward the door, motioning for Adrian to follow.

"Jacques!" I called out.

"No arguing with me!" he called back barely turning around. "You'll stay here where it's safe. I can't keep saving you—"

"Be careful!" I barked. "That…that was all I wanted to say."

He stopped. He met my eyes only for a moment, only to give a nod and turn back toward the door.

Adrian didn't follow Jacques right away. He reached out and took my hand in his.

"I feel like every time we say goodbye, we jinx it," he said with a laugh.

"Adrian…"

"I'll be back to say goodbye again," he replied. "So wait here for me."

He squeezed my hand gently and then released it. I opened my mouth to say something but didn't have the chance.

"Esmeralda…" the king whispered. "Come here."

With my mouth still open to speak, I turned around, shutting it on the way to his bedside. He reached up for my hand and I gave it to him, then sat next to his bed.

"Are you okay, Your Majesty?" I asked.

"Eventually, I'll be fine," he said. "You, on the other hand, are having great difficulties."

I swallowed. "If I had my wings, I might be able to help."

He gave a weak, breathy chuckle. "You think your wings give you power? Perhaps they do. But the question is, what kind of power will you have?"

"What do you mean?"

He let go of my hand, reaching his hand up to gently stroke my cheek. His fingers were cold, but not unpleasant, like a small breeze on a warm day.

"You had your wings once…" he said. "And with that power, you succumbed to great darkness."

I glanced at my arm, remembering what Jacques had told me. I had killed the Guardians. The king knew this as well. Perhaps he knew that even before Jacques read my arm.

"I don't have the power to give you wings," the king continued, "but I have just enough to give you sight."

He reached out, touching his hand to my forehead. It burned my skin, making me gasp.

"It's time for you to see," he said. "To see who you once were."

CHAPTER 40

SEPARATED

The horizon bled deep into the sunset. There were ships—specks in the distance—floating from one side of the sun to the next. I opened my wings and closed them again, letting the salty air pass through the feathers. They wanted to soar. They wanted to go to the ships and bring in the catch, but the sirens on duty had already been sent.

And they would bring back the wicked to be destroyed.

There was something exciting about a ship full of sailors that could possibly be sentenced to death. Like the world would be cleaner after it was finished. A little less evil in the world, fewer dirty humans to destroy the creation of the Siren King.

As I sat and watched the ships, a fluttering of wings came in behind me. I turned around to see Rhys as he landed. He plopped down next to me, a smile plastered hard against his face.

"Where have you been?" I asked. "The king was looking for you."

He shrugged. "I went back to the city."

"Again? That's the third time this month."

"There's just so many fascinating things there," Rhys said, practically glowing. "The humans have all these little inventions for their daily lives, like knives and umbrellas. They have tasty little things called pastries. And they can't fly, so they ride horses and these strange little open boxes with wheels… And their *stories.* They have the most incredible stories, Astraea! They're so similar to ours, but they involve human heroes slaying evil before it destroys them. Can you imagine?"

I laughed, shaking my head. "They're just human tales. Wildly unrealistic and disgustingly romantic."

"Yes! The men save women from horrific danger, and then they kiss."

I groaned. "Why would a human woman wait on a man to save her? Are the human females so weak?"

He shook his head. "They're strong too. But the human men seem to gain magical strength and courage when they have the kiss of a woman waiting for them."

"Is a kiss that powerful?"

Rhys's head cocked to the side as he looked at me. Something flickered in his eyes for a moment, and he gave a slightly sinful smile.

"It's incredibly intoxicating," he finally said.

I gasped, nudging him. "Rhys! Have you kissed before?"

He smiled proudly even though he was turning pink. He looked over his shoulder before leaning in closer to answer.

"A few times," he whispered. "The human women taught me."

I laughed. "You daring bastard. The king would rip your feathers off one by one if he knew."

"It's not a sin to kiss," he said, pouting.

"It's a sin to touch the humans."

"You want to try it too, don't you?"

I made a gagging sound. "The humans? You must be joking! I can't stand those slimy things."

He laughed and shook his head. "Not the humans. Kissing."

I pursed my lips, thinking about it. Rhys's fingers came to my chin, turning my face toward his. There was a different look in his eyes than normal. It was playful as usual, but with a hint of darkness in it. I had never seen it before.

"Would you like me to teach you?" he asked.

I paused for a moment, feeling a strange sort of flutter in my chest. It was a new feeling, and I wasn't sure what it was. Maybe it was the wind? But it was too warm to be the wind today. How strange.

I pulled back. "Maybe I'd like to try it. Someday."

Rhys's hand dropped to his side, his lips flat. "But not with me."

I shrugged.

"Maybe you'd rather have Renaldo?" he asked.

I folded my arms. He scoffed.

"I don't know why you have such a crush on him," Rhys muttered.

"A crush?"

"That's what the humans call it. You like Renaldo more than King Melchior."

"I don't love anyone more than the king!" I threw back. "But Renaldo… I feel differently about him. He's so fearless. And strong. And he has so much freedom."

Rhys brought his thumb to his lips in thought. "You've thought about kissing him before."

I shrugged again. "So what if I have?"

"Have you thought about being in bed with him before?"

I looked at him in shock. He only smiled.

"Trust me," he said. "That's a totally different feeling."

"Rhys…have you…?"

I didn't finish the question, but he understood it.

"Humans and sirens weren't built so differently," he replied, not looking at me.

Before I could respond, Rhys nodded to the horizon, signaling an arrival.

"It seems like Renaldo's ears were burning," Luc said.

Renaldo swooped in and landed next to us, a proud glow on his face as he smiled with full lips. His shoulders and arms glittered in the sunlight behind him, his smile doing something strange to my stomach. Whatever this feeling was, I liked it. Every time he was near me, I had this strange feeling, and I wanted to know what it was.

"You should have been out there with us, Astraea!" Renaldo said to me, full of life and energy. "It was thrilling!"

"You know I wanted to," I replied, "but the king never lets me go with you."

"We'll fix that one day. I promise."

He held my gaze for a brief moment, before noticing Rhys next to us.

"Rhys!" Renaldo beamed. "You finally made it back!"

Rhys stood slowly, his tongue roaming the side of his cheek.

"Yep," he replied flatly.

"I just got back from a siege myself," Renaldo replied, puffing his chest up as he pointed to a ship being pulled into the den.

I leaned over the side, using my wings to balance me. "Pirates?"

Renaldo nodded proudly. "Pirates, thieves, criminals …the dirtiest of the human world."

I rolled my eyes. "They're all equally disgusting, honestly. It's a shame we can't round them all up to be tried at once."

"That still wouldn't make you happy," Renaldo replied, laughing. "Some of them would survive. You would hate that."

I smiled. "You know me far too well."

Rhys coughed and gave a sour frown. He always had that frown around Renaldo.

"I'm going to head out," Rhys muttered.

"You okay?" Renaldo asked. "Already worn out from your play date? Did you ingest too many stories again?"

Rhys shrugged, not laughing at Renaldo's joke. "I have a lot of work to catch up on. See ya."

He flew off before I could say anything. Renaldo just waved after him, then turned to me, smiling.

"I have something for you," he said, reaching into his robe.

He pulled out a small silver ring, decorated with tiny diamonds. He took my hand in his and put it on my hand, the silver shining in the pale sunlight. I couldn't hold back a blushing smile.

"I knew you'd like it," Renaldo said.

"I feel like I'm in one of those human ceremonies where they exchange rings. What's it called?"

"A wedding, you mean?"

"Yeah, that. Why don't we have ceremonies like that?"

"Sirens don't get married, Astraea," Renaldo said, laughing. "We're far too busy for that."

I pouted.

"Why would King Melchior let the humans get married and not us? It's not like they deserve something so special. They're not loyal at all."

He shrugged. "Maybe that's why he lets them marry. It's the only way they can learn."

"Honestly, I think he favors the humans more."

Renaldo laughed. "I've never seen the king favor anyone. Don't be silly."

"Have you seen the way he treats the Guardians? He has the sirens bring them food and clothes, he invites them to our parties, he counsels them—"

"They guard the Eros."

"They're just humans. I don't see what makes them so special from the other humans."

Renaldo put his warm hands on my arms, smiling down at me. It soothed my angry nerves instantly.

"Don't worry about the humans," he said. "Just bring them to the king for judgment. That's all you have to do. Speaking of which, the Judges should come next month. So be on your best behavior, eh?"

I nodded but couldn't keep my eyes off the tiny, dirty ships in the sunset.

***

The Judges came. Renaldo was sentenced.

There had to have been a mistake. Renaldo was the most courageous of all of us. There wasn't a dark vein in his body. He was pure. I knew he was. He did so much for the king, and the king was just going to let him slip into a human body? A disgusting, wretched human body?

Renaldo didn't deserve that. No one did.

"You cannot see the king without a summons," Hugo said, monotone as always.

"I've requested to see him for three weeks!" I yelled back. "He hasn't even answered. Why is he refusing to answer me?"

"Are *you* the king?" Hugo replied. "Must he answer to you?"

"If he cared about his sirens as much as he says he does, he would. Instead, he lets them burn to death."

Hugo sighed, only making me angrier.

"You give me a headache, Astraea," he said. "Every day you act like you don't know any better. This is why I keep putting you on probation."

"Tell me what I should do to get through this door then, huh? Should I become one of your beloved humans? Is that it?"

Hugo's eyes flashed, as they always did right before he was about to reprimand me. Before he could, however, the king spoke from the other side of the door.

"Hugo," the king's voice echoed through the door. "Let her come in."

"Finally!" I huffed.

Hugo threw a hand in front of the door to block me. "Just because you got an audience with the king doesn't mean you're going to like what he has to say."

I threw his hand out of my way and stepped into the room, fists clenched. The king sat on his throne, chin on his hand as if he was already tired of our conversation even though we hadn't started yet.

"You refused to see me," I complained, not bothering with paying respects.

"I was giving you a chance to prepare yourself for truly listening," he replied calmly. "I see that you didn't take that opportunity."

"Renaldo was cursed."

"I know."

"And that means nothing to you?"

He slowly straightened, his eyes heavy but not sorrowful enough. "It means as much to me as it always does when I lose one of my own."

"But Renaldo was different. He wasn't like the evil sirens that murdered or stole or tortured the humans—"

"His sentence wasn't based on what *you* saw," the king said, "but what I saw."

"Maybe you saw wrong."

The king cocked his head to the side slowly, narrowing his eyes. I could tell that he was conjuring up his patience. I didn't know why he bothered. It wasn't like I had any patience left with him.

He stood from his throne, coming down the steps to meet me. He reached out and took my hand in his, looking down at the ring on my finger—the one Renaldo had given me.

"I know he was special to you," the king finally said. "In your pain, you can't understand my judgment."

I pulled my hand away. "You let the humans live. They sin far more than us, yet somehow they don't get sentenced."

"I didn't put them in charge of judgment. I gave the sirens that job. Because of your power, I judge you more harshly."

"You treat the humans better than us. We're practically their servants instead of their sentencers."

"And I serve you both, Astraea," he said firmly. "Do you think that you're higher than me?"

This time I had nothing to reply, my anger rendering me speechless.

"You need to see the way that I see," he continued. "If you don't, your heart will turn black, just as Renaldo's did."

I couldn't speak. I could only shake my head at him in frustration. He stepped forward and cupped my face in his hands.

"I don't want to lose you, Astraea," he said, his thumbs gently rubbing against my cheeks. "I don't want to lose any of you. I judge with my blood because I made you with it. How could I not love you?"

I swallowed. "You made the humans after us. Were we not good enough?"

He brought my head against his chest in a hug, but I didn't hug him back. He leaned his head on mine as he spoke.

"I made more creatures simply because I wanted to love more creatures. Not because I loved you less. I *can't* love you less. Do you believe me?"

After a breath, I pulled away, not looking at him. The room was unbearably silent. I crossed my arms, looking at the floor. The king only sighed.

"Don't come to me when you're ready to speak," he said softly. "Come to me when you're ready to listen."

I turned my head up to look at him. He didn't seem in pain at all. He didn't seem to care about my side at all. I hated how emotionless he was. How calm he was. How warm he was being when he should have been in as much pain as I was.

Saying nothing, I turned and left the room, fists still clenched.

How could he love the humans more than us? How could he love those filthy, vile creatures? Why did they have such power? Why could they sin and not us? Why could they love and not us?

The king didn't love us. He loved them.

And I hated them.

I hated them more than anything.

***

I gasped, falling to the ground on my knees as I opened my eyes to find myself in King Melchior's room once again. He looked down at me from his bed, still pale and only graying more.

Tears were streaming down my face before I could stop them.

"Your Majesty…" I sobbed.

He gave a weak smile. "Hello again, daughter."

He reached his hand out and I came to his side, lying against him and crying into his arm. I could feel his hand on my back to soothe me.

"Why didn't you tell me?" I cried. "Why didn't you tell me that it was all my fault?"

He didn't answer, but allowed me to cry, until I could find my words again.

"I killed them…" I said. "I killed the Guardians because I thought you loved them more than us. I thought you'd love us more if they were gone."

Hugo sighed. "Your hatred influenced many of the others. By the time you had gone through your second reincarnation, most of the sirens had been contaminated."

"So the king separated the worlds," Vito added. "The sirens and demons could see each other, but the humans lost contact with us completely. Only the Judges could go between worlds."

"And it's because the Guardians were killed and no more put in their place that Henrik's demon now has the Eros," I said. I looked at the king through blurry eyes. "Your Majesty… *Father*…you should have punished me far worse."

He smiled and brought his hand to the back of my head, lowering me down to kiss my forehead.

"My wish," he said, "is only to have all my children come home to me."

I clung to him as I leaned on his shoulder, his robe absorbing my tears. I couldn't remember everything, but I remembered enough. I remembered my own ugliness and corruption. I remembered my decision to kill the Guardians. I remembered how dark my heart was on the day I was sentenced to reincarnation.

I had earned it. My heart had been so black that I had come to the den twice more, only to be sentenced to another human body both times.

"You're no longer sentenced," the king said, as if hearing my thoughts. "You're now free from your evil. And now I think you're finally ready to listen."

I raised my head to look at him. He smiled, wiping his thumb under my eyes to clear away the tears.

"Just as I gave Rhys a gift, I give you one," he said. "You now have the ability to see your darkness and yet, hold on to your newfound light."

I sniffed. "What do you want me to do, Your Majesty?"

He smiled, his hand coming to mine with a firm grasp despite its pale color.

"Redemption," he said softly. "The siren who destroyed the Guardians of the Eros will now become one."

CHAPTER 41

CALLING

"Will you stop fidgeting?" Hugo asked. "Even in a human body, you still don't listen."

"At least she's willing to cooperate this time," Vito chimed in.

"Willingness to cooperate and the ability to listen are two different things."

I smiled and reached out to pinch Hugo's cheek. "I've missed you too, Hugo."

He cringed and took a step back, shaking off my hand.

"You didn't even remember who I was," he said, "let alone miss me."

I could swear that there was a slight pout in his usually stoic face.

"Yes…" I replied. "But now that I remember you, I've realized that I've missed you quite a lot."

His shoulders slumped, but he pulled them back instantly.

"Enough of your flattery," he said flatly, looking away and scratching the back of his ear. "Let's put that evil mind of yours to good use."

"I'm not sure how you want me to help," I admitted. "I can't approach the demon either."

"True," Hugo agreed. "But you can redeem yourself by dedicating yourself to protecting the Eros."

I knew the statement was meant to make me humble, not make me feel guilty, but it was difficult not to feel as humiliated as I did.

"Rhys," Hugo commanded. "Come forward."

Luc—Rhys, as now I recognized him—bowed his head and stepped forward. He had been completely silent this entire time, not a single emotion on his face clear enough to read.

"You and Astraea will both assist the pirates," Hugo commanded. "Be careful not to let the demon see you."

Luc nodded solemnly. There was no doubt in my mind that he had no desire to help the crew, but he seemed prepared to do as he was told.

"I wish I had my wings to help better..." I said absentmindedly.

Vito smiled. "You don't need them. You don't need what others have in order to do what you're meant to do."

I gave him a warm smile back, happy to see him again the way I was meant to.

"Enough encouraging nonsense," Hugo said. "We have business to take care of. Get moving, you two."

I glanced at Luc as he bowed solemnly.

"Remember that as long as Henrik has the stone," Vito continued, "he can control any creature of the spiritual realm that is in his sight and hears his commands."

"We'll stick to the air then," Luc said. "If we're quiet enough, Henrik won't look up."

"Let's hope you're right," Hugo said. "But there aren't a lot of options. Go do your best."

I gave a firm nod then ran over to King Melchior's bedside once more. He gave me a half smile.

"You'll do fine, daughter," he said.

I took his hand.

"I'm more worried about you," I replied. "Stay strong for me, Your Majesty."

He chuckled with a rasp. "I'm not going anywhere. I'll be here when you're ready to return to me."

There was a small glint in his eye even though his skin was pale. Luc stepped in beside me, bowing his head to the king.

"It seems you're tested time and time again, son," King Melchior added, looking at Luc. "But the test is to make you stronger. Remember that."

Luc chewed his lip and nodded, then took me by my free hand. I squeezed it, signaling that I was ready to go. Touching the king's hand with a gentle goodbye, I turned to Luc and he picked me up into his arms. He unfolded his wings, bursting from the ground and flying us out of the king's room.

Luc was silent, but I could tell that he was lost to his thoughts. There was no doubt in my mind that he was thinking about his task: to protect the humans he had intended to persecute.

"I really hated them," I said.

Luc raised an eyebrow.

"The humans," I continued. "It's strange to look back on how much I hated them."

"It's weird to see you defend them," Luc added.

I smiled. "But you always did. You always had a passionate interest in them."

He shrugged, holding on to me. "I never fit in with the sirens, really. The humans had such wonderful stories, inventions…possibilities. Freedoms we never had."

He flew us toward the other side of the caverns. We looked over the den, an eerie stillness to it. There wasn't a siren to be seen. The place had gone oddly quiet, the ones not helping in capturing Henrik or protecting the cavern most likely hiding in their rooms. It didn't look like anyone was daring to venture out on their own.

"Do you remember all your lives now?" Luc asked.

I shook my head. "Only my first life and this one."

"So you remember us now?"

I leaned against him, squeezing my arms around his neck. "I remember you, Rhys."

He didn't say anything, but I felt his arms tighten around me.

"What happened to the others?" I asked. "Have they returned?"

There was a long silence. "Honestly, I was too scared to ask. I only know that—"

He stopped. I brought my head up to look at him. He didn't look me in the eye.

"Renaldo hasn't returned, has he?" I asked.

Luc slowly shook his head. My heart sank a little, but I already knew it.

"The king saw a deep darkness in him, I think," I said. "Perhaps it was too dark. I never saw it, but I could have been blind to it. But you never liked him, did you?"

Luc sighed. "It wasn't that."

He glanced at me from the corner of his eye, then looked back down at the ground below us.

"Where do you think Henrik would be?" Luc asked, changing the subject.

He seemed uncomfortable, so I followed along.

"He has a stone that can control every siren in this place," I said. "Where would be the easiest place to control a bunch of sirens?"

"The throne room? The port? The courtroom?"

"What would a demon want to do with sirens?"

Luc's grip tightened. "He'd want them to do the work of demons, probably."

"And with that many demons—"

"It would destroy the king and the balance of good and evil."

I exhaled through my teeth. "Well, shit."

Luc chuckled. "I didn't think a lady such as yourself would say such colorful words."

I smiled, bringing a shoulder forward in coy innocence.

"Perhaps it's from being around too many pirates and their cook."

Luc chuckled. "So tell me, what do you miss the most: your home here, your home on land, or your new home at sea?"

I leaned back against his shoulder as we flew, thinking of the answer.

"I miss the way my father on land laughs when he's in high spirits," I said. "I miss the king who consoles and guides me. I miss the crew who treated me like an equal. I miss the captain and first mate who treated me like I was valuable. And I miss the siren-turned-cook who told me wild stories in both lives. These are all pieces of home. They can't belong in one place, and neither can I."

He cocked his head to the side, a smile slowly creeping onto his face. "It sounds like you're turning into a storyteller yourself."

I laughed. "I'm not even anywhere close to your level."

"Very true, but I'm willing to tutor."

I laughed, but the sound was quickly drowned out by the sound of a scream.

No, not a scream. A battle cry.

Luc and I looked at one another right before he dove toward the sound. It was coming from an unassigned room deep in the den, used mainly for relaxing and playing games.

Luc and I stayed completely silent as we came to the clearing, keeping close to the upper level. He flew us toward the corner of the room, putting me down on one of the rock formations built into the ceiling. We crouched behind the stones, watching below.

"Henrik!" a voice cried out from the room. "Stop!"

I bit my lip, recognizing Adrian's voice and praying it wasn't too late.

Henrik was in the center of the room, arm raised in the air. In his hand was the Eros.

And in front of him was a large group of sirens surrounding Adrian, Jacques, and the other pirates.

"Destroy them!" Henrik's strangled voice echoed. "Destroy them all!"

CHAPTER 42

WAR

Luc grabbed my arm to hold me back.

I wished we could have done the same for the others.

The sirens rushed the pirates. The pirates had swords, but it was useless since sirens could not die by the sword nor get tired while fighting. The pirates could do nothing but fend off the siren attacks until their own deaths.

"What do we do?" I whispered to Luc.

"We can't get close," he replied. "If Henrik sees us, he can control us."

"Can we blind him then?"

Luc snapped his head at me with a surprised look.

"Sorry," I said. "My old self was quite violent, wasn't she? Well, then what's a better way to…?"

I looked around, spotting the stream that surrounded the room. I glanced at the rocks beside me. Gasping, I tapped Luc's shoulder.

"The rocks," I said. "And the king's river water. If we combine them—"

"The earth and the spirit…yes." Luc licked his bottom lip, nodding. "Yes, that will work. But we'd have to—"

"Strike our own. But do we really have any other options?"

He gave a quick jerk of his head, keeping his eyes on the fight. "We need to get down without getting caught."

I looked around. After a couple breaths, I tore off a piece of my sleeve and rolled it up into a tight ball, sticking it in Luc's ear.

"Will this work?" I asked.

He felt his ear for a moment before nodding. "It's the best we have. Let's go."

We tore off tiny pieces of our clothes and stuffed our ears with them, blocking out the sound as much as possible. Even if Henrik saw us, we wouldn't hear his commands. But that was only one problem solved. The second problem was going to be dipping the stones in water and carrying them without burning ourselves in the process.

I motioned to Luc to take the rocks in a strip of robe, then dip them in the water and carry them to the pirates. He nodded. We gathered the rocks next to us, carrying as many as possible before Luc scooped me back into his arms to fly down to the fight. We had to fly toward the back, making sure that Henrik didn't see us coming.

When we hit the ground, we searched for the stream. It was hard to see through the blur of pirates and sirens in battle. We weaved through swords and wings, staying close together as we headed to the side of the room.

I put the rocks in a sling of cloth, dropping it down into the river. The water bubbled, as if it was boiling, assuring us that the magic was working.

I was suddenly jerked away from the river, the sling of rocks slipping from my hands. I had time to see a possessed siren aim a sword straight for my throat right before Luc blocked me. There was a muffled cry, and by the way Luc's chest seized, I knew it had come from him.

He huffed, his wings engulfing us. He hunched over for a split second. My lips said his name, even though he couldn't hear it, and I grabbed his face with my hands to make him look at me. He winced in pain, but he still had his typical smile, right before he shot open his wings and flapped them violently around us. The force knocked both the sirens and pirates around us off their feet.

He huffed again, and then I saw the cut in his robe. There was blood, but it wasn't a lot, siren blood being thicker than human blood. I touched his side, but he grabbed my hand and pulled it away.

I'm okay, he mouthed.

I swallowed my heartbeat down my throat. I knew sirens couldn't die, but knowing Luc was hurting…

Then it hit me. Luc couldn't die. But I could.

Luc had just taken a sword to his side to protect me.

Thank you, I mouthed back.

He shook his head and stepped back, snapping his wings once again to keep the fight away from the stream. While doing so, he untied the top part of his siren robe, loosening the strings around the wings so he could take off a side piece and wrap it around his hand. He then shoved his wrapped hand in the water, pulling out the burning rocks. I held out the bottom of my shirt for him, and he dropped the rocks in it.

When he had dropped about a dozen rocks into my sling, I took off running to the pirates. Dodging the swords, I tried to call to them, not sure how loud my voice really was. Some of them heard me. Some of them did not. The ones who did hear, however, turned and took a rock from my shirt, flinging the stones at their opponents. I couldn't hear the sirens clearly, but I could see their surprise and anguish as the stones made contact.

I could only apologize in my head.

I went back to Luc to resupply. He nodded and pointed to the ceiling, implying that he had to go back above for more rocks. I nodded, taking the last of the batch to the side of the room, resolving to give them to the first pirates I saw and then staying out of the way until Luc came back down with more rocks for the river.

There were a cluster of pirates on the side, and I shoved the rocks at them. They took most of them, fending off their opponents, but not without extreme exhaustion. They would need to retreat. They wouldn't be able to—

I turned my head, my eye catching one of the sirens elbowing a pirate in the face. The pirate hit the ground hard.

Adrian.

Adrian's sword flew from his hand, and the siren caught it, then pointed it back at Adrian's throat.

Without thinking, I grabbed one of the rocks from my shirt and flung it at the siren's head. It made contact, sending him backward and making him drop the sword. The pain suddenly hit me. I screamed as my palm burned from the stone. The flesh had turned red and blistered, a dark welt in the center just like the one Luc had in his back.

Tears pricked my eyes. It was true. I could die by both the spiritual weapons and the human ones.

I was easiest to kill in this room.

Adrian came to his feet, his eyes meeting mine. He broke his contact almost immediately, however, his head snapping over his shoulder to the front of the room. I followed his sight.

Henrik stood at the front of the room, his teeth bared in rage as he stared straight at me.

He pointed, his mouth opening wide in a command I didn't hear.

The sirens rushed me. Before I could even take a step to run, I was yanked into the air. I screamed until I looked over my shoulder to see that it was Luc. He pulled me in close, flying us out of the room. I gripped his neck, gasping in relief.

The other sirens weren't finished, however. Their wings were fully spread as they came for us. I couldn't hear their voices as they opened their mouths to scream at us, and it made it more terrifying than if I could hear.

Luc was fast—faster than I had ever remembered— and he sped and swooped through the cavern with ease as if he had never left. He stopped and snapped his wings backward, sending us behind all of our pursuers. He then bolted higher into the air, turning hard and going deeper into the cavern.

We made it halfway through the hall before we were hit from the side.

There was only blurring and pain. The hit from the side hurled us into the wall, and Luc gripped me tight on impact. The rocks above us loosened and fell, as did we. We tumbled down, farther and farther, until we hit the ground hard.

Everything went black.

Then white.

And when my eyes focused, I saw Luc lying next to me, unconscious and pale, boulders pinning him to the floor.

354

CHAPTER 43

RACING

I couldn't even bring myself to call his name. I came to my hands and knees, dizzy and shaking as I went to his side. He groaned in deep pain as I leaned over and touched his damp forehead.

I looked up overhead and saw none of the other sirens. Perhaps they had left us for dead. Perhaps they were hurt as well. Whatever the case, it didn't matter for now. All that mattered was Luc.

I turned his head toward me. "Luc? Can you hear me?"

His eyes fluttered open. He smiled, bringing a hand to mine.

"Is that you, little dove?" he asked. He curled up, hissing. "Shit… We may not die, but I forgot how much pain we can feel."

"Is it bad?"

He looked at his wings under the rocks and then back at me. "It's certainly not good."

I stood up and tried to roll the boulders off his wings. They were too heavy for me to move.

"Leave it, little dove," Luc said. "You have to go."

"I can't leave you here. What if the sirens come after you?"

"Then *you'll* be in danger," he replied. "Besides, the effects of the mind control probably wears off this far out. They have to be in Henrik's sight for them to obey."

"But they followed us all the way out here, and if they find you—"

"They can't kill me. You can't kill spirits without the Trials, remember?"

I dropped to my knees beside him, an annoying desire to cry. It wasn't an appropriate time and I didn't want to, but regardless, the tears were coming to my eyes before I could stop them. Luc raised his hand to my face.

"Are these for me?" he asked, collecting the tears on his fingers. "What have I done to deserve such precious little diamonds?"

"I can't fight them without you," I said.

"You can." His soft fingers left my face to grab my hand warmly. "Plug your ears. Keep your eyes open."

He squeezed my hand as he hissed again in pain, and I could tell by the way he was trying to hold it in that he wasn't faking it. I looked around the cavern, but I couldn't see a single soul that could help us.

What was I going to do?

Luc shook my hand to get my attention.

"Get going," he said. "You're in danger with me like this. Get back to the king and stay safe. If you die… I won't get to tell you…tell you so many things."

There was a dim light in his eyes as he said it, and I knew he was thinking of the people he had lost before. But it was Luc who had found me as a human and brought me to the ship, and it was him who brought me back to the

Den of Sirens. I knew that no matter what happened, I would find my way back to this place and him.

There was only one way to get him to understand that.

"You'll have the chance to tell me," I said. "Look."

I took his hand and pressed it to my wrist, my pulse racing against his fingers.

He laughed and rolled his eyes. "It's because we were just attacked."

"No," I replied, adamantly shaking my head. "It's because I thought I had lost you."

I held his gaze so he could read me. I wanted him to see it. I wanted him to understand that I was telling the truth.

His jaw slacked slightly, his fingers slowly tightening around my hand. He laced his fingers in mine and sighed through his nose.

"It's a promise, then," he said. "No matter what happens, you'll come home to me."

I smiled and nodded. "Whether it's in this life or the next, Rhys. I promise."

He held my gaze for a brief moment, his hand coming up to trace my jaw. I shivered against his touch. When I looked into his eyes, I saw that there was something different about them. Something soft and vulnerable, something vaguely familiar to a way he used to look at me when we were both sirens.

Wait… Did Luc…?

"This isn't the time," a voice said behind us.

I turned to Jacques's perturbed grimace. Adrian ran up beside him, smiling proudly as he caught his breath.

"Glad to see that you hate everyone who gets close to her, mate, and not just me," Adrian said.

"It has nothing to do with the woman," Jacques replied. "We just don't have time for this right now."

Jacques and Adrian came to us, looking at the boulders crushing Luc's wings. A couple of the other pirates fell in behind them.

"You two take the side," Adrian commanded. "Try not to roll the rock onto his face… although it might make it look better."

"Just go do your damn job," Luc snarled at him. "I don't need your help."

Adrian leaned against the boulder as he talked down to Luc. "And I don't want to help your mutinous ass either, mate. But if I want my brother back and you want your freedom back, you need to shut the hell up for a few minutes until this is all over with."

Luc gritted his teeth. I ran my fingers over his forehead to signal him to relax, standing with the men to help them push the boulders off Luc's wings. It took all of us to move the largest, and most of us to move the second and third. The rest of the rubble came off his wings easily, but it took effort for him to sit up even with his wings freed.

I crouched next to him, giving him support as he sat up. His wings were damaged, their feathers crooked, bent, and missing. He huffed, groaning as he tried to retract his wings close to his back.

"You need to regenerate," I said to him.

"It's quite a ways from the bathhouse," he replied.

The bathhouse. That's where I had met Jacques on that night, when he was half naked and looking at me like—

Wait. How was it that a Judge was able to soak in the bathhouse?

"Jacques," I said. "Does holy water not affect demons?"

"Holy water is for the holy," Jacques replied. "Demons are the rejected creatures of the king. They have no holiness within them; therefore, holy water is just the same as regular water to a demon."

"Then what is the actual weakness of a demon?"

Jacques tilted his head back to the ceiling to think. "Demons are complicated creatures. They aren't affected by holy defenses or human weapons. The only weakness they have is their human host. If the host is destroyed, then it's easier to capture them."

Adrian's hollow eyes showed that he already understood that option, but I wasn't going to accept it.

"There has to be another way," I said. "Every creature has a weakness or sin that—"

I stopped. That was it.

I pointed to Adrian's sword around his waist. "Give me one of those."

Adrian looked down to where I was pointing and raised a pointed eyebrow at me.

"The sword, you jackass," I replied.

He looked even more skeptical. So did Jacques.

"Are you going to try and stab a demon?" Jacques asked. "I know you can't be that stupid."

"Jacques?" I asked. "Why do demons possess humans?"

Jacques hesitated, but eventually decided to answer my question. "To gain power."

"Why do they need power?"

"To create more demons."

"And why do they possess humans and not the sirens?"

"Well, for one, sirens can't be possessed. And second, demons despise humans. Demons are rejected creations of the Siren King. Humans are not, even though they have no power."

I took a sword from one of the pirates and unsheathed it.

"Exactly," I said, staring at the tip of the blade of the sword. "The demons hate humans out of jealousy. Just as I did."

I glanced down at my arm, knowing I couldn't see it as Jacques did, but holding it up anyway. He looked between me and my forearm, his mouth slowly gaping.

"You *remember*?" he asked.

I nodded.

"I remember why I killed them," I said. "And just as importantly, I remember *how*."

"But how do you remember?" Jacques asked with genuine surprise. "You don't have your wings."

I smiled.

"I don't need them," I replied. "And I didn't need them to kill the Guardians either. There's another way to kill. To destroy any living creature, you just need to remind them of one thing: their lust for something they don't have."

CHAPTER 44

CAPTURED

The Guardians were on night watch.

There had always been too many of them. How many Guardians did there need to be when there was a cavern full of sirens? Nevertheless, the Siren King kept fifteen or twenty of them at a time, rotating every year with new Guardians in order to give the humans rest.

The humans were always weak like that. Always needing a break. Always needing family and friends. But sirens didn't need those sorts of things. Sirens weren't built to rest and have families. We were built to uphold the spiritual realm.

We didn't need the humans. The king would realize that once I showed him.

I watched the Guardians as they patrolled the hallways leading to the king's throne room. How could they even be allowed on the sacred tiles here? How could the king allow them inside a sacred space when they were so filthy? Fine, they were deemed pure by the trials. So what? Purity could always be corrupted. I knew that.

If the sirens could fall, so could the humans.

I approached the throne room. One of the Guardians, Wilton, bowed as I came forward.

"Hello, Astraea," he said with a smile. He was always oddly good at remembering our names. "I hope you are faring well this evening."

"I always fare well in my father's home," I replied, trying to make my smile reach my eyes. "Speaking of which, you've been with us for what? Three months now?"

He nodded proudly. "It's been quite the experience. To see the world as it really is…I wish everyone could see it."

"As do I." I leaned against the wall, doing my best to look downcast. "It's a shame you can't see your family. You must miss them."

His smile faltered a little. "Of course, of course. But what I do here is important."

I let a smile slip, but I hid it behind my hand.

"Is that so?" I asked. "Guarding a rock when the sirens could do it themselves?"

His eyes widened at my outburst. I patted my cheek in embarrassment.

"Forgive me," I said. "I didn't mean to speak ill. Perhaps it's because of what I saw…oh! Never mind. Forget I said anything."

With genuine concern—that foolish thing humans always seemed to have—he stepped forward to console me.

"It sounds serious," he replied. "What happened?"

I took a long breath for good measure.

"You know part of my job is to bring in the humans for judgment, yes? Well, this time our ship had a small child. Barely old enough to eat solid foods. We brought in her mother and father for judgment and—"

I made a fireworks gesture with my hands.

"The poor child wouldn't eat after that," I continued. "This morning we found the child…well, that is… Ah, such a tragedy."

When I put a hand over my mouth and shut my eyes to fake grief, he put his hand on my shoulder in condolence. It took everything within me to not cut it off.

"That's terrible!" he said.

I nodded. "So terrible, children being separated from their parents. We sirens have no children, so we don't think about those things. But the humans…why must they be separated from their children like that? Children would be so much better with their parents' love than anything else, it seems."

His face paled slightly as he took a step back and nodded.

"You have a young child, don't you?" I asked.

He nodded. "Three."

"Three! What a tragedy you can't see them for the rest of the year! If only the king would hire the sirens to…oh, well, that's not my place to say I guess. It's between the king and the humans."

He seemed lost in thought for a moment, processing my words.

"So sorry to burden you," I said. "Please forget I said anything about it."

I turned my back on him as I left him in the hall, this time not hiding my smile behind my hand.

***

Some of the humans were that easy to get rid of. The others, however, were more stubborn.

As humans, Guardians were susceptible to charm-speak, however, not in the Den of Sirens. How could you be deceived when you already saw the world for what it truly was? But getting the Guardians outside the den was quite the task. They had their missions from the king, and they chose to loyally pursue them.

I didn't understand why. They were disloyal to each other so easily.

And that would be their downfall.

"I heard that Fredrick and Gerrald were given special orders by the king," I told a small group of Guardians. "A type of promotion, I wager."

"Promotion?" one of them asked. "I didn't realize that was an option."

"Of course, of course," I said. "There's always a system of hierarchy, you know. Spiritual and physical realms alike. Anyway, it's cause for celebration, isn't it?"

A couple of them nodded enthusiastically, while a couple others looked confused. That was fine. I didn't need all of them to question it. I just needed one of the stronger ones to start questioning. When the strong ones questioned, the others followed along just to appear as equally strong.

"I think you all work so hard," I added. "I do hope you all see promotions as well!"

To this, they gave a small cheer, and they talked of grand dreams until I couldn't stand the sound of their voices anymore.

As I stood to leave, Silvan, another one of the Guardians, approached me.

"Quick question," he said, hesitating to ask. "Would you tell me when there's an opportunity for a promotion?"

I tried to contain my smile. "Of course. I'd be happy to."

***

Over the course of a month, five of them asked me that. They were incredibly anxious to prove themselves worthy, and even more so, determined to prove themselves more worthy than the others.

"I've had more years in the military than you," Silvan said, puffing up his chest. "Be careful who you're talking to."

Alain wasn't interested in backing down. "And I've been in much higher stations. Years doesn't outrank rank."

"You're not my superior."

"Maybe I should be."

Juanell rolled her eyes. "Oh, men and their show of power. How boorish."

Neva, with her arms folded close to her, nodded in agreement. "Quite. It would be much better if it was just us women."

"You read my mind!" Juanell exclaimed.

They smiled at each other right before turning their heads with a sharp expression and a distasteful pucker of their lips.

It was easy to turn the humans on each other. Not that I really needed to set it up. If I waited long enough, they would do it on their own.

I looked down on the ring on my finger, its shine beginning to fade. I didn't want to wait any longer. It was time to get rid of these *special* humans.

I stepped forward into the room, folding my hands in front of myself and giving my best smile.

"Thank you all for coming," I said. "I can't believe only a few brave souls came to rise to the king's challenge."

"What are our orders?" Neva asked.

"There are demons on the island north of here," I said. "If they get too close to the Eros, they'll gain in power. They're a threat to the king himself."

They all nodded seriously. Such loyalty to the king. My chest burned as I thought about his loyalty to them as well.

"Are you ready?" I asked. "Because even though all of you will try, only one will succeed in reaching the top."

I smiled, knowing that person was going to be me.

***

The storm hit the same time the ship was out at sea.

Of course, the crew of Guardians had become so divided—so paranoid and competitive with one another—that they couldn't survive the storm. The ship hit the rocks before it reached the island, and they didn't come back to the surface.

But I had missed the one who had survived.

I missed the one who had swam back to the king and told him of what I had done.

And I hadn't expected to be held responsible for their division.

But I was.

The humans and I both caused our own destruction: me by instigating the divide, and them for following it. My job as a siren was to separate good from evil, but I had failed to do that even in my own soul.

And now that I was an incarnate—now that the king had declared me a Guardian—I was going to do my job correctly.

I put a hand on the sword at my side, fingering the handle. My hands were beginning to sweat the more and more I climbed the rocks toward the room where Henrik had been before. He had probably moved by now, but I could pick up clues to where he had been. I tore new earplugs and put them in, hearing only my own breathing as I walked through the hallways. There was no one here. Everything was silent.

Suddenly, someone yanked my hair. I fell to the ground, looking up to see sirens reach for my arms. I couldn't hear what they were saying because of the ear plugs, but I had a good idea of what they were doing as they dug their hands into my flesh and dragged me to the open part of the cave.

When I looked up again, I saw Henrik in the front of the vast room, his eyes yellow again, a paleness to his skin that tinted it blue.

He gave a command, and the sirens held me fast, plucking the earplugs from my ears.

The demon in Henrik's body smiled.

"Little *sssiren...*" the demon hissed. "Say hello to your new master."

CHAPTER 45

LOST

"Hello, master," I said.

I shook my head, wondering how my tongue could form such disgusting words on their own. The demon laughed, holding up the Eros. The stone had no particular shape, but the flaming swirls deep in the stone showed just how unique and powerful it truly was.

"Your mind may be yours for now," the demon said in his raspy voice, "but everything else *belongsss* to me."

I took a step back, but he shook his head sharply.

"Hold *ssstill*," he commanded.

My feet and knees suddenly locked, gluing me to the floor. He stepped in closer to meet me, a wild look of pleasure in his eyes. He then brought a hand to my cheek. I flinched, the coldness of his skin nothing like Henrik's touch at all.

"The question *isss*," he continued, "what should I do with you, exactly?"

I assumed he didn't want an answer.

"My host is rather conflicted about you." He twirled a bit of my hair in his fingers, watching me. "I offered to kill you, but he refused. I offered to make you ours, and he also refused. I have all this power, and he seems *ssso* reluctant to use it on you. I wonder why that is?"

"Because humans are used to being weak," I replied.

The demon's hand stopped. He looked at me, stunned for a brief moment, then laughed.

"I hardly expected that from you, *ssiren*," he said.

I shrugged. "You assumed I cared for them. You made a mistake."

He stared at me for a moment, then smiled as he tapped his finger against his nose.

"I saw the way you fought to protect my host in that cell." He grinned knowingly. "You have a special place for the *humansss.*"

"That was before I remembered being a siren."

He glanced at my back. "You don't have your wings."

"Regardless, I regained my memories this morning. Do you want to know why I became human?"

He didn't answer, but his eyes told me that he was curious.

"Because I murdered the Guardians," I finished.

He scratched his nose with a smile, obviously not believing me.

"Interesting story, *sssiren*," he said. "But I don't find it very credible."

"I don't care if you believe me or not. It's the truth either way. I never had any love for the humans. I never understood why the king would give them such care when the sirens had more power."

He nodded bitterly. "And the demons have more power than you both, yet somehow, we're the exiled *onesss.*"

"The rejected creations of the king," I added.

I could see the demon's eyes flicker. I knew I couldn't read him like I could Henrik, but I didn't have to. I knew enough about the evil in myself to know what I had just triggered.

"Yes, but we can *possesss* the humans," the demon replied. "With our power, we can destroy the coveted *blessed creationsss* of the king."

"Or you could just kill them."

The demon cocked his head, his eyes widening in a bit of surprise.

I raised an eyebrow at him. "That's what I did in my former life."

"And now you're part human," the demon chuckled. "*Yesss*, that seems like something the king would do as a punishment."

I attempted to keep as cool a face as possible, trying to remember all the different ways I once hated the humans myself.

"If you're looking to get rid of the humans," I said, "let me offer my services."

The demon laughed, his high pitch echoing off the walls.

"Offer?" he asked, holding up the Eros. "I don't need you to offer me anything. I can take whatever I want."

"But you can't control sirens outside of your sight, can you?"

The demon's eye twitched slightly, but he shrugged it away. "I can speak into their souls in ways that don't need the Eros. Charmspeak may seduce your victims, but demonspeak *penetratesss* their souls."

"It makes your victims insane. You lose control too easily."

"So you want to offer your charmspeak?"

"No," I said with a shake of my head. "I want to offer you my body."

There was a puzzled amusement in his eyes, a slight hesitation that showed he didn't hate the idea.

"What game are you trying to play with me, *sssiren*?" he asked. "You think I'm a fool?"

"Not at all. I think you're limited in your power. As am I. We'd be much more useful together, don't you think?"

He cocked his head to the side; so far, in fact, that I thought he was going to snap Henrik's neck. It was proof that he liked the idea more than he cared to admit.

A demon couldn't resist the offer for more power. That's why they were so entranced by the Eros in the first place. It was in their nature.

"Demons don't *possesss sssirens*," the demon finally replied, regaining composure.

"They can't possess *full* sirens," I said, "but have you tried the reincarnates?"

The demon looked me over, hesitating.

"I'll only offer this to you once, demon," I said as calmly as possible. "Possess me instead of Henrik."

Something deep flickered in his eyes for a moment, the yellow fading momentarily.

Henrik.

It was in a demon's nature to want power. It was in Henrik's nature to protect.

It was the one thing I could use to divide them.

The yellow returned to Henrik's eyes, signaling that he wasn't fighting hard enough. I would have to push them apart further.

"You would be the first to possess a knowing incarnate, wouldn't you?" I asked. "Think of how much easier it would be to control the humans and the sirens in such a way."

His tongue ran against his teeth. "You hate them that much?"

"I hate that the king loves them that much."

It wasn't difficult to act while saying that line. I remembered that part of myself far too clearly.

His eyes drifted down to the floor and then slowly crawled up my body.

Too slowly.

Jacques…Adrian…if you are planning to step in…

"There's only one reason why I don't believe you, little *sssiren*," the demon said, sharply licking his lips.

He grabbed my wrist, pulling it up to his face as he looked at the scars from the stone I had thrown to protect Adrian.

The demon smiled sharply.

"If you hated them so much," he said, "you wouldn't have *thisss* pretty little pattern in your palm, now would you?"

He twisted my wrist hard, almost breaking it. Paralyzed in pain, I could only scream and drop to my knees. With his other hand, he reached for my waist, ripping away my sword.

"You also wouldn't have been armed," the demon continued, his voice seeming more lathered and twisted.

"A lady can't carry a sword to protect herself amidst a war?"

The scabbard fell to the ground next to me, and shortly I felt the edge of the sword come to my throat.

"You might be more trouble than you're worth," the demon said. "*Perhapsss* I should kill you now before you try anything else."

The blade pressed hard into my neck. I looked up into his eyes, the yellow in them glowing bright.

But he wasn't the owner of those eyes.

"Henrik!" I called out. "Save me!"

I gasped as I felt the sword cut through the skin of my neck. My heart clenched in terror for a brief moment before I realized that the demon had let go of my hand and stumbled backward. I brought my hand to my neck on instinct, realizing that even though there was blood, the cut wasn't deep.

When I looked back up, the yellow in Henrik's eyes was completely gone.

Henrik huffed in pain, his sword arm dead at his side. I could now read him, the fear and anger in his eyes clear.

"What the hell are you thinking!" Henrik yelled, his voice now back to normal.

I came to my feet, keeping my hand on the cut on my neck as the blood seeped through my fingers.

"You have two choices," I said to him. "Either you let Jacques burn the demon out of you, or the demon comes after me. Which is it?"

He forced a painful laugh. "You foolish, ridiculous woman. You knew the demon couldn't resist that kind of offer."

I nodded. Even though I had no intentions of letting the demon possess me, I knew he wouldn't be able to resist the temptation. And I knew Henrik wouldn't allow it.

"And about the Guardians," he continued, "was that the truth?"

I nodded again. "I once was a full-blooded siren until I betrayed the king. In my jealousy and pain, I killed the Guardians. And in yours, you took on a demon."

He blinked. His fingers slowly gripping his sword and then releasing it again.

I stepped forward, continuing. "The king, however, has given me another chance. And in return, I'm giving you one as well."

He hesitated for a moment, then screamed as he grabbed his head in pain.

"Dammit!" he snarled, his voice halfway between normal and demonic. "You need to get out, Esmeralda!"

He slipped the Eros in his pocket, gripping on to the sword with both hands as he kept it toward the ground.

His eyes flickered yellow, then back to brown.

"You need to go," he said again. He lifted his head to look me in the eyes, fear and pain weaved in them once more. "Because when I'm around you…I can't decide if I'm getting stronger or weaker."

The yellow consumed his eyes again. He held up his sword and lunged for my throat.

CHAPTER 46

POWERLESS

I dodged the blade as the demon struck for my throat. I picked up a rock as I jumped out of the way, throwing it at the demon's head. It stunned him just long enough for me to run to a mound of rocks and climb over. I dropped behind it, my heart lodged in my throat.

I had to stay out of his sight, or at the very least, block out the sound of his voice. The moment the demon had me in his sights and reached into his pocket, it was over.

Jacques, where are you?

"Come out, little *sssiren*," the demon hissed.

I felt a pull in my muscles to stand, but I didn't obey. Since he couldn't see me, I was outside of his total command. I scrambled to tear off another piece of my sleeve, momentarily hoping that Adrian wouldn't be angry at me for ruining his shirt in so many ways.

I had barely jammed the cloth in my ears with my shaking hands when the demon had jumped onto the wall. He looked over at me as he hung off the top, his lips moving in a command I couldn't hear.

I leapt to my feet and sped around the mound of

rocks, hopping across the creek of holy water that snaked through the room. The room was too wide to hide well, but not flat enough to be caught so easily. I hoped.

The demon was quick on my heels. He must have realized that his words were not working, because he stopped talking and swung his blade at me instead. I was able to dodge at the first swing, but he was much faster than I was.

He jumped in front of me, slicing at my side. I jumped back, but not fast enough. The blade cut my hip, and I stumbled to the ground. When I looked up, the demon had the blade raised to run me through.

I couldn't even suck in a breath to scream.

Suddenly, the yellow disappeared from Henrik's eyes and he stumbled back. He looked into my eyes, mouthing two words that I couldn't hear, but completely understood despite the silence.

"Fight back."

His left hand ripped the sword from his right and threw it at my feet. It hit my feet right as his eyes turned back to yellow.

I leapt for the sword. The demon spoke again, but I didn't hear it, and he reached for the sword hanging at Henrik's side.

When he swung, I blocked. Even though the demon was the one wielding the sword, it was still Henrik's body, and the demon used the same moves that Henrik had taught me.

But how could I fight back? I could keep myself alive, but in order to win the fight, I would have to...

The demon stepped forward with a jab, and I stepped to the side to avoid it. I sliced through his shoulder, gasping in horror as I watched the blood seep through Henrik's clothes. But his movement slowed momentarily, and I knew I had to slice through his sword arm in order to keep both of us alive.

I couldn't kill him. I just couldn't.

I went for his arm again, but he jumped back and blocked. My ears were still plugged, but I could feel the cloth in my right ear slipping. I didn't have a chance to put it back.

The demon took the opportunity of my distraction to step in from the side and drive his shoulder into mine. His power was far beyond that of a normal human body, and the hit sent me sliding across the stone floor. I screamed as the floor ripped open my skin, my ripped clothes brushing against and stinging the open wounds.

But most importantly, the earplugs had fallen out.

"Stand still, *sssiren*," the demon commanded.

Something pulled me to my feet, even though I knew that without the command I wouldn't have been able to stand at all. I tried to catch my breath, watching the demon hold the Eros in his fingers.

"Last chance, first mate," the demon said. "You wanted to control her, the *sssame* way she controlled you. The same way *she'sss* controlling you now."

"I'm not controlling him," I forced out. "You're the one possessing him."

"I give him power." The demon smiled. "You take it away. Which of *usss* has the better offer?"

I shook my head. "Henrik, don't listen to him. I would never—"

"Quiet!" Henrik suddenly screamed, the yellow from his eyes disappearing completely.

My mouth tightened, my tongue frozen against the roof of my mouth. Henrik huffed out his breath, turning to face me.

"I can't stand either one of you," he said, dropping the sword from his hand. "I haven't been able to control my own self since I agreed to getting on that damn ship."

His eyes raised to mine, the pain in them clear.

"Why am I even protecting you?" he muttered, seemingly to himself. "How have you had such a hold on me since the beginning?"

He stepped in closer. All I could do was meet his eyes, unable to move or speak, but able to read the deep emotions in his eyes.

He held up the Eros, the crimson light washing over his face. He looked at it, then at me.

"You have no choice but to follow my command as long as I hold this, right?" he asked. "How does it feel to be controlled in the same way you controlled us?"

I couldn't speak, but I shook my head, desperately begging with my eyes for Henrik to listen. He didn't seem to be paying attention. His eyes were piercing through mine, but he didn't see me at all.

"You know, I used to dream of you after we talked under the stars," he said, his hand coming up to my hair. "Was that your control too?"

I shook my head again, his fingers gently brushing against my neck as his fingers followed my hair to the tips. His touch was warm, nothing like when his demon had been touching me in a similar manner.

"Or the way my heart raced when you walked by?" he asked. "Was that my feelings for you? Or you controlling my emotions?"

I froze, not knowing the answer.

"Or when I thought that Jacques was your fiancé and I was insanely jealous whenever he was within ten feet of you. Was that my true jealousy?"

My heart broke with every word he spoke, his voice getting weaker with each word.

"Was it?" he asked softly.

When I couldn't answer, rage took over his face.

"Tell me!" he yelled.

"I don't know!" I yelled back, jaw suddenly loosened.

He clenched his jaw as I spoke.

"I didn't even know what I was until the night before the mutiny," I said. "I just thought people generally liked me. I never thought in a thousand years that I could… Henrik, believe me, if there was one person I would never try to manipulate, it's y—"

"How can I even believe you?" he replied. "I've watched men and women far less powerful than you give over their souls in a moment for greed. I've done it. I can't even say that I regret it. So even if you didn't want power before, that doesn't mean that now you hate it."

I swallowed, looking into his hollow eyes. "You're right, I don't hate the idea of power. I hate the idea that you can't stand me because of it."

Silence drifted between us, the tension in Henrik's muscles getting tighter. He looked at me from the side, head cocked, thoughts visibly racing through his mind.

"I don't hate you," he finally said. "But…I want to."

He came in closer, wrapping an arm around me and pulling me tight against him. When I put a hand to his chest to separate us, I felt his pulse race against my palm.

He was controlling me, and yet, he was the one affected.

He leaned into my ear, shallow, painful breaths coming from his lips.

"Touch me," he whispered.

My heart dropped to my stomach, but I had no choice but to obey. My hands moved against my own command, running slowly up his chest and across his shoulders. When my fingers reached his arms, he leaned his head against mine, his breath hitting my cheek. He grabbed one of my hands in his, and I could feel my hand twitching to try and continue its command. He slowly pressed his lips against my cheek, then leaned down further, his lips coming to my neck.

"Henrik," I gasped, "what are you doing?"

"Even if it isn't real…" he whispered, "I still want to feel it."

Words got stuck in my throat as he slowly pressed his lips against my neck again. It wasn't a possessive kiss or a demonic kiss but the kiss of a broken man who had lost everything.

He suddenly stopped and pulled back, his hands raised beside his head in surrender. I thought briefly that it was his moral compass that had stopped him, but then I saw Jacques behind him, the tip of the sword in his hand disappearing into Henrik's back.

"What a pathetic use of power," Jacques said flatly. "If you're going to be greedy, at least have some high ambition with it. Now step back slowly."

With defeated look, Henrik stepped back with his arms still raised. His warmth left me, even though it probably wasn't his real warmth in the first place.

"What took you so long?" I snapped at Jacques.

He scoffed. "*You* said you could get them to separate — Oh never mind. Captain, grab the ungrateful girl, will you?"

I turned just as someone took my hand in his and pulled me away from them both.

Adrian.

"Come on, Princess Blood," Adrian said. "You belong on my ship."

I looked over my shoulder at Henrik, his face pale with anger. When Adrian squeezed my hand and pulled me forward, I followed, not knowing what else to do.

"Don't go with him!" Henrik's voice shouted across the cavern.

My feet planted in the ground, nearly throwing me over. Adrian caught me before I could hit the ground face first. Holding me, he turned to his brother.

"You're better than this!" Adrian yelled to Henrik. "The brother I had would never use his power to hold a woman captive."

Henrik's breath shattered as he exhaled. "She held me captive first."

I shut my eyes, trying to keep out the pain.

"She's innocent and you know it," Adrian replied. "Don't do this. Don't take your revenge for me out on her."

My eyes shot open, looking at Adrian. He wasn't looking at me.

"I was the one who got you kicked out of the king's navy," Adrian continued. "I was the one to ruin the family name. Your abilities were a gift. I had none, and all I could do was make a reputation for myself in the only way I knew how: by destroying everything."

His hand squeezed mine again as he tried to steady his breath.

"You made me captain because you had hope for me, even when I had none for myself," Adrian continued. "You thought the responsibility would make me honorable, didn't you?"

Henrik didn't answer.

"But taking care of criminals, pirates, and the scum of the ship didn't make me honorable. Taking care of Esmeralda did."

I stared at the profile of his face, desperately wanting him to turn toward me so I could see if he was telling his true feelings.

But something in the way he gripped my hand told me that he was.

"Let her go, Henrik," Adrian said. "You can hate me more if you want, but at least let me keep you from destroying yourself."

I couldn't bear to look over my shoulder at Henrik, but I felt him staring at my back.

"Also," Jacques added, breaking the tension with his apathy, "remember that I have a sword in your back and your little rock doesn't affect me in the slightest."

There was another pause. Then Henrik huffed out a breath.

"Go then," he said. "Both of you get out."

The tension in my feet released, and Adrian pulled my hand to take me away from Henrik and Jacques. I couldn't look back, and I could barely raise my head to look at Adrian either.

"No, don't you—!" I heard Jacques yell.

There was an ear-splitting streak once more, shaking the den. Right as we turned to look at the sound, a rush of air blew past us. Adrian yelped right before letting me go, stumbling back with a hiss as he dropped to his knees on the ground.

There was a sword completely through in Adrian's side…with Henrik as its wielder.

There was a cruel, murderous glint in Henrik's yellow eyes that flickered out the moment Adrian twisted in pain. In the pause, Adrian grabbed the sword and pulled it from his side, right before collapsing completely on the ground.

Henrik's eyes flickered back to their original color, his face drained in terror.

"No!" Henrik howled, coming to his brother's side.

He rolled Adrian over, pulling apart Adrian's shirt to look at the blood streaming from his side. Adrian's eyes were only half open, his breath getting shorter and shorter.

"Adrian…" Henrik whispered, his hands shaking. "I couldn't stop him…I'd never…"

Adrian hissed again. "I'm surprised you didn't do it sooner, to be honest."

Henrik placed his hands on Adrian's wound as blood gushed out of his side.

"No! You don't deserve death!" Henrik replied. "You're my responsibility…you're my family."

Jacques stumbled forward, clutching the back of his neck. "Goddamn demons. I should put a sword through you for throwing me halfway across the—"

"Help me," Henrik begged, looking up at Jacques. "I beg of you, help me save him."

Jacques sighed with gritted teeth before glancing at me. He then looked back at Henrik.

"There's only one option," Jacques said.

He reached into his pocket, pulling out a small lighter. Henrik swallowed, flinching as Jacques lit it.

"Are you sure?" Jacques asked Henrik.

Henrik looked at Adrian, who was writhing in pain, blood gushing from his side onto the marble floor. He then looked back at Jacques.

Henrik nodded. "I'll do anything."

Jacques leaned down, grabbing Henrik by the arm.

"Then grit your teeth," Jacques said. "Because this is *really* going to hurt."

CHAPTER 47

HEALED

"This is hardly worth the time," Hugo said, his arms folded across his chest.

King Melchior gently held up his hand to quiet his left-hand advisor, his eyes focused on Adrian's body across the stone slab in front of him. With the Eros returned to the throne, the king had recovered instantly.

We couldn't say the same about Adrian.

Adrian had completely lost consciousness, his skin paled and discolored. His faint heartbeat was the only reassurance that he wasn't completely dead, but the way the color had drained from his face, we could all tell that there were only moments before his end.

All I could do was hold his hand, much like I did when the king was ill. There was nothing else I could do, and it made tears stream down my face as I turned to the king.

"Father…" I whispered quietly.

He dimly smiled at the title and gave a small nod, then motioned for me to step aside. I hesitated until Luc put his hand on my shoulder and pulled me close to his side. The king approached Adrian and put a hand on his chest.

"You returned my daughter to me and protected her from the demon that tried to destroy her," King Melchior said. "You assisted in restoring freewill to my creations, and so—this once—I will restore your body."

There was a teal glow from the king's hand that weaved deep into Adrian's side. The blood in his clothes disappeared, and the torn threads mended. For the first time in what seemed like hours, Adrian took a deep breath, but he didn't open his eyes.

The king took a step back, his face still solemn.

"Bring me his brother," the king commanded, his voice void of any emotion.

Jacques stepped forward, pulling Henrik forward by his arm. Henrik didn't attempt to stand straight, but instead, leaned to one side, his shirt burned and loosely hanging from his body. He kept his head bowed, but I couldn't tell if it was from pain or guilt.

"You've burned out the demon?" the king asked Jacques.

Jacques nodded. "Henrik's demon has been exiled, and the boy can become a Judge should you deem him as pure."

The king nodded. "You've done well, Jacques."

"Yes, well…I always repay my debts."

There was a shared look between them, but it only lasted for a breath of a moment. The king then turned his eyes toward Henrik. Henrik hung his head lower.

"Look at me, Henrik," the king commanded, his voice unreadable.

Henrik slowly raised his head, his jaw clenched tight, his eyes showing nothing but deep exhaustion.

"Yes, Your Majesty," he croaked out.

"You allowed a demon to possess you in order to gain power. I cannot overlook this."

"Yes, Your Majesty," Henrik replied, bowing his head. "I accept any punishment you command."

The king took a long breath. "You will be tried. Should you survive the Trials, you will work for me permanently. I saved your brother's life and spared yours. In return, you will hand that life over to me."

Henrik looked at Adrian, his eyes glossing over.

"Yes, Your Majesty," he said. "For my brother's life, you have my loyalty."

Henrik bowed his head out of respect, but failed to raise it, perhaps from pure exhaustion. The king cocked his head slightly to the side, a smile pulling gently at the corner of his lips.

"Come on," Jacques said, pulling on Henrik's arm. "Let's get this trial over with. I would say, 'Good luck,' but if you survive, then I have to train your ass for the rest of my life. So either *you* get hell, or I do."

Henrik said nothing, taking one long glance at his brother as he walked with Jacques toward the door. His eyes then lifted to mine for a brief moment, just long enough for me to read his shattered heart.

I smiled at him through the tears in my eyes and nodded, letting him know I understood.

He disappeared through the doors.

Luc squeezed my shoulder.

"You want to go, don't you?" he asked.

I chewed my lip, trying not to let my tears spill over.

"I'm scared to," I admitted.

Luc turned me toward him, bringing his soft long fingers to my cheek with a comforting smile on his face.

"You saw the grief in his heart, didn't you?" Luc asked. "That's a good sign. It's the ones with no grief that you should be worried about."

***

Ten days had passed.

None of us had planned on staying this long, but none of us had the heart or strength for sailing. The king had not spoken to me in all that time, but I knew he was preoccupied with more important things, and I had learned from my past mistakes of barging in unannounced. So I waited until he summoned me. Which he eventually did.

I made my way down the hall, to the throne room, stopping when I saw a familiar figure.

Henrik was in front of the throne room door, standing against the wall on duty but completely lost in thought. His eyes were glossed over as he looked at the empty space in front of him. He didn't hear me as I stepped in closer.

I watched him, waiting for him to look up. He looked completely different in the robe of a Judge, the uniform of the servant of the king. When Jacques wore that uniform, it looked like the leader of a cult. But when Henrik wore it, he looked like an honorable servant of the king.

He was meant to stand there, in those robes, from the beginning. I was sure of it.

He blinked, suddenly realizing I was there.

"Esmeralda…"

Henrik sharply straightened, but then stopped and grabbed his side in pain. I rushed over to hold his arm, leaning him back against the wall.

"Does it still hurt?" I asked.

Henrik pulled up his shirt slightly to show the blood-red burns in his skin. He tapped on it, hissing.

"It's my punishment," he said. "I deserved hell. Instead, I got the burning."

I rolled my eyes as I leaned against the wall next to him. "You sound just like your brother, demanding punishment when you've been offered grace."

Henrik's head lowered. "I put a sword through my own brother. I should have been sent to eternal punishment."

"But now the demon is gone, Adrian is healing, and you've already been tried." I took his hand. "I knew you were pure. I knew the moment I saw you."

His fingers interlaced in mine, and he squeezed my hand.

"I shouldn't have been saved," he whispered.

I put my other hand on his shoulder, meeting his eyes.

"Me neither," I replied.

He looked at me for a long moment, before turning his head back down toward the floor.

"I don't even know how to begin to apologize to you," he said, not looking me in the eye. "My demon had convinced me that you were controlling me the whole time on purpose. But after talking with the others, I know now that you were telling me the truth."

I shook my head sympathetically. "You had no way of knowing. And if we're being honest, the old me would have controlled you in any way she could. I spent multiple lifetimes paying for my crimes." I looked at the door of the throne room and swallowed. "And now, it finally comes to an end."

Henrik looked over his shoulder at the door. "You've been summoned."

I nodded.

"After you walk through those doors, you won't walk back out of them as a human, will you?"

I pressed my lips together and exhaled through my nose. "That's the plan."

There was a pause.

"Perhaps it's for the best," he whispered, seemingly to himself. He turned back to look at me, straightening. "I'll be here to serve you and the sirens either way, Esmeralda."

He clenched his jaw, his eyes searching mine. I could see his strength returning, the honorable first mate in my presence once again.

I leaned in and kissed his cheek with gratitude, giving him a knowing smile before going through the king's doors.

"Our heroine has arrived!" Vito cried, clapping his hands.

"Stop that," Hugo said, folding his arms. "It's already been more than a week."

"Should we only celebrate for such a short time?" Vito replied.

"We don't need to celebrate someone finally doing their job *correctly*."

I stopped listening to them, my eyes falling onto King Melchior as he stood from his throne.

He smiled warmly as he stood, and I couldn't hold myself back. I ran to his arms, embracing him tight. He chuckled.

"I missed you too, daughter," he said.

Hugo clicked his tongue. "She's losing her sense of place again."

"At least she's learned how to return her father's love now," Vito countered.

The king cupped my face warmly and kissed my forehead, stepping back.

"You summoned me, Your Majesty?" I asked.

He nodded. "I heard you had a request for me."

I nodded, trying to muster up my courage. "I did."

"Ask it, then."

I took a deep breath. "I've decided… I want my wings."

Vito audibly gasped. Hugo audibly rolled his eyes.

"Our siren wishes to return home!" Vito cheered. "How wonderful!"

"This means I have to start training her all over again," Hugo returned. "It was such a pain the first time."

The king raised his hand at his right- and left-hand men as they chattered. They went silent. He looked at me for a long moment, before opening his mouth to speak.

"My answer," King Melchior said, "is no."

My heart dropped into my stomach. The warmth on his face didn't fade, making me wonder if I had heard correctly.

"Forgive me," I said, confused. "What did you say, Your Majesty?"

"I decline your request," he said. "I can't give you your wings. Not now."

I blinked, trying to sort through my thoughts. "But I thought—"

He put his hands on my shoulders. "There is a man who needs you to return to him. As I have waited for you for decades, he has been waiting for you for months. His heart will not be at ease until you are home. I understand his anguish."

I gripped the king's hand, suddenly realizing that he was sending me away.

"But, I can't leave," I said. "I want to be with you."

He chuckled. "You'll return to me in due time. But I know that *his* heart will not settle in the afterlife until he has seen you again. And I know that regret will plague you for the rest of your eternal life if you don't see him."

I suddenly thought of my earthly father's face, tears building in my eyes.

I missed him so much. I had forgotten how much I missed him.

"You need to return to the human world quickly," he said. "The window of time is closing."

"Why?" I asked, looking up at him. "Is something wrong?"

He took a deep breath. "I'll have Rhys take you back. The ship won't be fast enough."

"What's—"

"I will wait for you to return to us when it's time," he continued. "But I need you to trust me, Astraea."

I stopped speaking, realizing that he wasn't going to tell me anything more. I nodded, understanding it as his command.

"Yes, Your Majesty," I said, my heart slowly breaking. "I will return to the human world."

He brought me in for another embrace, his warm arms telling me without words that he didn't want me to leave either.

"No matter where you go," he said softly, "I will wait here for you to return to me. You'll always be mine, Astraea. And I never abandon my own."

CHAPTER 48

RETURN

"So are you two siblings?"

Adrian looked between Luc and me as he leaned against his crutch. There had been awkward silence between the three of us as we waited for Jacques to come to the docks, and apparently this was the question Adrian decided to use to break the ice.

Luc and I instantly cringed.

"No," I replied, scrunching my nose.

"That would be like saying a desk and a chair are related because they both came from the same carpenter," Luc added. "King Melchior created everything, but the spiritual world doesn't have same family dynamics as the human world."

"But you can marry, yes?" Adrian asked.

Luc raised an eyebrow at him.

"I heard it somewhere," Adrian said with a smirk.

I looked down at the ring finger on my left hand, remembering the ring Renaldo gave me so many lifetimes ago. My heart sank a bit, remembering that he was gone, and that I was still betrothed to Jacques's father as a human.

"We can," I said, "but we don't."

"Our feelings come second to our duties," Luc added. "It's in our design."

"And they can't go against it, no matter how much they want to," a third voice cut in.

Jacques approached us.

"Sirens are controlled by duty," Jacques continued, "in the same ways that demons are controlled by desire and humans are controlled by emotion. That's why a siren going against their duties is so harshly punished."

"Seems rather unfair to be at the mercy of responsibility," Adrian said.

"Is it?" Jacques asked. "Humans have created both passion and crimes of passion. They're completely chaotic, inside and out, for better or worse. Without the judgment of the sirens, you would devour yourselves."

"And without the Judges?" Adrian asked, his eyes glossing over as he said it.

Jacques paused before answering.

"The Judges keep the balance," Jacques said, "so none of the king's creatures are lost to our own chaos. Your brother will be a strong enough Judge once I can break him of his self-hatred."

Adrian chuckled bitterly. "I think he's had that his whole life. Is it possible to cure him of it?"

Jacques looked down at his hand as he stretched it and clenched it slowly.

"It's normal for all Judges," he replied, his voice softer than normal. "Because of our demons, we can see the evil in ourselves easily."

Jacques met my eyes and cleared his throat.

"It's time to go," he said flatly. "We need to go now if we want to get there before sunset. Luc, are you ready?"

Luc nodded. "I'm ready if Astraea is."

I nodded. There was a tension in my shoulders as I took a deep breath, knowing that the king wouldn't have denied me my wings unless there was something urgent that needed to be seen to in the human world.

My hand came to my necklace, praying that my father was all right.

Jacques turned to Adrian with a sigh.

"I suppose since your brother is now under my command," Jacques said, "I'll have to see more of your face from now on."

Adrian smiled and winked. "Looking forward to it, mate."

Jacques frowned and walked off. Adrian turned to me.

"Shall we say yet another goodbye, princess?" he asked me. "We've said so many of them."

I couldn't even bring words to my throat as I looked at him. He leaned against his crutch with a cocky smile, as if he hadn't almost died while helping us. I couldn't say anything. I could only wrap my arms around his neck in gratitude. He embraced me tight with one arm.

"Whether or not it's from a spell," he whispered in my ear, "a piece of me will always love you for saving me."

He released me from the embrace, a proud smile on his lips. Luc cleared his throat. Adrian met his eyes and took a step back, his cockiness slightly dimming.

"It was quite the adventure," Adrian said with a huff of air. "I look forward to our next goodbye."

He smiled. I smiled back.

I looked over his shoulder toward the entrance. He turned to look back with me, sighing.

"I told him to come," Adrian said. "But he said didn't have the courage to look all of you in the eye."

I nodded, understanding.

"Then tell him that I look forward to seeing him when I return to the den," I said.

Adrian nodded. "I will."

"Perhaps I will see you as well," I said. "So don't forget me, Captain."

"Not even if I wanted to, princess."

I smiled, the bittersweet reality being that he would forget me eventually.

Before I could say another word, I was pulled into someone's arms and swept off my feet into the air. Luc looked at Adrian coldly, holding me close to his chest as his wings pulled us off the ground.

"You too, Luc?" Adrian said with a laugh. "I suppose that's understandable."

"She was mine first," Luc replied. "I mean…she was ours first."

Adrian chuckled. "Sure. That's what you meant."

Luc grunted, going higher into the air. I tightened my arms around his neck as we flew toward the den entrance.

"You're being petty," I scolded.

"Just because I let him live doesn't mean I like him," he returned.

There was silence between us; Jacques and his siren carrier came up from behind. We bolted from the docks into the caverns before the den, zigging and zagging until we made it out the other side into the sunlight.

I automatically shielded my eyes, the fresh sunlight feeling completely new and foreign. My back and my heart both ached as the den got farther and farther away, turning into a small spec in the middle of the ocean.

I gripped Luc's shirt, but not from fear of falling. It was simply the only thing I had to hang on to, to endure the pain.

"Will you come back to us?" Luc asked softly, rising higher into the air.

I heard the pain in his voice before I saw it in his eyes. I nodded.

"I'll come back to you," I said. "You know I will."

He pressed his lips together and nodded.

"Somehow even knowing that," he said, "still doesn't make it any easier for me to let you go."

***

The sun had just set by the time we arrived back in the city.

It was strange to think that the home I had grown up in as a human child and the home I was created in were only one day's flight apart. It had taken months by ship, but with Luc's wings, it had taken only hours. The world suddenly felt a bit smaller, which made my heart ache less.

Maybe it wouldn't be so difficult to go between homes.

The city lights spread out below us, taking my breath away. I had only seen the lanterns at eye level, and to see them from the eyes of the birds was a completely different experience. I fell in love with the city all over again, the ache in my heart overpowering the ache between my shoulders.

"Where is your home?" Luc asked.

I hesitated, realizing that he wasn't asking me a deep question, but a practical one. I tried to figure out the lay of the land. I soon saw the landmark closest to my home: the city library. I pointed to it and Luc swept down. Guiding him closer and closer to the house, my heart clenched—nearly stopping—as we reached the balcony.

He fluttered down to the balcony, his bare feet barely touching the floor as his wings fluttered beside us. I looked over Luc's shoulder, seeing that Jacques and his siren were not too far behind.

Luc kept his arms around me as he set my feet on the floor. There was a tense pause, a hesitation as he formed his words.

"Before he gets here," Luc said, nodding back to Jacques, "I want you to know that however long it takes, I'll wait for you to come home to me."

He spelled out his words slowly, as if each word was cutting him bit by bit as he spoke. I knew it was painful for him to let me go; he had let go of so many people. And now that I knew who I was, I didn't want to let go of him either.

I wrapped my arms around him in an embrace. "Somehow we always find each other, Luc. As sirens…as humans…I'll always find a way back to you."

He gave me a small smile, the warmth of the cook onboard the *Quetzalcoatl* pouring through his eyes. He leaned forward, placing a single kiss on my temple and giving me another warm embrace.

Jacques and his siren landed next to us. Luc slowly released me as Jacques looked at us, unamused.

But he was never amused at anything anyway, so I wasn't bothered.

"Thank you," Jacques said to his siren carrier. He turned back to Luc. "And to you as well."

Luc nodded.

"This won't be the last we see you," Jacques said to Luc.

I raised an eyebrow. "We?"

Jacques raised his eyebrow back at me. "What? Did you think I was just going to abandon you? I have to go back to train Henrik eventually. I assumed you'd go with me."

He said it as if I had already decided on it.

I smiled. "You understand me better than I do, it seems."

"The sirens may read souls," he replied, "but I have the gift of being able to read you quite easily."

He almost smiled, but then seemed to think better of it. I was distracted by Luc's hand on mine and turned to his sad eyes.

"I have to leave now, little dove," he said. "Remember your promise."

I nodded. "I may forget the lives before this one, but my heart hasn't forgotten its home."

Luc extended his wings with a painful smile, lifting himself in the air with the other siren. He gave me a slow wink, shooting in the air and flying toward the stars. I wrapped my arms around me, the wind of his wings fanning over my skin.

Jacques stepped in to meet me, a softness in his eyes. He pointed to the sky, just under the moon.

"Do you see that star?" he asked.

I squinted, focusing my eyes on a faint star under the moon, to the right.

"Yes, I see it," I replied.

"That's the Den of Sirens," he said.

He lowered his hand, not saying anything else. But I already knew his intentions.

"Thank you, Jacques," I said, putting a hand on his arm in gratitude.

He glanced at it for a brief moment, before his eyes settled on my neck. It took me a moment to realize what he was staring at.

"That's a beautiful necklace," Jacques said.

I touched my mother's necklace, looking at the deep green gem as it reflected in the moonlight.

"Do you know what emerald means?" he asked.

I shook my head.

"Rebirth," he said. "Suitable for you… Mademoiselle *Esmeralda*."

Then, truly, he smiled.

There was a clattering from my room as the door swung open. Lina burst through the door, huffing as she walked in.

"Lina!" I yelled, running to meet her.

Her hand flew over her mouth, a cry of joy and fear coming from her throat. She took me into a motherly embrace, practically sobbing as she spoke.

"I thought you were a ghost!" she cried into my hair. "Why didn't you come to the doo— Oh, never mind it. Never mind it! You're home and that's all that matters! How did you—?"

Jacques took this as his cue to step in from the balcony, standing tall. Lina nodded to acknowledge him.

"So it was you," she said. "You kept your promise. Thank you, my boy. Thank you."

It was the first time I had seen Jacques blush.

"You're welcome, Lina," he said.

Lina grabbed my face frantically. "Oh, but we can't waste another moment. Come! You must see your father immediately before it's too late!"

My stomach sank. "Too late? Lina what's happened?"

Lina fanned herself then grabbed my hand. "Oh, dear girl. His heart couldn't take you being gone. I'm afraid it's given out on him completely. If he doesn't see you right away, maybe he won't recover."

CHAPTER 49

CEREMONIES

I looked at myself in the mirror as Lina straightened the train of my white gown. Her frown was heavier than mine.

"Is the doctor coming today?" I asked her, breaking the uncomfortable silence between us.

She sighed. "Yes, yes. He said he would come check on your father today. He seems to be gaining his strength back these days. My dear, with that in mind, are you sure you want—"

"I've made my decision," I said firmly.

Lina nodded solemnly, and it broke my heart to see her so disappointed. Even though she had been the one to encourage my arranged marriage in the beginning, she hadn't stopped sighing and frowning since I actually agreed to it.

When I had seen Father for the first time after returning, he was pale and cold. I hadn't seen him so weak since Mother had passed. I had never known that his heart had started to fail him since the day of her funeral.

That's why his business was failing.

And that's why he had betrothed me to Monsieur De Villiers.

Now that I had returned, Father was healing, but I couldn't bring myself to give him any bad news lest his heart failed completely. He was already teetering on death, and I couldn't be what sent him over the edge. Regardless of my life before this one, I still loved Father and Mother dearly, and it was still painful to lose them both.

So I agreed to the marriage.

I knew now how small my human life was compared to my eternal one, and I was willing to make this sacrifice for a short time. Maybe I would be freed at death and put in another body. Or perhaps, when I was widowed and my future children grown, I could go back to the den.

I would have to think about the long-term later. I could only think of keeping my father alive now.

My room was scattered with white veils, ribbons, shoes, and pearls that belonged to my mother. I kept my hand on her necklace, praying that she would guide me through.

I didn't know how much strength I had.

Knock, knock, knock.

Lina and I both turned to a face I hadn't expected to see.

My betrothed.

"Mademoiselle Esmeralda and Madame Lina," Captain De Villiers said, tipping his hat at us individually. "Have I caught you at a bad time?"

"Of course not, Monsieur De Villiers," I said. "You're always welcome."

I stepped away from the mirror to face him. He gave me a quick glance and a warm smile.

"You look quite lovely," he said sincerely. "I was wondering if I might speak with you, my dear."

I nodded to him in agreement and motioned for Lina to give us some privacy. She shut the door behind us. Monsieur De Villiers took off his hat and coat, placing them on the chair next to him.

I had only met with Monsieur De Villiers a few times since I had returned, but never alone. He always brought doctors with him to look after Father, and our conversations had been nothing but small talk with my father in his bedroom.

Monsieur De Villiers had been paying for all of father's medical expenses, according to Lina. He never breathed a word of it, and he never made me feel like I owed him.

"I wanted to see how you were feeling," Monsieur De Villiers said.

"I have nothing to complain about," I replied. "My father is beginning to recover, and I'm home once more."

He nodded in thought. "Of course, of course. But I was thinking more of your feelings toward this wedding, my dear."

I tried not to show my shaky breath as I exhaled. I lifted my skirts and sat on the bench next to the window, unsure of how to answer. He stepped forward and sat down next to me.

"Arrangements like ours are not uncommon," he said, "and your father thought the best way to protect you was to make this arrangement. He knew his health was failing, and he couldn't find any other means to provide for you."

I gripped my hands in my dress, frustration pricking the back of my eyes. "Why didn't he tell me he was sick? I would have—"

"You would have worked yourself to the bone in his place," he finished for me. "Your father would have become even further ill with guilt if that were to happen, and he would have sentenced himself as a failure as a father. I understand him. I already feel like a lifetime isn't long enough to make up for my lack of care regarding Jacques and his mother, and I would despise myself should anything happen to my two daughters."

He folded his hands in front of him, turning to look at me.

"That's why I agreed to this arrangement," he continued. "If, at the very least, I could put the old fool at ease for a few moments. His health was already failing, and I couldn't refuse him, as it would only aggravate his condition. But understand that I had no intention of forcing you to marry me."

I looked up at him in confusion. He smiled warmly.

"I intend to take care of you and your father, with or without this marriage," he said. "Your father would have refused me if I simply offered my resources, so I agreed to his proposal instead."

I laughed ironically. "It seems we're quite similar in our thinking. We both agreed to this in order to spare Father pain."

There was a pause between us.

"But there's no point in causing more pain for *you*, my dear," he said quietly. "I will be happy to take care of you as my wife, should that be what you want. If it isn't, then I won't take your rejection personally."

He smiled again. I suddenly felt overwhelmed, tears forming at the back of my eyes. I sniffed them back, trying to keep my composure.

"I'm grateful for your kindness," I said. "And thank you for being so considerate of both my father and myself."

He nodded firmly. "Your father saved my life. On many occasions, out on the sea and on land. I owe him as much."

He came to his feet and walked back toward the entrance of the room, picking up his jacket and hanging it over his arm.

"And for the record," he said, "your father never officially announced our engagement. It won't be difficult to brush it off as a simple rumor."

He gave an innocent shrug before putting on his hat.

"You can let me know your decision at any time," he said, putting on his coat. "But now, I'm going to go to my physician and request that he take care of your father exclusively. So put your mind at ease, hmm?"

Overwhelmed by emotions, I came to my feet and ran to him, throwing my arms around him in gratitude.

"Thank you, Captain," I said sincerely.

He gave me a light pat on the shoulder as he chuckled. "It's my pleasure, my dear. Wherever your happiness lies, I want you to go to it. I'll watch over you and your father no matter where your feet want to go."

He gave me a quick nod of encouragement, breaking away from our embrace to go out the door.

All the tension in my body released in a single wave, sending me to my knees on the ground. I shuddered, not sure whether to laugh or cry. Instead, all I could do was breathe heavily into my hands, grateful to anyone who could hear how hard my heart was beating.

I was free.

There was no one holding me here. There was no one holding any power over my life.

But now that I was free, what would I do? Where would I go?

Where was my happiness?

JACQUES'S ENDING

Before I could even come back to my feet, the door swung open. I expected it to be Monsieur De Villiers again, but I was even more surprised to see his son instead.

More frantic than I had ever seen him, at that.

He looked at me, his eyes drilling right through mine. He didn't say anything right away, looking me over with intense interest. Perhaps it was the wedding gown that had him stunned.

He shut the door. I forced myself to my feet to meet him.

"Jacques…" I said, my mouth dry at the intense gaze he was giving me. "What are you—"

"I've decided that this is unacceptable," he said, stepping in to meet me. "I won't allow you to marry my father."

"Jacques, your father just—"

Before I could finish, his lips met mine. A rough hand came to the back of my head, pressing me closer against him, and a gasp escaped me, giving him the opportunity to kiss me deeper. I put my hands on his chest to push him away, but stopped as soon as I touched him. The heat of his body was inviting. The warmth of his kiss was intoxicating. I couldn't help but accept it.

His lips left mine, a puff of air hitting them as he stepped back.

"There," he said, wiping the bottom of his lip with his thumb. "They won't allow you to marry one man when you've kissed another."

Coming out of my daze, frustration suddenly struck me.

"Wait," I stuttered. "Did you kiss me just to break off my betrothal?"

He huffed, agreeing to my statement.

"Oh, you idiot!" I snapped. "You were willing to ruin my reputation when the wedding has already been called off?"

"How am I the idiot when you're the one marryi— Wait, what?"

It was the first time I had seen him completely confused, and I couldn't hold back a laugh. He almost looked innocent.

I knew better.

"As I was trying to say," I continued, "before you so rudely interrupted, that is, was that your father is here now. Our engagement has been called off."

He brought his fingers to his lips. "So you're saying I did that for no reason?"

I nodded smugly. He ran his tongue against his teeth, his skin turning pink.

"Unless you *wanted* to kiss me," I added.

He glared at me. "Why would I want to do such a thing?"

"You've been quite adamant about me not marrying your father," I said. "You never told me a real reason."

"I did. You're a gold digger."

"A gold digger who tried to get her wings and was rejected?"

He paused as I looked over my shoulder at the sky, looking toward the star Jacques had shown me—the one over the den.

"You said I was easy to understand," I said, turning back to face him. "You must know what I want most, even now."

His eyes met mine. After a moment, he turned his head away, muttering to himself.

"I'll see that you make it back," he said eventually. "I already gave you my word."

"Another thing you didn't have to do," I returned. "Why are you helping me, Jacques?"

He paused. "Because it's my duty as a Judge."

"We both know that's not true. That's not one of your duties. And even so, you are not bound to duty as I am."

He glared at me. I returned the favor. Suddenly, he reached his hands out, gripping my waist and lifting me onto my dresser. With a yelp I grabbed his shoulders, looking at him in bewilderment.

"What?" he asked, back to his cocky self. "Are you waiting for a confession? As if I'm under your siren spell, unable to live without you?"

"I only want the truth." I held his gaze. "Why are you going this far for me?"

He seemed to lose his words for a moment, swallowing as he looked at me in my wedding gown. He shook his head, confusion still across his face.

"I'm intrigued," he said.

Regardless of the monotone of his voice, there was heat pouring off his body. He didn't move, holding my gaze. My fingers traced around the back of his neck, and he closed his eyes as he deeply breathed in.

"You said it was dangerous," I whispered. "A Judge and a siren."

He nodded, leaning his head against mine. "If danger bothered me, I wouldn't be who I am."

He pulled back a little, his eyes glancing at my lips once more before he looked away.

"Did you really only kiss me to break the betrothal?" I asked.

He didn't look at me. "Why else would I kiss you?"

I leaned in to get his attention. "If all you wanted to do was break off the engagement, you could have just said that Henrik kissed me. You witnessed that for yourself."

He then finally turned his head at me, looking at my lips once more. His fingers came to my face, his thumb brushing lightly against my lips.

"Yes," he replied, "but I hate thinking about that."

"Why?"

He didn't answer right away, still touching the curves of my face with his fingertips. He suddenly pulled back, standing straight.

"I don't know," he finally said.

I couldn't hold back my smile as he turned pink. I didn't have to read his eyes to know his feelings.

"Admit it," I said. "You like me, Jacques De Villiers."

He snapped his head at me in annoyance, his lips then pulling back into their usual smugness.

"There it is again," he said.

"What?"

"Your aura," he said. "It's rose."

I hunched my shoulders up, suddenly feeling naked. "You can see my aura? It has a color?"

He put one hand on each side of me on the dresser and leaned in closer.

"Rose is the color of infatuation," he said. "It was that color the night you met me in the hot springs. It was that color the first night we met, when you thought I was your betrothed."

He stared into my eyes, but I couldn't hold his gaze. I felt sheepish, as if I had been caught in a crime. But I hadn't, had I? I hadn't done anything wrong.

I folded my arms coyly. "Honestly, you'd be lucky to be my betrothed."

He leaned in closer, his eyes dropping to my neck before coming back to my face.

"I don't need luck," he whispered. "Not when it's obvious how much you're attracted to me."

He met his lips to mine again, and before I could even think, my hands were in his hair pulling him closer. The heat of his fingers came to my back, gently pushing me closer to him as he kissed me over and over again.

Yes, we barely knew one another, but there was an electricity to him that pulled me in. It did when we first met, and it had every time we were together since. Perhaps it was the same for him.

I broke the kiss, pulling back and looking over my shoulder.

"What's wrong?" he asked.

"I just remembered that your father is in the next room."

He chuckled darkly in my ear. "Who cares? Let him know that I'm the only one that can touch you like this."

I blushed. "Y-you realize that since I've rejected him, I have no dowry. You'll be with a broke, rejected siren."

"You were not rejected," he objected. "You were temporarily denied your request for obvious reasons. It will be granted in time. And second, do you really think a Judge of the spiritual world would be broke?"

He smirked. I shook my head at him in confusion.

"What do you mean?" I asked.

"Just because I don't have an inheritance doesn't mean a thing. How do you think I fund my travels between this world and the Den of Sirens?" He cocked his head to the side in pride. "You think just because you never imagined me rich, that I really wasn't?"

I lost my voice for a moment, processing his words. "So you mean…"

He pecked my lips in satisfaction. "It means no matter which life you choose—the human realm or the next—I'm the one in charge of your fate."

***

I had five more years with my father before he was laid to rest next to my mother. Jacques's father paid all the outstanding debts of the funeral and my father's business, saying that it was nothing compared to the life my father had given him.

After Father passed, I sold all my belongings except for my mother's necklace and my father's wedding ring. I kept them together around my neck at all times, remembering my blessed life on earth with them.

Our staff was dismissed to other jobs, and Lina found herself in Monsieur de Villiers's home as an assistant there. A year after she settled into his home, Jacques and I announced that we were moving across the ocean for Jacques's business. No one thought it was strange. After all, Jacques was a successful trader, and as his wife, it made perfectly logical sense that I accompany him to his new headquarters.

But the truth was, I was going home.

Jacques and I packed our things and sailed back to the Den of Sirens. King Melchior welcomed us back with open arms, a glint in his eyes showing that he knew that Jacques and I had married behind his back. But he didn't seem angry with it.

Eventually, my request for my wings was granted, and I was turned back into a siren. All my lives collected together in my memories, and the evil I had seen and done made me stronger as a siren, my perspective broader after experiencing so much.

Jacques and I were paired together in our missions: him judging the sirens, and me judging the humans. We worked well together, even if he had to pull me out of the reckless situations I frequently got myself into.

Luc, my dearest Rhys, became a close friend to me once again, and it felt like I had never left the den even though it had been centuries. After the years passed, his broken heart turned into deep wisdom, and I saw him blossom into a wise, honorable siren that anyone could look up to.

And when it came to honor, Henrik regained his. He was loyal to the king in every way, the pain of his evil past keeping him on track. Our relationship was restored, but remained distant, as Jacques was his employer and Henrik refused to get too close to me out of respect for his superior.

I heard and saw Adrian rarely. When he came to the den to see Henrik, he remembered me. When I flew into the city, he didn't recognize me. He eventually married, proving that his infatuation for me didn't override his sense. And watching him play with his children made me realize how pure his heart truly was now, how much one heart could influence others.

The humans who knew Adrian and Henrik were affected in positive ways. Although many still gossiped about the wayward pirate and the expelled naval son, those who knew them both personally were better for it.

Their pure hearts made my job easier.

Luc had been right. To live as a siren and make a difference in the balance of the realms was much more than I could have dreamed, and with Jacques as my most intimate confidant, I was made even better for it.

After all, Jacques had once been possessed by evil, and I had once succumbed to it. Knowing this—knowing the difference between our transgressions and our purity—we could see the world for what it was: blended.

A mix of light and dark, a combination of good and evil.

Knowing good and evil, we could heal ourselves. Knowing the good and evil within ourselves, we could heal it in the world.

ADRIAN'S ENDING

It had been eight weeks since I had come home.

Father had been healing well, but slowly. There were times I thought he might not wake the next morning, making me grateful that I had come home to take care of him. The Siren King must have known how ill my father was, and that's why he had denied me my request for my wings.

But even so, this meant that I was a human with the power to charm. This power was more than I understood. I didn't want to abuse it, if nothing more for the fact that I knew I would answer to King Melchior in the end if I did.

But could I live for a lifetime with the knowledge that those who loved me were under a spell?

Evenings had become cooler, the summer fading into fall. When the sun had fully set and my father had gone to sleep, I stood on the balcony, looking out over the sea as the moon and stars shone above it. Every night I looked at the star that hung over the Den of Sirens, wondering about the people who lived there. I missed the king. I missed Luc. I even missed Hugo and Vito and their constant bickering.

Jacques had left back to the den to train Henrik, and now I was left alone with no proof that anything had happened at all in the last few months. The loneliness was chilling. All I could do was go on the balcony each night and look at the star that hung over the Den of Sirens.

I would make it back home someday. Whether it was in this body or the next, it didn't matter.

I sometimes imagined hijacking a ship myself to get there, but I couldn't leave my earthly father behind. Even so, as I dreamed of sailing on the sea, I couldn't help but think of the crew I once knew. And as I stood on the balcony each night, I couldn't help but think of the captain of the ship himself, who had once kidnapped me from this very spot.

I remembered the way my heart had fluttered the moment I saw him…the way his velvety voice made me shiver.

Even though I was the one with the power to charm, perhaps he, too, was a siren in another life.

Because in the end, he had me completely charmed.

"Even if you don't remember me fondly, at least remember how warm it felt sleeping next to me."

I wrapped my arms around myself, wishing I could feel that warmth once more.

But how could I ask for that? How could I ask him to come back to me when I knew it was a spell?

"Are you making a wish?" a voice asked behind me.

Every muscle in my body seized. That voice… It was my imagination, right?

"A woman only looks at the stars that intensely when she has a deep wish," the voice continued.

I turned. Adrian stood right behind me, the same smile on his lips that he had the night we first met. The autumn breeze brought over the scent of cinnamon and rum, and I realized I wasn't dreaming.

"Adrian…" I whispered, my heart racing. "How did you get here?"

He made his way toward me, nodding over the side of the balcony. "I wanted to see if I was strong enough to climb again."

I huffed, pointing to his side.

"Honestly! Why would you risk such a thing?" I asked. "Don't you know how much you could have gotten hurt—"

"Seeing you again made it worth it." He stopped right in front of me, close enough for me to reach out and touch his face. "It may have been reckless, but as soon as they released me, I had to find you."

He smiled. My heart fluttered and broke at the same time.

"I thought the distance would have broken the spell," I said. "You realize that these feelings aren't real."

He stepped in even closer. "Aren't they?"

When I didn't answer, he stepped to the side and leaned against the balcony rail, facing me but looking at the stars over his shoulder. The wind blew through his hair, making my fingertips eager to touch the tresses.

"Even when we were apart," he said, "I still couldn't get you out of my mind. Aren't your charms only supposed to work when we're in the same room?"

I thought about it and shrugged, trying to let go of my hopes.

"The effects can last for a few minutes or a few days," I said.

"But it's been weeks, months, in fact," he replied. "And I missed you every moment."

He came in closer, putting both of his warm hands on my elbows and drawing me close. He smelled of cinnamon and the sea, hints of leather and citrus. It was a smell that took me back to his ship, where I slept every night in the same room as him.

"Y-you know that I can manipulate you," I said. "I just have to change my voice and you will do—"

"Then manipulate me," he returned. "Command me whenever it pleases you. I know I'm safe under your spell, princess."

He took my hand and put it on his chest, over his heart.

"You made me look at my own darkness until I could find light," he said. "Your power didn't harm me, Esmeralda. It made me who I am now."

He drew me in closer, my hand still on his heart. The heat from his body mixed up all my senses, making me wonder which one of us was the one with power over the other.

"Whether it's a spell or a curse," he said, "I want nothing more than to have you by my side."

I wanted to speak, but I couldn't, all the words stolen away from my throat. He leaned in closer, and I couldn't resist the temptation to close my eyes and let him take over.

Which he did.

He pressed his lips against mine, soft at first. There was a warmth in his lips that stole away all of my resistance, and when he knew I was at his full mercy, he kissed me stronger. Wrapping an arm around my back he pressed me in closer, his kiss deepening until I could barely breathe.

My voice may have controlled his actions, but his lips were now controlling my heart.

He broke away slowly, leaning his forehead against mine.

"I'll do anything you ask me," he said, "but don't ask me to leave. Even if this is just a result of a spell, it's a spell I want to be under."

I looked up into his eyes, sincerity filling them. Looking at him I knew that even with the power to make him do my every desire, I could never hurt him. I wanted to use this power to protect him. I wanted to keep him close to me even if his love wasn't completely true.

Because even if his feelings weren't real, mine were.

"Remember your words, Captain," I said. "Don't regret them when I grant you your wishes."

He smiled as he looked down at me. "I won't regret my wish, Siren Princess. Does this mean you will grant it?"

I nodded, running my fingers through his hair as I brought him back in close.

"I'll grant it," I said, "but only because you have me under your spell too."

We kissed again, the wind and the moon the witnesses of our vows.

***

I had five more years with my father until he passed.

Jacques's father paid for all the expenses for the funeral. I sold him our house for only a single franc, telling him to do anything he wanted with the estate. All I needed was my mother's necklace and my father's wedding ring around my neck to go where I was going.

Adrian and I were married only weeks after he had returned from the den. Perhaps it was the spell he was under that made him so adamant about marrying me so quickly, but I was the one who agreed, so I wasn't any better. Jacques had told King Melchior of the event, and when I asked him what the king had said, all Jacques replied was that no one was surprised.

Adrian and I had our first child a year after our wedding, our second child two years after that. I was grateful that my father had seen his grandchildren before passing. Perhaps that's what helped him to live as long as he did.

And even though my parents were gone, Adrian's parents took me in as their own. Adrian's mother healed in due time, his father still crippled physically but not spiritually. Adrian's parents loved watching and playing with their grandchildren, which came in handy when Adrian and I went out to sea.

Adrian had become a ship trader for Jacques's trade business—a business none of us realized he had. Apparently, Jacques had created an entire trade business while sailing between the den and the city (that was the reason he could pay for his passages between worlds), and he put Adrian in charge of one of the ships. It made Jacques's job easier, and it was the best way for Adrian to see Henrik on a regular basis.

Henrik was strong under Jacques's command and guidance, and he was given a strong position among the Judges. He was able to be himself—with no one fearing his abilities—and to see a new peace in him because of it made my heart soar.

My relationship with Henrik mended, and he became a dear friend to me once again. He was no longer under my spell, and the demons that once haunted him didn't bother me; after all, I had my own demonic past.

Luc became a dear friend of the family as well, and when we weren't on our way to see him in the Den of Sirens, he came to visit us in the city. He flew into the children's bedroom window once a week and told them grand stories at bedtime. He never truly forgave Adrian, but they seemed to decide that me and the children were a type of neutral ground, and that no blood would be shed between them on account of us. (For now, anyways.)

I knew that someday I would return to the den and get my wings, but I had no intentions now. I wanted to watch my little ones grow, and grow old with my husband. If I came back home in this body or the next, it didn't matter. I was content. Adrian's love was pure and enchanting, adventurous and thrilling. That was all I wanted.

Whether it was a spell or reality wasn't important. Being together—loving each other whether it was genuine or delusion—made me crave nothing else.

HENRIK'S ENDING

"Father, you must rest now," I said, making my voice light. "Remember the doctor's orders."

Father laid his head back against his pillow, his eyelids fluttering open and shut.

"Yes, yes," he said, complying. "You're quite right."

I pulled his blankets up to his shoulders, tucking him gently as he submitted to sleep. There was a weight in my stomach as my fear for his health and my guilt for using charmspeak intertwined.

This is the only way I can help you, Father...

When he had fully fallen asleep, I stepped outside his bedroom, shutting the door behind me and putting my face in my hands.

It had been three months since I had come home, my father's health improving slower than the doctors had wanted. There were times he went into fits of rage from his illness, and I started using my charmspeak to keep him calm and stable.

But it tore me apart to do so. Just knowing I could affect people in such a powerful way was overwhelming. Even though I had broken off my engagement to Jacques's father, could I actually marry for love? I'd forever be a natural charmer, my feelings undoubtedly real but my husband's always questionable.

I swallowed, wondering if someone could love me truly as a woman; if there was someone who could care for me beyond a spell.

Even if it isn't real, I want to feel it.

I understood Henrik's words so well now. Because even if a man couldn't love me without power, I still wanted to love someone with every fiber of my heart.

I felt so unsettled here, trapped between wanting a normal life with a family, and thirsting for the sea and my home beyond it.

A strong knock came to the front door. I lifted my head, looking toward the staircase to the first floor in curiosity.

Who would come to call so late?

"May I help you?" Lina asked downstairs.

"Yes, I apologize for coming so late in the evening and unannounced," a familiar voice said. "I was wondering if I might speak with the lady of the house."

That formal tone…

My heart jumped to my throat as I rushed to the top of the staircase. Henrik stood frozen in the doorway, his eyes meeting mine as he swallowed. I froze as well, unable to say a word, not even his name.

Lina cleared her throat as she reached for Henrik's coat.

"You two can visit in the parlor," she said. "I'll make you some tea."

She nodded sharply at me, her way of telling me nonverbally to act presentable and come down. I came down the steps, trying not to show how much I was shaking.

He was still as handsome as the day I had met him. Not a trace of demon in his eyes, pure and mature, every bit a gentleman.

But how did he see *me* now? As a siren he was meant to answer to? Or as a woman?

I stepped down from the stairs, meeting him only a few feet apart. He abruptly broke eye contact, opening the door for me to the parlor. We both took a seat on opposite sofas, not able to speak at first. It seemed that neither of us knew how to start the conversation.

Lina brought in the tea and left it on the table, closing the door behind her.

Neither of us touched it.

"It's good to see you, Henrik," I finally said.

He laughed ironically. "Is it? I was worried about what you might say when I came to your door."

He looked at his folded hands.

"And then," he continued, "I forgot everything I wanted to say once I saw you."

Silence passed again as I felt my face flush. I leaned forward and poured us both some tea as I collected my thoughts.

"Is Jacques training you well?" I asked, picking up a cup of tea and offering it to him.

He nodded, taking the cup from my hands. "I've been treated well, considering. No one is afraid of me under this king's command. Thanks to the king, my family is safe and I am in a position of purpose. I can't ask for anything more."

He took a sip of his tea, the cup clinking against the saucer.

"I'm glad to hear that you and your family are well," I replied.

He nodded in gratitude. "And your father?"

"His healing hasn't been smooth, but he's becoming more stable."

Henrik sighed. "If there's anything you need, please allow me to serve you as—" He stopped. "As a servant of the king."

He quickly drank more tea, coughing as he swallowed.

"Please, Henrik," I said quietly. "Don't act like my servant. Not when I've spent so much time looking up to you."

He dropped the cup from its saucer, the tea spilling on his clothes. I quickly grabbed a napkin from the tea tray and dabbed his shirt. When the burn marks on his abdomen peeked out from between the buttons on his shirt, I couldn't help but stop. Without thinking, I reached out and touched them.

"Do they still hurt?" I asked.

He shifted in his seat. "No."

Suddenly realizing, I pulled my hand back.

"Forgive me," I said, stepping back. "I didn't mean to touch you so mindlessly."

He shook his head. "I knew you had no ill intentions."

He paused, staring at me with such an intensity that I couldn't help but look at the floor in front of me.

"But there's something I just don't understand," he finally said.

He lifted his shirt showing more of the burn marks.

"Even with these runes etched into my skin," he said, "these markings drawn to protect me from your spell, even now, you're still the only thing I can think about."

My hand fluttered to my chest as my heart fluttered along with it. He let down his shirt, dropping his head.

"I know I hurt you," he said. "My darkness enslaved me, and I lashed out at you for it. But…but I wanted to tell you that with or without magic, you're the one who has captivated me most."

I swallowed down my heartbeat. Henrik laughed nervously, running his fingers through his hair. He then stood to his feet.

"I realize that you're engaged—perhaps by now, even married—and I don't wish to make things any more difficult for you." His hands shook. "I just…had to tell you in person myself. I had to apologize for my actions and wish you the greatest happiness."

"Henrik—"

"So please consider this my formal apology," he said, bowing. "I wish you the greatest happiness, Esmeralda. I won't forget what you—"

I cut him off, jumping to my feet and throwing my arms around his neck.

"You fool," I said in his ear. "How can you wish me great happiness when my greatest happiness is you?"

I held his face in my hands and pecked him on the lips. He jumped, taking a step back in surprise.

"Esmeralda? What are you…?"

"I thought about you every day since I returned," I confessed. "Every time I looked at the swords on my father's bedroom wall, I couldn't help but think of the naval gentleman who always made me feel at home, even when I thought I'd never find home again."

His lips pulled back in a half smile, but he shook it away. "I hurt you, Esmeralda."

I pulled him back into my embrace. "And now? Do you still want revenge against me?"

His hands came up to my arms as if he were going to break free, but his touch was light against my skin.

"Of course not," he replied. "Not when I—"

He stopped. I nudged him.

"What is it?" I asked.

He shook his head. "Nothing."

"Tell me?"

I lifted my voice, smiling when he met my eyes. We both knew that my charmspeak had no effect now.

One of his hands came from my arm to my face, and he gently rubbed my cheek with his thumb.

"I'm in love with you," he said. "I'm completely obsessed."

I smiled in return. "What a coincidence. I love you too."

A smile burst onto his lips, and he pulled me close into an embrace. He leaned down and nuzzled the skin behind my ear, sighing in confusion.

"But why?" he whispered. "After all that I've done?"

I leaned my head against his shoulder. "You act as if my hands are clean. I murdered the Guardians in cold blood as a siren. How can I judge you so harshly for sins when I have so many of my own?"

He leaned back, realizing. "Your curse. I had forgotten." His eyes were frantic and wide. "Esmeralda, if you don't become a full siren, then—"

"Then I finish this life and live another. But if I become a siren, it would be quite difficult for us to be together."

His fingers came to my hair, brushing it away from my neck and shoulder.

"As deeply as I feel for you, I don't want to be the reason you are cursed forever," he said. "If you want your wings—"

"I don't," I said firmly. "Not in this life. In this life, I want my family. I want my father, my future children, and you. If I live a thousand more lives with a thousand more families, it won't be so bad. There are worse punishments."

I embraced him tighter.

"Did you just imply that you want to have children with me?" he asked with an airy chuckle.

Heat rushed to my cheeks as I pulled back. "That wasn't…I mean…"

He leaned back to look into my eyes, a new mischievous glint in them. I looked away, not knowing what to say. He chuckled once again before gently directing my chin back to face him.

"A family with you," he whispered, "would be the best future I can possibly imagine."

The embarrassment ebbed from my body and I relaxed, getting lost in his sweet and dark eyes. He glanced at my lips, before parting his own.

"Can I kiss you?" he whispered.

I leaned forward. "Every day until the day I leave this body."

He smiled before leaning in and capturing my lips in his. Affection flowed from his fingertips as they crawled up my back, pressing me closer against him. This was not possessive and controlling as the kiss in the cavern had been. It was deep and intimate, slow and drowning. Feeling his chest rise and fall with his breath along with each kiss, I melted slowly into his embrace. He was every bit a gentleman, but his true feelings were communicated through his kiss.

His demons may have been gone, but he still wanted me to be completely his.

***

It was five more years before my father passed. Luckily, he was able to meet his first grandchild before his passing.

The union between a siren and a Judge was technically frowned upon; however, because I was an incarnate siren, Henrik and I were allowed to bend the rules. Henrik, being the gentleman that he was, asked both my earthly father and King Melchior for permission to marry. To Henrik's surprise, they both agreed. He had believed his reputation would doom his future forever. My fathers, however, had decided otherwise.

Henrik spent time back and forth between the Den of Sirens as a Judge alongside Jacques, and I stayed at home to care for our, eventual, three children. I couldn't go to the den with them so young, and although I missed it, I knew that eventually I would return sooner or later. Whether it was in this body or in another, I wouldn't know. But I knew I wanted to be there for my children and family for as long as I could.

Luc visited us all at night, telling my children wild stories before bed. They all became adventurous souls thanks to Uncle Luc, Uncle Adrian, and their father, and I couldn't have been prouder.

As it so happened, Jacques was in charge of a large ship trading company that none of us were aware of. It was apparently how he afforded to travel between the den and the city. He offered Adrian a job on one of his ships, allowing Adrian to see Henrik in the den on a regular basis.

Henrik forbade Adrian to be alone with me—unsurprisingly—as my charms on him never fully wore off. His visits to the children became far and few between, and I knew it was because he was trying to respect his older brother, no matter what feelings he thought he had. He always blamed his work at sea for the infrequent visits, but I could tell by his eyes that it was because he never wanted to hurt his brother again.

The skin between my shoulders ached often, but my heart did not. Every moment with Henrik was precious and full of pure joy. To watch him judge good and evil, and give that wisdom to our children was better than I had anticipated.

Perhaps I couldn't judge the world as a siren for now, but I knew that in loving my husband and children that the world was a little purer than it was before.

LUC'S ENDING

Night fell, the lanterns shedding light on the streets below.

I folded my arms close to my chest as the ocean wind blew across the city. I spent my evenings standing on the balcony, staring at the ocean horizon at the star that hung over the Den of Sirens. I spent much of my free time wondering how I might return, wondering how the sirens were faring without me.

It had been eight weeks since I had returned home. Father was stable, healing slowly. Jacques's father had taken care of all necessary expenses even though he had not taken my hand in marriage. I was grateful.

But something still tugged at my heart, no matter how at peace I should have been.

How long would it be until I saw the den again?

The wind chilled, encouraging me to go back into my room. I turned around to go in, until a sudden rush of wind caused me to jump and turn back around.

I gasped when I saw what had caused the sudden burst of air: large, black wings.

Luc stood before me on the balcony, his wings fully extended.

He smiled.

"Luc?" I asked. "You returned?"

His wings fluttered as he began to close them. Before he could answer my question, I ran to him and wrapped my arms around him.

"You have no idea how much I missed you," I said.

He held me tight. "I missed you too, Astraea. Far more than I should have."

Neither of us broke the hug right away, lingering in our reunion as long as possible. He then pulled back a little, not fully breaking the hug.

"And your father?" he asked. "Is he well?"

I nodded. "He's healing. He might be sick for some time though."

Luc inhaled slowly. "The king knew about your father. That's why he sent you away. I understand why you left, but nevertheless…"

He reached up, gently combing his fingers through my hair. I knew the gesture was meant to be endearing, but something about his touch was different. There was more heat in his fingertips than usual, and his silent stare at the top of my head uneasy.

"Why did you come back?" I asked.

He kept combing my hair, his eyes following his own hand. "I wanted to know that you were cared for, little dove. In our lives as sirens, in our lives as humans…I guess I just got used to being responsible for you."

"Oh, Luc." I laughed. "You were never that responsible."

He burst into laughter, his smile making my heart flutter. When his laughter subsided, he took my hands in his, seeming to hesitate before he looked down at them.

"Your fingers are bare," he finally said. "Are you still engaged to that man?"

The twinge of annoyance in his voice was something I hadn't heard before. I was tempted to tell the truth, but even more tempted to find the cause behind his sudden sharp tone.

"I haven't been wed yet," I replied. "How do you think the king would feel if I decided to wed instead of to return?"

Luc's tongue ran across his lips before he looked up to meet my eyes. There was a darkness in them now, even though I could tell he was trying to hide it.

"He…he would allow you to make your own choices, I suppose," Luc replied.

There was even more bitterness to his voice now. It made my heart pound, encouraging me to risk a dangerous question.

"Would you come to my wedding?" I asked.

He searched my eyes for a long moment, the air seeming to thicken as he swallowed. He gave a bitter smile, shaking his head.

"I'd ruin it," he said.

"Ruin?"

He pulled me in close, holding my hand to his chest. He leaned forward, his breath softly hitting my ear.

"Haven't you heard?" he asked. "I steal other men's wives."

His wings surrounded us, blocking out the entire world. The dark feathers brushed against my skin, sending chills up my neck. He brought me in for a second embrace, this one more intimate than the first.

"Luc—" I managed to say.

"I'll wait for you to come back to us," he said, cutting me off. "But you need to know, it kills me to wait like this."

He pulled back, touching his thumb to my lips. I stood still, his touch warm and comforting. He swallowed again before speaking.

"It's ironic, really," he said, stroking my face. "Working with you side by side on that ship, I started to fall for you, not remembering that I had already loved you as a siren."

My mouth went dry, heart pounding in my ears. "What?"

I heard, but I needed to hear it again.

He gave a small smile. "I always had different feelings toward you. But sirens always expected to live with their feelings second. I suppose that's what I envied most about the humans. That's why I left the den so many times: to live as they did.

"When you came aboard that ship," he continued, "there were pieces of you that made me feel at home. And now that I've found my true home, it still doesn't feel right without you."

I put my hand on his. The air seemed still for a moment as we locked eyes, the swirls of blue and green in his usually black irises stealing my breath away.

"Is my confession too much, little dove?" he asked.

I held my hand out toward him, palm up.

"Check for yourself," I said.

He looked down at my wrist for a moment then smiled, bringing his fingers to it. He then smiled wider.

"It's a little fast," he said, stepping closer.

I nodded. "It's your fault."

He brushed my hair from my neck, tucking loose strands of it behind my ear.

"Yet somehow," he added, "I'm unsatisfied."

His wings tightened around us and pushed me close to him, our bodies now fleshed against each other. Blood rushed from my toes to my head so fast that it would have knocked me off balance had Luc not been holding me so close by his arms and his wings.

"Come back to the Den of Sirens with me," Luc whispered. "Come accept your wings, so you can be mine."

I put my hands on his chest, my feelings bubbling in my stomach. But the rush soon crashed, my heart sinking.

"I want more than anything to be with you. But my father's illness…"

He nodded. "I won't ask you to abandon him. I would have never abandoned Maria's family given any circumstance. I won't ask you to abandon a man who has treated you with such affection." He stroked my cheek. "But regardless, I will offer my own affections to you whenever you're ready to come home. Eternally."

My lips parted in surprise. "That's a very large promise to make, Rhys."

"And I'm a man of my word, Astraea," he returned.

My eyes searched his, trying to decide on an answer. He smiled.

"You keep yearning for it, don't you?" he asked. "You keep looking at the sea from your window, wishing you were on it again?"

I laughed. "I forgot that you can see all my dreams and desires."

He leaned forward. "And you can see mine, too, you know."

I stared deep into his eyes, noticing the colors swarm once more, before something undoubtedly bubbled up in my mind.

Luc loved me.

No… Rhys loved me. Rhys had always loved me.

We were from a world where feelings were regarded as afterthoughts, but he had me first in his heart from the beginning.

He smiled. "You saw it."

He held me close, his arms around my back in an embrace like a child holding a teddy bear. It was warm and affectionate, yet desperate for comfort.

"Please, Astraea," he whispered, his lips grazing my ear. "I spent half of my last human life looking for the spirit of the woman I loved, only to lose her forever. I can't go through that again."

Something in my heart ached, knowing deep down that if I reincarnated again, Luc wouldn't be able to find me for some time. Leaving him alone shattered something in me.

"Come back with me," he said again. "I'll make sure you and your father are taken care of completely, in whatever realm you want to live."

His fingers dug into my hips as he held me close, the desperation in his voice sweet. I ran my hands from his chest to his neck, twisting the hair on the back of his head gently with my fingers.

I didn't need to check his pulse to know that it was racing.

"I want to live in whatever realm you're in," I whispered back. "I want to stay by your side until you know how much you are loved."

Luc seemed to freeze for a moment before his eyes locked with mine. He clenched his teeth, his eyes watering until a few stray tears spilled over. He smiled, licking the drops from his lips.

"Aye, my heart must be weak today," he said. "You touched it so easily."

I leaned forward and kissed the tears on his cheeks, the salt from his tears and his skin dancing across my tongue. His hands glided across my waist, pulling me impossibly close to him as I kissed his cheeks up to his eyelids.

I stopped, and his eyes fluttered open. His hand crawled up my back and pressed firmly between my shoulder blades, bringing me in as his lips pressed against the corner of my mouth.

The sensation was cosmic. It made my whole body tingle.

He kissed me again, full on the mouth, inviting me to trust him as he sucked slowly on my lips with each consecutive kiss.

Each kiss was sensual, adventurous, and comforting. Much like Luc himself.

Our lips parted, but not our bodies. He randomly planted kisses around my face and neck, chuckling softly as I became shy from his affection. His fingers came to my wrist, satisfaction beaming off his face as my pulse raced against his fingers.

"Are you happy now?" I teased.

He shook his head like a playful puppy. "This is only the beginning."

I squealed as he leaned down and wrapped his hands behind my knees, lifting me up into the air. He smiled up at me.

"There are so many things I've wanted to do to make your heart race," he whispered seductively. "And now, I finally get to try them."

***

I had five years with my father before he was laid next to my mother.

Jacques's father paid for not only all of Father's medical bills, but also for all the funeral expenses. He even purchased Father's estate from me for a single franc; after all, I didn't need it where I was going.

Luc escorted me back to the Den of Sirens not long after Father passed, and the king granted me my wings. I remembered all my lives before, overwhelmed with gratefulness for every one of them—painful or pleasurable—as they had turned me into what I was now.

Although sirens usually didn't marry, King Melchior allowed Rhys and I to be partners. His only response to Rhys's passionate confession of love for me was, "I knew you would find your bravery eventually."

(Followed up with Hugo's comment: "It took you long enough.")

Jacques and Henrik worked for the king as Judges, and I only saw them at times of the trials. Adrian sometimes accompanied them as captain over one of Jacques's trade ships. Apparently, Jacques had created an entire trade business traveling between the den and the city so many times. This meant that Jacques was even richer than his father. And needing help with his business, he had put Adrian in charge of one of his vessels.

Because of my true form, I knew that Adrian couldn't recognize me outside the Den of Sirens. It seemed, however, that nothing was kept secret in the den itself, and because of this, Adrian knew who I was in this place. But he was still susceptible to my charms, and this kept Luc on his toes at all times.

Henrik and I were able to reconcile our relationship, and he became a dear friend once again. He served the king and sirens well, his reputation nothing but honored in the den. He was a great leader among them. Possibly the best in centuries. And when the king walked by him and smiled, I couldn't help but wonder if the king had known that would be the case all along.

And I was forever by Rhys's side. Nothing between the human world or siren world was forbidden to us, and we worked each day collecting humanity for judgment.

Our task as sirens was painful but necessary. Although we could not cure evil entirely, we could address the evil in front of us. And since we both had already addressed our own evils, we were much more effective in cleansing the world the rightful way.

There was nothing easy about purity. It was an endless commitment, with no immediate reward. But we knew that evil had a devastating outcome, even if it rewarded us for a short time. Living in the world we knew we were meant to live in—serving the king, dwelling with the people we loved most, and saving others from their own evil—that was the most satisfying life I could think of.

Satisfied with what I had, I needed nothing else. Satisfied with what I had, I could give more to the world instead of taking from it.

SCENES FROM HIS POV

Don't like any of the endings? Well then, write your own! At the end of this book are blank pages for you to write whatever ending you want.

For further inspiration, or to spend more time with your favorite leading man, here are some scenes from the points of view of Adrian, Henrik, Jacques, and Luc. Get to know them better by seeing the story through their eyes!

ADRIAN

ONE

I could hear music flowing out of the windows.

It wasn't my place to ask why a broke man was throwing a hell of a party. It was better just to join in the fun. It didn't matter whether or not I had been invited. I had crashed many parties before in the past, and this one would be just as fun to sneak into.

Of course, this was the first time I had to cut someone open and steal their blood, but I always enjoyed a new challenge.

Going through the front door was obviously a bad decision, so I settled for the next best thing: a high window. Party guests usually hung around the first floor, so if I snuck in the lower windows I'd be easily caught. (Knowledge gained from personal experience.) The upper floors, however, were usually empty and not difficult to get to if you had nimble feet.

There was a beautiful white lattice climbing up the stone walls of the house, and it held my boots better than I expected. Of course, there was always the chance that the lattice would snap under the pressure, but this particular fence seemed too happy to accommodate my mission.

Once I reached the top of the lattice, I checked for any straggling guests that might report me. When the coast seemed clear, I hopped over the balcony rail, straightening my hair and stolen jacket.

I checked the door for voices before opening it and

letting myself inside. The room was dark, but there was a hint of floral perfume that hit my nose. This was definitely a woman's room. Looking at the full gowns in her closet, it was a woman of high quality.

Ah, the woman I was looking for, perhaps.

I helped myself to her dresser and vanity drawers, wondering if there was anything else I could take from this woman besides her blood. To my surprise, the drawers were quite empty. She had many clothes, but no jewels. There was a small stack of books. A few paintings on the walls that I didn't recognize. Nothing else.

What a boring woman. Such a typical aristocrat.

I checked myself in the mirror, looking as rich as I could for the occasion. I couldn't lower myself to that level, though. I was far too handsome and rugged. It was just a curse I would have to deal with.

I took the tiny flask out of my pocket, making sure that I hadn't damaged it while climbing. It sparkled a bit in the moonlight as if it were winking at me.

I just needed a few drops of blood. Nothing terrible. The girl would be traumatized for life, maybe, but she wouldn't die.

Exiting the bedroom and slipping down the stairs to the main room was a bit harder than climbing up the lattice, but I knew the trick: look like you belong there, and everyone will think you do too.

I threw open the door, doing just that.

It had been awhile since I had broken into a house, and it gave me a good buzz of energy. Bouncing down the stairs, I took a glass of wine for myself at the bottom and made my way through the chattering crowd.

Damn, there were some beautiful women at the party. It was a shame I had to focus on only one tonight.

If my last plan for seducing a rich woman to marry me hadn't gone so badly, I would have abandoned this whole mission and gone after one of these swans. But I didn't need another knife in my neck.

This was the last chance I had for success.

I could have asked who the lady of the house was, but it would be obvious. All I had to do was find the most confident girl in the room, and she was bound to be the owner. She was probably also the loudest, yet somehow perceived as graceful, probably attracting a crowd because everyone wanted to kiss up to the host of the party. She was probably…

…wearing a red and gold dress, dancing with a tall man, smiling like she owned the world and had no intentions in giving it back.

Yep. That was definitely her.

I drank the last of my wine, keeping my eyes on her. That smile of hers was alarmingly mesmerizing. She certainly didn't look broke. She looked like she was related to the king himself, and he had just given her half of France. I could have stayed here for half the night and—

I frowned, rubbing the scar on my neck.

Focus, mate. Focus.

The song ended and the woman bowed to her suitor, who seemed as stale as an aristocrat could be. I stepped forward to cut in, but she bounced over to an older gentleman before I had the chance to even say a word. She looped her arm in his and he glowed with pride. By the look of their matching eyes and long noses, I guessed they were related. Her father, perhaps.

They walked out of the main room, arm in arm, something twisting in my stomach as they walked down the hall. Perhaps it was something to do with the memory of linking arms with my mother in the city gardens and talking about mindless things. Now she was restricted to her bed.

I traded my empty wine glass for a full one and downed it.

That woman's smile…the way she beamed like she owned the world…I wanted that.

I wanted more than blood. I wanted more than gold.

I wanted it for myself more than anything.

EIGHT

"Here, sip this."

I handed Esmeralda the glass of purified water, this time, with *extra* rum. I could tell by her face that she smelled it.

"Are you trying to take advantage of me?" she asked, her eyebrows raised indignantly.

"No, I'm trying to keep my sanity," I replied. "If I have to deal with your anxiety the whole night—"

The ship lurched sideways again with the wind. I grabbed on to Esmeralda before she could fall flat on her face and dump rum all over my sheets. She tried to pull out of my hands automatically, but I held fast to her. She was acting defiant, but her hands shook like a small, hairless dog.

"Drink it," I commanded. "It will help you sleep through the storm."

She hesitated, a wavering look passing through those large eyes before she looked down at the glass.

"This is a ruse to get me drunk and have your way with me isn't it?"

"I would have done it already if I was interested," I said flatly. "Drink. It."

I shoved her glass up to her face and made her drink. She didn't fight me as hard as I thought she would. Instead, she took the drink like a small child. It was adorable, actually.

She grunted in disgust when she finished, wiping her mouth and squeezing her eyes tight. I couldn't help but laugh at her reaction.

"It's not enough to get you drunk," I added. "It's just enough to get you to sleep."

The ship got caught in the wind once more, and she fell straight into my arms, the glass clinking its way across the floor.

"Are you sure you're not trying to take advantage of *me*?" I asked her, holding her close.

She shoved me away. "Not in a million years, you disgusting, ridiculous pirate! There is nothing on earth or sea that would make me come on to such a heathen!"

***

Lightning struck. It took two seconds for the thunder to roll.

And that's when my bed creaked.

I groggily opened my eyes, trying to figure out why small hands were gripping my shirt.

Was I having that dream about that girl from Barbados again?

"Adrian!" a frantic voice whispered. "Are you awake?"

"No," I replied. "I'm fast asleep."

"You fool, wake up!"

I opened my eyes all the way, squinting at the face far too close to me. I wasn't sure whether to push her away or pull her in closer.

"What's your problem, princess?"

The thunder boomed again. She gripped her fingers into my neck, giving me a mix of feelings I wasn't about to share with her.

"Please don't leave me," she said. "I'm so scared."

I wrapped an arm lazily around her waist and pulled her in close. She molded against me, laying her head on my chest as she held on to my neck.

"I've got you, princess," I said. "Just relax."

She shuddered as she held me tight, her nails going deeper into my neck. It was starting to turn me on, honestly, until I realized it was right next to my scar…where I had taken a knife after trying to seduce a rich woman only months before.

As much as I wanted to seduce this woman, it would end badly.

"You really belong on the floor," I muttered, mostly to myself.

I need you away from me. Something about you…is too enchanting.

"Just hold me for a little bit," she begged. "Just until it stops."

I gripped her, harder than I had meant to. The way her voice went up, her vulnerability and innocence, something in that tone stirred every fiber of my being.

"One night only," I said.

I held her in my arms, grazing my fingers against the skin of her arm back and forth until she stopped shaking. It was not long after until she fell asleep completely, not conscious of the storm at all.

But I was. I was wide awake and aware of everything.

Looking at her long eyelashes and rosy lips, feeling her hands around my neck…

This was dangerous. It was getting more and more dangerous as time went on.

EIGHTEEN

She was in my bed again.

This had become a habit I didn't approve of. It wasn't that I hated the idea of a beautiful woman sleeping next to me, of course, but I hated how attached to this woman I was becoming. If she didn't get back on that floor, I was going to do something we'd both regret.

So instead, I dragged myself out of bed and went to my desk. One of us had to make wise decisions. I was out of practice, but I could probably figure it out.

I lit a candle to break up the dark and poured myself a heavy glass of rum. I downed my liquor, the candlelight next to me catching the edges of the glass.

"Aren't you in pain?"

How could she read me so easily?

Men had died under my command before. That was part of being…whatever I was. An outlaw? A criminal? Regardless, I had never lost this many men. I hadn't sent men to their spiritual doom before.

The first time I lost a man, it nearly killed me. The guilt and pain of being irresponsible with the lives of someone else…it was too much for me. I was too young to handle it at the time. I still felt too young to handle it now. So instead, I decided to have no interest in protecting life at all. I wouldn't get attached. I wouldn't feel that guilt again.

And now here I was, drinking large amounts of liquor and thinking about how I'd lost my men, and how I could have lost her too.

Her fiancé had come for her. There was no mistake about that. The siege was so that he could take her from me. My chest tightened at the thought. It made me want to go down and slit their throats in their cells.

But I knew if I did that, she would never respect me.

I shook my head to myself, pouring another glass of rum.

"Why do you care so much, Captain?" I whispered to myself. "She's just a woman. You've never acted like this."

There were a few times in my life when I thought I was in love with a woman. The one who stood out to me the most, however, was when I was thirteen. She was the daughter of a regular customer in my father's shop before his accident. She was incredibly shy but graceful. The way she looked at me through her long eyelashes sent me into first-love bliss. When she moved away for her father's business, I was completely shattered as a boy, wondering how I could let a girl like that slip out of my fingers.

Esmeralda made me feel like that boy again. That stupid thirteen-year-old boy who was obsessed and possessive.

But her fiancé was only a few feet away from us.

"With him as your prisoner, you can command me to do anything you wish."

I swallowed a mouthful of rum. *Anything?* You stupid girl. Do you know what kind of thoughts a man has when you say that sort of thing?

I was no angel. I knew exactly what I could do to her, and I knew I was capable of doing it.

Suddenly that guilt came over me again. I felt the guilt of lives in my hands that I had no business being in charge of. My men died to protect her on my orders. But now she was in my bed, and all I could think about was ways I could make her mine.

Of course, I couldn't. She was too pure. Too innocent. Dirty hands like mine shouldn't touch women like her.

Instead, I opened the drawer of my desk, taking out my notebook and dipping my pen in ink.

I couldn't trace the curves of her jaw and lips with my fingers—not in this life—but on paper I could do anything I wanted.

I couldn't love her. I didn't know how to do such a thing anyway. But I could capture pieces of her on paper to keep with me for when she left me. After all, she wouldn't stay. She couldn't.

Princesses like her didn't love demons like me.

FORTY-EIGHT

"You'll never measure up to your brother."

My father's words echoed in my head as I ran my hand against the handle of my sword. My family had always praised Henrik for his accomplishments, but I had never done anything worth praising. I struggled with reading, and so my studies were useless. On top of that, my classmates found out about my alchemist uncle, and they mercilessly mocked Henrik and me until I was forced to punch them in the mouth about it.

Henrik was the one who taught me how to fight, but I never caught on to the part about honor.

And now I would possibly have to kill my own brother to learn that lesson.

"Are you sure you can do this?" Jacques asked. "If you hesitate for a single moment—"

"Yeah, I know," I said. "Everyone gets enslaved by my possessed demon brother. I picked up on it."

"I don't appreciate your humor."

"I don't appreciate your lack of it."

We followed Esmeralda deeper into the caves, as she was the lead on this mission. I didn't like using her as bait. If anything happened to her—

"Grab her."

My brother's voice echoed through the cave. At least, the remnants of his voice. There was something inhumane about it now, like his throat had been burned on the inside. He sneered as his two siren minions grabbed Esmeralda and began to drag her toward him.

Jacques grabbed my arm to stop me. He then grabbed me by the collar, dragging me to the corner of the room. He eyed the two sirens and Henrik, his eyes narrowing.

Esmeralda stayed cool, her posture straight and unafraid as she spoke directly to my demonic brother. I didn't understand how she could be so calm. My heart was about to rip out of my chest.

She could die. And so could my brother.

I didn't care if it was a spell or not; I couldn't stand the thought of something happening to her. And my brother, could he even be saved?

"I want to offer you my body," Esmeralda's calm voice said loud and clear.

My mouth opened, but Jacques spoke first.

"Shit," he cursed. "The demon can't resist the idea of more power. And if she's offering him her body then…"

He caught my look.

"Not sexually," he added. "She's offering to let him possess her."

"You can do that?"

"All possession is at first willing."

I jumped to my feet, but he pulled me back down.

"She said she could separate them," he said. "Wait."

"One of them is going to end up dead."

"This spell she has on you is so damn inconvenient…"

"Henrik!" she screamed. "Save me!"

I turned to see a sword at her throat, but Henrik pulled it back, his arm dropping to the side. He shook, the power suddenly gone from his face.

"So that's what she's doing," Jacques muttered. "What an interesting strategy."

He seemed to have no intention of moving from his place, even though everything in my body told me to run to them both. It would only take a moment for me to lose them again.

Maybe for good this time.

I had cheated death too many times already, and I doubted Fate was kind enough to let me off again.

Henrik's voice was too soft to hear, but I could at least tell that it was normal. My brother was still in that body.

Please…I need my brother back. I'll die myself if that's what it takes.

I reached for the sword at my side, and not too soon.

"Dammit!" Henrik yelled, grabbing his head in pain. "You need to get out, Esmeralda!"

He lunged for her. She dove away, barely missing the blade.

I drew my sword.

"That's a signal as far as I'm concerned," I said to Jacques.

I stepped forward. Before I could even get two steps, however, my brother turned. His yellow eyes met mine, and I felt frozen to the ground.

He saw me, but he didn't recognize me. My brother didn't know me.

"Why are you hesi—" Jacques started.

But he didn't get to finish.

"Get the humans!" Henrik commanded.

The sirens that had brought Esmeralda to Henrik swooped in to obey their commands. Jacques grabbed my arm and pulled me back just before one of them nearly slammed into me.

"Get it together!" Jacques barked, knocking me back to my senses.

I turned my focus away from my brother to the sirens, unable to shake the image of my brother's hatred from my sight.

"Incoming!"

Jacques opened a flask of holy water and doused the rocks in front of him. Then he grabbed one of the sirens by the neck and slammed his head against the wet rock. The siren screamed in agony but didn't quit his fight.

I jumped in to aid him, swinging my sword at the sirens with a new burst of energy in my blood.

I had nothing to lose at this point.

I had ruined my family name. I had no honor. The love I felt for a woman was a spell. And my brother—the only one who held out any faith in my redemption— wanted me dead.

The least I could do was make my final act an act of honor.

ENDING

"Just hold me for a little bit…until the storm stops."

I rubbed the ache out of my chest. Whether it was from being laid up for the past two months or from memories, I wasn't sure.

The sirens were hospitable even if they were somewhat awkward. Maybe they were just in awe of my incredible heroism, or maybe they just weren't used to humans staying with them for so long.

Henrik and Jacques were always in training, and my brother seemed lost in thought most of the time. We spoke little to one another. I knew he didn't hate me; he just felt guilty. In time he would relax and maybe things would be a little more normal. Well, at least as normal as they could be with my brother now being someone who divided good and evil souls in the spiritual realm.

I wondered how Mom would feel about that one.

I was too restless to stay in bed. There didn't seem to be much entertainment in the siren world, except maybe destroying humans. I suppose that took up enough time. Regardless, I wandered around the caverns, looking for something to do.

There was a flutter behind me, the wind hitting my back.

I rolled my eyes. "Still keeping tabs on me, eh?"

I turned around to Luc's stoic face. His jaw clenched.

"It's my job," he replied flatly.

"The king's orders, I take it?"

He didn't reply. I chuckled.

"I suppose he likes that kind of irony, doesn't he?" I asked.

There was silence for a moment. As we stood across from one another, there was a second ache in my chest.

My own guilt.

"There wasn't supposed to be anyone inside that night," I finally said.

Luc cocked his head for a moment. I saw his eyes flicker when he caught my meaning.

"I counted," I continued. "But it seems I miscalculated."

Again he said nothing. I could still feel his hatred for me, and I didn't blame him.

"I won't insult you with an apology," I said. "It wouldn't be enough."

He swallowed. "You're right. It wouldn't."

I nodded in acknowledgment. "But let's not forget that you also put a spell on me, planned a mutiny against my crew, sent a large chunk of them to their deaths, tried to kill me when I went after your woman—"

"Esmeralda is not my woman," he said.

I clicked my tongue. "I never said her name, mate."

He rolled his eyes and looked away.

"You're not under a spell like I am," I continued, "but your feelings are pretty obvious. I'm surprised you didn't stay in the human world with her."

He was quiet. He looked as if he was thinking of what to say, so I didn't interrupt.

"Despite what she decides," he eventually said, "I know that after her life as a human is finished, she'll eventually return to me. This is her home."

I licked the salt from my lips.

"So who will love her in *this* life?" I asked.

I said it mostly to myself, but there was no denying that he heard it. It looked as if he was going to ignore my sentiment for a moment.

"The charmspeak has limitations," he finally said, looking annoyed.

"As in?"

"As in the symptoms wear off. The charm only works in the presence of a siren. Those deeply enchanted usually lose all interest in about three to four weeks."

"And?"

"You've been here twice that long."

He looked away, sighing.

"Don't cause any trouble," he said. "I'll be watching."

And with that, he flew off.

***

The lattice was much harder the second time around. Probably because of the hole in my side.

I didn't think knocking on the front door would be beneficial. After all, it was nearly midnight. Not to mention, I was the pirate who kidnapped Esmeralda in the first place.

But I had to see her.

There was an ache in my side as I made it to the top of the balcony. The bedroom balcony was too high, so I climbed the ballroom balcony instead, but it was still a little too much for my aching muscles.

It was nothing, however, compared to the ache in my chest when I saw her.

I knew it was a spell. It had to be. Nothing else would make me think such dramatic, disgustingly romantic thoughts. I wasn't a man of romance, really. Seduction was entertaining. Flirting was a good pastime. But this woman, she entranced me so instantly.

Yes, it was a spell. But I didn't mind it.

She hadn't noticed me yet. She was looking up at the stars, the same exact look on her face the first night we met.

What charming thing had I said to her that night? Ah, right.

"Are you making a wish?" I repeated. "A woman only looks at the stars that intensely when she has a deep wish."

She turned to me, her eyes widening and narrowing as if she was trying to make sense of reality. I chuckled, unable to ignore the fact that even though she was the siren, I somehow stole her breath away.

"Adrian…" she whispered. "How did you get here?"

That was her question? She was supposed to run into my arms, openly weeping with joy.

No matter.

I nodded over the side of the balcony. "I wanted to see if I was strong enough."

"Why would you take a risk like that?" she asked, pouting and rolling her eyes. "You could have gotten hurt—"

When I stepped in front of her, she stopped speaking. Her lips were still parted as if she had more to say, but she didn't. Instead, the wind whipped through her hair, teasing me mercilessly.

"Seeing you made it worth it," I admitted. "As soon as they released me, I had to see you."

Her eyelashes fluttered, a flash of pain shooting across her face as she looked down for a moment.

"These feelings…" she said. "You realize they aren't real."

She sounded so heartbroken at the fact. It encouraged me.

"Aren't they?" I asked, leaning in closer.

She went silent, and I could feel her apprehension. Everything in my body was begging to kiss her, but I held myself back. We both knew this was a spell, but I was going to convince her it was worth it first.

I stepped away and leaned against the balcony rail, giving her some space to breathe.

"Even when we were apart, I couldn't stop thinking about you," I said. "Isn't the spell only supposed to work when we're in the same room?"

She shrugged. "The effects can last a few minutes or a few days."

"But it's been weeks, and I've missed you for every moment of them."

She held her arms as if she were cold, and I could tell that she was on the fence. Yes, she was a siren. Yes, I was under a spell. But I needed her to understand that I didn't care. I was happy this way.

Spell or not, this was the first time I felt happy.

I moved away from the balcony rail and closed the gap between us, taking her by the elbows and bringing her in close to me. Her shoulders came closer to her ears, and the shyness made me even more obsessed with touching her.

"Y-you know that I can manipulate you," she stammered. "I just have to change my voice—"

"Then manipulate me," I said, unable to keep my fingers out of her hair at this point. "Command me whenever it pleases you. I know I'm safe under your spell, princess."

Her shoulders laxed, and I took the opportunity to grab her hand and put it against my chest.

"You made me look into my own darkness until I could find my light," I whispered. "Your power didn't hurt me, Esmeralda. It made me who I am now."

I felt her body mold closer to mine, and I could tell that she was giving in. I had seduced the siren, and I had never been so proud of an accomplishment in entire my life.

"Whether it's a spell or a curse," I whispered in her ear, "I want nothing more than to have you by my side."

I sealed my words with a kiss. I waited, expecting her to back away like she had the time I kissed her in my room, but she didn't. I brought her in closer as she submitted to me, deepening my kiss as a stronger seal.

If it wasn't true love, I didn't care. I never believed in such a thing anyway.

But I believed in feeling truly alive.

That's how I felt with her. That was all I needed.

HENRIK

THREE

His name was Dagon.

I had no idea why I knew this; he had never spoken his name to me. It wasn't often that creatures of the spirit world introduced themselves, and I had never been given a name before.

But I knew his name was Dagon. And I knew he was a demon.

You don't think your brother is capable of his tasssk, do you? Dagon asked.

I rubbed the bridge of my nose.

"He'll be fine," I replied. "He's used to doing questionable acts."

Yesss…but just how many more will he do at your expenssse?

I laughed ironically to myself.

"Expense or request?" I asked. "I was the one who told him to get her blood."

And you've been unsettled about the whole thing ever sssince. I may not need sleep, but you do.

My body felt heavier at the mention of sleep. I hadn't had any since we had boarded this ship. How could I? My delinquent brother was captain of a ship heading toward disaster, my parents were at home ill, and there was a demon speaking to me. How could anyone sleep with such a hurricane of problems?

Someone knocked at the door.

I turned toward the door and opened it. On the other side was Luc, looking dazed and slightly uncomfortable.

"Yes?" I asked him. "What is it?"

"The captain has returned to the ship," he said, rubbing his bottom lip with his thumb thoughtfully. "And you're not going to like it."

I didn't have time to question why the cook was telling me this instead of one of my brother's men, but truth be told, I hated everyone equally on this ship and it didn't matter. What mattered was it sounded like there was another mess I had to clean up.

I went to the deck to meet my brother.

I had sent my brother to collect a vial of blood, not a woman in a blood-red dress.

She was slung over his shoulder, unconscious, her hair draping down his back as he met me with a smile.

Luc was right. I didn't like this at all.

"You absolute moron," I growled at him, nodding at the girl. "This was not part of the plan."

"Yes, well," he replied nonchalantly, "call me old-fashioned, but I wanted some better insurance for the deal. If your voodoo methods fail to work, I need another route for cash."

"You mean another route for prison! Did you even think about the consequences for this?"

"Are they much better than the consequences of cutting a woman open and taking her blood? Face it, Henrik, this wasn't going to end well either way."

A couple men came forward to see what was happening. Adrian caught my glare—I know he did—but he ignored it completely.

"Get her to my room," Adrian commanded his men. "Be careful where you put your hands. None of you are allowed to touch her, understand?"

The men agreed and took the girl from his shoulder. I caught a glimpse of her full red lips and long neck, the soft curve of her jaw and nose. When my heart skipped a beat, I cursed myself.

I knew the demon had felt my heart as well. He didn't have a face, but I could feel him smiling.

"I want no part of this," I said. "Of all the stupid, brainless activities—"

"It'll be fine," he said, brushing me off. "I have it handled."

"You have nothing handled! You never do! If you could handle things, then we wouldn't—"

I stopped. No. I wasn't going to bring it up. It wouldn't do any good. Besides, it wasn't like I had brought honor to our family either.

I huffed, shaking my head to myself.

"I want no part of this," I said, waving my hand at him. "You deal with this yourself. I'll find the path for you. Nothing else."

Before he could give me any excuses, I turned away and went back to my room. I slammed the door behind me, putting my face in my hands.

A ssstunning creature, Dagon said. *If only you weren't scorned by so many…perhaps you could find a bride like that for yoursssself.*

I tried to shake him out of my head, but I knew it wouldn't work.

"Keep those thoughts to yourself, demon," I replied.

Are they my thoughtsss, or yoursss?

I swallowed.

You've sssuffered with your thoughts alone for so long, he continued. *It's nice to have sssomeone to share them with, isn't it?*

"I don't trust you."

I'm not your enemy, you know.

"You're not my ally either."

How ssso? I've offered to help you gain your honor back. I've offered to help you become a name respected and feared among the seasss so you're never scorned again. You can provide for your family. You can start your own family. Everything you ever wanted—

"If I submit to you," I finished. "That doesn't make you an ally, that makes you my owner."

And yet…you haven't gotten rid of me yet. I'm ssstill here.

I chewed my bottom lip, knowing he was right. If I had wanted to rid myself of him, I could have done it by now. He wasn't possessing me, but I was keeping him close by. I wasn't rejecting him.

It was the thing I feared most about myself.

NINETEEN

I looked down at my hands as they shook.

I should have been dead. I had been cornered by pirates, their swords drawn. They were ready to run me through.

And then Dagon…

You don't have to thank me, he said. *I was jussst doing my job as your protector.*

I couldn't form any words. I could only play that moment in my mind over and over again.

I had thrown two men overboard, at the same time.

This is only a sssmall amount of the power I can give you, Dagon added. *Remember that.*

"I don't want power," I said, as if speaking out loud would make it true. "I simply want to save my family."

You have to sssave yourself first, don't you?

My hands shook harder. I needed to get rid of him. I needed to find a way to extract him before I—

There was a knock at the door.

It took me two tries to get my shaking hand around the doorknob to open it. Adrian was rubbing his neck with his hand on the other side, looking lost in thought even though he had just knocked.

"What is it?" I asked, feeling sweat drip down my neck.

He continued to rub his neck. I glanced between him and the door as he did, realizing this was the first time he had actually knocked instead of barging in.

He stepped in, not looking at me but instead at the swords on the wall.

"I spent a lot of time trying to figure out why you would teach her to fight," he finally said. "It seems really obvious now."

I swallowed my heartbeat. "What are you talking about?"

He looked over his shoulder at me. "Esmeralda. You like her, don't you?"

I laughed, far more awkwardly than I should have. "Of course not. I'm simply trying to keep us from getting imprisoned for life."

"I think she likes you too."

I froze at his words, not sensing any irony in them. He folded his arms, tapping his fingers in thought. I could only swallow again, no words coming to my lips.

"After all," he suddenly said, sucking in a breath. "I'm incredibly charming and ruggedly handsome, and yet, she insists on spending time with you. You treat her better, I'm guessing."

I shifted my weight. This was more uncomfortable than when he was being an idiot.

"And since when did you start caring about how you treat people?" I asked honestly.

His shoulders slumped, and I nearly apologized. Most of the time, he was someone I didn't know. He was a reckless criminal, caring nothing for consequences. He had changed so much from my little brother who dreamed of following in my footsteps, far from the teenage boy who applied to be a privateer for the king and was rejected due to his weaker physique and lower education.

Despite his shattered dreams, I had continued on into the navy without him.

And in turn, he became an enemy of both me and the king.

"Treating people well isn't beneficial in my line of…er…*work*," he replied. "But it is in yours. That's probably why you have better foresight than me."

I laughed bitterly again. Foresight, huh? If I had looked after him properly as the elder brother—training him for the navy instead of leaving him to ruin himself—then we wouldn't be where we were now.

He thought I was training Esmeralda to impress her. In reality, I think I was just trying to find redemption for abandoning my brother.

"She saw right through me," he said, licking his bottom lip. "She knew how I…"

He sighed, a painful laugh escaping his lips as he shifted his weight and cleared his throat.

"I've had blood on my hands before, Henrik, but not this much." His eyes glossed over. "There's a lot of things I'm willing to take. The lives of my men isn't one of them."

He stood as still and empty as a statue. When he didn't move or blink, I stepped forward and put a hand on the back of his neck, bringing him down to my shoulder. He leaned his weight on me in despair. I kissed his temple.

"You know," I said, "sometimes when I think your soul is completely gone, you prove me wrong."

He didn't respond, resting himself against my shoulder.

I let him stay there as long as he needed, knowing that the blood on his hands was partly my fault.

***

I had been too distracted by Dagon to even catch wind of the mutiny.

It was my own fault.

The crew that was once ours now held Adrian and I captive. They threw us into a cell together. The rest of the crew that had not submitted to Luc's command were also dragged into their own cells. Some locked themselves in cells, obviously enchanted by charmspeak.

"What the hell is happening?" Adrian asked, inspecting the locked bars.

"Siren enchantment," I replied. "Luc used the power in his arsenal to put a spell over the crew."

"And Esmeralda?"

"Also a siren. An accomplice, seemingly."

"The fiancé as well?"

I thought for a moment. I wasn't sure what the prisoner's role was at all. The markings on his chest were certainly from the spiritual realm. The patterns were quite vivid.

"I decide whether you get your wings, or if you're sentenced to endless reincarnation," he had said.

He'sss a Judge, Dagon whispered.

"What's that?" I asked.

"What's what?" Adrian asked me.

I held up a finger for him to be silent.

A Judge puts the creaturesss of the spiritual realm on trial, Dagon continued. *He decidesss if they are punished or given their original power.*

"What original power?" I asked.

The power to destroy humansss, like you and your brother.

"Are you talking to the spirits in your head again?" Adrian asked. "This isn't really the time for that, is it?"

I gritted my teeth, throwing my hands up in frustration. "I don't have time for your opinions! There's things about this world you don't understand, Adrian."

"I understand that Uncle Leo is dead!" he threw back. He grabbed my face, making me look at him. "I understand that Uncle Leo lost himself to this bullshit and now he's dead! You'll end up the same way!"

We both know that'sss not true, Dagon said. *I'm the one that'sss been keeping you alive.*

I pulled out of Adrian's hold, grunting. I was about to tear him verbally limb from limb, until I saw the fear in his eyes. We stared at each other for a few tense moments, my breath getting stuck in my lungs.

He needsss you, Dagon said. *You can see it, can't you?*

I ran my tongue through my dry mouth, nodding. My brother needed me. The look on his face told me that he actually wanted me around. He hadn't looked at me that way since we both applied for the navy.

But I wasn't strong enough. I couldn't protect either one of us.

I can help you with that, you know, Dagon continued. *I can keep both of you alive.*

"I can't do this on my own, Henrik," Adrian said, cutting into our conversation. "I need you to keep it together."

I brought my hand to the back of his neck, bringing him into my embrace. In my arms, he was just my little brother, and I was the older brother responsible for his safety.

There was no one else. If I wanted redemption, this was the only way.

"All right," I said. "You win."

And although Adrian heard it come from my lips, Dagon was the one who understood.

THIRTY-SEVEN

I vaguely recalled the ship landing into a crystal-teal port.

There was something about trials.

There was a bright red light.

And then I awoke to a prison cell.

I couldn't tell how long I had been there. By my thirst and hunger, it couldn't have been too long. But I had been going in and out of consciousness, so there was no way to know what Dagon had done. What I had done.

"Where's my brother?" I yelled down the hallway. The guards didn't answer. They seemed to be deliberately avoiding my questions about Adrian, only wanting to discuss my demon.

If I had asked about Esmeralda, then would they…? No. She wasn't mine to ask for.

The girl is sssafe, Dagon said. *This is her home, after all. Your brother, on the other hand…*

I shook my head violently. "Don't lie to me, demon."

Even as a demon, I have limited power against the sirensss. They've captured his mind, turning him completely against you. Don't you remember what he said at the Trialsss? Let me help you.

He returned a small piece of the trial to my memory.

"He's snapped completely…"

I huffed, my throat suddenly starting to close up.

They've all turned against you, Henrik. I'm all you have now.

I swallowed, my hands trembling once more.

I'll get you out of here alive, he continued. *I'll get you back to your family. With my power, you'll gain back everything you've lost and more.*

I leaned against the bars, out of breath. The cold metal bit into my sweating forehead.

I couldn't fight anymore. I couldn't. There was nothing else worth fighting for anymore.

I slid to the floor, everything turning to black once again.

***

She wantsss to talk to you.

"Who?" I asked, my lips not actually moving.

The woman who ruined you. The woman who took your family from you. The little siren who's suffered nothing for her crimesss.

I felt my heart clench, a conflicting pain of hate…and the desire to see her.

Don't forget the pain she's caused you.

Suddenly, it felt like I had been struck by lightning. I screamed, the sound echoing off the walls of wherever I was.

It hurtsss, doesn't it? Dagon asked. *I can get rid of her, if you want.*

I knew what he meant by the phrase *"get rid of,"* but I wouldn't allow that.

I didn't know why, but I just couldn't.

Suit yourself, he said. *Why don't you talk to her then; I'll stay with you. I'll protect you from her. I'll keep you from her ssspell.*

I felt myself sit up against a cold wall.

The prison. I was still in prison.

Then my eyes blurred and she came into sight. I exhaled, wondering if I could be entranced so quickly. Why was she so beautiful?

Remember what she did to your brother, Henrik. Remember what she did to you. She made sssure you're still a laughingstock.

I clenched my jaw.

"You shouldn't be here," I said.

Her eyes widened in shock, then closed in relief.

"Oh, Henrik, is that you?" she asked, her voice light and airy.

That's how sssirens capture you, Dagon reminded me. *I'm protecting you from that voice now. Ssshe's using it to charm you.*

"Don't worry," she continued. "I'll get Jacques. He can get rid of the demon—"

"And why should I get rid of him?" I barked. "So I can be controlled by creatures like you?"

She froze. I stood from the floor, my body aching. Her hand came to my shoulder, but I stepped out of her grasp.

"Get out," I warned. "There's no telling what we'll do to you."

"You won't hurt me," she said, her voice just as high as before. Was she still trying to charm me? "You won't let him."

"And why shouldn't I?" I asked, turning to her. "Shouldn't I have a way to protect myself from your power?"

She met my eyes, not answering. Perhaps she realized she couldn't control me with Dagon present. Her shoulders slumped in defeat.

"I had no idea…" she started. "I care about you. You've always been strong and kind—"

"And where did my kindness get me? Kicked out of the navy? A laughingstock to the king himself? I've been possessed by both a demon and a siren. Has my *kindness* led me anywhere profitable?"

She seemed to fumble around for her words.

Ssshe's trying to strategize, Dagon said. *I can give you power over her.*

I felt him start to take over, but I pulled him back.

I didn't trust him either. I didn't trust either one of them.

"Fight him," Esmeralda said. "Don't let him take over—"

I grabbed her hand before she could try and touch me—before she could use her fingers to control me—and pulled her close to look her in the eyes.

Even like this, I wanted her.

"If I get rid of him," I said, "will you come to me?"

She didn't speak at first. Dagon interrupted.

You don't have to get rid of me, he said. *We can take her for ourselvesss right now.*

I stepped back from her before he could do what he was implying.

"No!" I said out loud. "I won't—"

Don't you want her? Don't you want to know how she tastesss?

"We'll get rid of the demon," Esmeralda said, cutting into my thoughts. "We'll get rid of him so—"

"So you can possess me?"

Dagon took my hands and forced her against the wall.

What are you doing? I asked him.

Protecting you from her ssspell, he replied.

Why were they both torturing me? I didn't have power. I had nothing at all worth tricking me for. And I had done nothing for her. There was no reason for her to save me. I helped kidnap her, sacrificed her blood, and kept her from her family.

There was no reason for her to come to me. Not unless she wanted to own me.

"Do you want my soul to play with?" I asked her.

She shook her head. "No, let me—"

"I'm tired of fighting. Against you. Against this demon. I don't have the strength anymore."

Let's take her, Henrik. Show her she can't possesss you.

No.

You want her.

Yes, I want her.

Then take her.

No, I won't take people the way you do.

Sssmall problem with that, Henrik. I'm you.

Before I could stop him, he put my hands through her hair and forced my lips against hers. She trembled and twisted under my touch, showing me how much it was hurting her.

Stop. I commanded. Not like this.

Why are you commanding me? Isn't thisss what you imagined?

My stomach clenched. He was right. This was how I had imagined taking her away from my brother and her fiancé. This was how I imagined making her mine. I wanted something to belong only to me. Something that couldn't be taken away. Something I could possess.

Dagon wasn't the demon. I was.

He returned my control back to me. I pulled back, just far enough to speak, but not far enough to look her in the eyes.

"Save me," I begged.

I was ripped from her side, just long enough to see the look of terror on her face.

Then everything went black.

FORTY-EIGHT

The guards binding my hands behind my back were the only reason I wasn't lying on the ground in pain.

Every inch of my skin felt like it was on fire, even though Jacques had only burned the skin on my chest. It was enough to set my whole body on flame, however. And although I didn't know the true location of my soul, I could feel it ache from the way it had now been split in two.

Dagon was gone.

But seeing my brother pale and bleeding from his side, it felt like I had never been possessed at all. I was the demon the entire time.

"Let her go, Henrik," Adrian had said. *"You can hate me more if you want, but at least let me keep you from destroying yourself. Let me do one honorable thing for us both."*

I knew he had changed when he said that. My younger brother cared nothing for honor. But if Esmeralda had saved him, how could I damn him again?

You can't let them leave, Dagon had said as Adrian took Esmeralda's hand. *If he leavesss, your family is over.*

It wouldn't be because of him, I replied. I did this.

"Go then," I huffed out, ignoring Jacques's sword in my back. "Both of you get out."

I made it a command. Both Adrian and Esmeralda needed to be free of me.

And I, even if there was nothing I could do to redeem myself, at least wanted to die with a clean soul.

Don't you dare, Dagon warned. *I've given you everything.*

Give it to someone else, I replied.

"Jacques," I said over my shoulder. "About the demon…"

Dagon took over before I could finish, not even allowing my permission this time.

I never told you my price, Henrik.

What price?

The price everyone is judged with in the end. The only price that mattersss in this realm: blood.

After that, everything went black.

There was a flash of light.

And I awoke to my brother on the floor and bleeding, the bloodied sword in my own hand.

And now, my brother's lifeless body was lying in front of the Siren King, the same king I had tried to kill. The same king whose children I tried to destroy.

I had no hope for mercy.

They laid Adrian's body in front of the king. The way the king looked at me showed that knew me quite well, even though I didn't remember us meeting at all. It was from his posture and mannerisms alone that I assumed he was king.

Part of me knew to pay respects. The other half hated myself too much to act with any pride.

"Father…"

Esmeralda's broken whisper made me raise my head. With tears falling down her cheeks, she held my brother's limp hand and looked to her leader.

She was a siren, I knew. With that power, she could manipulate and destroy humanity in any way she wanted. But here she was, holding my brother's hand, pleading for his life.

Forgive me, Esmeralda, you were exactly who you said you were. I was the liar. I was the deceitful one. I was the demon.

The king stepped forward, putting his hand on Adrian's forehead.

"You returned my daughter to me," the king said to my brother as he lay unconscious. "And protected her from the demon that tried to destroy us all."

I dropped my head.

"You assisted in restoring freewill to my creations," the king continued, "and so, this once, I will restore your body."

I raised my head to see a beautiful turquoise thread spring from the king's hand and weave into Adrian's body. Tears of relief sprung to my eyes as his color returned. He wasn't conscious, but I knew his life had returned to him.

I was too exhausted to express my gratitude.

"Bring me his brother," the king commanded.

If I was to be sentenced to death, I accepted. My actions had been evil, blinded by my own pride. I put a sword in my own brother. I commanded the killing of the sirens. I almost even destroyed an innocent woman who had done nothing but show concern for my family.

I would take death. I had earned it.

I lowered my head.

"Look at me, Henrik," the king commanded.

It took all my strength to do it. Whether it was from exhaustion or fear, it was hard to say.

"Yes…" I whispered out. "Yes, Your Majesty."

"You allowed a demon to possess you for power," he said firmly. "A demon cannot possess without permission. Therefore, I can't overlook this."

I lowered my head again. "Yes, Your Majesty. I'll accept your judgment."

There was silence for a long moment. I assumed he was contemplating the worst possible punishment. I had no intentions to resist. My own personal judgment had been so poor. Better it was left in his hands than mine.

"You will be tried," the king said finally. "Should you survive, you will work for me permanently."

I raised my head. It seemed too gracious a judgment to believe. The king's gaze met mine, his face both fearless and wise.

"I saved your brother's life and spared yours," he said. "In return, you will hand that life over to me."

I convulsed, my legs buckling under me. The guards held me up, the tears in my eyes falling freely. I looked at my brother nodding.

"Yes, Your Majesty," I said, still unable to believe my ears. "For my brother's life, you have my loyalty."

I could barely take a full breath in as Jacques approached me.

"I would wish you luck," he said, "but if you survive, then I have to train your ass for the rest of my life."

The guards escorted me to the door, my knees buckling under me from the flood of emotions. I looked over my shoulder to look at Adrian once more, desperate to see him one last time.

His body was still, at peace. Perhaps he was grown enough now to live without me. Perhaps he was the man I knew he could be.

As we reached the door, I caught Esmeralda's eyes. She gave me a warm smile through her own tears, and my shame consumed me again.

I could never repay her. I could never even apologize.

So I only whispered to her in my thoughts.

Thank you, Esmeralda. Thank you for looking past my demons.

ENDING

I crumpled the paper again, throwing it to the side of the Judges' room with the others.

Words weren't enough. No matter how much I tried to apologize or explain—

"Not skilled in the art of love letters, are you?"

I turned to see Adrian unrolling my crumpled pages, reading them with his nose scrunched in amusement. I stood and snatched the paper from his hands.

"Aren't you supposed to be resting?" I scolded. "You're not even healed—"

"I can't stare at the ceiling forever," he replied. "Besides, I'm fine. There's no damage."

He tapped on his side for emphasis. He then winced in regret, but shook his head as if he was just teasing. I knew he wasn't.

"How's training?" he asked, changing subjects.

"Brutal." I sat back in my chair, leaning my head against it. "But I deserve it."

He shrugged. "Maybe. But you deserve some credit too. You'd be dead if you were completely evil, right? The paintings on your ribs indicate you're not a complete loser."

My lip twitched. "Thanks."

He paused, tapping his fingers against the desk.

"Perhaps we both got the justice we deserved," he said, "and the mercy we didn't."

I raised an eyebrow. He caught my eye and cleared his throat.

"Don't get used to great insights like that," he said.

"I wasn't planning on it."

I sighed putting elbows on the desk and my head in my hands.

"You know," Adrian said, "a woman much prefers an apology in person."

I laughed behind my hands. "An apology couldn't cover it."

"Maybe, maybe not. You never know unless you try."

I picked up the pen and tapped it against the paper, the ink making incoherent splotches across the page.

"Besides, you want to see her again," Adrian asked. "Don't you?"

I swallowed, avoiding his gaze. "Does it matter?"

"It would to her."

I met his eyes and turned away when I saw the seriousness in them. I sighed, not answering.

"In other news, Jacques hired me for a job," Adrian said, filling the silence. "I leave in about a week. Maybe you should come back with me. See Mom and Dad, maybe a few other people worth seeing."

He lingered for a moment, waiting for my answer. I nodded, but I wasn't sure if it was simply in acknowledgment or in agreement.

He smirked as if he had won a game of cards.

"You'll have enough time to think of your apologies on the ship," he said as he started to walk out the door. "But if you ask me, I'd say you won't be needing them."

***

"This is it?" I asked.

Adrian nodded, walking up to the door with me. He was the only one of us who knew where Esmeralda lived, and he had offered—or, I should say, forced—his escort to her house. I had to keep wiping my sweaty palms against my coat, hoping it would help them from shaking.

"It's late," I commented. "Maybe we should come back tomorrow—"

"It took us over a month to get here," he said. "Don't you think you've made her wait long enough?"

He reached up to knock on the door, but I grabbed his arm.

"She has to hate me," I blurted out. "She has to."

His eyes lingered on me for a long moment, and he lowered his arm.

"Esmeralda? Hate?" He chuckled. "I kidnapped her, threatened her family, and nearly got her killed. In the end, she still pleaded for my life. You think that woman would hate you?"

I swallowed. "I did far worse."

He puffed out his cheeks and gave a rough sigh. "Yeah, yeah, you messed up. How about you ask her directly how she feels instead of making up stories that make you miserable?"

With that, he banged hard on the front door and ran off, leaving me at the doorstep alone.

"You rat!" I called after him.

He turned back, laughing. "I won't wait up for you!"

Before I could scold him further, the door swung open. An older woman answered the door, her face clearly worn from exhaustion.

"May I help you?" she asked flatly.

The words spilled out of my lips in rapid fire. "Y-yes, I apologize for coming so late in the evening, but I was wondering if I could speak to the lady of the house?"

"She's with her father now," the woman said. "Perhaps—"

"Is her father healing?" I blurted out. "I heard he was ill. Is he faring well? Is she? Has she been we—"

I stopped, suddenly realizing how much I had rambled on my questions. The older woman smiled fondly and nodded, waving me in.

"Perhaps you should come inside and wait?" she asked.

I nodded, the blood coming to my face. "Yes, thank you. I appreciate the generosity."

She helped me to remove my coat as I stepped in. When I raised my head, I saw a beautiful creature atop the staircase, so lovely, in fact, that I forgot to breathe.

Esmeralda's blonde hair was tousled around her shoulders, much like she had while we had been at sea together. Her gown was simple but flattering, the hues of blue bringing out her eyes even from where I was standing.

Someone cleared her throat.

I jumped, forgetting the kind older woman next to me. She hung my coat in the foyer with a smile much like Adrian's.

"You two can visit in the parlor," she said. "I'll make some tea."

I nodded. Esmeralda said nothing as she descended down the stairs, staring at me as if I were a stranger. Maybe she thought I was here to harm her? Maybe she was filled with so much anger and hatred for me that she was unable to speak?

Whatever it was, when she stood directly in front of me, all I could do was stare. There were dark circles under her clear eyes, but they didn't make her any less beautiful.

I knew I was no longer under her spell, but this feeling certainly felt like one.

She nodded to the parlor room gently, her gesture timid. I swallowed, wondering how the bold woman I met the first day of the ship had suddenly become so shy in my presence. I must have truly hurt her.

I sat on one of the large sofas, and she sat across from me. I opened my mouth a few times to speak, but nothing came out. It was just as if I were writing her a letter again.

The older woman returned with tea, the warm, cinnamon scent suddenly filling the room. As she shut the door behind her, the steam from the pot twisted up in the air between Esmeralda and me, reminding me of that night the sky split apart.

"It's good to see you, Henrik," she said.

A relieved, bitter laugh escaped my mouth.

"Is it?" I asked, unable to look her in the eyes. "I was worried what you would say when I came to your door. And then…"

I swallowed.

"And then I forgot everything I wanted to say when I saw you," I finished.

Without a word, she leaned forward. I thought she'd scold me for being so forward, but she only poured the tea into the cups and handed me one.

"How is your training?" she asked.

I accepted the change of subject.

"I've been treated well, under the circumstances," I replied. "Thanks to His Majesty, my family is safe and I'm in a position of purpose. I can't ask for anything more."

I tried to steady my hand while sipping the tea.

"And your father?" I asked.

"He's healing, but not…"

Her face fell. It wasn't the face of a powerful siren but of a caring daughter struggling with the idea of losing her family. And if it wasn't for her, my family would have been ruined. My brother and I wouldn't now be making enough salary to take care of our parents. My brother would be dead. And I would still be a demon.

"If there's anything you need," I said, "please allow me to serve you as—"

I stopped. I couldn't say what I wanted: *As the man who loves you.*

"As a servant of the king," I finished.

She looked at me and sighed, visible pain in her eyes.

"Please don't act like my servant," she said. "Not when I look up to you."

The teacup slipped from my hand, the hot water splashing on my shirt. In a moment, Esmeralda had jumped to her feet, a napkin in her hand to assist me. As we both scrambled to get the burning water out of my shirt, the skin underneath became exposed, showing off the burn marks that reminded us both that I had once been a demon.

Her gentle fingers grazed my skin.

"Do they still hurt?" she asked.

I pulled back, her touch making my whole body heat up.

"No," I replied. "There is, however, something I still don't understand."

I looked into her eyes, far too eager to give my confession.

"Even with these runes etched into my skin," I said, "you're still the only thing I can think about."

She answered only with silence, but I couldn't control my honesty.

"I know I hurt you," I said. "My darkness enslaved me, and I lashed out at you for it. But I wanted to say that with or without magic, you're the one who has captured me the most. I realize that you're engaged, and I don't wish to make anything difficult for you, but I had to tell you in person myself. I had to apologize for my actions and wish you the greatest happiness."

I stood to my feet, realizing I had overstepped and that it was now time for me to leave.

"I wish you the greatest happiness, Esmeralda," I said in closing. "I won't forget—"

Suddenly I was in her embrace, her lips against mine.

I pulled back, too shocked for words. She smiled up at me, her arms around my neck.

"You fool," she said. "How can you wish me great happiness when my greatest happiness is you?"

I swallowed, words rushing back to my lungs. "I hurt you," I said.

"Do you still want revenge against me?"

"Of course not. Not when I—"

I stopped. She smirked knowingly, nudging me.

"Tell me?" she sang.

We both smiled. Her spell wouldn't work on me, we both knew that. But she didn't have to have me under a spell; she already knew I was hers.

"Because I'm in love with you," I whispered. "Completely obsessed."

She smiled brighter, the light in her eyes turning into my soul's lighthouse.

"Good," she said. "Because I love you too."

I chewed my lip, holding her in my arms. I had once been a demon, but the look in her eyes showed that she saw nothing less than a man.

That was all I needed. It was more than I could ever ask for.

JACQUES

ONE

"This is some of the best wine I've tasted," the captain said, trying to make small talk for the thirteenth time this evening.

The wine in Spain was much better, but I wasn't going to tell him that. There was no need for him to know about my own lifestyle. The captain still thought I was his poor bastard child, and I didn't mind making him feel a bit of guilt for the last twenty-five years of negligence.

"It's palatable," I replied cooly.

He nodded, taking another sip of his wine and losing his words again.

I could tell he was nervous. His aura was tinted gray. Whether he was nervous about me coming to this party with him or about the gold digger he was taking as his new wife was what I couldn't determine.

From what I had heard of her, she was beautiful and graceful, charming and sophisticated. There wasn't a tarnish on their family name. Her mother had passed— same as mine—and now my supposed father was stepping in to save the day. Perhaps it was guilt because he never stepped in to save my own mother, his ex-lover. That was the only reason why he would drag me into this in the first place. I had no business with the girl.

"Perhaps I could ask for the label and provide it at the wedding," he rambled. "At least I know one thing the lady enjoys."

He chuckled, but his aura darkened, meaning he hated his own joke. I decided to pry.

"It's Burgundy wine from the northeast," I replied. "I know a trader of it, if you're interested. But it's a high price. It's not the wine chosen by a man about to go out of business."

His aura changed to a saturated red before going back to gray. Apparently, I had irritated him momentarily.

"Don't start rumors, my dear Jacques," he urged. "Simon has not lost his business from poor management skills or lack of character. So don't ruin the reputation he will leave behind for his daughter."

"You make it sound like the man is ill."

The captain suddenly went silent, his aura darkening once again. I swallowed my drink roughly.

"Wait, is that it?" I asked. "Is that the reason you're marrying this woman?"

Before he could answer, everyone stopped talking and turned their heads toward the staircase. Confused by the sudden shift in environment, I had no choice but to look in the same direction.

Perched at the top of the stairs was a woman in a crimson and gold ball gown, her long, pale and slender arm touching the rail as she smiled proudly to the audience below. Her golden hair was pulled back, blue eyes bright enough to see from the bottom of the stairs. As her audience looked up, their auras all slowly changed to a glowing rose.

The aura of attraction.

"Thank you all for coming so far to see us today," the lady atop the stairs said. "I'm grateful that our family has so many good people to call friends. My handmaid will take your thoughtful and expensive gifts on the way out."

They all chucked at her joke, which was not witty enough for that kind of a reaction. But her voice was light and airy, and her own aura deepened to purple, meaning she was giving off a powerful imaginative feeling.

That aura—purple interlaced with hints of gold— was only for the spiritual realm. And it was pouring off every inch of the woman.

Wait… was she a creature from the spiritual realm? But who would be able to charm…

…*a siren*? The woman of the house was a siren?

She would have to be an incarnate. She clearly had no wings. But she was undoubtedly using charmspeak. There had been a few times that incarnates found out their real identities, through fortune tellers and the like. She must have known. She was far too confident as she spoke. Yes, she knew what kind of power she held, and she was enjoying the use of it.

Her eyes met mine, her eyes freezing momentarily. I raised my wine to my lips, not taking my eyes off of her.

I know what you are, little siren. Do you know what I am?

She descended the stairs, taking an older man's arm. That must have been her father, Simon.

Hmmm. His aura was quite faded. The man was truly ill. Did the daughter know? I couldn't tell by her aura.

I took another sip of wine, processing the information.

My new father leaned over to my ear.

"Best foot forward," he said. I wasn't sure if he was talking to me or himself.

The woman of the house and the older gentleman came to greet us. Her eyes met mine once more, her aura turning from purple to rose. I tried not to smile. The little siren found me attractive. How amusing.

You should be afraid of me, woman. If you know you're a siren, then you should know what I can do to you.

"I'd like you to meet former Naval Captain Theodore de Villiers, and his son, Jacques," her father said. "Gentlemen, this is my daughter, Esmeralda."

With a rosy smile she held out her hand for us to kiss. My father did so with a gentlemanly manner. I couldn't hate him for it; she was undoubtably beautiful in many senses, and her siren charm was probably affecting him. I, however, only brought it up toward my lips but didn't make contact. If this woman was a siren, I didn't want to get myself in any more of a mess with the spirit world than necessary.

"I was afraid he was exaggerating," my father said, "but I'm pleased to find that your father's quite accurate in his praises of you."

She brought a delicate hand to her expensive necklace. "My father should save some of those praises for himself. All of my accomplishments are from his spoils."

And yet you asked the entire room to leave you expensive gifts, I thought.

I wasn't buying this woman's affections for her father. It was obvious how interested in money she was.

My father and hers joked together about their time in their navy, helping me piece together why my father had agreed to this arrangement. The father was a dear friend and ill. The woman, however, didn't seem suitable.

And there was no way I was going to allow my father to marry a siren. To mix more people I knew with the spiritual world would only end in disaster.

It always had.

"Have you danced yet, my dear?" Esmeralda's father asked.

She patted his arm affectionately. "Looking for a suitable partner, Father. All in good time."

"Perhaps someone nearby would be suitable?"

"Are you volunteering, Father?"

"Me? Heavens no. You know I haven't the slightest ounce of rhythm."

Her father looked at mine.

My father shifted uncomfortably. "As much as I would enjoy asking for the first dance, I'm afraid I've forgotten all the steps after this blasted knee injury. Jacques, my boy, would you do the honor?"

Why was I getting involved in this again?

I took another sip of wine and put down the glass. I held out my hand, her aura turning even more pink. Even if I couldn't read her aura, I could read her eyes. There was an anticipation in them, as if she thought I was her betrothed instead of my father. She should have known that a man like me could never be betrothed to a woman like her.

I wondered how long it would take for her to realize what I was, and how mortified she would be when she found out.

"I warn you," I whispered to her as I escorted her to the dance floor. "Once we dance, you'll lose interest in taking my hand again."

"Is your dancing so bad?" she said with a flirtatious giggle.

I tried to hold back my smile, amused that she didn't realize how much danger she was truly in.

"No," I said in her ear. "But once you find out who I am, you'll keep your distance, just like everybody else."

THREE

I couldn't get drunk enough at this party.

There were far too many women eager to compliment me based on either my looks or my father, and I wasn't interested either way. Their comments wouldn't be worth anything if they had found out what I *actually* did full-time. Damning the souls of spiritual creatures didn't add me to anyone's Most Desirable Bachelors list.

I needed some air.

The house had a balcony, so I made my way to it. When I walked out, however, I wasn't expecting to see a man and woman standing on the balcony ledge, ready to jump.

The man turned toward me, his aura a mix of pride and enchantment. His face, on the other hand, was dark and twisted, childish and too smug for its own good.

"Is she yours, mate?" he asked.

It took me a moment to realize that he was holding Esmeralda, whose aura was completely black with fear.

"I'm going to borrow her for a bit," the man continued, his hand over Esmeralda's mouth. "I hope you don't mind."

They dropped off the side.

I rushed to the edge, hearing Esmeralda scream as they plunged into the darkness below. Her scream brought about the interest of a few others close to the balcony, and they ran over to see what was happening.

"Who was that?" one of them asked.

"Did someone just commit suicide?"

"Someone call the police!"

I winced at their annoying banter in my ears. I took off my jacket, handing it to one of the women standing next to me.

"Hold this for a moment, please," I said.

I climbed over the side and down the wall. There were a few noisy cries as I did so, but I didn't pay much attention to what they were saying. They certainly had enough energy to talk, but not enough energy to do anything about the situation. Typical.

Halfway down the side of the house, I dropped down and hit the streets, taking off in the direction I saw them go.

I didn't know these streets like I knew the streets back home. It wasn't often that my men even had a chance to come to this city, and if we did, we kept to the slums. Ironically, the poor paid more than the rich for our products. Probably because the rich actually knew the worth of their money. The poor were still foolish enough to think they could buy happiness. The rich had already bought happiness and realized it was a scam.

There were too many winding streets in this city. I had to climb up another house and stand on the roof just to get a better look.

Where was our little thief?

Adjusting my eyes to the shadows, I looked over the city and tried to scan for him. It took quite a few minutes, but in time I found an abnormally thick shadow heading toward the docks.

Pirates?

Well, this was complicated.

***

"Sit down, sir," the handmaid, Lina, said to Simon. "Think of that heart of yours."

Esmeralda's father was completely red from his forehead to his fingertips. His aura was a fierce black-and-red mix, but it flickered from strong to nearly invisible. He was fighting with his illness and his emotions at the same time.

I didn't say anything as Lina held his hand and tried to soothe him. The way she patted his hand reminded me of someone from a lifetime ago—the young priestess who had freed me of my demon.

But she was gone now. Same as my mother. And same as my demon.

I tried to shove the memory down.

"I'll do whatever it takes to bring her back," my father said firmly. "She'll return safely home. I promise you, Simon."

Simon got up from his chair, pacing the room frantically.

"I'll put a sword in them!" he yelled. "A bullet! I'll send a whole firing squad!"

Lina and the captain attempted to calm him down, but it didn't go as smoothly as planned. I decided to step out of the room, not finding myself particularly useful in the situation. The guests had already abandoned the party, proving themselves just as useless. They'd no doubt gossip and slander while they were at home, making it worse on the entire family as a whole.

It wasn't my business. Even if struck too close to home.

"A priestess running about with the scum of the city! This taints the purity of the church!"

"But he's so young, and he needs our help—"

"His whole family worships the devil himself! So let Satan deal with his own. If you want to help him, then you can leave this church and go to Satan yourself!"

"Young Master de Villiers?"

I turned around at Lina's voice. She wrung her hands together, her aura twisted in worry.

My shoulders loosened. "Please call me Jacques. I'm no master."

Her mouth ticked with a smile as she stepped forward to talk to me. "You must be hungry. You've stayed with us far past midnight barely knowing a soul in front of you. Come with me and I'll get you some bread and tea."

She didn't even give me the chance to object, stalking off to the kitchen before I could open my mouth. I followed only to tell her that it wasn't necessary, but she was deep in her own thoughts, muttering as she sliced some bread.

"My dear girl…she must be so frightened. Who would be so twisted as to take an innocent child?"

"Pirates," I said as she placed the buttered bread and tea on the table. "Criminal scum that will do anything for some quick money."

She poured the tea, and I felt there was nothing I could do but take it as she motioned for me to sit at the table.

She huffed. "Ahh, criminals like that…don't they realize their salvation isn't in their wallets?"

I chewed the bread slowly. "There are more opportunities for those with deep pockets."

"What good is an opportunity when you have no character to sustain it?"

I tried not to smile as I swallowed. Lina was exactly like Samantha. If Samantha had had the chance to grow into a middle-aged woman, that is.

Lina sat in front of me, the gray strands of her hair seeming brighter as she fanned her round face in anxiety.

"That girl isn't my blood, but I can't help but feel like I've lost my own daughter."

She dabbed the corners of her eyes with her sleeve. I couldn't tell if the girl had charmed Lina—charmspeak could take up to a month to wear completely off, depending on the victim—but Lina's blue aura was honest enough. The same blue aura Samantha had right after the church excommunicated her for helping me, right before the end of everything.

The words left my mouth before I had the chance to think them through.

"Don't worry, Madame Lina. I'll bring her back."

***

"We got the information you wanted, Jac," my contact said. "The guy's name is Adrian. He's a wanted criminal in a few places for arson and vandalism."

It had been awhile since I had met one of my former subordinates in a back alley for information. So long, in fact, that I had completely overdressed. I had been so used to meeting businessmen that I forgot how to dress for scum who did honest business.

"Seems mild compared to kidnapping," I replied.

"Maybe he's trying to level up his criminal status? Either way, he seems like a lunatic."

"How so?"

"He's been going about the city asking about something called the Eros."

My ears perked. Our thief is interested in the siren world? Is that why he stole a siren?

"Apparently," my subordinate continued, "it's supposed to be some sort of fancy rock that controls—"

"I'm aware of it," I said. And I did. More than I cared to know. "This is more than useful. You've done well."

"Then the payment we agreed on?"

"On its way to your house now," I said. "I wouldn't dream of carrying cash on me in this part of the city. I know you bastards."

He grinned with two missing teeth and bowed at the waist. "That's 'cause we learned from the best."

"Don't try to flatter me. It doesn't pay extra."

He tipped his ragged hat to say goodbye. I clutched his shoulder before he left, pulling him back. I flung off my long coat and threw it over his head.

"Don't you dare sell it," I commanded.

He pulled it off, wrapping it around his shoulders. I had taught him not to show gratitude, so he didn't, but his aura showed me that he was thankful.

"Next time, Jac," he said with a smile.

"If one of us isn't dead by then," I replied.

With a nod, he left.

The Eros. It had been some time since I had been to the Den of Sirens. A while since I had damned spiritual creatures to heaven or hell.

Perhaps it was time to pay them a visit.

THIRTY-FIVE

I forgot how strong demons were. And loud.

"You cannot stop us!" Henrik's demon shrieked as we drug him down to the cells. "The Eros is in our grasp!"

"The only thing in your grasp is eternal damnation," I replied, grunting.

He kicked and twisted between the four of us, the Judge bonds making it hard for him to break out but also digging into my hands. I didn't appreciate it. We tossed him in his cell, giving us just enough time to sprint to close the door behind him.

As expected, Henrik broke through the bonds in a matter of moments, shrieking once again and slamming into the cell bars. Henrik was going to feel that when he snapped out of his trance.

"Get the candles," I ordered two of my men. "Once he calms down, we'll try to approach the human host."

Henrik cackled. "Who says I'll allow it?"

I licked my lips in annoyance. "You don't have infinite energy, demon."

"But my host has plenty of anger, bitterness, and greed for me to feed on."

I ignored him and motioned to my third man. "Go get his brother. We need to question him."

He nodded and ran down the corridor, and I turned to walk away myself.

"You're going to fail, Judge," he taunted.

I waved behind me, not interested.

"After all, you have a long history of failures, right?" he continued. "If it wasn't for you, that sweet innocent priestess would still be part of her church. Still thriving. Still so happy."

My heart pounded, but didn't race. It maintained a steady rhythm, already accustomed to these accusatory thoughts.

"So sad that she was excommunicated after helping you," the demon continued still. "So sad that she slipped into such a deep depression. So sad that poison is so easy to come by…"

I turned back to the cell, meeting the demon in the eyes. I could see the pride in his them, as if he was happy to know my pain. I stepped in close, leaning my arm against the bars as I stared him straight in the eyes.

"You've made a mistake, demon," I said. "You assumed my feelings hold power over me still."

"Aren't you guilty?" he asked me.

I chuckled. "Of course. But the reason creatures like you don't control me anymore is because I grew up to realize that we're all guilty."

The demon raised Henrik's eyebrow pointedly.

"So you don't take any responsibility? Are you sure you're holy, Judge?"

"I never claimed to be. But I don't take morality lessons from demons."

He stared at me, possibly analyzing my aura. I had no idea what he saw. That was the only drawback of seeing auras: you couldn't see your own.

I cleared his words from my head, putting my mission toward the front of my mind. I leaned in as close as I could between the bars.

"I'm going to send you back to hell," I whispered. "And if my soul goes with yours, so be it."

With a screech and a hiss he slammed against the bars. I stepped back to allow him the temper tantrum.

He couldn't break through the bars, and I wasn't going to let him break through my mind either.

"You'll pay for your sins, Judge," he yelled. "You think you can escape it?"

I chuckled. "No. We all pay for them eventually. You will too. Don't forget it."

***

"I don't have the time to babysit," I said.

King Melchior only stared at me. I wasn't sure why he had called me in for a status report. He knew already that it was going to take time for me to extract the demon out of Henrik's body. That is, if Henrik *wanted* to have the demon extracted.

"Adrian stays near the cell constantly," I continued, "making it impossible for my men to do their job."

The king nodded thoughtfully. "And what is their job, exactly?"

I tried not to roll my eyes. He was asking questions he already knew the answers to again.

"To find the demon's weak point or the human host's strength," I replied, monotone.

"And just what could the host's strength be, I wonder?"

He rested his chin on his hand, waiting for my reply to his fake rhetorical question.

I sighed. "I've thought of it too. But the problem is, if Adrian is Henrik's strength, that means that the demon is going to try and get rid of Adrian."

"Then exploit the demon's weakness before he can hurt the brother," Hugo said.

"But Adrian's presence may remind Henrik of his ultimate purpose," Vito added. "We shouldn't keep them too far from each other."

"Allow Adrian to see his brother, as agreed," the king finally said. "But your priority is to extract the demon, so do whatever is necessary, even temporary blockades, in order to do so."

Even after all this time, it still was unnerving to watch the three of them talk as one conscious thought. It was something I had never gotten used to. Maybe it just reminded me too much of a sharing my body with a demon for so long.

"But my worry," the king continued, "extends to you and your men as well."

I shrugged. "It's nothing I haven't done before."

"Demons are strong," the king replied.

"They can read auras, same as the Judges," Vito said.

"So while you look for their weakness, they look for yours," Hugo added.

I looked between the three of them and shrugged again. "I don't have any more weaknesses. They've been beaten out of me."

The king nodded thoughtfully. "You're incredibly strong, Jacques. To that, I agree. But there are new things in your life now that the demons can use against you."

"Like what?" I asked with a laugh. "My wealth? I've lived without it before."

He shook his head. "No, Jacques. Your family."

I licked my lips, glancing to the wall and not answering.

"The boy who watched his mother's tragic spiritual trial and then tried to kill the king himself because of her sentence did not go unnoticed by the spiritual world," the king said. "Now that you've united with your father, they'll try to dig open your soul until you break."

He stared at me, but I didn't reply.

Yes, I knew it. Which is exactly why my father needed to stay as far from me—and *her*—as possible.

There was a moment of silence. I broke it with a dry laugh.

"Don't worry, Your Majesty," I said. "Should my father suffer the same fate, it won't affect me as it did my mother. I've learned that everyone rightly pays for their sins eventually."

"That wasn't my point."

"I should get back to my men," I said. "Do I have your permission to be dismissed?"

He rubbed his finger against his lip and then twirled his hand in a gentle motion to leave. I did, not looking back.

Honestly, I wasn't sure who I hated bringing up the past the most: the demons, the king, or myself.

THIRTY-EIGHT

"Stop taking your shirt off in front of me," Esmeralda snapped, folding her arms across her chest but not *actually* looking away.

I whipped the shirt off for extra emphasis. "You're the one who jumped out of a siren suite. This is your own fault. Get used to it."

I changed into a pullover shirt, throwing the previous shirt in the corner of the room. I hated how physically exhausting demon extraction was. It was soaking sweat into all my shirts.

I glanced over to check Esmeralda's aura. I couldn't hold back my laughter when I saw that she was both attracted and annoyed at the same time. She was pretending not to be looking at me through the corner of her eye, but I could tell that she was. For a siren, she was quite awkward around men.

No, she was awkward with only me, come to think of it. Charmspeak worked on everyone else.

"I don't know why jumping out of Luc's room means I have to share a room with you," she eventually replied.

"I can lock you in one of the cells with the demons if you'd like. It'd be easier to keep track of you."

"And where do you expect me to sleep, exactly?" She pointed to the bed. "There's only one bed here."

I stepped in close to her. "We only need one."

Her aura switched to attraction and fear at the same time. I bit back a smile. She was getting more and more fun to play with.

"Y-you're joking," she replied.

"Since when do I joke?"

"That's a fair point."

I leaned in closer until she backed down, slowly sitting on the bed as I came closer and closer. Her aura became genuinely nervous, so I decided to stop being an ass.

"We only need one bed," I whispered, "because I'm going to sleep on the floor."

I pulled back and let her breathe for a moment. I tried not to laugh as the color rushed out of her skin.

"How long do I have to stay here?" she asked.

"Until it's time to take you home," I replied. "I made a promise to your family. I intend to keep it."

"I thought you said you weren't coming for me?"

She folded her arms again, her aura a bit...sad?

I huffed. "You want to marry my father that badly?"

She shifted on the bed, her sad aura getting stronger. She didn't answer me, but she didn't have to.

"Is he kind?"

Her words echoed in my head. They had ever since that night.

I had wanted her to be twisted, sinful, and greedy. I wanted to find reasons to dislike her or make her my enemy.

But she wasn't. And I couldn't. Her biggest sins were that she was too pure and too damn foolish.

"Decide what you want," I said eventually. "I'll do my best to take care of it."

I didn't look at her, but I could feel her head turn toward me.

"Why would you do that?" she asked.

I shrugged. "There's no point in making everyone suffer if no one wants this arrangement. Not to mention, your soft spot for the pirate captain is quite obvious."

She laughed ironically. "You said it yourself: it's just a spell."

"For him. Not for you."

Our eyes met for a brief moment, but she looked away. Her aura didn't change at all, refusing to show me her true feelings.

Or maybe I was looking at them this entire time and just not accepting them.

"Why are you doing all this for me anyway?" she asked. "I thought you hated me."

I took a long breath. Perhaps the truth wasn't out of order.

"You're a siren," I said. "And I don't want the spiritual realm anywhere close to my family. It's already done enough damage."

I blinked hard, as if I was watching my mother disappear into the light of the afterlife all over again. I didn't think I had my back turned for so long, until Esmeralda's hand came to my shoulder. I turned to face her, her eyes and aura full of sympathy.

"I want to know more of your story," she said.

I put a hand on top of her head to stop her, uncomfortable with her sudden affection. "Still trying to bond with me, eh, dear mother?"

The nickname tasted sour this time. I didn't want to call her that. I didn't want her to be part of my family. Not like this.

I thought of her in the light of the bathhouse, the way her skin felt on my fingertips as I teased her about her obvious interest in me. Even if her rose aura hadn't given it away, the look in her eyes that night did. I couldn't let her pursue that interest.

I was starting to wonder how much I'd let her pursue, and how long it would take me to eventually respond.

ENDING

I fed a piece of ham to the dog. His tail beat rhythmically against the floor, his toenails scraping the tile in delight as he scarfed down the meat under the table.

"So satisfied with something so simple, huh?" I asked him, finishing my breakfast.

It was a luxury to be simple. If I could have survived, I might have considered being a simple person myself, but my path didn't leave that opportunity.

At the very least, I had to continue as a Judge. For Samantha's sake.

I wondered what she would have said if she knew I no longer embodied evil, but now judged it?

The captain's footsteps came down the steps, and I caught a glimpse of him straightening his coat and heading toward the door. He caught my eye and stopped.

"Jacques," he greeted. "How long have you been here, son?"

My innards shifted oddly at the nickname. I didn't hate it, really, but there was something about it that made me uneasy. I stood from the kitchen table to meet him.

"Clara invited me shopping in the square," I said. "I came a bit early."

He nodded in satisfaction. "Enjoy the time with your sister, then. I'd like to stay and visit, but I need to attend the Dupont's this afternoon. I'll be back by evening."

I gritted my teeth as he put on his hat to leave. As he opened the front door, the words slipped out of my mouth.

"Are you sure you want to go through with this?" I asked.

He stopped in the doorway. He then leaned one hand against the frame and slowly tapped his fingers against it.

"You realize that she's only after your money," I added.

He chuckled as he turned to face me. "Of course. I'm the one who offered it."

There was silence between us for a moment, my shock probably quite visible. He half smiled.

"You know," he started, "when you're young, you believe that marriage for love is the most successful or meaningful, but in reality, marriage is a partnership. It's two people who build each other up so they can thrive, even on days when they don't particularly like one another."

"So you would marry a woman half your age to entertain you?" I asked.

"No. I'd marry a woman half my age to protect a family that I owe my life to."

His eyes went straight through mine. It was the most intimidating I had seen the man since meeting him. Regardless, I had not been one to look away when challenged, and so I returned his stare.

He took two steps forward from the doorway toward me.

"I loved your mother, Jacques," he said. "Truly. When I met her she was wild and free-spirited, something I hadn't experienced in my youth. But..."

He stopped, nodding to himself before continuing.

"That wild and free spirit was probably what encouraged her to disappear suddenly without telling me about you."

His aura turned to grief, and I couldn't think of anything to reply. He put a warm hand on my shoulder. I flinched. I still wasn't used to his affections.

"A good partner is not someone you always love," he said, "but someone you can always depend on. Someone who has the same vision for life you do. Esmeralda Dupont has agreed to this arrangement, understanding what it is."

Yes, she agreed to it. A siren didn't say no to their duties. They couldn't. But her true feelings…was I the only one who could see them? She didn't want this marriage.

And I didn't either.

***

I didn't knock. Not at the front door, not at the bedroom door.

It was my own fault, really, to walk in on Esmeralda in a wedding dress—my punishment for being ill-mannered, perhaps.

But to hell with it. I didn't care about any of that anyway.

She was sitting on her ankles on the floor, the white train of her dress pooled around her. Her aura shifted from happy to confused when she saw me, which pissed me off. Happy? Was she happy trying on her gown and thinking of her comfortable life after marriage? A marriage that ignored everything she truly was?

No, I wasn't going to allow that.

I shut the door behind me.

"I've decided this is unacceptable," I said as she stood. "I can't allow you to marry my father."

She opened her mouth, and all I could think was that I was tired of hearing her giving me excuses. She needed to shut her mouth just one time and listen.

That must have been why I kissed her.

She gave a muffled moan as my lips met hers. I expected her to throw a tantrum, but instead, she quickly submitted. I already knew she was attracted to me. At least she was brave enough to admit it with her kiss.

I stepped back and she only stared at me, stunned. I couldn't blame her. I was stunned myself.

"T-there," I said, trying to act as if I had planned that. "They won't allow you to marry one man when you've kissed another."

It was true. Society wasn't kind to…well, anyone if I was honest, but least of all to the disloyal.

Her aura flashed instantly to anger. "Then you mean, you just kissed me to break off my betrothal?"

I nodded.

"Oh, you idiot!" she yelled. "You were willing to ruin my reputation when the wedding has been called off?"

"Why are you calling me an idiot when you're the— Wait, what?"

Her shoulders slumped as she pressed her lips together, her aura suddenly amused. What the hell was she amused about?

"Like I was *trying* to say," she continued. "Your father is here now. Our engagement has been called off."

It took me a moment to get my head around it. Who called it off? Him? Her? Why suddenly did— Wait, that wasn't the issue now. I had just kissed the woman.

"So you're saying I did that for no reason?" I said, rubbing my lips.

She nodded, not holding back her smile any longer.

"Unless you *wanted* to kiss me," she teased.

"And why would I do such a thing?"

She tapped an amused finger against her chin. "You've been quite adamant about me not marrying your father. You never gave me a good reason for it."

"I did. Because you're a gold digger."

"A gold digger who asked for her wings and was rejected?"

Her tone dipped, and I didn't have to see her aura to know how much being away from the den was hurting her. She wanted to be part of the spirit world once more, the world she was built for.

"I'll see that you make it back," I said. "I gave you my word."

Why I made such a promise, I still wasn't completely sure. It wasn't that her happiness was my responsibility, was it? Perhaps as a Judge with the responsibility to look after the sirens, and her responsibility to look after the humans, we had similar goals. That's why I looked after her, even though she was quite irritating from time to time.

But all in all, we had the same objective. A type of ...*partnership*.

She stepped in closer to me, and the light and airy scent of her soap stirred my senses.

"Why are you helping me, Jacques?"

I tried to brush off the question. "Because it's my duty as a Judge."

"We both know that's not true."

Her aura changed to affection once again. I was tired of her looking at me in a such a way. If she had looked at me with lust, it would have been different. Lust was self-serving and possessive. But her aura was pure fascination, nothing selfish in her affection at all.

That also pissed me off.

I grabbed her by the waist, and set her on the dresser. She only blinked at me in surprise.

"Do you want me to confess to you?" I asked, leaning in closer. "Do you want me to tell you that I'm caught in your siren spell and can't live without you?"

Perhaps she wanted me to be as obsessive and needy as the pirate captain and first mate. Hell, even her little siren friend had obvious feelings for her, and sirens weren't even supposed to have such strong feelings.

But I wasn't that kind of man. I didn't have feelings like those.

At the same time, this woman was one of the few in the world who understood my world and everything that went with it. And even though she had her own power, she still needed me to come save her. I was oddly… needed.

"I just want the truth," she whispered. "Why are you going this far for me?"

I swallowed before answering truthfully. She would see it in my soul eventually.

"I'm intrigued," I replied.

The longer she looked at me, the more I lost my interest in keeping my walls up. And when her hands went from my arms to the back of my neck, I knew I was in trouble.

This woman had a lock on me.

I couldn't call it love—not as it was—but there was something that constantly drew me to her, even though her powers had no effect on me. It was something else that kept me around her, even at times like this, when there was no reason to stay.

I wanted to know what it was.

I wanted to know why I was so drawn to her, and what would happen if I had surrendered.

I had already surrendered to evil once.

I wanted to know what it would be like to surrender to something pure.

LUC

ONE

I stepped back to eyeball the fluffy green dress on the mannequin. Women's fashion was always so much more complex than men's clothing, which was maybe why male fashion designers found themselves so interested in it. It certainly held more of a challenge for the designer. And what creature didn't love a good challenge?

I pinched the rough fabric between my fingers, sniffing with disinterest. Maria never agreed to wear such itchy things like this. She always wore simple cotton and lace, straight gowns with no petticoat. She had no interest in crowds, which is maybe why she never went to parties that required dressed like these.

My current target, on the other hand, was another story.

It was a long search to find one of the descendants of the Guardians. I had never even tracked down my own genealogy—quite impossible for orphans anyway—and yet I had spent the last six months trying to track down someone else's. It took just as long to sift through the legitimate and fake fortune tellers to find someone who even believed in the Eros.

But it would be worth it. If I could avenge Maria, it didn't matter what I had to do.

"Can I help you, sir?" the sales clerk asked.

My face bounced into a smile as I turned to her.

"Ah, just browsing, my dear," I replied, trying to keep my voice light. "I saw your beautiful fabrics in the window and just couldn't help myself."

She returned my smile. "Do you have a special lady you'd like to shop for?"

"Of course. I'm thinking of a dazzling woman in high society, known for her interests in the arts and jewels. Her father is a prestigious arts dealer and her mother—may she rest in peace—was the grand hostess of lavish parties at their estate."

The saleswoman blinked. "That's quite specific."

"Yes," I replied, turning my voice into a bit of a song. "Do you have any customers like that around here?"

Her eyes glazed a bit. She blinked a few times, as if she was trying to remember.

"Yes…" she said slowly. "I think we have someone like that."

"Could you tell me what days she might come in?" I sang.

The doorbell jingled. It broke the trance I had on the saleswoman, who instantly forgot our conversation and stepped toward the door to greet her new customer.

I checked the door myself, but it was only an elderly woman. My target was much younger. I'd have to wait until the saleswoman was through with her customer before I could charmspeak her again for more information.

To kill time, I walked down the aisles of fabrics and gowns, grazing my fingertips along the fabrics. So this was how the upper class lived, eh? It was a shame I wasn't interested in wealth. I could have worn these threads fantastically. But what I wanted was bigger than money. Bigger than status. Bigger than life itself.

Lost in thought, I bumped into someone at the end of the aisle. She gasped and I reflexively grabbed her shoulders to steady her.

"Forgive me," I said. "I wasn't watching where I was going—"

I stopped at the sight of her. Two of the purest, most radiant blue eyes I had ever seen were looking back at me, accented by a blue gown of the most current fashion. She smiled at me with innocence.

"It's quite all right," she replied, her voice naturally breathy and high. "It was just as much my own fault."

I then realized I still had my hands on her shoulders. I plucked them off, stepping back as I straightened my coat.

"Nothing injured, I hope?" I asked.

She dramatically searched her bodice and hands, then smiled at me once more. "I'm in one piece, thank you. So sorry for the trouble."

"Not at all. It was my pleasure to bump into you," I said, taking in her round face and eyes, Roman nose, blonde hair, and a curvy body only the upper class could accent properly. "An absolute pleasure, indeed."

I gave her my best wink, but she only returned a mildly amused pout.

"Esmeralda!" someone shouted across the room.

The woman in front of me turned her head toward the name and then waved at the salesclerk, making her way across the room.

Goosebumps. *That* was Esmeralda?

My target was far more enchanting than I thought she would be.

"What brings you in today, Esmeralda?" the clerk asked.

"Father's throwing me a celebration for my birthday at the end of the month," she replied, bright as the sun in the spring. "My twenty-first birthday! Can you believe it?"

I swallowed. She would be of age after the end of the month. That meant that her blood could open up the spirit world once again.

And once it opened, I could go home.

I couldn't help but watch her for a moment. There was something familiar about her. I knew we had never met, but there was something warm and nostalgic that vibrated in my chest when I looked at her. What was this strange feeling? Was this what they called love at first sight?

I laughed to myself. How amusing! To fall instantly in love with the woman I needed to trade in for revenge.

It was a pity I couldn't stay to play with her. The way she held herself straight as she talked to the store clerk showed a confident, most likely adventurous, woman. Her smile was uniquely bold, like a child who had no sense of danger.

If she had, perhaps she wouldn't have reacted to me the way she did.

No matter. I had one of the descendants in my grasp. That was all I needed.

I will avenge you, Maria. I promise.

***

The darkest part of midnight fell.

I didn't like being in this part of town at this time of night, but it wasn't as if I was completely helpless. Growing up a homeless thief gave me a strange set of skills that I hadn't anticipated to be useful.

Thankfully, pirates were easier to locate than spiritual creatures. All you had to do was follow easy money and easier spending.

I walked into the tavern, instantly squinting at the noise and strong alcohol. To think I'd have to endure a voyage of this made me nearly queasy, but I'd have to simply get through it.

I scanned the room, looking for the most arrogant individual in the place. Only captains pretended they were kings. In comparison, everyone else were just greedy dogs, waiting for the scraps of their master.

Then I saw him.

He wasn't intimidating, but he was confident, sitting at a table surrounded by those obvious greedy dogs. There was a cheap woman on each side of him, but he was focused on his hand of cards.

"Royal flush," he said with a smile, throwing down his cards.

The men at the table groaned in loss, while the women giggled. The captain playfully took his money from the table, as if he had no worries in the world.

I gritted my teeth.

How could the man who murdered my fiancée be so damn relaxed?

I approached the table without a word. The men at the table turned to stare, and after a delayed moment, the captain looked up at me as well.

Captain Adrian Moreau.

"Can I help you, mate?" he asked.

I reminded myself that I needed to keep him alive to get home.

"I heard you're looking for someone who can guide you to a little red rock," I replied.

He cocked a defensive eyebrow at me, tapping his cards against the table. His smile vanished.

"Did you come to insult me?" he asked sharply.

"I came to help you."

It was silent as he stared at me, trying to size me up. He was trying to intimidate me. How useless.

He stood, making a show of his power by slowly walking over to meet me. He stared me in the eyes as he spoke.

"Are you a descendant then?" he asked.

I shook my head. "No, but I know a young lady who is. I also know what party you can sneak into at the end of the month to meet her yourself."

I changed my voice ever so slightly to charm him. His interest piqued. Whether it was from charmspeak or natural interest, it was hard to tell.

"And in exchange?" he asked.

"Transportation. I need out of the city. If you agree to make me part of your crew, then I'll tell you where the girl is."

I tried not to grip my fists while he considered. It was difficult to be this close to the bastard and not slit his throat. But killing him wasn't enough. I needed the spiritual world opened again. And if I killed him now, they'd never accept me back into the Den of Sirens.

He nodded thoughtfully. "I believe I might have an opening for you."

I held out my hand for him to shake. He looked confused for a moment, then amused, as he gripped my hand in a firm shake. He stepped back, suddenly uninterested in the people behind him.

"Tell me about the girl," he said.

"Her name is Esmeralda," I replied. "And you'll need to buy her a birthday present."

ELEVEN

She loved my story, but for the wrong reasons.

I could see that she wasn't entranced the same way the men were. Henrik was the same way when I first met him: he had no interest in my charmspeak either, and it was difficult to get him to a place where I could control him. His touch with the spiritual world had made him more resistant to my powers.

But Esmeralda, she didn't respond at all.

"A load of bullshit," Adrian said, interrupting my thoughts.

The captain, on the other hand, was always entranced by my stories but never took them seriously enough.

"There is no man completely pure or evil," he continued. "Sirens, merfolk, the spirits and what-have-you…there is no such thing. They would have swept half these bastards off my ship."

The crew laughed emptily at their captain's joke, somehow not taking any offense to being called scum. It was true, however, that most of the crew would be wiped from existence.

And if I had anything to say about it, Adrian would be first.

"You'd do well to respect the spirit world, Captain," I replied. "Just because you pay no mind to them doesn't mean they won't search your heart."

Adrian rolled his eyes and shrugged.

"I have no concerns for my morality," he replied.

"No truer words spoken," Henrik interjected.

The two glanced at one another, Henrik's glare making Adrian shrink back in his chair. It was a small pleasure to see the great captain writhe under the disapproving look of his older brother.

With no other words, Henrik left the table. The table was silent for a moment until Esmeralda, still nestled in Adrian's lap, looked at Adrian with genuine concern.

He didn't take it in a very gentleman-like manner.

"You wanna stare closer, princess?" he asked, leaning in close to her.

I took this as my opportunity to step in. I hopped off the table and offered my hand to Esmeralda.

"I hate to steal this one away," I said, "but there is a hot stove waiting for our attention."

The men groaned in disappointment as Esmeralda took my hand. Adrian's eyes flashed red as she took my hand and followed me.

"She'll return to you in only moments, my dear captain," I added. "Never you worry."

His shoulders slumped back as he took my spell, and I was able to get her away from the table without any riots.

"Thank you, Luc," Esmeralda said as we left the table and started down the stairs to the kitchen. "That horrible captain just can't keep his hands to himself. So many childish games…"

She trailed on, but I only half listened. There was something about her that was incredibly familiar. What on earth was it?

"The captain seems quite infatuated with you, little dove," I said with a laugh, pretending to be joking. "He always wants you for himself."

"And for what?" she replied in confirmation. "He doesn't enjoy my company, really. I think he just likes to bully people."

I cocked my head to the side in thought and then shook it.

"It doesn't seem that way to me," I said. "It seems like the captain has a bit of an infatuation."

She gaped her mouth in disgust. "Don't make such vile accusations, Luc. Even if that were true, I wouldn't accept such horrible affections."

She started ladling soup into bowls, seemingly trying to distract herself. I bounced up behind her, my curiosity piqued.

"You must have this trouble often," I said. "I bet men flock to your side on land as well."

"I've had a fair share of suitors," she replied plainly. "None of which measured up to my father or his standards."

"You think of your father pretty highly."

"The highest," she replied.

I scratched my chin, eyeing her. There had to be something that would break her.

"Do you really have no interest in rebelling against his wishes and marrying anyone of your own choice?" I asked.

I put my hands on each side of the counter, trapping her. She turned to face me, raising an eyebrow in disapproval. I smiled in return.

"What if I asked you to run away with me?" I said. "Abandon your father's expectations and marry the man who can make all your dreams come true?"

She shrugged her shoulders with a laugh and frowned at me. "I won't abandon my family, nor the standards laid out for me."

"You have no interest in defying your father?"

She pressed her lips together, shaking her head slowly from side to side.

"My father is my greatest strength and my most important love," she said softly. "I could never betray him. It would break my heart more than it would his."

I held my breath.

Not only did she not respond to charmspeak, but she always obeyed her father to the point of personal sacrifice. That wasn't a human trait. The humans were always thinking of their emotions first, not their duties. They didn't speak like Esmeralda spoke, as if she was betraying the king of the spiritual realm instead of a man.

She didn't respond to charmspeak.

She didn't follow her own desires.

Her heart didn't race when I spoke.

And Adrian and Henrik were obviously both infatuated with her even though she had only been on the ship a short time.

That meant…

I grabbed her chin and directed her eyes to mine. She flinched—and rightly so since I had grabbed her rougher than I intended—and looked at me with a twinge of fear.

"Luc, what are you—"

"Don't move," I ordered.

I tried to read her. The spiritual realm had given me the power to read people's emotions, fears, and desires, and if there was any time to use it, it was now.

I kept my eyes on her, trying to dig into her soul. And as I looked, I found the confirmation I needed.

She wasn't charmed by me at all.

And there would only be one reason why I couldn't put her under my spell.

Esmeralda was a cursed siren like me.

I stepped back, the shock overwhelming me. How on earth was this woman one of my kind? Did she know about it like I did? No, she couldn't, could she? It was strange that I even knew.

"Luc?" she asked.

I blinked, trying to compose myself.

"You have a strong will, little dove," I said, trying to act natural. "Those eyes of yours show it."

She scoffed and rolled her eyes. "You have no interest in personal space, do you, storyteller?"

She threw the bowls on a tray, furrowing her brows, and then made her way up the stairs. I rubbed my chin in thought as she walked away.

"Not especially," I whispered after her. "But you'd be surprised at how close we truly are, little dove."

TWENTY-FIVE

It was my turn to feed them.

I had been trying to avoid the prisoners on board, especially on today of all days. To charmspeak the men into pushing our upcoming planned mutiny up had taken all my energy, but seeing how Henrik was already losing himself to his obsession with Esmeralda made it clear that it was time to put them behind bars. The technicalities of shoving them into prison without the current prisoners getting out was the largest problem, but there was no time.

Perhaps the biggest problem was that the pirate leader—whose name I kept forgetting—couldn't be charmed, and I didn't know why.

There wasn't much time before the mutiny, but I was still on kitchen duty. I should have gotten someone else to do it, I supposed, but at the same time, the pirate leader had knowledge I wanted. Knowledge I needed.

I could tell by looking into his soul that he had answers I had been searching for.

And if he died in my mutiny, then it would be a waste.

I put on my best smile, per habit, and strutted down the stairs into the brig.

"Good evening, gentlemen!" I called out. "Supper is served, courtesy of the great captain."

The last three words came out rather sharply, but no one noticed. They were too busy grasping for the bowls between the bars. They slurped it down sloppily as I made my way to the back of the cells.

Their leader was still with his back against the wall, staring straight ahead. He didn't look upset or agitated, but only waiting, like a lion watching its prey.

I didn't want to face him. Somehow I knew he was connected to the spiritual world. He didn't respond to charmspeak at all. He seemed entertained by it. He knew what I was, I was sure. But I didn't know exactly what he was.

He turned his head toward me. He then raised an eyebrow, as if he was asking me why I was staring at him and not saying anything.

"Dinner?" I asked, holding up a bowl.

He shrugged. "Not necessary."

The way he stared after his answer made my hair stand on end. He slowly rose to his feet to meet me, and I stepped back.

He chuckled.

"You act scared now," he said. "You weren't so timid when you cut down three of my men and then put a sword at *my* throat."

I swallowed, but didn't answer. The soup bowl was warm against my palm.

"You're obviously courageous enough to be on this ship," he continued. "I'm interested in how you got the captain to let you aboard the ship headed straight for the Eros. Was it your impressive resume or something else?"

He stared me down. I held my breath in order to steady myself, but it didn't keep me from sweating.

"Who are you?" I asked.

He raised one shoulder and dropped it. "Someone who knows a reincarnate when I see one. My question is, how do *you* know what you are?"

I licked my bottom lip, glancing at the bowl of soup. "Fortune tellers."

This time his laugh was more bitter than amused. "Leave it to them to screw up the spiritual realm, then poorly attempt to fix it in order to look like saints. I bet they charged you every last penny for it too."

I didn't answer. He folded his arms and leaned against the bars.

"I assume you know the woman is an incarnate as well?" he asked.

Again, I didn't answer.

"Let me guess," he said. "You found another one of your kind, and now you're running home together. Rather romantic for sirens, really. But the king will be pleased to have two of his children home again."

I almost forgot to breathe. The Siren King really did exist. I had heard stories from the fortune tellers, but to hear it from another source was breathtaking.

The leader of the prisoners nodded approvingly. "I hate romance, but at the same time, you whisking the woman siren off to the den will take care of my problems as well. So I'm willing to cut you a deal."

"A deal?" I scoffed. "What could you offer?"

He leaned against the bars as he smiled at me.

"Let me out of this cell," he said, "and I'll take you both home."

The word hit me straight through the gut. *Home.* Oh, how much I had wanted to say that word on my own lips. And when I searched his eyes, I saw no dishonesty in his proposition.

But how could he know where it was? Not unless…

"Are you returning as well?" I asked.

He snorted distastefully. "I have no interest in your king or his domain."

So he wasn't a siren. And he clearly hated fortune tellers. So that meant he was either a Hunter or a Judge.

"Swear to me that you won't hurt Esmeralda," I said.

He didn't blink as he searched for his words. I saw his desires once more—the same desire I had seen when I first met him with Esmeralda—causing me to pull her out of his way.

His desire was to see the sirens destroyed.

"There are no choices in my world, little siren," he said. "Your destruction is your own doing. I can't force you toward it, nor can I save you from it."

I stepped back again. His desire was not only for our deaths, but our deaths were also his job.

Which meant…

"Boss, it's time."

A voice echoed down the stairs. I recognized it as one of Adrian's men and hushed him.

"Silence," I commanded. "Not until my signal."

"Boss, huh?" the leader of the prisoners chuckled, long and deep. "I see you haven't wasted time in using your gifts. I hope that pleases the king."

"Boss?" the man asked again.

"Just a moment," I sang. "The games will begin soon."

I stepped away from the cell to attend to my scheduled mutiny, the pirate leader's voice echoing behind me.

"So they will, little siren. So they will."

THIRTY-SEVEN

"Escort Adrian back to his room," the king ordered two sirens in the throne room. "And you, Rhys, shall remain here."

I caught the stern look in his eye before bowing my head.

"Yes, Your Majesty," I answered.

I didn't lift my eyes as Adrian left. I had only intended to confront him—to ask him why his heart had changed so much in such a short time—but as soon as I saw his face, I lost control. My hatred for him had consumed all logic, and I hadn't noticed until it was too late, until the king had to force himself between us.

When Adrian left and the doors shut behind him, the king stood to step away from his throne.

"Be careful not to return to your own habits," he said. "The consequences may be worse than the first time."

"Yes, Your Majesty."

"I've given you the gift of another chance," he continued. "Do not allow your heart to return to its former darkness and ruin that gift."

"Yes, Your Majesty."

Silence.

"You cared for the humans in the beginning," he said when some time had passed. "You even saved them from those who would destroy them without a second thought."

I caught his eye, knowing exactly who he was talking about.

I could still remember the blood of the child and its mother on Renaldo's hands. I barely made it to the second child in time. But I had only been able to save one of the three. There was plenty more innocent blood before and plenty more innocent blood after that I couldn't save.

But I had never told the king. I had never told anyone.

It was foolish, however, to think the king didn't already know.

He continued. "And in their pain, and your own, you tried to give and take pleasure. But that was also against my rules."

I nodded in agreement. "Yes, Your Majesty."

"You loved the humans, and then you lost what real love was. So I had to teach you."

Maria's eyes flashed in my mind for a brief moment. I knew I could never see her again. The siren world and the world of the dead didn't cross. Our mission was to judge humans on Earth. Nothing else.

But from that pain, and a few other tragically lost loves in my other lives, I understood what the king was trying to teach me. I understood how I saw love incorrectly. Selfishly. Possessively. And emptied.

"Love isn't destructive," he said, stepping closer to me. "Did you learn it?"

526

I nodded, looking down.

"Since you learned the pain of destruction, you must show me your repentance."

"Yes, Your Majesty."

"That's why I'm commanding you to keep guard over the humans."

I raised my head to protest, but the firm resolve in his eyes told me to keep silent.

I swallowed.

"Yes, Your Majesty."

He pulled his lips to the side in a teasing scowl.

"You're allowed to call me *Father*, you know," he said. "You did once."

I bit my lip, nearly ripping the skin off with my teeth. Clearing my throat, I shook my head.

"I haven't earned it, Your Majesty."

He stared at me for a long moment. He then cocked his head gently to the side and nodded.

"That's true," he replied. "And the fact is, you can't earn it."

The truth struck my gut, and I bowed my head further. The king, however, put both his hands on my shoulders and prompted me to look at him.

"And because you can't earn it," he continued, "you can't lose it either. Do you understand my meaning, son?"

I stared back at him, realizing he wasn't talking about calling him *Father* anymore.

It struck me once again in the gut, tearing open my grief. As tears spilled from my eyes he pulled me close, allowing them to stain his pure robes as he comforted me.

ENDING

The sunset wasn't as glorious as it used to be.

I could see the entire world, it seemed, from the top of the Den of Sirens, and before I had become human, it felt like the greatest power in the world. Now it was only empty colors across the horizon. Perhaps it was because I was here alone—and I didn't want to be alone.

"So this is where you come to think," a voice said behind me. "It's quite beautiful, if I do say so myself."

I turned to see the king behind me, his eyes scanning the water and sky as the wind tousled his hair and robes. I jumped to my feet.

"Your Majesty," I said. "How did you get here?"

He cocked an eyebrow at me. "I created the entire spiritual realm and you think I can't climb a rock?"

I swallowed and chuckled, embarrassed. He came and stood on the edge of the den with me, his hands gently clasped behind his back.

"Also," he added, "do you really think I would create all this and never come out to look at it?"

I had forgotten how easy it was for him to read my thoughts. I don't know why it was so hard to remember. After all, he had created all of us with the ability to read souls as well.

"I just didn't expect you to come to me," I said honestly. "I didn't think it would be worth your time."

It was too honest, perhaps. I wished I could take it back as soon as I said it, but it didn't matter anyway. The king could already see it.

"I do as I wish," he replied flatly. "And my wish was to see why your heart was so heavy now that you're standing on top of the world."

I sighed, looking out onto the water as I arranged my thoughts.

"The human world has so much suffering," I said. "As a human, I had thought the spiritual realm would have less suffering. And though I finally feel at home, I have to admit, Your Majesty, my soul still aches in some places."

He was silent for a moment.

"Both realms have their responsibilities," he finally said. "The weight of a siren's responsibilities are not light. To condemn the physical world to life or death is no easy task."

I nodded my head, even though that wasn't what the weight in my heart was from.

"I know that I'm home," I said, the wind encouraging me to voice my thoughts into them. "But that loneliness I felt as a human, sometimes I still feel it."

He was silent for a longer moment this time. I doubted that I had offended him, but it made me uneasy that he would be silent for so long.

He then spoke.

"Your heart is pulled in too many directions," he said. "That pull causes so many tears in you that can't be filled." I thought about it for a moment. The human realm. The spiritual realm. My past lives. My current life. The king. My friends here. My friends on Earth.

"Perhaps loneliness is not your issue, Rhys," the king said. "Perhaps it's restlessness. You're separating yourself into so many pieces."

"What do you mean, Your Majesty?"

He smiled as he inhaled.

"You want to be in the sky, you want to be on land. You want to be with us, and you want to be with the humans. You want to fulfill your duties, and you want to be in love." He looked over his shoulder at me with a smirk. "Am I incorrect?"

I met his eyes and then slowly hung my head. "You're correct, Your Majesty. Please forgive my greed."

He chuckled. "When I made you, Rhys, I made you with an adventurous spirit and an eye for beauty. Although this design may have led you down dark paths, I made no mistakes when I made you."

I swallowed my emotions back down my throat, wondering if my desire to cry was also a design.

The king looked up at the sky and took a deep breath.

"It's a beautiful day to take to the skies," he said. "Why don't you go and see what you can find?"

I could only look at his feet. When he turned to walk away, I reached out and grabbed a bit of his robe. He stopped.

I steadied my voice to speak. "Thank you…Father."

His hand came to the back of my head and brought me in, his lips coming to my forehead. He patted me on the shoulder and left me to look at the skies.

***

The sky fell into darkness, and my heart felt different than before. It was longing for something, some connection with beauty of some sort.

Perhaps that's why I flew to her.

I just wanted to see that Astraea was well. I wanted to make sure that she hadn't been sent to another body in the last couple of months.

Did she marry? Did her father recover? Was she happy or in pain?

My concern for her heart outweighed my fears of her rejection.

I circled her house, wondering where I could land to see her better. There were a couple of balconies to choose from, and there was a tiny figure on one of them. I hovered around the corner of the building, realizing it was her.

Her skin was pale with exhaustion and sadness. Was it her father or her marriage that made her frown in such a way? I had to know.

I had to know that she was okay.

She turned to go inside, but I didn't want her to. I didn't want to be this close and not speak with her. I jumped on the balcony, my wings starting a current that got her attention.

"Luc?" she asked as she turned.

I smiled. She ran to my arms and held me tight, her embrace filling the loneliness I had been feeling.

"You have no idea how much I missed you," she said.

I laughed to myself. "I missed you too, Astraea. Far more than I should have."

I swallowed, pulling back to look at her face.

"And your father?" I asked. "Is he well?"

Her eyes dimmed, giving me the only answer I needed. Her words, however, faked optimism.

"He's healing. He might be sick for some time though."

In other words, his body had given up on him. That was the beautiful paradox of the humans: to feel so much but to be so easily broken.

"The king knew about your father," I said. "That's why he sent you away. I understand it, but…"

I couldn't finish my sentence. She looked so lovely in the moonlight with the wind caressing her hair, and I had to do the same out of jealousy. I combed her hair with my fingers, the soft tresses stirring emotions in me I had long forgotten.

"Why did you come back?" she asked softly.

I swallowed. "I had to make sure you were cared for, little dove. In our lives as sirens, in our lives as humans…I guess I just got used to being responsible for you."

She laughed. "You were never *that* responsible."

I laughed with her, the feeling more freeing than taking to the skies. Seeing her delicate hands, I took them in mine, looking for the ring on her finger. She had always wanted one, and perhaps now she would have one. But for now, her hands were bare.

"Are you still engaged?" I asked.

"I haven't been wed yet," she said with a shrug. "Do you think the king would be upset if I decided to wed instead of returning?"

I licked my bottom lip. Maybe the king wouldn't. But I had a few things to say about it.

"He would allow you to make your own choices," I said honestly.

"Would you come to my wedding?" she asked.

I met her eyes, trying to see if she was joking or not. She had to know that sirens couldn't attend human events, and at the very least, I had no intentions on watching her be with another man.

Something in her eyes told me she knew that. She was joking with me. How had she become so cruel?

It seemed like she wanted to know my true feelings. Well, if she was going to fool around with such serious things…

"I'd ruin it," I finally answered.

"Ruin?"

I pulled her in close, leaning down to her ear.

"Haven't you heard?" I asked. "That I steal other men's wives?"

I felt her shiver under my touch. This was the closest we had ever been in hundreds of years, and I wasn't about to give up the opportunity. I wrapped my wings around us, attempting to keep her from running away from me. Not until I said what needed to be said.

"I'll wait for you to come back to us," I said. "But you need to know, it kills me to wait like this."

She didn't speak or move, allowing me to trace the lines in her face. It was not the body she had been born with as a siren. I remembered her so differently. But her soul was exactly the same, and no matter what shell she had now, the beauty I always saw in her was still there.

"It's funny," I continued, "I started to fall for you on that ship, not remembering that I had already loved you as a siren."

Her eyes flashed with disbelief and surprise, her lips gaping.

"What?" she asked, swallowing.

"I always had different feelings toward you, but sirens are expected to live with their feelings second. When you came aboard that ship, there were pieces of you that made me feel at home. And now that I'm truly home, it still doesn't feel right without you."

The king was right. My heart was pulled in so many directions that it was impossible to find peace. But he also must have known my feelings toward Astraea, considering he knew my heart more than anyone.

And because he knew, I felt no guilt in my confession.

My words, however, made Astraea freeze in her place.

"Is my confession too much, little dove?" I asked with a chuckle.

She seemed to come back to reality for a moment, her eyes softening as she looked at me. I had always wanted her to look at me in such a way.

She smiled, holding out her palm. "See for yourself."

I looked down at her hand and then reached out to put my fingers to her wrist. Her heart was beating fast, faster than I thought was possible for an incarnate. That was my confirmation. Although sirens felt feelings second, we still had them. They were there. And the woman I had loved for centuries was in my arms.

This was the love I had been searching for when I had taken so many women for myself. Those women didn't belong to me, and so they had never felt right.

But Astraea…she was mine. Rightfully. Wonderfully. Beautifully.

It gave my heart peace.

The king said I hadn't suffered from loneliness, and I realized in this moment that he was right. It wasn't loneliness I felt, but restlessness.

Maybe it was part of my design. Maybe I would never be satisfied.

But with Astraea in my arms, at this moment, I felt like everything was the way it should have been. That was enough for now. Even if there were holes in my spirit, one less hole was enough.

WRITE YOUR OWN ENDING!

Not satisfied with any of the four endings of this book? Have a great idea of your own? Write your ending to *Gods of the Sea* here!

WRITE YOUR OWN ENDING HERE

WRITE YOUR OWN ENDING HERE

WRITE YOUR OWN ENDING HERE

Like the book? Leave a review!

Your reviews help make my books better.

TURN THE PAGE
FOR AN EXCERPT FROM
THE REBELLION

A Choose the Ending Novel

"You can't take him!" I screamed.

The guards grabbed me before I reached the door, pulling me back into the living room. I was strong, but not strong enough to twist from their hold. My younger brother looked at me over his shoulder as the emperor's guards dragged him outside into the darkness. They forced him to his knees, pointing a sword at his throat.

A man in heavy boots stepped between us, his broad shoulders bringing back memories I had thrown away long ago. He had once been a shadow of my past, but now, he was a shadow that divided me from my brother.

"It's too late, Jaehwa," the shadow replied, not turning to face me.

I narrowed my eyes, the guards' hands gripping hard into my arms as I struggled to step forward.

"You expect me to back down?" I asked. "He's all I have left, Saejun! You know that!"

The shadow turned and stepped back into the house, his dark eyes showing no regrets nor sympathy as the living room candles lit his face. The crimson robes of the emperor clung to his skin like blood, a testament to his position of power. He stood tall and arrogant, as if he had never been the poor farmer's son he once was.

"He's a murderer," Saejun said. "He brought this upon himself."

"You're wrong!" I tried to twist out of the guards' hold, but they held fast. "Kiwan would never commit treason against the emperor! You know that. How can you take him away to be executed?"

I tried to catch my breath, my eyes beginning to burn. Saejun stepped in closer, but I only stared at his expensive boots, refusing to let him intimidate me. His fingers curled under my chin, lifting my head up to look at him. His features were just as I remembered - his sharp eyes and strong jaw - but there was a new darkness in him that wasn't caused by the late hour.

"Stop fighting against me," he replied. "You won't win. You know that."

I jerked my face from his hand. "Get out of myhouse."

"I hate to say this," he said, his hand dropping to his side, "but this house is no longer yours."

I looked up at him. "What do you mean?"

His jaw clenched before he opened his mouth again.

"This house was in your brother's name. Now that he's been arrested, it has defaulted to the emperor."

"Saejun —"

"You can live here for the time being," he continued, "but you can be thrown out at any time. These are the orders of the emperor."

I twisted hard, breaking free from the guards, but only for a moment. They pulled me back again, bringing me down to my knees.

"Who the hell do you think you are?" I spat at Saejun.

"Enough," he warned.

"You disappeared for five years, become captain of the guards, and then show up at my door to take my brother and my home away from me?" The guards twisted my arms in an attempt to silence me, but I continued. "Who the hell do you think you are? What right do you have to come back here?"

"Put her under house arrest," he told the guards, not even blinking. "Secure the first floor."

He turned his back on me. It was something he was good at.

"Saejun!" I called.

He stopped. With two heavy footsteps, he turned back.

"That…" he said, "will be the last time I allow you to say my name and live."

AUTHOR'S NOTE

Do you want to hear an incredible tale? It's a true story. One of my own, in fact.

This story is strange, but I can't refrain from telling it since it's so incredible that I still can't believe it's true myself.

It's related to this book in the most magical way possible.

I grew up without a father, knowing nothing more than his name. It wasn't a lot to grow up with, and the mystery crushed me. So in my early teenage years, I used the newly available internet (no one misses dial-up, do we?) to track him down. It went poorly, and I gave up on the search by the time I was sixteen.

In my late twenties, I decided to do a DNA test. I simply wanted to know my genetic origins and thought it was the best route. Nearly seven years later, coronavirus began. I began writing *Gods of the Sea* around this time, directly after finishing my first semester of spiritual formation and theology classes for my master's degree in philosophy.

For *Gods of the Sea*, I wanted to explore the idea of fathers: the earthly father versus the heavenly one. It was my reflection on the character of God, how He would act as the Father of Creation, reflected in the character of King Melchior.

The main character of the story became Esmeralda, the French debutante daughter of a powerful retired naval officer, and her run-in with pirates who were looking for the stone called the Eros (named after the Greek god of love who was created after the god of chaos) that controlled the freewill of the spiritual realm.

Halfway through writing this book—after just finishing the chapter titled "Reunited"—I was contacted by a random woman on Facebook, who wanted to know if I knew a man named Lonnie. That was my biological father's name. As it turned out, while coronavirus had contained everyone in their homes, this woman—who turned out to be a cousin of mine—had begun searching for the missing daughter of my father. Me.

Apparently, my father's side of the family had been searching for me for over thirty years.

My biological father, unfortunately, passed away when I was three years old, which is why I had never heard from him. I was put in contact with his sister, who was overjoyed to finally find me. She sent me some of my father's belongings, including his navy yearbook.

I never knew that my father was in the navy. I had never even seen a picture of him until then.

Suddenly, *Gods of the Sea* became much more personal than it already was. And that's why the dedication reads: "To the father I never knew, and the Father who took care of me in his place." The God of the Bible is truly the Father to the fatherless. Praise to His name that I've been reunited to my earthly father's side of the family in His perfect timing. This book will stand as a reminder of God's goodness to me.

The poem, "Eros" by Ralph Waldo Emerson speaks of the cross between the spiritual realm and the human realm:

The sense of the world is short,—
Long and various the report,—
To love and be beloved;
Men and gods have not outlearned it;
And, how oft soe'er they've turned it,
'Tis not to be improved.

While life here is tragically short, and its meaning is overwhelmingly inconclusive, it seems that in both the spiritual and physical realms that there is something that can never be changed or improved: to love and be beloved. It is the design of both realms.

It is in your design. Never forget it.

As always, I thank my wonderful beta readers for their feedback and encouragement, as well as my Tigers who continue to support me and my stories. You all make the hours, days, weeks, and years worth the hard work. Thank you to my wonderful editor, Darya, as well, for taking on the task of editing this tome.

And of course, it would be incomplete without thanking my heavenly Father, Who is the greatest storyteller of all time and the Author of Life. That has been proven, if only microscopically, by me writing this book, and the events that came along with it.

I am not a great theologian, nor a woman of wealth and reputation; nor am I pure or blameless in character and heart; but I am called a daughter of the King of Kings, and I can think of no higher honor than that.

And as Esmeralda's heart belongs in both worlds, so does mine.

- Deidrea

OTHER WORKS BY DEIDREA DEWITT

CHOOSE THE ENDING SERIES

The Five Princes

The Rebellion

Gods of the Sea

POETRY

Love and Other Broken Things

SHORT STORIES

The Exchange

You can read more short stories and poetry by
Deidrea DeWitt on her website at
www.deidreadewitt.com

ABOUT THE AUTHOR

Deidrea is a California native who currently lives in South Korea as an author, teacher, and philosophy/theology major. She is the author of the CHOOSE THE ENDING series, the romance series that lets YOU choose how the story ends.

Her greatest loves include classic and Gothic literature, the struggle of good and evil in the human soul, and pancakes.

Learn more about the author at
http://deidreadewitt.com/